# THE
# BRAIDED
# STREAM

## THE REPLACEMENT CHRONICLES: PART FOUR

# Harper Swan

# OTHER WORK BY HARPER SWAN

**Raven's Choice**
Part One: The Replacement Chronicles

**Journeys of Choice**
Parts Two and Three: The Replacement Chronicles

**The Replacement Chronicles Omnibus Edition**
Parts One-Three

**Gas Heat**
(This story is offered free for those who join my mailing list.)
http://eepurl.com/b3MpEv

For Barb who is always a great help and a friend as well.

*Dueling Megaloceros artwork by Philip Newsom*

# CHAPTER 1

*Raven*

RAVEN'S NAMESAKE BIRDS HADN'T COME around for some time, not even in her dreams. They'd always sought her out, but lately she'd only spotted them flying in the distance. That morning, however, one of the largest she had ever seen was on the ground across from the clearing. It rested there, as black and still as a burnt stump.

The raven started hopping closer upon seeing that she'd noticed it, then it flapped a few times to close the distance. Landing on top of a nearby log, the enormous bird cocked its head to one side, watching her curiously. She frowned and turned away, not about to be distracted from her duties by an overly bold raven.

Raven's tongue tapped against the small gap between her front teeth while she observed the patient standing to one side of the fire. The young woman held her shoulders stiffly. That rigidity would only prolong her headache and suffering.

"If you'll allow me, I would like to take a look at your shoulders and back."

After a wary glance at Raven, the woman gave a quick nod.

"Good, I need you to unlace your tunic and slip it down a bit."

Turning her back, she complied. Raven grasped the woman's braids in one hand and lifted them to check underneath for swelling and other signs of injury. Her own shoulders stiffened when she saw what the hair had covered. Several yellow-green splotches stood out against the brown skin. Smaller bruises were higher up, as if someone not long ago had grabbed the woman by the nape. Raven gently ran several fingers across the discolored areas. They would be impossible to see on one's own body; it was doubtful the woman even knew the marks were there.

Raven could guess how they were made—and she had an idea about what might be contributing to the frequent head-aches. Her patient's mate was a somewhat brusque man who obviously had a temper. Living with someone who might strike out at the slightest provocation would cause anyone to tense up. Raven didn't feel that she knew the woman well enough to gain her confidence about the matter, though. The young childless couple had only recently arrived from the coast, com-ing to dwell at the edges of the Great High Plains with Raven's band.

Raven lowered the braids and moved around to face her. "Shake your arms and shoulders for a good while," she said. "I believe I remember that your name is Gale."

The young woman nodded.

"Like this, Gale, but longer." Raven gently shook her own arms and shoulders for a moment.

Gale readjusted her tunic. "It's not my arms and shoulders that ache."

"You're holding yourself stiffly," Raven said patiently. "That may be a reason why you have headaches. You need to shake out all that tenseness."

Gale began shaking, and Raven unfolded the mat she'd finished weaving that morning from stalks of medicinal plants. She placed it beside her patient's cooking hearth and knelt upon it. While taking out the things she needed—powdered poplar bark, waterskin, and a gourd—from her pouch, Raven became aware once more of the raven perched on the log directly in front of where she crouched.

The bird croaked and gave her a long sideways stare that somehow reminded her of Leaf. It was the same look he gave her whenever he thought she wasn't telling the complete truth or when he knew something she didn't. The suddenly human-like countenance of the raven sent a chill down her spine.

Leaf had left camp earlier to check his fish traps. Wren had begged to go, so he'd taken her along. Raven imagined what his response would be when they returned and she told him about seeing a raven that favored him in appearance. He would laugh and make light of it.

"Now that's a strange bit of flattery," he would say. But the bird was possibly a warning from the Earth Mother, and she needed to tell him so whether he took her seriously or not.

She broke eye contact with the raven, turning her attention back to sloshing the powdered bark and water together in the gourd. When Raven stood and turned around, she recoiled slightly. Not only were her patient's arms and shoulders shaking, but she was trembling violently all over. Then she stopped and became still, her body visibly relaxing.

Gale's facial expression took on a smooth quality. Her eyes fluttered several times before staring vacantly into the fire. By all appearances, she'd fallen into a trance. Raven placed the gourd on the ground and took hold of Gale's arms, gently tugging her down to sit on the mat.

Slowly, Gale's eyes came back into focus. When she saw Raven peering into her face, she started and looked about self-consciously. "What just happened to me?" She wiped the back of her hand across her mouth and glanced at the drool on her knuckles. "Once I started shaking, I couldn't stop."

"I believe you were in a trance. Do you remember seeing anything before it broke?"

"No, all I remember is shaking and then nothing." Her worried eyes looked at Raven hovering above her. "I've never lost myself like that before."

Her reply caused a fleeting sense of disquiet that left as quickly as it came. The young woman had simply experienced her first trance. She would probably have many others during her life. "You're fine. I'm sure you've seen people fall into trances while they dance. Happens to me quite often. Shaking as hard as you were is enough like dancing that it caused your trance." Raven ran her eyes over Gale from head to toe. "All that movement may have actually done some good. You aren't holding yourself as rigidly now. Do you still have your headache?"

Gale pressed several fingers against her forehead. "Yes, it's still there."

"This will help." Raven reached for the gourd, swirled the contents a couple of times, and handed it over. "Drink this potion as quickly as you can."

While Gale gulped the medicine, Raven looked in the direction of the log. The raven was still there, running wing pinions through its beak as it preened.

Gale poked Raven's arm with the gourd, bringing her attention back. "That was bitter," she said, making a face.

Raven took the emptied vessel and set it aside. "Then you'll enjoy this next remedy. It's not bitter at all." She slid a wooden bowl across the mat and uncovered two small chunks of honeycomb that were inside. "Put one piece in your mouth and chew. Tell me when all the honey is gone out of it."

Bending over so that the sticky drips wouldn't spoil the tunic she wore, Gale popped a piece into her mouth then licked her fingers before chewing.

Raven pushed herself up and opened her pack. She took out a feather and began circling around Gale, running the feather tip lightly over the woman's face, neck, and back. As Raven stroked, she chanted to the bee spirits, thanking them for the honey.

After chewing for a while, Gale gestured toward her mouth. "The honey is gone," she said, words slurring around the depleted wax.

Finished with the feather, Raven slipped it into the bag. She bent over so that her face was in front of Gale's and looked directly into the other woman's eyes. "Listen closely. When I tell you to, but not before, spit the wax onto the ground. The empty wax is absorbing your pain, becoming full with it." Raven waited several heartbeats, letting the tension build, then straightened. She tilted her head back, hands reaching toward the sky. "Earth Mother, hear my plea. I beg your help in healing one of your daughters." She lowered her hands and turned to her patient. "Spit it out now!"

Gale spat to one side and eyed the glistening clump intently, as if searching for the evil thing that had caused such discomfort. She gasped, and her hands flew to her face. "My headache is gone."

Raven tried not to feel overly self-satisfied. The rituals didn't always work. It was difficult to say which had helped the most: the willow bark, the honey, or the prayer to the Earth Mother. Or perhaps none of them was the reason the headache had vanished. Raven suspected that a malady sometimes went away simply because a person thought a particular remedy would help. Just believing seemed to make the body heal.

Gale stood from the mat, interrupting Raven's musings, and gave her a quick hug. "When people say you're the best healer in all the tribes, they're being truthful."

Warmth encircled Raven's heart. Since childhood, she'd

wished to be the best healer possible. She patted Gale's arm. "It's good of you to say so." Raven picked up the bowl and held it out to her. "I'll leave the other piece of honeycomb. If your headache returns, just repeat what you did here. Make sure you've swallowed all the honey before spitting out the wax. You can return the bowl later. Do you have any other problems—any at all—that you'd like help with?"

Taking the bowl, Gale darted a startled look at Raven then turned away abruptly. "No, no. Thank you, healer, but I'll be minding my chores now." She left the hearth fire, heading for the tent behind it.

Raven stooped to pack her bag. Information traveled rapidly within the camp. A woman who'd known Gale while living at the coast had told Raven the night before that the couple had lost several babies due to miscarriage. Raven was familiar with certain medicines that helped prevent the loss of a child, but the problem might lie with her abusive mate, not with Gale.

She'd almost forgotten the raven when a scraping sound came from the log. The bird was rubbing its beak noisily back and forth across the bark. When finished, it looked at her for only a heartbeat before flying up and away, its large wings flapping furiously into pink-tinged clouds.

Raven gazed up at the brightly colored sky. The sun was already setting. She must go for her two youngest children who were being minded by her sister-in-law. As Raven started down a path, she wondered if Leaf and Wren had brought back fish for that night's meal. She would pass by her hearth on the way to Shell's tent and find out. If the catch was a big one, she would take some along to share.

Leaf and Wren hadn't yet returned when she walked into the clearing. The empty silence, broken only by the chattering of a squirrel, seemed ominous. Raven remembered the way the raven had looked at her with Leaf's face, and her stomach knotted. She tried not to give the incident too much importance. The raven's visit was just a curious bird stopping by to see what she was doing. And perhaps Leaf had already thought to share fish with his sister. He and Wren were probably at her hearth that very moment. Raven left the medicine pouch in the tent and went on.

There wasn't any sign of Leaf or Wren when she approached her sister-in-law's hearth. Sky and Windy were playing with Shell's children off to one side, and Raven paused at a distance to watch them. How Sky had grown. He was as tall as his two male cousins, even though they were older than her son's six summers. The boy was going to be as tall as Leaf someday. He appeared to be arguing with the others over a game they were playing with pretend spears—probably a game he'd made up himself. At three summers, Windy was exactly the same size as Shell's youngest girl, who'd been born only a few moons before her. The pair were happily making dolls out of asters they'd laid on the ground, poking tiny pebbles into the large centers of the blooms to make eyes and mouths.

Before Windy could spot her, Raven darted over and scooped the little girl up. "I've got you," she said.

Her daughter gave a squeal, dropping the pebbles.

"Now all we need is your brother—and your big sister and father." She felt her stomach knot again.

Raven put Windy down but held her hand tightly so she couldn't run away. She was willful, though not as headstrong as Wren had been at that age. Raven smiled wryly to herself. Wren was still difficult, even though she was in her tenth summer.

Shell came out of the tent.

Raven greeted her and walked over, Windy in tow. "Have

you seen Leaf and Wren? They went to check Leaf's fish traps. I thought they may have come back this way."

"No, I haven't seen them. If they do come by, I'll let Leaf know you're looking for them."

"I can't help but worry, because it's already twilight."

Shell glanced at the sky. "Yes, night is almost upon us." She laughed nervously. "Now you have me worried. If you see them first, send Wren by here for a moment."

Sky deserted the game and came over to stand beside Raven. She ran her fingers over his hair to smooth it. "If the catch was good, I'll send fish with Wren."

Shell smiled. "I hope that it was."

As she turned to leave with her children, Raven cheerfully returned Shell's farewell wave, but her thoughts were dark. She remembered the disquiet she'd felt after Gale came out of the trance. Perhaps the raven had been sent by the Earth Mother to gift Raven with a trance that held a vision, but because she'd been so irritated by the bird's untimely appearance, Gale had been given the trance instead. If so, it was wasted. If Gale had a vision, she didn't remember it. Any possible message was lost.

As Raven walked down the path, bats darted about overhead, already hunting for their evening meal. The band's leader, Fin, ambled toward them in the dusk, heading for his hearth. Raven didn't care for the man. Most of the Wind tribe people were easygoing compared to the Fire Cloud tribe she'd grown up in, but not Fin. Normally, she passed by him with the briefest of greetings, but that evening, she needed his help. She stopped in the middle of the path, the children pausing with her.

He looked up and saw her. "Ah, Raven. You're out late. I hope no one is seriously ill."

"No, nothing like that." She waited a moment until he was standing before her. "It's just that Leaf and Wren haven't come back from checking his fish traps. I'm beginning to worry since the sun is almost down. Did you happen to see them?"

Fin had a way of not answering at once, always eyeing a person doubtfully as if information were deliberately being withheld. When he didn't respond, she spoke again. "It's possible the way back is cut off by animals, and they've had to wait." A night cicada nearby began its whirring song. She lifted her voice over it. "Or perhaps Wren got separated from Leaf, and he can't find her."

"No, I haven't seen them, but I wouldn't worry." His voice became mildly sarcastic. "Leaf knows the steppes well. Of that he assured us more than once when he brought us here from the coast. As for Wren, Leaf knows what a handful his oldest daughter can be." He gave Raven a knowing look. "I suppose it's the way of a mother—fretting over a wayward child."

Raven's forehead puckered at hearing his condescending tone, and she regretted mentioning Wren's tendency to wander. Several times, the whole band had to look for her when she'd disappeared. "She's more careful now that she's a bit older." Windy and Sky were listening silently, their upturned faces shadowed by the fading light. For their sakes, Raven tried not to lose her temper, but her words came out edged with anger. "Regardless, some of us should take torches and go search for them." She jabbed a finger at the sky. "The sun has already met the earth."

"I know where the sun is, Raven, and there won't be a moon tonight. We'd be wandering around in the dark once the torches burned out. If they had to return a different way, then we'll miss them—and run into whatever it is they're avoiding." He ran a hand over his beard. "Don't worry so much. Leaf probably didn't realize how late it was, or he wanted to check traps that were farther away. He'll simply build a fire wherever he is, and they'll return at first dawn."

Raven looked at him doubtfully. "Leaf didn't take much with him to the traps, certainly not enough to make a comfortable camp for him and Wren."

"They'll be fine. It's summertime. Piles of leaves are all anyone needs for covering up these mild nights. For all we know, they're at your hearth as we speak, wondering where you are."

She hoped he was right, even though he was only mollifying her so he could retreat to the comfort of his tent. She made as if to leave then turned back. "If they haven't returned by morning, I'll come by your hearth."

Fin's eyes narrowed at her harsh tone. "I would expect you to," he said and went on his way.

*** 

Raven slept poorly that night. Every noise brought her awake, her heart floundering, then she would listen in vain for the entry flap to open. She missed the sound of Wren's noisy breathing mingled with the gentler respirations of the two younger children as they slept peacefully, and she yearned to feel Leaf's warm body pressed against hers.

As soon as the tent began to brighten with morning light, she gave up trying to sleep and woke Windy to nurse her. Raven was almost finished when she saw Sky watching them, his sleepy face petulant. She'd weaned him when he was barely two summers, earlier than normal, because she'd wanted another baby right away. He still resented the displacement. Raven was thinking again of becoming pregnant, so she would soon finish weaning Windy.

She didn't want to waste time by breaking night-fast but decided it was best to do so. At least Shell wouldn't have to feed Sky and Windy that morning while Raven tried to find the rest of her family. Even if she didn't complain, Shell's hospitality had limits. Raven brought out leftover bits of venison for Sky

and heated them beside the tent hearth instead of going outside to the larger hearth. After giving Windy several softened
pieces to placate her, Raven forced herself to eat some. There
was no way of knowing how much of the day she would spend
on the steppes with only dried meat for sustenance.

Although Sky hadn't asked after his father and big sister,
the boy was subdued and could barely eat for opening the flap
to look outside. "The draft is making the tent fill with smoke,"
she finally snapped. "It's not going out the top anymore. We'll
soon be coughing up soot." Without looking at her, he turned
away from the opening.

As soon as they were done eating and clothed, Raven
packed a leather pouch with things to take with her. Then she
threw the bag over her shoulder and looked for Windy. Her
daughter was burrowing under the sleeping furs. Raven threw
the covers back, lifted the child, and propped her on a hip
with one swift movement.

Windy began wriggling to get down.

"Stop that," Raven said sharply, and the small body stilled.

Sky fell in behind Raven without being told to as she left
the tent. He was still sulking from the scolding he'd received
earlier. She would regret being short with her children for a
long time to come, but that morning, Raven's ill temper had
no bounds.

Her patience was tried yet again when she found that
Dune, Shell's mate, had left camp earlier. Raven had hoped he
would help her search, along with Fin and whomever else the
headman asked along.

Shell spoke hesitantly. "He went with several other men to
scout for bison. I was sure that Leaf and Wren had returned,
or I would have asked him to talk to you before leaving." She
wrung her hands. "I feel bad. Because there wasn't a moon last

night, I thought you'd decided not to send Wren to tell me they were back."

Of all the people in the camp, Shell was the least deserving of Raven's temper. "It's all right. I appreciate you taking care of Sky and Windy again." Raven placed her hands lightly on their shoulders. She was surprised that Windy hadn't run off to play. Her expression was as solemn as her brother's, and the two of them craned their necks to gaze up at Raven. "Do you know if Fin went along?"

"No, I heard he wasn't going."

"Well, I'm off to see him then." After taking a final look at her children's faces, Raven turned to leave.

"Be careful out on the plains," Shell called out. "Don't worry about Sky and Windy. I love my little kinsmen."

The sound of playful shrieks followed Raven. Looking back, she saw Shell had started a game of tickle to distract the children. Instead of cheering Raven, their laughter made her miss them even though she'd barely left.

Fin's two boys were sitting near the outside fire, shaving bark off poles.

"Is your father awake?" Raven asked them.

They stopped working and shook their heads. "No, healer," they said in unison.

Raven nodded toward the tent. "Go wake him for me," she said to the oldest one.

He got up and did her bidding. After a few heartbeats, Fin's head came from under the opening flap. He stepped outside, a skin wrapped around his body.

Raven forced herself to be polite. "Good day to you, Fin. I came to let you know that Leaf and Wren still haven't returned."

He stifled a yawn. "They probably holed up somewhere because lions were close by or a pack of hyenas came along—although I haven't seen any hyenas in a while. If so, those beasts moved on to their dens at sunrise. You said yourself that the way back was probably blocked." Fin kept his head down for a moment then gazed up—not at Raven, but at a point over her. "Give them a while to reach home. If they're not back by midmorning, that will be the time to search."

Raven looked at him in disbelief. He was treating her like a bothersome child. She didn't understand why he refused to heed her appeal for help.

The people of the Wind tribe were just as uncomfortable with anything to do with the spirits as the people of her old tribe, the Fire Cloud tribe, were. Both groups left the appeasement of those sometime-malevolent beings to their healers. That discomfort, unfortunately, extended to the healers as well. Raven had always struggled to fit into tribal life, so she was reluctant to use her status to manipulate him. But she didn't seem to have a choice.

"I saw an unusually large raven yesterday," she said. "It had Leaf's face." He wouldn't dare ignore that.

Fin's feigned drowsiness disappeared as his gaze met hers.

"When the raven landed, I was tending Gale, the woman recently come to the band. She fell into a trance. Ask her, if you don't believe me."

Fin moved back a step. He'd fallen into a trance once while leading the men in a ceremonial dance. The experience had unnerved him so much that he refused to discuss the incident with anyone.

"If she had a vision that contained a message, she doesn't remember it. Regardless, the bird itself was a message. Leaf and Wren are in some kind of danger. I truly believe this, or I would not be pestering you."

"I'll get together several men. Wait at your hearth. We'll

come by to let you know when we leave." Fin started back under the flap.

Raven breathed a sigh of relief. "I'm coming with you."

Fin looked over a shoulder. "Do you think it necessary? You'll slow us down."

Raven folded her arms over her chest. "Slow? We're starting out slow. Besides, you don't know—"

The flap fell; he'd already gone inside.

Hot anger coursing through her, Raven crossed over to the tent. She'd only wanted to point out that she knew where the fish traps were. They would need her help if they lost Leaf and Wren's trail.

She paused with her hand on the flap. Barging inside would irritate him, and he might delay their departure yet again.

Gull, Fin's youngest mate, burst out of the tent and collided with Raven. "Oh, I'm so sorry," Gull said, moving away to one side. "I just wanted to tell you how worried we all are about Leaf."

Gull had neglected to mention Wren. Raven looked at her sharply.

The young woman flushed, and Raven remembered how Gull had fluttered around Leaf on a recent day when the band feasted together. Perhaps that misplaced attention had something to do with Fin's reluctance to help find Leaf. Raven's voice was stiff with chilly politeness as she strode away quickly. "I appreciate your worriment."

*** 

While waiting for Fin, Raven braided coarse strands of horsehair into stiff cord. Leaf had come across the animal's carcass on the plains only a few days before. Not much had been left to salvage, but the tail had still been intact. She smiled briefly as she finished a length. He was always on the lookout for anything that would be helpful. Once, when she was using her own hair to make finely plaited cords, he'd bent down so that she could slice off some of his with a stone knife. Her blue-black strands braided with his brown-black ones went into making a thin, supple twine to tie off her smallest medicine pouches. Raven had fashioned a bracelet for herself out of a short length. She still wore it even though it was beginning to fray.

After a while, Raven put down the cording. In her mind, there were no longer any doubts that something was wrong. She ached inside with a pain similar to what she'd felt after Willow, her older sister, had died. Struggling against despair, Raven stood. Too much time had passed. She would have to go around Fin's authority and raise a search party herself.

Just then, voices called to her from outside. She hurried over and lifted the flap. Two of the camp's trackers stood there, leaning on their spears. They carried small packs on their backs. Many members of the Wind tribe, such as these brothers, had names that referred to the sea instead of the wind. When Raven had remarked upon the duality to Leaf, he'd explained that giving children sea names was a tradition reflecting the fact that most Wind tribe bands lived along the coast. The oldest brother was named Long Wave because his body had been long and thin at birth. The youngest had been a smaller baby and was named Short Wave. After a time, they were simply called Long and Short by everyone, just as Leaf's name had been shortened from Blowing Leaf.

Raven looked behind them. "Where's Fin?"

They shifted on their feet. Long replied, "He didn't say he was coming."

"Well, that's typical."

They exchanged glances at her hard, abrupt voice, but Raven didn't care an owl's hoot if she made them uncomfortable.

At last, the search was underway. She fell into step with the two men as they left, matching them stride for stride.

They soon picked up Leaf and Wren's trail from the day before. The tracks wound through steppe-land grasses and small thickets of trees as father and daughter had gone from stream to isolated stream. Everything about their course appeared normal until the fourth trap site.

From the direction her footprints took, it was obvious that Wren had gone off by herself to a nearby patch of blueberry bushes. Leaf had stayed behind. His prints on either side of the stream showed that he'd straddled the water to pull up the trap.

Long put his feet in Leaf's footprints and bent over to heave it up. The trap sloshed out, full of fish. They flopped about as the water drained away. Long let out a loud grunt and dropped the trap back in. "Whatever happened, it made him forget the fish."

"It looks as though Leaf followed the girl." Short pointed at footprints a short distance from Wren's that went in the direction of the blueberry bushes.

The three of them headed over. Numerous large bushes laden with fruit spread out in front of them. Normally, Raven would have been delighted, but being distracted by worry, she barely noticed the berries. After going a few steps into the patch, Raven and the two trackers stopped. Leaf's prints had disappeared, but there were a lot of other prints that weren't his.

Raven looked in dismay at the impressions in the sandy soil. Leaf had been set upon, although she didn't see many signs of a struggle. The area wasn't unduly roiled the way it would have been if he'd fought them.

Long glanced at Short. "I'd say that two full-grown men

came upon him in these bushes. One had on moccasins, and the other was barefooted."

"I agree," Short said. "Big men." Clearly awed, he squatted down beside the prints. "They have feet larger than any I've seen."

Raven's hands strayed to her mouth as she stared at how the toes of the barefooted man had splayed in the sand. Those feet were indeed large—and very wide. Beyond that, they were familiar. She'd seen prints like those before.

# CHAPTER 2

*Leaf*

L EAF STRUGGLED UP A SLIPPERY slope of awareness, his head throbbing with pain. His first cognizant thought was that he should go ask Raven for some of her powders to stop his head hurting. Upon attempting to rise, he found he wasn't able to move at all, much less go anywhere. Leaf tried to see what held his arms and legs so tightly, but solid darkness surrounded him, blacker than a cloudy night sky.

Twitching around in frustrated confusion, he found that even though his arms were bound alongside his body, he could still move his hands a bit. Leaf wriggled his fingers against his thighs and felt coils of rope. He'd been trussed tighter than a skewered grouse before roasting. At the thought, his head cleared a little. Leaf remembered that he'd been with Wren at the fish traps, hoping to find enough trout and perhaps some eels in them for a good meal. Perhaps she was also tied up nearby.

"Wren," he croaked several times, but no one answered. The empty silence was not unlike the vast quietness found deep within a cave.

He struggled to understand what had happened. The closest traps hadn't held any fish, and even though it was a much longer walk, they went to the stream where he was often lucky. When they got there, he'd reminded Wren to stay close by and strolled down to the submerged trap. At the other streams, the cages had come out easily, but the present one was stuck underwater. The frame's wooden lattice was entangled with a branch. He couldn't see the trap through the murky water full of debris from recent heavy rains, but he thought it might be full.

After wrestling with it for a while, Leaf raised his head to check on Wren. She'd wandered over to some large blueberry bushes that were a little too far away, but she was in plain sight, so he continued his efforts. When Leaf finally freed the trap, he could no longer see her. Somehow, she'd vanished during the short time he was bent over the stream. He muttered a curse, dropped the fish-laden trap back into the water, and hurried to the blueberry bushes.

That was when someone attacked him. Leaf tried to recall if he'd gotten a glimpse of whoever had hit him in the head. He frowned in concentration, flinching as another pang went through his skull. That blow had made thinking surprisingly difficult. Leaf remembered wandering among enormous blueberry bushes, taller than a man, calling to Wren, galled at how she'd slipped away from him so quickly. He'd popped a few blueberries in his mouth right before hearing footsteps behind him. Thinking it was her, he'd started turning around. The world had immediately gone black. He hadn't really seen anyone.

Perhaps his attackers were desperate outcasts from another tribe. But as far as he knew, no other bands or tribes lived in the area. The lack of competition was one of the arguments Leaf had put forward in persuading his tribesmen that they should come with him to the edges of the Great High Plains. The hunting would be better. Besides, it didn't make sense for tribal vagabonds to take him prisoner. They would have been better off killing him after taking his things and the fish so that he couldn't raise a group to track them. If they'd taken Wren—that unfortunately was more understandable. Lately, she'd begun to look a little more woman than child.

"Wren," he called out once more into the darkness, but there was no response.

Raven would worry when they didn't return. She would not blame him, but whatever had happened to her oldest daughter was surely his fault. Leaf had given in to Wren's wheedling. He should have told the girl to mind her younger brother and sister, so that her mother could accompany him instead. Raven always needed fresh medicinal plants, and they could have been alone together for a change. But instead of putting Wren in her place, he'd brought her with him, even though he knew he would have to watch her like a hawk.

Wren behaved as though she were already fully grown. It didn't help that she was large for her age; her size only gave her false confidence. Not much frightened her, and her bravery made her foolish. Leaf often wondered if Wren's lack of fear and early physical maturity was because her blood-father had been a Longhead man. A person only had to hunt with the Longheads once to know they were fearless. Even the Longhead women had multiple scars on their bodies from encounters with animals while out foraging. Leaf went rigid within his bindings. He let out a loud grunt.

He'd forgotten that one particular tribal band could be living on the grasslands. For a few days, during the time they'd traveled from the mountains to the coast, he and Raven had shadowed the Longhead band led by Elder Woman, Wren's grandmother. The woman hadn't wanted them near her, so he and Raven had struck out on their own across the plains, searching for the Wind tribe and Leaf's family. That grandmother had caused Raven and Leaf a great deal of worry when they'd lived with her band. Raven had always believed that Elder Woman wanted to steal Wren away after she was born and was only kept from doing so by the lack of nursing mothers within the Longhead band.

Surely the aged woman wasn't still living, but if she was behind their capture, then he didn't understand why she'd taken him. Wren was the one she wanted. Elder Woman disliked Leaf. She would have killed him rather than take him prisoner. It made more sense that outcasts had been behind his kidnapping.

Leaf tested his bindings again, but to no avail. The woven ropes didn't give. The irony of the situation was that he'd been trying to catch fish. The main reason they'd moved from the coastline was that Leaf had decided his scouting skills were wasted fishing in the Big Waters. Although he still wanted to be part of the Wind tribe, he'd become more like the Fire Cloud tribe that he'd lived with for so long. He missed hunting the large grass-eating animals that lived upon the steppes. The coastal Wind tribe bands rarely traveled onto the plains for any reason. A few groups did live a little farther out, and Leaf's band traded with them, swapping fish for game. But those outlying tribesmen were still very close to the coast, whereas Leaf craved to be in the middle of where all those horses, bison, rhinoceroses, aurochs, and various types of deer roamed.

When he told Raven that he'd be happier living on the Great High Plains, she'd pointed out that the caves overlooking the Big Waters were safer. The grazing animals rarely came to the coast, and therefore, the predators that followed them stayed away. But he hadn't listened, so strong was his desire to be a hunter rather than a fisherman. When she saw that he was set on leaving, Raven had compromised by agreeing to stay on the edges of the Great High Plains. After all, she was a woman of the steppes herself. But she wasn't in favor of going deeper into the plains. The winters there were longer and colder than they were nearer the coast.

By that time, the group they lived with had become overly large, and the typical quarreling that came from overcrowded caves had broken out between certain families. The traditional way to relieve that kind of pressure was for some of the families to move elsewhere, but none of them would agree to do so. Their discord worked to Leaf's advantage. Those nights when the band gathered beside fires down on the shore, he'd begun bringing up the idea of moving inland. Some of the more adventuresome families, including Shell's family, had thrown in their lot with him. Shell's mate had been badly beaten during an argument with another man in the band and was more than ready for a change.

Before long, a group had formed, and they'd moved a day's journey from the Big Waters. They'd no sooner stopped traveling than Fin, an older man, challenged Leaf for leadership of the new band. Leaf had happily relinquished that role so he could concentrate on scouting and hunting.

Having been fishermen all their lives, the other men weren't as skilled as Leaf at hunting. He was kept busy for a long while teaching them the finer points of tracking and ambushing. Although most of the men became competent enough, none of them ever became as good as Leaf. That was partly because of his eyesight. He was able to see distant animals, prey or predator, before anyone else did. But his eyes hadn't helped him while at the fish traps. Just because he could see far into the distance didn't mean that he was exempt from being ambushed by a people who excelled at catching prey that way.

A sudden blaze of light revealed the stony walls of a small enclosed area that must be part of a cave. He turned his head toward the glare. Someone holding a torch stood within an opening in the stone. Straining to see through the flames, Leaf blinked in disbelief. He thought he'd glimpsed Chukar—Elder Woman's youngest son, Wren's real father. Then the light withdrew, plunging Leaf once more into darkness.

But Leaf couldn't have seen Chukar, because Chukar had died from a spear wound a long time ago. The burly form Leaf had seen behind the light must have been one of Elder Woman's other sons. The four brothers had all favored one another. The blow that had knocked him out had obviously affected Leaf's eyesight.

In the distance, he heard Longheads arguing, the cadence of their speech unmistakable. They were too far away for him to understand what they were saying, and to Leaf's disappointment, they soon stopped talking. He'd wanted them to come nearer so he could shame them for their despicable behavior. Dumping him on a stone floor after knocking him out and tying him up was no way to treat an old hunting companion who'd helped them feed their children.

By rocking himself back and forth, Leaf managed to flip over onto his stomach. After several twists and rolls, his feet touched a cave wall he'd seen in the torchlight. He would try to sit up with his back against the wall, but first he needed to rest.

He didn't know how long he'd been asleep before the cavern lit up again. Although he'd wanted to confront them earlier, Leaf felt a twinge of fear. Perhaps they'd decided to kill him, after all. He was a bound animal lying there, awaiting the knife. His legs were not tied as tightly as his arms, and Leaf struggled until he was sitting upright. They would have to look him in the eyes before slicing his throat.

He froze when he saw Elder Woman standing there, holding a torch. With a large hooked nose, white-streaked hair, and withering gaze, she reminded him of the ancient gnarled trees seen occasionally on the plains, a survivor from an earlier time.

Her knobby fingers gestured at the man accompanying her. He
brought a wooden water bowl over to Leaf and raised it to his
mouth. Leaf relaxed within the bindings. They wouldn't give
him water if they were going to cut his throat.

Leaf recognized the bearer of the bowl as the son they
called Jay. He must have been the man Leaf had glimpsed
earlier. The water slipped down his throat, fresh and cool, but
after only a few gulps, he jerked his head back. Now that he
wasn't afraid of dying on the spot, Leaf wanted answers, and he
wanted them immediately. Water sloshed over Jay, who started
and stepped away.

"Why have you done this, old woman?" Leaf shouted at
Elder Woman. The language he hadn't used for so many turns
of the seasons was still there. His arms struggled in vain to
make the habitual arm gestures that would have completed the
meaning behind the words. "And where is the girl who was
with me?"

Her hand not holding the torch moved slowly and deliberately. "My granddaughter is fine."

"That girl isn't Wren."

"Harrumph! You are lying. That girl is the child of Chukar's
body." She handed Jay her torch and took the bowl. "Everyone
can see the resemblance. Her hair is more like his, and even her
head is better shaped than your overly rounded skull." Groaning, the old woman knelt awkwardly and pressed the wooden
lip against his closed mouth. "Drink. We are almost ready to
leave. Our travel won't pause just because you're thirsty."

The water spilled over his chin. He opened his mouth and
swallowed before it was all wasted.

"I need to empty my bladder," he said as soon as she took
away the bowl. He shifted on the stone floor. "I'm too old to
lie in my mess like an infant." His urge was strong, it was true,
but Leaf was hoping they would take off his ropes. Perhaps

then he could escape. Once he determined the way back, he could return to the band and put together a group of men to rescue Wren.

Elder Woman slowly rose onto her feet. She looked down at him, her large brow lowered in thought over deep-set eyes. Finally, she said, "I will return shortly."

Leaf remembered Elder Woman as being somewhat spiteful. He watched her and Jay leave, hoping that he hadn't given her an idea for humiliating him. A urine-filled loincloth would make him rawer than a neglected baby. He rotated his neck, loosening the muscles. At least his head had cleared while he'd slept and didn't ache as much.

She was as good as her word, though, and quickly returned with Jay, another man, and an almost-grown boy. Leaf recognized the enormous Longhead as Whit, the oldest of Jay's brothers. Although the boy did seem familiar, Leaf didn't recognize him. He felt strangely gratified that she thought he needed to be so strongly guarded. They stood Leaf up and began unwinding the ropes while Elder Woman looked on.

"Chukar told us how *Them*—your people—tied ropes around his neck so that he wouldn't escape," she said. "We will bind you in the same way to take you outside."

"Chukar's capture wasn't my decision, and neither was the way he was tied. But you want me bound in the same way. Well, I can tell you that we—*Them*, as you call us—wouldn't wind someone in a cocoon of rope to keep him from escaping. It's a waste of effort. Just tying my ankles and wrists would stop me from going anywhere." He nodded at the brothers. "Look at how long it's taking them to undo the ropes."

"Harrumph. Be quiet. I'll ask if I want your advice." From the way she eyed him malevolently, Leaf knew he shouldn't try her. At any moment, she could order her sons to snap his neck with their large hands.

They forced the looped end of a leather rope over his head and down around his neck, pulling the loop too tightly. When Leaf gagged, Jay hurried to loosen it. The leash was disappointing. Escape would be more difficult, although not impossible.

Jay passed the leash to Whit, who took the lead. Leaf's arms and legs tingled painfully as blood rushed back into them, but he hurried after Whit, keeping up so that the rope wouldn't strangle him. The others followed, holding their torches high so that the dark passageway was illuminated. As they went, Leaf kept an eye out for any sign of Wren. The chamber where they'd dumped him was a small room of a larger cave. He looked down every side tunnel they passed, but she was nowhere in sight.

After pausing at the cave mouth to stick their torches into the ground, the Longheads led him outside. Rock pigeons ceased their cooing and burst into the air, abandoning the lip of the cave mouth. Leaf blinked in the bright sunlight, trying to take in his surroundings. A gully snaked through the earth down the slope. He would have to stay out of that once he made his break. A large cluster of trees grew out on the plains. He could head in that direction.

Leaf was encouraged that none of them had brought their spears along for the short outing. All he needed was an opportunity. The muscles in his legs tensed the same way they did right before a sprint toward game. He'd always paced himself in the past when hunting with the Longhead men so as not to outdistance them with his longer legs. Otherwise, he might have faced an angry aurochs or boar without help. Once he pulled the rope out of Whit's hands, he could outrun every one of them.

They gathered around Leaf while he relieved himself. He found it disconcerting that Elder Woman had come along. The Longheads were usually as modest about their bodily functions as the other tribes were. Men and women never left the cave together when taking care of those matters. That she would ignore such a taboo indicated to Leaf how reluctant Elder Woman was to hand over control of him to her sons.

He tried to scan their positions without being obvious about it. The largest gap was between Elder Woman and the youth. Leaf suddenly recognized the boy as the son of another one of the Longhead brothers. Leaf wondered where that brother was. Perhaps, like Chukar, he'd died. If he remembered correctly, the boy's name was Skraw. The younger man had heft to him, but he was smaller than his uncles. Leaf had a better chance of getting past him than the other two. Elder Woman wasn't as steady on her feet as she used to be. He would shove her aside if she tried to stop him.

As soon as he'd readjusted his loincloth, he grabbed the rope and snatched it. Whit gasped as the rope burned out of his hands. Leaf dashed toward the gap between Elder Woman and Skraw, but before he cleared them, the young man leapt upon him. Leaf staggered under the weight, tripped, and fell. With startling speed, Skraw picked up a large stick from the ground and began beating Leaf with it as if he were a pesky badger.

"Skraw, Skraw!" Elder Woman yelled at the top of her lungs. "Do not kill him, Skraw!" The blows stopped, but the coil around his neck tightened painfully as someone caught hold of the rope. His breath rasping, Leaf scrabbled at the rope until he managed to loosen it. He rolled onto his stomach and panted into the earth. Someone kicked him hard in the side, forcing him onto his back again. Elder Woman was yelling above him, her arms slicing the air as she ranted. Leaf strained to make sense of her words.

"I have a use for you," she was saying. "But if you are too much trouble, I won't need you anymore."

"I'm afraid that I'll be useless then. Let me return to my people."

"Harrumph. Never—that will never happen."

It sounded as if she wanted him to do something for her and that if he didn't comply, she would kill him. *Could she want to make me a slave?* Anger gripped him. "Well, get on with it. I won't be your slave. So do what you will."

She frowned down at him. "I was going to feed you before our journey, but you can do without. Beat him some more, Skraw. Just not too hard."

When Leaf looked up at the boy, he regretted arguing with her. Skraw grinned in anticipation as he moved forward, lifting the stick over his head. Elder Woman stepped back out of his way. She wasn't exactly smiling, but her face was set in a satisfied expression. Before the first blow landed, Leaf glanced at Jay and Whit.

He'd made stone tools and hunted with the two men many times. They'd been his comrades, but the uneasy expressions on their craggy visages gave him little hope. He knew that even if the two brothers disliked what their mother was doing, they would never defy her.

Skraw hit him over and over. Every blow took away his breath, pain blossoming wherever the stick fell.

"Not so hard," Elder Woman kept yelling. But the boy was either defying his grandmother, or he didn't know how to temper his strength.

# CHAPTER 3

*Raven*

RAVEN TORE HER EYES AWAY from the large footprints. She glanced at Short, who was still kneeling beside the tracks, then at his brother. The two trackers obviously had no idea who'd left them. "Those footprints were made by Longheads," she said.

They stared at her, jaws dropping. Without saying a word, Long fell to his knees beside Short to better see the marks. Their shock didn't surprise Raven. For all they knew, their own tribesmen could have made the prints.

The Longheads had become mythical beings to the Wind tribe, known only through fireside tales. The elders of the band told stories of powerful creatures, part human and part beast, that had elongated skulls. They'd once dwelled upon the land but had disappeared before the present day. Raven and Leaf listened quietly without comment when they heard the lore that had been passed down from the elders' grandfathers. Neither of them ever corrected the erroneous beliefs about the Longheads, although when the elders spoke of mammoths as though they were all gone, Leaf let them know that those great beasts did still exist beyond Fire Cloud lands.

The stories, told around the hearth fires at night, were full of disturbing images. It was said that Longheads not only hunted and devoured the peoples of other tribes but also ate their own kind whenever they died. The men always expressed disgust upon hearing that part of the tale, while the women shuddered, and the children's eyes widened with fright. Raven and Leaf would glance at each other, the only reaction they allowed themselves. They knew there was some truth in what the elders said when it came to the Longheads eating their own dead, as they did follow that practice during times of starvation.

After the first night hearing the stories, Raven had told Leaf she thought it best they not tell the others he wasn't Wren's father. "I don't think we should ever tell Wren, either," she'd whispered.

He'd nodded, although his eyes hadn't met hers. "I agree. It's best not to." She hadn't detected any malice in his voice, but as always, Raven wondered if somewhere deep down inside, Leaf was resentful about what had happened between her and Chukar before she'd joined up with him.

From then on, they rarely discussed the Longhead band they'd lived with during a long-ago winter. Raven had tried, somewhat unsuccessfully, to push all memories of that mysterious tribe into the dark, deep waters of her mind. But their footprints were blatant reminders they existed.

Short stood up abruptly. "These can't be from Longheads, because spirits don't leave tracks."

"The men who made these tracks aren't spirits. Longheads breathe the same air as you and I do."

"Are you telling us that those ancient beasts are still around?" Long sat back on his heels and peered through the surrounding blueberry bushes as if expecting them to suddenly appear.

Raven hesitated only a heartbeat. "Once, when I lived with the Fire Cloud tribe, I saw them hunting bison."

"Why haven't we ever heard you mention that before?"

She waved a hand nonchalantly. "I didn't think it important, and I didn't want to frighten the children. With all the cave lions in the area, the little ones have enough to be afraid of. Besides, I didn't think the Longheads ever came this close to the coast."

Long snorted. "They have now. Perhaps they're staying nearby in a cave. If so, that's where they took Leaf." He traced one of the prints with a finger then looked at his brother. "They'll be easy to track."

Short's hands fidgeted on his spear shaft. "Perhaps we should go back for more men? We don't even know why they stole them. All the stories say—"

"Most of the stories you've heard aren't true," Raven said. "The Longheads are people like you and me, even if they do look a little different. They aren't part beast. And I've never heard of them eating anyone," she lied. "If we return now, Fin will make us wait until tomorrow before going out again. And we don't know for sure if the Longheads are at one of the caves in the area, or if they were just traveling through. Before we return and talk to Fin, we need to find out more."

Long stood up. "I, for one, am curious to get a glimpse of these people." He squinted at Raven. "If, as you say, they *are* people."

"Then let's follow their tracks. Once we find them, we can return to camp, probably before nightfall, and tell everyone what we discovered."

Short grunted. "What if they see us? They might follow *our* tracks back to camp and try to steal more of us. I know what you said, but what if they do actually eat people?"

Raven stamped her foot at Short's cowardly grousing. While Leaf and Wren were who knew where and the day was getting older, they were standing around talking. "We'll stay hidden," she hissed at him. "From what we've seen, there's only two of them, two men, just as there are two of you. We won't find out if there's more unless we follow them."

Short's face flushed, and he shrugged. "Just as long as we get back before dusk. I'm not spending the night out here with those creatures around."

The three of them started out, but then Long stopped with a jerk. "We didn't finish following Wren's tracks."

At that point, Raven wanted to scream curses at the two men, but she forced herself to remain calm. A quarrel had to be avoided; she badly needed their help. "They have Wren. These two may have caught her after they took Leaf, or she'd already been taken by other Longheads. Either way, she's with them."

"But how can you be sure when we haven't even seen where her tracks lead?" Long waved a hand toward the bushes. "She could be hiding somewhere."

Raven was certain that if Wren had remained free, she would have returned to camp the day before. Raven was also sure that she knew exactly who'd taken Leaf and Wren. Why they'd taken Leaf wasn't clear, unless they'd been afraid he would track them. But she had a good idea for the reason behind Wren's disappearance. The memory of Elder Woman's harsh face softening while dandling her baby granddaughter on a knee flashed through Raven's mind. The woman's affection had gone far beyond the natural love of a grandmother for her grandchild. Elder Woman had coveted Wren from the moment she was born. Raven understood what had happened to her daughter. Even so, Long's words gave her hope that Wren had possibly eluded her captors.

"I suppose we should determine exactly what happened," she said.

As Raven suspected, when they followed Wren's tracks,

they saw she'd also been caught, the prints surrounding hers made by two people.

"The footprints here are a little smaller than the others." Long pointed at several. "I think those are made by an old woman. She's a little unsteady on her feet." He rubbed his chin as he bent over a different set of tracks. "The others are made by a younger person, most likely an almost-grown boy." He glanced at Short for affirmation.

Short nodded and gestured toward Raven. "If those tracks had been made by yet more men, I'd demand that we go back." He sniffed loudly. "But an old woman and a boy? I won't argue with you."

Raven permitted herself a wry smile. He'd finally found his courage.

Wren hadn't gone easily. For a good distance, she'd been dragged. Eventually, she'd stopped fighting and begun walking. Raven bit her lips as she followed her daughter's footsteps. She hoped they hadn't been overly harsh to make her come with them. The tracks of the two men soon joined those of Wren and her captors. Leaf's footprints were still nowhere to be seen. It was obvious from the moccasin tracks sunk deeply in the sandy soil that one of the men was carrying Leaf—probably over his shoulder.

Raven's heart sank. He hadn't been able to walk. "They hurt Leaf."

"At least there's no sign of blood," Long replied.

His words comforted her very little. As a healer, she knew that many serious injuries were bloodless.

Raven and the two men followed the tracks into a canyon. The dry gully was relatively clean of brush and wood debris, and they were able to travel quickly. As they hurried along, dark, heavy clouds formed far out on the plains. Raven considered the massed blackness. The storm was off to the side and so remote that it was unlikely rain would wash away the prints they were following. Rumbles of thunder muttered, and from time to time, the horizon throbbed with lightning. Soon, a broad waterfall of rain hazed the distance down close to the earth. Raven shivered as if the dark clouds were overhead, pelting her with cold raindrops.

When they'd gone farther, the Canyon curved sharply so that it faced the dark horizon. Raven had to rethink her earlier assessment. Luckily, the deluge didn't seem to be coming any closer, but she wished that the canyon would turn again, away from the storm. Leaf and Wren's captors had a large head start, and if they were traveling a long distance instead of being holed up nearby in a cave or rock shelter, they might have been caught by the rain. If so, the trail was effectively obliterated whether the kidnappers had stayed in the canyon or left it.

The three of them stopped to drink water from the bladders they carried in their packs, sitting for a moment on the canyon floor. When they started out again, the darkness in the distance had already lightened, and the canyon twisted away from where the storm had raged. Raven breathed a sigh of relief, but she knew their success in catching up with the captors that day was still uncertain. She glanced at Short trudging along beside his brother. Her greatest worry was that he would soon insist that it had become too late to continue.

They'd walked a goodly distance when several rabbits bounded past. Then a flock of crows flew out of the gully, cawing in alarm. Raven stopped in her tracks, as did the men. Something around the next bend had frightened the animals. As Raven stared along the passage, the ground ahead of them seemed to writhe as though full of snakes. She took a few steps backward just as the canyon floor started shaking. The dirt around her feet began leaping as high as her calves, and looking down, she saw her moccasins were completely covered by the soil. A muted roar from farther down the canyon vibrated the air with terrible purpose.

"Flood!" she yelled and turned to race back the direction they'd come.

As she ran, Raven looked from one side of the canyon to the other, frantically seeking a way out, a collapsed area or a path made by animals that led up the walls. All she saw was sheer rock. Both men caught up, passing her on either side. She glanced over her shoulder, and the sound of water crashing through the narrow channel drowned her scream. A herd of horses was bearing down on them, fleeing in front of the torrent.

To get out of their way, Raven quickly scrambled up the side of a small boulder. The herd passed by but quickly ran down the two brothers. Men and horses were swept away together, the horses kicking mightily as they attempted to swim. Raven strained to see what had happened to the men, but they'd vanished.

The cascade lifted the boulder, tilting it precariously to one side. Raven leapt from the stone surface. The water hurled her toward the canyon wall, and she crashed into a tree that was growing on a ledge. Raven tried to climb the branches, but her pack straps had become twisted around her, tightly holding down one of her arms. She pulled the straps up and over her head with her free arm. The heavy pack flopped onto the rapidly moving water, the flow snatching the straps from her grasp. Raven gave a small cry as the leather bag disappeared in the froth. Everything she needed in case they had to make camp for the night was gone.

The rising water forced her higher. An ominous creaking, barely audible over the gushing roar, came from the slender trunk bending over the flood. Raven feared it would break or her weight would pull the roots out, sending her and the tree twirling down the canyon. But the tree held, and after a short while, the floodwaters abated rapidly. Eventually, only a stream ran down the center of the passage. Raven cautiously lowered herself to the ledge, then she slid down a mud slope until her feet reached the canyon floor.

Her moccasins had somehow stayed on through it all. Muck sucked at them as Raven began stumbling back the way toward camp. The bodies of animals—rabbits, squirrels, a fox, and a lynx—were scattered about, predators and prey alike, all dead. She didn't see any sign of the brothers or her pack. Her jaw tightened with regret. They'd been foolish to stay in the canyon with rain in full sight.

She'd only gone a short distance when she realized she was limping badly and that her thigh burned painfully. Small rivulets of blood ran down one leg. Her tunic had been shredded above the knee, and upon lifting the tatters, she saw a gash that had probably been made when the waters dashed her into the tree.

Raven stopped walking and looked around in desperation for the pack. Not that she could have immediately treated the wound with any herbs from the medicine pouch inside it. Everything would be soaked with muddy water, but without the medicine pouch, she felt as if a part of her were missing. Raven pressed her hand over the worst part of the wound and limped on, shivering. The stone walls blocked the sun, and the breeze coming through the canyon cut to the bone. At least the brisk air was drying her; the wet surroundings made it impossible to find rubbing sticks and tinder for a fire.

A splashing sound from behind alerted Raven that someone besides herself, or perhaps an animal, was also moving through the canyon. She looked over her shoulder. Although she'd seen the men washed away, Raven hoped that the water hadn't carried them very far. Perhaps Long or Short had been left half drowned under a debris pile and had become conscious enough to crawl out only after she'd passed by. But instead of a man, a small colt came around the bend. It froze upon seeing her, tossed its head, and nickered. Relieved that the animal wasn't a bear or a lion, Raven continued on.

The colt stayed at a distance, not attempting to pass, and every time Raven turned around, it whinnied. The sound somehow seemed like a question, as if it were asking her if she'd seen its mother—or if she intended to do it harm. A readily available, unprotected baby animal would normally make Raven think that the Earth Mother was providing an easy meal. But at the moment, she felt sorry for the small creature. It must've been left behind by the stampeding herd then somehow survived the waters.

The colt's long-legged youthfulness made her think of Windy and Sky, and she yearned to see and hold them. A glance at the sun told her she could be with them before nightfall—if she gave up her quest to find Leaf and Wren. Her chest tightened. If she returned to camp, Raven was afraid that she would never see them again. Fin wouldn't help her mount another search, especially if Long and Short hadn't survived.

Raven crossed the canyon to avoid walking upon a stretch of rough river cobbles. She saw when she glanced back that the colt was directly behind her. Shortly afterward, she spotted a man's legs protruding from under a large pile of brush. The legs were stripped of their leggings, and their bared stubbiness told her they belonged to Short. She trotted over and began untangling him from the branches but stopped when his severely crushed forehead made her realize she could do nothing for him.

Her eyes brimmed with silent tears. What she'd taken as cowardice may have only been a premonition on his part that he wouldn't survive the trip. She dreaded facing his family's grief that night. She hoped Long had survived and would invite his brother's mate and children to live at his hearth. Raven pulled the brush back over him, wiped her eyes, and continued on.

She noticed a musky odor pervading the air just before the chuffing of a cave lion came from around a sharp curve in the canyon. Raven froze in her tracks. She glanced back at the colt. It had also stopped and was watching her silently. By the way its eyes were rolled back with the whites showing, she knew it had heard and smelled the lion.

Raven carefully moved to a place farther along the wall and eased her head forward to look around a bulge in the stone. Movement on a ledge near the top of the canyon caught her eye. She remembered seeing a small cave or hollowed area at the back of the ledge when she'd passed through the channel earlier with Long and Short. Two lions stood on the flat stone in front of the hollowed-out rock, one with spots and the other without. They were looking down the soggy ravine in the opposite direction from where Raven hid.

The sound of the flood had most likely awakened them from their usual daytime sleep. Barely breathing, she moved her head back. It wasn't possible to continue forward, but Raven did not want to turn around; the colt might whinny if it saw her coming toward it. Raven again peeked around the side. The lions stood blinking in the sunlight. After a heartbeat, the largest made a rumbling sound, and they both turned and went inside their lair. Raven let out her breath. She wasn't worried they would come out again. The Elders said the lion's nocturnal behavior was part of the Earth Mother's wisdom. While they slept during the day, the tribes hunted, unmolested by one of the most fearsome animals of the land. Likewise, the lions were left in peace at night to find their food without interference from tribal hunters.

Raven walked slowly down the ravine, trying to avoid stepping on anything that might make noise. She hoped that if the colt trailed her, it would follow her example and move as carefully as possible. After she'd gone on a while, Raven stopped to look back. The distant ledge remained empty, and the colt was close behind her. As she watched, quivers rippled up and down its thin legs and over its back. Then its flesh became still, and it looked at her tranquilly, eyes dark without any white showing.

The colt's reaction to the lessening danger provided Raven with sudden insight. Now that the colt felt safer, it no longer needed to be afraid. She believed that the animal's shaking had somehow dissolved or released the fear it had felt upon sensing the lions. Raven recalled how Gale had felt better after her body shook, and she thought about the way Leaf always trembled when he was emotionally overwrought. Perhaps the shaking and trembling was the Earth Mother's way of relieving the strain of living in a dangerous world. She'd never heard the Elders speak of such, but it might be true. A cricket landed on her hand and sprang away immediately, reminding her that she had to keep moving. She couldn't become distracted while traveling alone.

A little farther down, the flood had eroded the wall badly, loosening a landslide. Raven paused before the incline of crumbled earth and eyed the colt. It stared back, its tail switching. Although a very young animal, the colt had long legs nimble enough to follow her if it so chose. She limped toward the scree-filled soil and began climbing up through the muck. As soon as she reached the top, she bent over and rested her hands on her knees, breathing in slowly and deeply.

A challenging neigh caused Raven to straighten. Several horses watched her from a short distance away. A large mare turned to face her directly. Clearly disturbed by a human presence, it pawed the ground with a hoof, snorting, its head

jerking up and down. Raven heard scrabbling hooves coming up the ravine from behind. With a shrill whinny, the colt
clambered over the edge, bolted past her, and ran for the mare.

Nickering all the while, the mare sniffed and nudged her
little one, then she turned and trotted away, the colt running
by her side. The other horses quickly followed. Raven watched
them vanish in the distance, happy for the colt, although its
sudden absence caused her vision to blur.

The breeze was even stronger than it had been in the ravine,
and a gust quickly dried her eyes. She hadn't been so alone
since she'd struggled to survive on the steppes after fleeing
the Fire Cloud tribe. That was far in the past, but Raven still
remembered the sweet relief she'd felt after Leaf had managed
to find her.

She looked at the sun. Midday had passed already. Although Raven hadn't come across Long's tracks, she hadn't
encountered his body, either. They should have decided on a
pre-arranged signal for locating each other in case they became
separated. If she still lived with the Fire Cloud tribe, a series
of owl hoots would have let anyone within hearing range
know that she was there. The Longheads used wolf howls, but
strangely, the Wind tribe didn't have any such set signal.

Raven had a feeling that Long had survived and was well
on his way back to camp. Raven should also turn in that direction. Windy was probably fretting for her mother's breast, and
Shell would be sorely tried until Raven arrived. She didn't have
much hope about Fin sending out another search party, but if
Leaf was alive, he would eventually find a way to escape. Of
that, she had no doubt. And although losing her daughter left
a large hole in her heart, at ten summers, Wren would at least
survive without her mother's care even if she could never be
rescued.

The day was leaking away slowly, yet Raven's indecision

kept her feet firmly rooted to the edge of the ravine. No one could possibly have a better mate than Leaf, and Wren was her beloved firstborn. And though Raven knew she was being disloyal to Leaf, she had to admit that her oldest child was also a cherished reminder of the dead man who'd fathered her. They'd barely known each other, but Raven would never forget him.

"No," she shouted down into the channel. It just wasn't possible to return without Wren. She didn't want to shed her child and past the way a snake did its skin. Her cry was wiped out by the excited calls of a multitude of birds scavenging drowned insects and animals in the depths below.

Raven looked out across the land. She focused her eyes. It seemed to her that the canyon might end in the distance, not much farther than the bend where she and the men had rested. Before returning to the band, Raven could at least go to that point and find where the kidnappers had left the gully. Eventually, rain would obliterate their tracks, perhaps that very day. If she knew the direction that Elder Woman had taken Leaf and Wren, then she would at least have a chance of persuading Fin to search more.

A sharp twinge from her thigh reminded Raven that she had to take care of her wound. Although the bleeding had stopped and the scraped skin around the cut didn't look bad, she still needed to bind the area with a part of her tunic. But first, Raven wanted to clean the wound with fresh water.

Limping, she followed the edge of the ravine, searching for a spring as she walked, each step taking her away from the Wind camp. When she reached the area that she thought contained the lion's den, she gave the gully a wide berth before coming back to the edge.

With hope pushing her along, Raven closed the distance fairly rapidly, but upon approaching where they'd rested before the flood, she realized the end of the canyon had been an illusion. The bend was yet another sharp change in direction, and the gully, although it narrowed, continued far into the distance. Slightly higher land on either side of the turn had blocked her view earlier, providing a false impression.

Raven again checked the sun. At that point, it couldn't be denied—she was too far out to reach camp before dark. The only thing to do was to keep going and find shelter for the night. She'd passed several partial overhangs in large outcrops of rock, but just ahead, a series of rocky hills began. Caves had to be in those hills, though cave lions were probably there as well. Any cave she found would have to be investigated carefully. She limped forward, looking for any evidence of the big cats—a scratched tree or their covered scat.

Instead of lion tracks, Raven found footprints emerging from the canyon and heading toward the hills. She bent and placed her hand over a print made by Wren's moccasin. If only the flood had come later—after she and the men had followed the tracks out of the gully. Although Leaf's prints weren't among them, Raven had high hopes she would soon see both him and Wren. Her heart beat faster at the thought, and she began to trot until the pain in her leg reduced her progress to a fast hobble.

The tracks led to a cave in the side of a hill, and Raven hurried toward the mouth. Partway there, she stopped. Elder Woman would take Raven prisoner if she entered. But then, at least, Raven would be with Leaf and Wren. Her only other option was to survive the night somewhere else and return to the Wind tribe on the morrow. Her throat tightened with the difficulty of deciding, but then she noticed that there was no smoke. Just as the other tribes did, Longheads made guard fires near a cave mouth to ward off predators and curious animals. The way in should be full of swirling smoke. Raven moved slowly forward.

Only dead coals filled the front of the cave, although they smelled of recent fire. Raven stepped over them and went to another hearth farther back in the chamber, and there, she got lucky. When she dug a stick into the charred wood, red glowed beneath the ash. Some of the coals were still alive. Thistledown and unused firewood were conveniently lying nearby, and she soon revived the fire. That done, she took a look around. Three dark passages led off the main chamber. Having used all the available wood, Raven had nothing with which to make a crude torch. She left the cave to gather more brush and limbs. Besides wood for torches, she needed enough kindling to last the night.

Because Raven's leg complained whenever she tried to carry a heavy load, she collected less each trip than she would have normally. She made herself return outside over and over even though she was impatient to explore the rest of the cave. Upon coming across some grubs, she gathered them into a folded leaf for cooking later. She wasn't fond of grubs, but they would at least sustain her until morning. She also found dandelions nearby and pulled them up whole, her fingers digging through the soil for their roots. Every part of those plants was edible, and eating them would also help the swelling around the wound.

During her last foray, Raven made out the footprints of several people where the ground was less trampled. To her excitement, Leaf's were among them. She became alarmed, however, when she followed the tracks into a brush-filled hollow. Apparently, a struggle had occurred. The prints were all mingled together, and the crushed grass showed where someone had ended up on the ground. Raven scowled as she looked at a large stick that lay nearby. She crossed her arms for a moment, hands kneading her biceps in agitation. Then Raven picked up the stick, and while gathering more wood, she kept watch for other tracks. Somewhere out there was the trail left when they'd continued their journey.

Once back in the cave and after the ends of several long sticks were flaming, Raven went down a short passage that ended in a small room. There, she discovered areas on the gritty cave floor where skins had been put down. At least a handful of people had spent the night on them.

She returned to the central cavern and followed a different corridor until it ended in yet another small chamber. Although the dust was full of numerous footprints, only one place showed where someone had lain. An image popped into Raven's mind of Leaf lying there with his arms and legs bound. She searched the room diligently, even going so far as to sniff the cave floor with her mouth open to see if the heavy telltale odor of blood would hit the back of her throat. All she smelled, though, was the musty odor of a cave bear that had once hibernated there.

"At least there's no sign of blood," she said, repeating Long's earlier observation. But as before, the words did little to soothe her.

***

When Raven awoke the next morning, the cave mouth was barely outlined by first light. The fire in the mouth had burned out, but she was so hot that the one she'd slept beside was surely blazing. Raven saw, however, that it was almost out. She struggled up. A wave of dizziness made her sway, and Raven realized that the heat consuming her was from a fever. She gently touched the area around the long cut. Her upper leg had swollen badly during the night. Raven was so uncomfortably warm that she almost decided not to replenish the fires, but the ways of the Fire Cloud tribe were deeply ingrained within her. The more flames, the better, they believed when it came to keeping safe from predators.

Tormented by a terrible thirst, she staggered outside to find water. She pushed aside her rent tunic to take a better look at the injury. A scab had formed, but it was oozing pus. When Raven saw faint red streaks going up her thigh, she drew a shaky breath. She needed to drink elderflower tea and make a paste of comfrey or yarrow right away for the wound, or she wouldn't be traveling anywhere for a very long time, if ever.

Her fever and the accompanying dizziness had abated a little. From her experience healing others, she knew the reprieve was only temporary. She had to move quickly before the fever flared once more. Her mouth and throat were parched, but the air against her skin felt relatively humid, which meant some of the nearby plants possibly still contained dew. She limped over and licked the moisture off a few leaves, but it wasn't enough to slake her thirst. The canyon snaked by not far away. There would be water there left from the flood. She rubbed her face with a hand to get her bearings, then started out.

Using bushes growing from the canyon sides for handholds, she made her way down and found several puddles against the shadowy walls that were still full from the flood. After drinking heavily from the one that held the cleanest water, Raven looked around the area for a turtle shell that could be used for heating water. She could at least clean her leg.

Unfortunately, Raven didn't find anything that would hold water. Continuing to search wasn't an option. The exertion of climbing down into the canyon had weakened her, and Raven dreaded the trip back up. She rested occasionally as she forced herself up the wall, but she was completely out of breath when she entered the cave and collapsed beside the inner fire.

Raven pressed her fingertips against her face; the fever had come back stronger than ever. She was in a bad situation, with only herself to blame, she realized with the clarity given by hindsight. After surviving the flood, the best course would have been to temporarily give up her search, but that error could still be remedied, Raven desperately told herself. While walking toward camp, she could locate the medicinal herbs she needed to treat her leg and fever. Even traveling at a snail's pace, she would be with Windy and Sky within a few days. She would be on her way just as soon as she rested a bit more.

When a wolf's mournful howl pierced the cave, her eyes jerked open. The world had gone strangely dim while she rested. Raven lifted her head but couldn't make herself sit up, and she thought she was probably dying. A part of her mind railed, demanding that she rise and fight to stay alive. She had to if she ever wanted to see her children again.

After a short struggle, Raven managed to prop herself on one elbow, but anything more seemed impossible. She flopped back down. *Perhaps it isn't necessary to get up.* In the past, Leaf had always found her no matter where she went, even locating her on the steppes after she'd had several days' head start on him.

Raven vaguely knew that something wasn't right with that idea, but her mind had grown so sluggish that she couldn't determine how she might be wrong about him coming. Maybe if she slept a while longer, she would be able to think more clearly.

The darkness was broken only by the fire's embers when someone or something entered the cave. Raven's eyes opened reluctantly; she was almost beyond caring whether the intruder was man or beast. A dark figure stood over her and called her name. His voice was a deep, vibrating moan.

Tears leaked from the corners of her lids. He'd come just as she'd thought he would. Perhaps she would see her children again after all. Relieved, Raven allowed herself to drift back into unconsciousness.

# CHAPTER 4

## *Elder Woman*

E LDER WOMAN WAS DREAMING ABOUT a specific time
during her youth. She'd been brought by family members
to the band of her soon-to-be mate, Eagle, the one who would
become Elder Man when he reached his prime. Her family had
remained with her until the ceremony and feasting were over.
The morning they'd left, Elder Woman's new band made ready
to take an animal from the land, their food supplies having
been depleted by her kinsmen's large appetites.

She and the other women were outside the cave to see off
the men, when Eagle came over and took her arm. He looked
past her at the other hunters, his face defiant. "This one will
come with us," he said.

Several of the men frowned and flexed their hands in preparation to speak. Eagle quickly held up her arm, bending it at
the elbow so they could see the large muscles that ran up to
her shoulder. "She is strong and quick. We won't be hindered."
When they saw that he was determined she should go, no one
spoke against her.

Elder Woman hunted often with Elder Man during the
time he was called Eagle. During that particular afternoon, she
and Eagle helped force a large stag to flee into an ambush.
They chased it through a gap in some brush, running with all
their might. When Elder Woman came out the other side, the

animal still stood. The stag was raking its antlers at the men who were trying to close in on it. Holding her spear tightly, she ran directly up to the deer from the side and brought the beast down with a well-aimed thrust to the heart.

Anyone who killed an animal outright was entitled to the liver, and she'd signaled her rightful claim by placing a foot on top of the animal. They'd allowed her to have the hide too, and the leggings she'd made from it had lasted many seasons.

But in her dream, Elder Woman was having difficulties. The tunnel through the brush was much longer than it had actually been. If she didn't run faster, the stag would be killed before she got there, or even worse, it would get away.

Elder Woman came awake, her legs thrashing the sleep pallet with so much force that the furs flew off. She propped up on an elbow and took a quick look around the chamber before pulling the coverings back over again. All of the band still slept, except for her daughter, Chirrup, who was cooking a piglet they'd butchered the night before. If she'd noticed her mother's vigorous awakening, she pretended not to.

Elder Woman didn't like the way her dream had ended so abruptly. It left her with the sense of things gone awry, a familiar feeling as of late. Waking before the kill had deprived her of seeing the awe on Eagle's face once again as he marveled at the prowess of the woman who'd become his mate. That distant day, his eyes had met hers while her foot rested on the deer, his gaze slowly filling with lust.

After he became Elder Man and she Elder Woman, they'd jointly led the band for many moons, but he'd eventually died, failing to awaken one morning. She missed him still. He'd been a good mate and provided Elder Woman with many strong children, who, for the most part, were respectful and did her bidding. Only Chukar, her youngest, had ever been any trouble. And that one remained a problem. When he'd reappeared after his supposed death, strolling one day into the cave warren where they'd settled, Elder Woman had thought him a spirit.

Everyone leapt from the hearth and fled outside. Elder Woman hadn't understood why he wasn't dead. Death had been all over Chukar when the band left him in the overhang. Elder Woman had seen enough people die to know when to give up on them. Yet there he was, thin and wan, but alive. When she recovered from her fright, Elder Woman went back inside. Chukar was sitting calmly before the hearth, devouring venison from a skewer as if he'd just returned from a hunt instead of from the dead.

"How did you survive?" she asked. "That type of chest wound can't be healed."

He answered plainly, but his accompanying hand speech conveyed a certain smugness as he told her that the healer, Raven, had given him medicines before she left him.

"I took her herbs; they healed me," he said, plucking off another piece of venison.

Elder Woman didn't believe that. To her knowledge, no medicinal plant in the world could have fixed the dripping puncture in Chukar's chest. That conviction was behind her belief that he was probably a spirit, a particularly devious one, trying to convince them all he was a living man.

Chukar didn't attempt to live with the band at the cave warren, but he occasionally came by then left again in the same day. She was glad that he didn't visit often. Every time Chukar reappeared, Elder Woman got a small fright. And although it was the way of the People to leave behind anyone who wasn't able to keep up, Elder Woman couldn't help but think Chukar resented the way they'd all deserted him and that he might someday seek revenge.

Chukar had suffered his chest wound while trying to

protect Raven from one of the healer's own tribesmen, a man named Bear. Elder Woman breathed out a heavy sigh over the foolishness and poor judgement of her son in becoming involved with a Them woman.

The only understandable explanation for Chukar's strange behavior was that although Raven was Leaf's mate, she'd birthed Chukar's child while she was living with Elder Woman's band. They were shocked when Wren was born, as it became clear the baby girl was Chukar's and not Leaf's. Just as lions and leopards never mated, no one had considered it possible that the two different groups could join and produce a child. All they could think, though, was that Chukar had gotten her pregnant during the time he was a captive of Raven and Leaf's tribe.

Leaf had known before Wren's birth that Chukar was the real father. Elder Woman begrudgingly admired Leaf's tolerance and restraint. Bands were often torn apart by jealous hatred. Once it began, the fighting was hard to extinguish. Without ever discussing the matter with Leaf, Elder Woman's family had conspired with him to keep Chukar away from Raven.

Raven and Leaf had no sooner moved in with Elder Woman's band during that long-ago winter when Chukar began completely ignoring his own mate, Chirrup. That she was also his sister made the slight even worse. Elder Woman and Elder Man had been greatly offended.

Elder Woman had come around to thinking, though, that Chukar's defection had to do with the fact that Chirrup *was* his sister. She and Elder Man had tried to find mates from another band for the two siblings, but the People had become so few that they'd been unsuccessful. That dearth of mates had been behind her decision to seize Wren and Leaf, an entirely distasteful undertaking.

She threw off her sleeping furs, her mind too busy to sleep more, and rose with a groan to start the day. Her body was so stiff lately. Elder Woman had watched other elders fade rapidly and knew that her days were limited. She must move quickly to do those things that she had decided were necessary. Now that she had her granddaughter, as well as Leaf, under her control, she could go forward with her plan. The mouthwatering aroma of roasting piglet saturated the air. "Is the meat done cooking?"

"Yes," Chirrup replied cheerfully. "Done enough."

"I'll take some to the girl this morning. Freshly cooked meat is hard to resist. Has she been eating any better?"

Chirrup shook her head. "Wren never even looks up to see what we have brought her. It is as if we hurt her eyes. She pulls the large cape she wears tightly around her body and tucks her chin on her chest."

Elder Woman frowned. The girl was resentful about the rough treatment she'd received, but capturing someone wasn't that easy. Skraw was only supposed to restrain Wren when Elder Woman gave him a signal, to simply grab her from behind. But in his excitement, he'd run over and knocked her into a large blueberry bush.

While the girl was stunned, Elder Woman had hurried over and gagged Wren's mouth tightly with a strip of leather. The girl refused to walk and had instead fallen down every time they stood her up. They'd resorted to dragging her by the legs. But after only a short distance, her head hit a rock, and so she began walking. Then she'd tried to run away, and Elder Woman had lost her patience, hitting Wren about the head with her fists. Perhaps Elder Woman shouldn't have done that, because from then on, Wren cringed whenever Elder Woman went near her.

After the girl saw Leaf hanging over Whit's shoulder, the

problems with her ceased completely. Wren's eyes became watery and red as if she thought he were dead. When Elder Woman asked if he was alive, her sons said they hadn't hit him hard enough to kill him. That had been a relief. The band needed Leaf as much as the girl. Fortunately, he'd recovered enough during the night to be able to walk, and they were able to resume their journey the next morning without Whit having to carry him.

Upon reaching the cave warren where Elder Woman's band was living, Whit and Jay had secured their captives in separate small chambers, blocking both entries with a couple of the large boulders found everywhere in the passageways. Elder Woman had decided to leave Wren alone for a while, but that was about to change. She had to be won over as soon as possible. Her defiance had to stop.

So preoccupied was Elder Woman that she ate very little before folding some of the steaming meat into fresh leaves, making sure she'd included pieces streaked with juicy fat. Whit and Jay had awoken by then, and she took them with her. When they reached the chamber, the two men moved the boulder from the opening. Motioning to them that they should stay outside, Elder Woman entered. Ideally, Wren's time alone over the last days had made her more desirous of company.

But it wasn't so. Just as Chirrup had described, the girl settled into herself. She refused to raise her eyes, leaving her grandmother staring down at her hair, woven in the same strange manner that Raven had kept her black tresses. Most of that should be cut off soon, so that Wren would look more like one of the People. At least the reddish-brown color resembled Chukar's.

The girl almost hadn't survived her birth. Everyone had been sure that Raven would die and take the baby with her into darkness. For almost a day, Elder Woman had watched that woman's ridiculously narrow body strain and struggle without success to squeeze out the infant. But then Raven had taken herbs that weren't familiar to Elder Woman, and the child had come.

Everyone always hoped a baby would survive the ordeal that was birthing, but Elder Woman had been made uneasy when Raven's medicines managed to bring it about. She'd felt the same type of discomfort as when Chukar claimed later that Raven's medicine had healed him. It was unthinkable that Raven might know more about healing than Elder Woman did.

She focused again on her granddaughter. Elder Woman had to admit that Chukar and Raven had made a very satisfying child together. The girl did look a little strange with that darker skin and smallish nose, but in spite of those faults, she was somehow very appealing—as a child should be to a grandmother.

Elder Woman placed the meat on top of a flat rock that was near Wren, opening the leaves so the smell would tempt her. With a withering look at Elder Woman's food offering, the girl rose and strode over to stand in front of a rocky wall. The room was warm from the fire, and Wren wasn't wearing her shaggy cape. Elder Woman finally got a good look at her. Inside her tunic, Wren's breasts seemed to be nicely filled out, and although her hips were a little slim, they were much better sized than her mother's. Elder Woman didn't think Skraw would mind that she was a bit tall. He would overlook that for a chance to mate. Hopefully, their children would look more like the People than Wren did.

A growing excitement filled her. Elder Woman would soon have a special kind of grandchild that not too many women lived long enough to see—one born from a grandchild. And the band would increase in size. The only thing that held her back from immediately planning the mating ceremony was

that she didn't know if Wren had started having her moon
blood. Elder Woman strolled over to take another look at her
from the side. Wren certainly looked mature. Surely she'd already become a woman.

But her granddaughter still shrank from Elder Woman's
eyes. Perhaps Wren was an easily frightened girl. After all, her
mother was one of Them, and they were known to be cowardly
in some ways. From what Elder Woman's sons told her, Leaf
had always hunted in a very timid manner. He threw his spear
from a distance rather than making sure of a kill by approaching the animal closely. Cowardice was a serious defect. Maybe
the girl had enough of the People in her blood to overcome it.

Or the problem could be that Wren considered Elder
Woman a stranger. Elder Woman made a slow cradling motion
with her arms. "I held you as a baby," she said loudly.

Elder Woman was disappointed when Wren didn't respond,
but of course, the girl only understood that unnatural speech
spoken by her people.

"Wren," Elder Woman uttered, forcing her mouth around
the strange sounds.

Surprised, the child turned her head.

Elder Woman garbled out another word she'd learned long
ago. "Raven."

Eyes wide, Wren whirled to face her.

Elder Woman dipped her head several times, preparing to
say another difficult word. "Leaf."

The girl suddenly let out a torrent of gabble. That was how
Elder Woman stumbled upon the idea of using Leaf to tell
Wren that she was her grandmother. Although he often said
the words badly, at least he knew how to speak like someone of
the People.

Pleased at having come up with a way to communicate
with her granddaughter, Elder Woman left the chamber. Whit

stayed to guard the entry while she took Jay with her down the passage. She wanted to talk to Leaf before he saw Wren. Elder Woman and Jay rolled the rock away from the opening of the room Leaf was kept in.

Although bound tightly, Leaf had managed to sit up, his back and shoulders against a wall. The look on his face made her think that she might one day have to kill him—before he tried to kill her. That wasn't something that she would do any-time soon, not if she wanted more grandchildren at her hearth. He would have to be watched carefully, though. Except for those days when she would undo the ropes so he could do her bidding, he had to remain tied. Elder Woman must survive so that she could be the one to grasp those future babies as they left their mothers' bodies. Only then could she peacefully die.

The People had always been a small presence upon the land during her lifetime, but now, they'd completely vanished from the High Plains. Search though she might for other bands, the only evidence they'd ever existed were old campsites—very old ones. The hearths in the caves that had once been used for cooking and warmth had become so buried by dust that a person had to dig before finding the spent coals. Elder Woman couldn't fathom the reason for her people's disappearance. All she knew was that the lack of suitable mates made it difficult for her family to grow again after the strange illness that had decimated them upon arriving at the cave complex.

Elder Woman had lived at the complex several different times in her childhood, and she'd led the band to the place. It was as convoluted as a rabbit warren, full of small hollow rooms that could be easily heated with hearth fires during the winter. They currently occupied only a small part of the maze, rattling around in it like so many stones. It was easy to become lost there.

She stood looking at the cave floor while she thought—not

staring at Leaf in the rude way he was eyeing her. He didn't understand that a person's eyes were powerful and capable of offending whomever they looked at. One's gaze should be re-served for aiding communication, both spoken and unspoken. And he always talked too much, never realizing that words often weren't needed at all.

Elder Woman made him wait a while longer before lifting her arms and beginning the dance of hand gestures and words. "We will take you to Wren. I want you to tell that girl my name and that she is the grandchild of my body. Tell her about Chukar."

He glared at her. "No, I'm the only father she's ever known." His hands and arms pushed against his bindings as he tried to use them while speaking the way one normally would. "She doesn't need another shock after what you…" He pressed his lips together tightly for a moment. "Just let me comfort her now. We can tell her that you're her grandmother some other day."

Elder Woman thought about what he'd said but decided against waiting. She must start putting her plan in place right away. Her voice might croak like an old woman's, but he shouldn't think he could tell her what to do.

"Harrumph. We all know who the real father is, and now Wren must know." Her hands made short choppy movements. "Will you do what I ask, or must I keep you apart?"

Leaf's glower was so full of hate that Elder Woman thought he might actually refuse her. He swallowed hard. "If it's the only way I can see her, then I'll do it."

Jay looked at Elder Woman.

"Only untie his legs," she told him.

"Tell me why you stole *me* away," he said as Jay bent over him. "What do you want with me?"

"You'll know soon—very soon."

When Jay pulled him onto his feet, Leaf almost fell. He uttered a small sound as the other man hurried to steady him. "Wait a heartbeat for the blood to flow," Leaf said. "The ropes have made my legs into deadwood."

While Elder Woman stood impatiently with Jay in the passageway, he stamped his feet for a while before coming out. She could barely wait to get back to her granddaughter.

When they entered, Wren darted over and tried unsuccessfully to grasp one of Leaf's tightly bound hands. Her words were shrieks as she gave up on his hand and threw her arms around him, making him stagger. Elder Woman shook her head, aghast at the display. Leaf's appearance probably did distress Wren. He had a large bruise on his forehead, and his lip was cut. But still, the girl should have better self-control. In her haste, Wren had almost knocked the choice pieces of piglet off the rock that Elder Woman had brought her. A closer look showed that she had at least eaten some of it.

Leaf replied to her ravings with a low, steady voice, talking to her at length. Elder Woman thought she was calming, but then the girl jumped back as if he'd slapped her. Wren's eyes rolled when she caught sight of Elder Woman and Jay standing behind Leaf. She snarled some words and pointed rudely at her grandmother. Then she stamped her feet and turned back to Leaf, using a word that Elder Woman recognized. It was something she'd heard Raven say to Wren when she was small and misbehaved.

"No, no!" she yelled over and over.

If it hadn't been for the torches and hearth fire illuminating the room, Elder Woman might have thought she was listening to a small child throw a temper tantrum. Annoyance turned into an ache that settled just above her brow line. She didn't understand why her granddaughter behaved in such a manner. The girl should be happy to hear who she really was. Wren should have already noticed that the People were stronger and better formed than Them.

Leaf seemed to be trying to soothe her, murmuring softly in her ear, but she kept interrupting him. After watching her granddaughter's unseemly behavior for a few more moments, Elder Woman shrugged in disgust and headed for the corridor. She motioned for the brothers to bring Leaf along.

When the girl tried to follow him out, Elder Woman pushed her back inside. Wren's resentful face stared out at her, and as the rock slid in front of the opening, she stuck out her tongue. Never had any of her children or grandchildren done such a thing, but Elder Woman grasped at once that the gesture was one of defiant disdain.

For most of the day, Elder Woman simmered with anger about the way things had gone with her granddaughter. Although there was much to be done, it was difficult not to allow bitter thoughts to distract her from working. She finally took some skins along with her to sit at the main hearth during late afternoon. Elder Woman began softening the skins with her mouth, thoroughly chewing one area before moving on to another. A twinge in her jaw warned her that she should rest her teeth for a moment.

Everyone had already come inside ahead of the darkness, and Elder Woman felt something akin to panic at once more noticing how few they'd become. Skraw and his cousin Coo were the only two grandchildren who remained after the terrible illness. Of Elder Woman's own children, three had survived—Jay, Whit, and Chirrup. She didn't include Chukar in her tally because of her uncertainty about whether or not he truly existed. Besides, he didn't live with the band anyway. Jay's mate, Finch, had lived, although Whit's woman had died. These few people were the remnants of the band she and Elder

Man had formed with a couple of his brothers and their mates all those moons ago.

Her eyes lingered on Chirrup. If that one and her brother had birthed a handful of children, things wouldn't presently be so dire. But the lack of offspring probably hadn't been their fault. Elder Woman remembered the miscarriage Chirrup suffered halfway through her one and only pregnancy. She may have lost other babies even earlier on; she'd sometimes complained about moon blood days that came at strange times. The reason Chirrup and Chukar hadn't produced a single living child was possibly because they were siblings.

Elder Woman thought back to the few brother-sister pairings in her childhood band. The babies who did survive birth were often malformed and had to be smothered. She'd also noticed that sibling couples didn't seem to join very much. From their earliest days, children saw animals mating on the steppes, and it wasn't difficult for her as a girl to figure out what certain sounds meant in the cave during the night—although everybody always pretended not to notice. If the couple wasn't too far from the hearth's flickering flames, then the furs covering them could be seen moving vigorously. She always had to resist giggling at the sight, or she would receive a sharp kick from her mother.

Those sibling couples, however, hadn't produced that interesting, amusing display very often—and neither had Chukar and Chirrup after their ceremony. His neglect made Chirrup unhappy. Not that she desired him any more than he did her, but Chirrup had wanted a baby more than he had—or so Elder Woman had thought until Wren was born. It was partly the way Chukar's eyes brightened whenever he looked at the baby girl that had helped Elder Woman realize Wren was his. That—and his yearning for Raven.

Elder Woman rubbed her jaw. The pain wasn't going away

very quickly. She would soon have to stop softening skins with her mouth. Although she couldn't see them, Elder Woman suspected that all of her back teeth were cracked. Once the teeth went, a person's life was nearly over. Elder Woman didn't have enough days left in her for putting up with a rebellious granddaughter.

She glanced at Skraw, who was busy cutting the wing feathers away from a vulture carcass. He seemed to be enjoying the task. Elder Woman hadn't told him that the long black feathers would adorn his clothing and hair during the joining ceremony that would take place someday soon. Once Wren realized she would not be allowed to see Leaf again, her loneliness would become unbearable. Then Elder Woman would begin taking that virile boy along with her whenever she visited her granddaughter. She shouldn't be overly concerned that Wren would continue her scornful behavior. The girl was ripe enough that she would eventually respond to Skraw in spite of herself.

Running a finger over her throbbing gums, Elder Woman turned her attention to Coo. Elder Woman, along with Finch and Chirrup, Coo's aunts, had somehow saved her during the illness. The young woman, unaware of her grandmother's appraisal, sat eating a ground squirrel she'd caught and cooked. Coo's eyes were large and clear, her reddish-brown hair glossy. Her ample but firm body was full of vigor—and all that potential fecundity was being wasted. She should have birthed several children by this time in her life, but there hadn't been any man for her to join with—until now.

If Chukar could produce an adequate child with Raven, then Elder Woman was sure that Coo could do so with Leaf. She stopped exploring all the cracks in her back teeth that her fingers had found. Beyond having someone pull out every ruined tooth, she could do nothing to make them go away.

Elder Woman slept deeply that night, without dreaming.

She awoke with a rare feeling of contentment brought about by knowing she was doing something helpful for her people. Whit had never showed any interest in finding another woman, and Chirrup's unhappiness at being childless would occasionally permeate the air, but at least Coo and Skraw would have mates now that she had Wren and Leaf in her clutches. The time-consuming search for more of their own kind could stop. And best of all, Elder Woman would soon have more grandchildren around her at the hearth—just as it should be.

Jay, Whit, and Skraw left to go hunting that morning. After they were gone, Elder Woman went with the women to a nearby stream for water. She straightened from filling her waterskins just in time to see Chukar top the slope in front of the cave and slip through the mouth. She felt a lash of anger that his brothers were once more neglecting to stop him—until she remembered that they'd gone hunting. Against her wishes, they almost always allowed him inside even though Chukar made them just as uncomfortable as he did Elder Woman.

But they couldn't be blamed entirely because, at times, Elder Woman didn't chase him out either. She would only turn her head, pretending not to see him. He would slowly ease down upon a log at the fire, quietly taking a place among the group. Everyone always sat stiffly with their eyes averted until he left again.

How Chukar managed to survive by himself, she couldn't fathom. Although he'd always been different from her other children, disturbingly so at times, his mating with Raven had somehow changed him into someone she didn't recognize. In spite of the strong resemblance to Elder Man, he was a stranger. Because she'd somehow known when he was born that he was her last child, Elder Woman had nursed him until he'd passed four turns of the season, a ridiculously long time. Perhaps all that mother's milk had ruined him.

She didn't see him come out of the cave, but when they returned with the water, Chukar wasn't inside. The spirit-like way he'd disappeared set her teeth on edge, making her jaw ache again. Elder Woman found the pain so distracting that she went to find her herbal bag. Some powdered poplar bark would at least help temporarily.

To her dismay, the pouch was nowhere to be found. It was usually beside her sleeping skins, but that morning, it wasn't.

The women stopped what they were doing to help her search. They looked everywhere in the parts of the cave they were living in except for the rooms where Leaf and Wren were being kept. She hadn't taken the bag with her to either place. Finally, Elder Woman gave up and ordered the women to stop searching. Although she'd never done so in the past, perhaps she'd carelessly left the bag somewhere outside. If so, her mind was weakening.

Chirrup went with her that afternoon to begin finding the most important medicinal plants to replace her lost ones. It would take many days of foraging to replenish her stores, and she wouldn't be able to replace the powdered poplar bark anytime soon. None of the trees grew nearby.

The summer air was mild, neither too warm nor too cold. A bird dear to Elder Woman, a nightingale, sang its cheerful strident song nearby, but seeing Chukar had put her in a bad mood. She snatched flowers and stems off plants, all the while keeping an eye out for fennel, which was good for jaw pain.

In contrast to Elder Woman's frantic pace, Chirrup worked placidly, pinching the feathery leaves off a wormwood shrub. But then her daughter was almost always even tempered. She'd seemed upset, however, when she found out that Leaf had been taken captive and that both he and Wren were prisoners. Although she had known that Elder Woman and the men had gone on a quest to bring Wren back, Chirrup hadn't realized they were going to steal her. Elder Woman had told Chirrup and the other two women only that she wanted Wren to live with them for a while. Leaf's forced presence at the cave had been a complete surprise.

Elder Woman's explanation that they'd brought Leaf along so that he wouldn't immediately track them down and make trouble was the truth, even if that wasn't the primary reason she'd taken him. Chirrup's eyes, however, had remained full of accusation. More so than the rest of them, Chirrup had befriended Leaf and Raven when the couple had lived with the band. It was good she hadn't been around when Skraw disciplined Leaf for trying to escape. She may have tried to intervene.

Elder Woman didn't know how her daughter would react when she found out Wren and Leaf had been brought to the cave for the purpose of providing Elder Woman with more grandchildren. She must come up with a way to make Leaf cooperate. Elder Woman was so very fond of Chirrup. She didn't want to antagonize her further by making him disappear.

# CHAPTER 5

*Raven*

R AVEN WAS CONFUSED AS TO the identity of the shadowy form that frequently floated into the surrounding dimness. The spirit-like visitor had the musky smell of a man, but his presence didn't feel at all like Leaf's. Whereas Leaf was tall and lean, the shape that loomed over her was large and broad, and she sensed a difference about the man that went beyond size. He was different but somehow familiar. Raven's mind wasn't alert enough to untangle her impressions and tease out where she'd met him; all she understood was that if she died, someone would notice her passing.

Whenever he wiped her body down with cool water, she almost came to, as the raging temperature lowered enough for her to capture a few stray thoughts. But all too quickly, mind-numbing chills seized her again, making her shiver, and the fever would flare. Occasionally, he pushed chewed pieces of meat into Raven's mouth. When she tried to spit them out, he pressed his cupped palm over her lips and stroked her throat until she swallowed. Then he would tilt her head back and pry open her mouth with his fingers. As the water dripped onto Raven's tongue, her dry gullet would convulse greedily.

Raven understood somewhere deep down inside that he was struggling to keep her from joining forever with the Earth Mother. Occasionally, he lay down on the cave floor with her

while she fought to throw off the fever, his arms wrapped
tightly around her, his body becoming soaked with her sweat.
He called out Raven's name while he held her, trying to coax
her toward a lucidity that she couldn't quite reach. Although
his cries reminded her of a young raven pleading to be fed, his
voice was much more melodious than the harsh sounds of her
namesake bird.

When at some point, the man lifted her, Raven came awake
a little. He sat her against a wall, gently easing her body into
a slight depression so she wouldn't collapse. Raven moaned at
the effort of sitting upright. She kept her eyes closed against
the whirling dizziness.

Something dropped heavily onto her lap. Raven's eyelids
cracked open, and she saw large strong hands opening a bag.
An herbal smell scented the air, and she blinked to focus on
the bag's contents. The neatly stacked leather packets caused a
small stirring of interest. Someone had found her medicines—
but then she saw the bag was different. Her herbal pouch was
made of deer leather. This one was of wolverine.

Bewildered, she looked up to see who owned the bag, and
her breathing almost stopped. Although everything in front
of her floated erratically, she was able to make out his features—the large nose, heavy brows, and well-notched lips. But
his green eyes blazing with concern were what made her heart
race so hard, she thought it would leap from her chest. She'd
only known one man who had eyes that color. A muted shriek
escaped her. Everything went dark again.

She wasn't allowed to linger for long within the blackness.
Sharp pricks on Raven's arms like stinging bees made her
flinch. She came partly to and started swatting away the bees.
They immediately attacked her legs. Bending from the waist,
Raven slapped at them. Her eyes flew open to see Chukar, a
man who, by anyone's reckoning, was dead.

He slipped off one of her moccasins then picked up a long thorn and held it at the ready, pointed at her foot. She didn't know whether she was dreaming or if his spirit had been sent to her by the Earth Mother, but he was making sure she couldn't ignore him.

Raven managed to detach her dry tongue from the top of her mouth. "Stop," she said hoarsely, her hand making the correct sign in the Longhead language.

His eyes held hers while he kept the thorn near her toes. "Look in the bag, Raven. Find the medicines to heal your leg."

Raven became aware of the pain that had been deadened by her delirium, and she recalled her injury. She began slowly taking out packets, opening them, and smelling their contents. A few she put aside. "I need hot water, for the herbs and to clean my leg."

He dropped the thorn and stood up.

"I must be dreaming," Raven murmured after he'd gone out. Not once in all the seasons since she'd last seen him had the Earth Mother gifted her with a dream about Chukar. Now the Earth Mother sent one in which he stuck her skin with a thorn. Raven ran her fingers over an arm, searching out any irritated areas. She found them in abundance. Every time a finger touched one of the raised bumps, her skin stung in a very un-dreamlike manner.

Her attempts to think clearly were exhausting, but she made herself stay awake so she could take another good look at him if he came back. When she'd left Chukar in the rock overhang, death's jaws had been opening to swallow him. It was difficult to believe that he'd recovered.

When the apparition Chukar returned, he brought with him a tortoise shell brimming with water. He set about building up the fire, and the heat soon reached the wall she was reclined against. Perhaps he was a spirit come to help. Raven closed her eyes tightly, slipping away from her confusion.

She hadn't dozed long when she heard his voice as if from a long distance.

"The water is hot." He nudged her foot, gently at first then more insistently.

She opened her eyes. He was holding a small turtle shell full of steaming water that he'd dipped from the larger tortoise shell. Raven remembered how she'd been unable to find anything in the canyon that held water, much less a turtle's shell.

He put the water on the floor beside her then pressed the packets she'd chosen into her hands. "I can't make medicines. You do it."

If he didn't know how to use the chopped and powdered herbs, the bag wasn't his. Raven wondered where he'd found it. She sifted scant handfuls into the turtle shell.

"I need a small stick," she said, her hand pantomiming stirring.

He broke a twig off the firewood, and she used that to mix the herbs into the water. After letting the larger flakes settle to the bottom, she took a sip. The bitter taste of the mixed poplar bark, feverwort, and ground juniper berries roused her somewhat. The feverwort could also be used as a poultice to treat her inflamed wound, and she was very glad for the ground poplar bark. Nothing worked better for pain and swollen flesh.

As Raven cleaned her wound with a square of soft leather from the bag, she saw Chukar staring at her bared leg. The Chukar watching her was a fully mature man, an older, even more powerfully put together version of the Longhead youth Raven had known. He took some dried meat from a food pouch and began chewing it. A spirit wouldn't need to eat. Her insides quivered at the thought.

Raven started to ask him if he *was* a spirit, but she couldn't recall the correct Longhead words to use. She used language that came more easily. "Are you alive?"

Chukar took the chewed meat out of his mouth. "I did not die." He looked at her strangely but didn't seem overly surprised by her confusion.

"I don't understand how you lived."

He started rolling the softened meat into small balls, which he put aside on a piece of leather. "Your medicine was strong. It healed me."

Raven stared at him. The powdered willow bark she'd given Chukar that day couldn't have saved him. She'd only been trying to ease his pain. One of Raven's eyelids began twitching from the effort of thinking. As they always had, his bright green eyes muddled her. She closed her own in order to think more clearly and to stop the annoying twitch. Chukar believed the medicine she'd given him was strong enough to heal him. That was something similar to Gale when she'd sworn her headache was gone even before the poplar bark had time to work. Before Raven could speculate further, her breathing deepened, her consciousness slipping once more.

"No, Raven," Chukar said loudly. "You must stay awake longer."

She heard him move closer. Remembering the painful pricks, Raven forced her eyes back open. But in place of the thorn, he held a ball of worked meat in front of her face, suspended between his thumb and forefinger.

"I'm not hungry."

"You must eat."

"After I sleep more." Her eyelids fluttered wearily. To struggle against death was exhausting. Raven could truly understand why many of the old ones seemed to welcome their inevitable melding with the Earth Mother.

Raven felt herself lifted away from the wall. She made a startled sound and clung tightly to his tunic.

He sat down carefully, holding her in his lap as if she were a child. "Open your mouth."

Although Chukar's voice was nothing like Elder Woman's gravelly one, his demanding tone reminded her of his mother. And she realized that, like Elder Woman, he would persist until she obeyed. She closed her eyes in protest but opened her mouth, expecting to feel one of the food balls land on her tongue.

Instead, he spoke a single word uttered in a low and husky voice. "Aulehleh."

Raven's brow tightened. *Aulehleh* was the first word of his language that she'd learned. It meant *eat* and was what one said when offering someone food. The word often included hidden meanings, the various connotations not always clear, but Raven had always sensed the deep emotions felt by the Longheads whenever they said or heard the word. Her eyes opened in surprise as his warm mouth covered her own, and when the food came onto her tongue, she swallowed. He was attempting to feed her the same way mothers fed their children while weaning them.

Raven moved her head back. "You are truly alive," she murmured, the words lilting up as if she'd asked him a question.

Because of their heavy features, Raven couldn't always figure out what a Longhead was thinking, but one of their facial expressions had always held her attention whenever she noticed it. It was an expression—or actually a lingering glance that someone would occasionally bestow upon a mate or child. Chukar had looked at Wren that way when she was a baby.

Chukar was currently eyeing her the same way, but with an agonizing intensity that resembled pain. She felt her face grow hot under his startling gaze that shone on her like a burning sun. He put another food ball in his mouth, and Raven opened her own to meet his. She swallowed once more. Neither of them broke contact, his heavy breathing mingling with her weaker respirations. An odd contentment crept over her, and Raven felt that life was possibly worth fighting for.

Eventually, he removed his mouth. Holding Raven closely, he struggled to his feet and returned her to the wall. After placing the piece of leather with the remaining food balls beside her leg, he gave her a stern look, once more in control of himself. "Eat them. Then you can sleep."

She plucked a ball from the leather. When Chukar saw her chewing it, he turned and left. His footsteps paused in the corridor, and he belatedly responded to her earlier questioning words. "I am truly alive, and so you must live as well." That was what it sounded like he said, although she couldn't see his hand movements to know for sure.

***

Over the following days, Raven focused on becoming well. She ate as much as she could of whatever Chukar provided, and he aided in making poultices from the herbs in the bag he'd brought. The skin around her suppurating wound was still flaming red and tender to the touch. When he saw how she struggled to wind a leather bandage around her thigh, he took the strip from her. She moaned as he gently bound the paste-covered wound.

"Whose medicines are these?" she asked to take her mind off the pain.

"They are yours," he replied. "For as long as you need them."

Raven didn't press him. She thought she knew to whom the medicinal pouch belonged, but she doubted it had been freely given.

He helped her stumble to one of the other chambers whenever she needed to relieve herself, but by the third day of having regained her senses, Raven craved to breathe fresh air and to see the sun. She asked Chukar to take her outside. As he carried her toward the mouth, Raven realized that he'd tried very hard to make the cave safe during his frequent absences. Not only was there ample kindling for the small fire in the chamber where she stayed, but wood, dung, and brush were stacked high near the main hearth and beside the fire in the cave mouth. She could tell by the large amount of spent ashes that the blaze in the mouth had been built up at times to be a bonfire. Collecting that much kindling filled much of a day.

"I'll help you gather firewood when I feel a little better," she said.

He shook his head. "Not until your wound has healed."

Once outside, he put her down within some bushes. While squatting, she saw him through the branches, prowling the area, his eyes alert, darting about for predators. She remembered the lions in the gully. They weren't very far away. He had to know they were there, yet he hadn't hesitated to bring her out when she'd asked. Now he was guarding her as though she might be snatched away at any moment. Raven regretted that she'd imposed a task on him that he probably thought foolish. She must try not to be overly demanding.

*** 

Chukar continued helping Raven tend her leg daily, and together, they cooked the few roots he gathered, the small animals he trapped, and the larger ones he hunted, emptying the partially digested contents of their stomachs so as to have more vegetation along with the meat. But mainly, her days were blurred with sleep as she slowly healed. Raven stayed in the small hollowed-out room and didn't ask again to be taken outside. The only way she knew that night had come was if she awoke and saw him lying on the other side of the fire. His presence reassured her during those times, and she would float away once more into dreamless sleep.

Her leg eventually improved, and although Raven remained weak, her temperature was almost gone. She started using fewer of the herbs and began staying awake for longer periods. Her mind cleared enough to figure out that because Chukar had found her so quickly, Elder Woman's band probably lived close by.

Raven had no doubts that the old matriarch was behind Leaf and Wren's disappearance. She desperately hoped that Chukar hadn't been part of the plot to take them. The footprints in the blueberry bushes had showed that besides a woman and boy, two adult males had been involved in the kidnapping. Regardless of whether or not he was involved, he knew where Leaf and Wren were. Surely, he would take her to them.

"I have two other children besides Wren," she blurted one day. "I must return to them soon, but first, I want to find out what has happened to Wren and Leaf. Can you tell me?"

Chukar's large body visibly stiffened. "You are too weak." He immediately rose and left the cave.

From his reaction, Raven suspected he was guilty of taking part in Leaf and Wren's capture, and her heart sank. But she wasn't sure of anything. His distress could be for an entirely different reason.

Just as she had a fondness for him, Raven was certain that Chukar had feelings for her. That insight had been reaffirmed by his present healing care. Raven's abrupt declaration that she would leave had most likely taken him aback. But how could he not realize that she would eventually return to her previous life—even if it meant never seeing him again? A lump filled her throat at the thought, and because she understood how difficult their parting would be, Raven left off asking him for more information.

She couldn't help but wonder, though, if he'd told Elder Woman about finding her half dead—not that the old woman would've cared if she lived or died. And she wanted to know how he'd become reunited with the band. Some of his brothers must have eventually returned to the overhang where he'd been left and found him still alive. Raven had so many questions for him, but they only talked about her immediate needs. It wasn't long, though, before her desire to find Wren and Leaf bubbled again to the surface.

Several mornings later, Chukar worked in the cave mouth, busy warming glue made from birch bark that he would use for setting a flint point into a spear shaft. Because of the pungent odor, Raven sat at the main hearth farther inside the cave. She waited until he finished with the spear then carried over a turtle shell filled with the hot venison soup that she'd found the energy to make. After he took it, she returned to ladle some into a shell for herself.

Raven intended to try him once more. Chukar rarely told her the reason for his comings and goings, but she had a hunch that he would leave sometime that day to go wherever the band dwelled. He was edgy, not at all calm and confident the way he was on the days he went out to bring back game or other foods. If her health had returned fully, she would have insisted on going with him, but that wasn't yet possible.

"The medicine bag is Elder Woman's, isn't it?" she asked, sitting down beside him.

He didn't look up from the soup.

"Well, can you at least tell me if she and the band are nearby?"

Bristling, he gestured at his bowl, giving her a hostile look.

She was reminded of the way one wolf warned another that it should be left alone while eating.

"Talking, too much talking," he said. "We will talk when you are better."

She stifled a sigh. He would ignore anything else she said. Raven plucked a piece of meat from her soup and placed it between her teeth, blowing over the chunk to cool it. The air made a small whistling noise as it went through the small gap between her top front teeth.

He looked over, smiling a little, apparently amused at the sound.

When Raven saw that he was in a better humor once more, she let the meat drop back into the bowl and grasped his arm. "I'm grateful for your concern, but I'm well enough to talk. I know that Wren and Leaf are with the band. How far away are they?"

He lowered his eyes to her hand holding him tightly.

Raven became aware of the warm, muscular flesh beneath her fingers and took away her hand.

He frowned. "We will talk about these matters soon."

"Where is our daughter? I want to know."

Chukar's head reared back. "Ot," he said loudly. His hand moved as quickly as a striking snake to cover her mouth.

Tears sprang to her eyes. Raven had always despised that word full of negative meanings. She couldn't bear that he'd used it to frighten her into silence.

Her unhappiness seemed to disturb him, yet his hand remained over her mouth. He held her watery gaze for a long time, his furrowed brow working. Finally, he spoke. "I will say this then. I do not stay with them."

It surprised her to hear that he didn't live with the band, and he seemed to be telling her that he didn't know the whereabouts of Leaf and Wren. Although disappointed, Raven was glad to know that at least he hadn't been involved in the kidnapping. She wondered how he managed to survive by himself.

He slowly took his hand away and stood. "Sometimes, it is enough just to live."

Raven didn't know whether he was referring to her, himself, or the both of them. She watched him prepare to leave, and the unspoken question hung in the air—where was he going that day, if not to the band? Raven decided to bide her time. Eventually, she would be well enough to travel. She hoped Chukar would help her search for their daughter, even if he truly didn't know where she was.

\*\*\*

Raven finally requested that he take her outside again, once more craving the sun on her face. He helped her, and she clasped his arm while limping along, walking so that he could carry a spear. "What is the source of the fresh water you bring to the cave?" she asked. "I'd like to bathe before long."

In response, he dropped the spear and picked her up, carrying her as he followed a path around the side of a hill. In spite of her weakened state, remnants of the old, familiar desire for him stirred—a tickle left over from the frustrating itch that she'd fought to ignore in the past. She watched his face through her lashes, wondering if he sensed her restlessness, but his expression didn't change.

Chukar followed a ledge that curved steadily downward until they reached a hollow area surrounded on three sides by cliff walls. Tall reeds grew around a pool formed by a spring flowing down the rockface. He put her down.

A plethora of turtles disappeared with a splash, and Chukar gestured at the water. "Turtle meat is good when there's nothing else."

Raven watched the ripples spreading over the surface. She

may not have been able to find their shells in the canyon, but there were lots of turtles at the pool. Just as interesting were the reeds. Their long fibers made sturdy baskets.

"We can't stay long," he said. "Many beasts water here."

She realized that he put himself in danger every time he went for drinking water. The three-sided space was potentially a trap for anything that entered. When she and Leaf had crossed the steppe lands together, both of them kept an eye out for predators. As long as her mobility was limited, she wouldn't be able to help Chukar that way very much.

He cleared his throat, his face serious. "If you wish to bathe quickly, I'll go back a distance and climb up high to watch for animals. If any start this way, I will come for you at once."

She gazed intently into the clear spring water for a long moment. "I've changed my mind about bathing. The fever hasn't gone completely, and I might catch a chill. As much as I want to get clean, it can wait until another time." She pointed at the edges of the pool. "Those reeds around the water are good and sturdy. I'm well enough to make a few baskets. If you'll gather some, I'll keep a lookout."

He immediately took a stone knife out of the pouch he wore at his side.

Raven slowly climbed up the hill until she could see out of the enclosure. Her eyes scoured the area vigilantly until he finished. Because his arms were full of reeds, she walked without his help, but right before they reached the cave, dark spots began dancing across her vision. She bent over so blood would rush to her head.

Seeing her distress, Chukar dropped the reeds and scooped her up. "I'll come back for them."

Raven had just settled in his arms when he grunted and spun halfway around. When she looked to see what had alarmed him, movement in the distance caught her eye. A cave lion slunk along the edge of the canyon below, its tawny colors standing out against the dark gully behind it. It was late enough in the day for the big cat to have come out of its lair. Again, Raven felt foolish. She'd asked him to gather reeds even though she'd seen him leave his spear behind earlier so he could carry her.

They watched the lion move away from the canyon toward the walled-in hollow where the spring was located. A tremor went through Raven. He felt the movement and glanced down at her. Neither spoke, but they both knew that she wouldn't be bathing at the pool. They couldn't do without water, however. She had to get well soon. It was too dangerous for him to go alone.

As her stamina increased over the following handful of days, Raven wove several baskets tight enough to hold water. Chukar gave her a small amount of beeswax, which she warmed before waterproofing the sides of each basket. He could make fewer trips to the pool by taking them to carry water instead of using small deer bladders and the bulky tortoise shell.

While she made the baskets, Chukar often stayed in the small chamber, sitting by the fire, silently watching her weave. Raven enjoyed his company, but she noticed that his eyes often roved over her as if she were terrain he was about to cross. His attention made her fingers clumsy and plying the reed strips difficult.

Raven felt that he was restraining himself only because of her illness. She was grateful for his consideration, but now that she was better, Raven didn't know what she would do if he approached her, wanting to mate. She hadn't given up on Leaf; he was her life-mate and deserved her loyalty. But she found it increasingly difficult to ignore the powerful feelings and urges that Chukar set off within her. And then there was Wren, the evidence of their undeniable carnal bond. Each time Raven had asked him about Wren's whereabouts, she felt as though she were pointing out what had happened between them all those moons ago.

***

The fever eventually went away completely, and she stopped taking the ground poplar bark and feverwort. The gash looked to be healed; the red streaks had faded. Because long-term use of juniper berries caused stomachaches, she began using wormwood against any lingering infection.

The baskets were long finished, the reeds all used up, when he entered the room one day, carrying a small wooden bowl in one hand and a bone scraper in the other. "I know that you like to be clean." He held out the bowl, and she looked inside.

It was full of the unguent that Raven had seen the Long-head people use to clean their skin and bodies, massaging it in and then scraping it off. Raven had been using a chamois and water occasionally to bathe herself, but the unguent would provide a more thorough cleansing.

Chukar had only recently returned from being gone for several days. Raven imagined him walking over the steppes then entering a large cave. In her mind, she saw him go inside a chamber within the cave and take the bowl out of someone's bag. That was what she thought he'd done so that he could offer her the unguent. He was standing there, waiting for her response.

"Thank you. I've never used it before," she heard herself say, "but I would like to try it."

He immediately jumped into the opening that she'd unwittingly made. "I'll show you how."

The heated flush that went through Raven almost paralyzed her. He put the unguent and scraper down near the fire.

She managed to make her tongue work and stuttered, "It-it seems easy enough."

But he was already pulling Raven up and tugging the tunic over her head the way he had when he used water to cool her fever. Raven told herself that Chukar had brought the unguent because of the lions; he'd come up with a way that she could be clean while remaining safe.

He didn't try to remove the narrow loincloth Raven always wore, and that was consistent with what she'd seen in the past when one person cleaned another. The person being worked on always remained partially clothed.

"You took care of me when my shoulder was injured. Now I will take care of you." His words pacified her anxious misgivings, being what someone returning a favor to a friend might say.

She had indeed helped him during the moon he was held captive by her tribal band. After she'd reset his dislocated shoulder, Raven had rubbed his skin regularly with her own ointment to keep the blood flowing and to hasten movement. She'd also made sure that he had food and water each day. That was as far as it should have gone, but while providing him food for his travels after he was released, she'd ended up taking care of yet another need. The experience had left her shaken.

The waxy substance full of dried flowers and herbs gave forth the familiar aroma that had often filled the cave where Elder Woman's people had dwelled. She closed her eyes as he began. If it weren't for his fingers keeping her firmly rooted in the present, she could have imagined that she was back there again.

Chukar went about cleansing her in such a practical manner that Raven wondered if she was wrong in thinking that he wanted her. First, he briskly massaged the wax over her skin. Upon reaching her injured thigh, he used a lighter touch over the tender pink scar. When Chukar finished with the wax, he put it aside and started scraping her. Raven's skin tingled under the narrow bone. He paused when he again reached the scar, making the small clicking sound that indicated sympathy.

By the time he'd finished with both legs and feet, she was having difficulty keeping her breathing level. Certainly, she'd enjoyed joining with Leaf throughout all the turns of the seasons they'd been together. Never, however, had she ached for him with the same hunger that Chukar's hands were presently instilling in her. Perhaps it was his otherness, or maybe it was how he was so similar in spite of the differences that proved irresistible to Raven. She couldn't say.

The unguent had become an oily liquid in the bowl as it melted in the heat from the fire. Chukar dipped his fingers in the fragrant oil, preparing to begin the light rubbing that was the final step of the process. Facing Raven, he looked into her eyes, his own glistening like leaves freshly cleaned by rain. He began with her neck. The large splayed fingertips of his hands had frightened her the first time she'd noticed them, but they were capable of great tenderness.

The slow and gentle movement of his hands down her body undid any lingering resistance. Her eyes narrowed, and her mouth slackened in a way that she knew he could not help but interpret as desire. At the moment, though, she was beyond caring what he thought. When he tugged off her loincloth, she gave a small cry and grasped at the skins covering his chest. He took her hands away and pulled off the skins, along with the rest of his clothing. The scar on his chest from the old spear wound was as pink as the scar on her thigh.

She slowly reached out a hand. "You survived." The way the firelight played over his heavily muscled body made her words a gasp. She pressed her fingers along the scar and felt his heart thumping deep inside. "As I have survived."

Perhaps he was right. Sometimes, it was enough just to be alive.

# CHAPTER 6

## *Leaf*

LEAF STOOD BEFORE THE SMALL fire after they left him alone in the stone room of his imprisonment, legs and arms tightly bound once more. They'd neglected to help him sit, but he didn't want to anyway. If only he could pace the chamber to calm himself. Wren's distraught reaction when Leaf told her that he wasn't her real father had left him aching inside. She hadn't believed him. To convince her, he'd reluctantly begun destroying what she'd always thought to be true about herself.

As soon as they brought him to Wren, she'd run over and grabbed on like a frightened animal that still had some fight left in it. She yelled at them to untie the ropes, her flashing eyes daring the Longheads to separate her from him. His ribs were still sore from Skraw's blows, and the sudden contact momentarily took his breath away. He staggered but quickly caught himself, trying to avoid the humiliation of falling down before her. Even though she'd seen the ropes, Wren began loudly begging him to take her home. He was trying to reassure her, but then he caught Elder Woman's impatient eye. Leaf feared that she would have him beaten in front of Wren if he didn't follow her orders, so he calmly told Wren that Elder Woman was her grandmother—just as the old woman had demanded.

Wren's face became clouded by confusion, and she yanked

her arms from around him, jumping back as if he were hot to the touch. When Leaf then told her that her real father was Elder Woman's son, a man of the Longheads, she stared at him in openmouthed disbelief. His bound arms twitched from wanting to take her hand, from his desire to do something— anything that might lessen the shock of what she was hearing. "You must understand me, Wren. I'm telling you the truth. His name was Chukar."

She shook her head. "*You* are my father."

"Yes, but I'm not your birth father. Before your mother and I joined in ceremony, she knew that Longhead."

"How?" The word was a howl.

"He'd been injured, and your mother healed him."

Her shrill voice filled the room. "How does that make him my father?" She whirled toward Elder Woman, pointing a finger at her. "That's not my grandmother!" Wren turned back to Leaf and stamped her foot the way she had when an unruly toddler. "No, no, no! Why is she making you lie?"

Leaf was spared further explanation by Elder Woman's response to Wren's tantrum. Her hands chopped at the air. "Enough."

After a couple more movements of her arms, Whit seized Leaf by the shoulders, turning him away. Panic flickered over Wren's face. As he was prodded toward the outside passage, she lunged after him. Looking over his shoulder, Leaf saw Elder Woman shove Wren back into the room.

Because he and Raven had, by unspoken agreement, rarely discussed the past after they'd gone to live with the Wind tribe, the knowledge that Wren wasn't actually his child had become a shushed whisper inside Leaf. He'd begun his life anew when he and Raven located his tribesmen; he never dwelt on the unpleasantness that had come before. In his mind, Wren was his, and he felt the same affection for her that he did his birth children.

But now he found that those almost-dead husks of memories contained seeds that stubbornly grew, throwing up bitter shoots that pushed to the surface. He remembered the day when the band had released Chukar, allowing him to return to his people. Leaf had followed Raven as she tracked the Longhead man up the slopes leading out of the valley. She'd caught up with him at a pool, and Leaf had hidden in nearby bushes.

He saw her give Chukar what looked like dead steppe hamsters, and Leaf begrudgingly appreciated her thoughtfulness in providing the freed captive food for his journey. When the man tossed the hamsters aside and pulled Raven down with him onto the grass, Leaf's primary emotions were shock... and envy. If only he were in the grass with her instead of the Longhead. Biting despair followed as he crouched there. Because of his youth, she'd never even considered him as a potential mate. To Raven in those days, he was just a pesky boy who constantly followed her around.

Although he couldn't see them well because of the surrounding foliage, Leaf recalled that she hadn't fought Chukar and had stayed in the grass with him for a long while. After Raven and Chukar left together, Leaf returned to the lake camp, forcing himself to acknowledge that she was gone forever. When he encountered Raven in camp close to dusk that day, his relief over her return was such that he suddenly noticed how the sunset lit up the landscape with colors usually only seen in flowers.

The ropes were chafing his arms. They'd bound him as tightly as a cocoon, but the pain of the ropes against his bruises wasn't nearly as bothersome as the realization that the untroubled calmness he'd carefully maintained since wooing Raven to his side was draining away rapidly. The old rancor that had erupted after he'd escaped his childhood captors to live with the Fire Cloud tribe was rushing back. How could it be that he'd been taken again by the Longheads—wasn't once in a lifetime enough?

It crossed Leaf's mind then that if Raven had actually gone with Chukar all those moons ago, then he wouldn't be in his present situation. He would certainly not have become attached to a child who wasn't entirely of his own kind.

At least they would not make Wren a slave. Being of Elder Woman's blood, she would be treated better. They would busy Leaf with curing and softening skins just as that other group of Longheads had when he was a boy. During the time they'd wintered with Elder Woman's band while waiting for Wren's birth, Leaf had sworn that he would never be a Longhead slave again. He told Raven he would have to leave her with them, if it came to that, then return in the spring for her and the baby. Fortunately, he hadn't needed to desert Raven that way.

Leaf was determined not to bend to Elder Woman's will. When he refused to work for her, she would probably have that young wolf beat him. He shivered. If he didn't break away soon, she'd tire of feeding him and have the boy kill him.

His thoughts turned to Windy and Sky, and he couldn't bear to think of some other man in his place as their father. Leaf knew several men in the band who would quickly offer his family their hearth when he didn't return.

"No," he muttered under his breath. Although he felt an animosity toward Raven that hadn't been there before his capture, he still wanted to continue his life with her. He should be planning his escape instead of thinking about dying, but it seemed to Leaf that his fate was slipping from him. It was as though the Earth Mother had willed that he live much of his life as a Longhead slave. If so, she was a cruel spirit, and death was much more preferable.

Leaf tried to think of a way to break free, but his prospects weren't good. He began writhing within the ropes, trying to wriggle out of them. When he was unsuccessful, he lost all restraint and began hopping, bounding mindlessly about like a deer caught in a pit trap. The only thing he accomplished was crossing one calf over the other so that he fell onto the floor.

His mind clawed out of the darkness possessing him to focus on the jagged stone near the bottom of the wall. If he used the edges to cut the ropes from his arms, then he could unwind the ones around his legs. Without thinking about how he would get out of the room once he was free, Leaf rolled over the cave floor until he reached the wall. He pressed his chest against the stone and began rocking his shoulders back and forth. After a while, he rolled away and took a look. The plaited fiber coils going around his middle were beginning to fray, but it was very little to show for his efforts. Groaning, he flopped onto his back to rest before continuing.

His body twitched within the ropes, and he came to without any idea as to how long he'd slept. He cursed the Earth spirits loudly for not keeping him awake so that he could escape, his agitated voice filling the small space. Rolling onto his side, Leaf once more began rubbing his front against the wall.

He'd barely started when the boulder covering the gap began scraping across the stone floor. He quickly struggled up and sat so that his back faced the entry, hunching over with his head hung down as if deep in sleep. If they'd come only to leave water in the stone basin, then he wouldn't have to expose the damaged cords by turning around. They always untied his arms for eating but never for drinking. He was expected to lap the water like an animal.

But the two brothers pulled him onto his feet. Leaf hoped that his lack of luck wasn't a quick slap from the Earth Mother, offended by the way he'd cursed the spirits. He wished Raven were there. The spirits had always favored her because she was a healer and understood them better than anyone. *But where is Raven?* More than enough time had passed for her to raise an alarm and for the band to form a search group.

Jay started unwinding Leaf's leg bindings. Leaf watched him, sure that the man's eyes would go higher and see what he'd done, but Jay remained focused on the leg ropes. Leaf breathed a small sigh of relief when they led him away without incident.

Once they were outside, Jay partially undid Leaf's arms so he could use his hands in a limited fashion to take care of his bodily functions. After his earlier escape attempt, they never untied him completely and always used a leash around his neck. Strangely, Jay still hadn't noticed anything different, not even while he loosened the ropes. At least their mother hadn't come along as she usually did. Her hawk eyes would have spotted the worn places at once.

But when they returned to the small chamber, Elder Woman was there, stoking the fire with more wood. Not for his benefit, Leaf was sure. She didn't want to be cold for however long she stayed. Before he could turn away, her eyes squinted at him. Leaf glanced down at his chest. The ropes had been replaced so that several of the frayed ones were still showing. She hobbled over and ran her hands down the coils, her foul breath swarming all over him.

She pushed him hard in the chest so that he almost fell, then she turned to look at her sons.

They both hung their heads, not meeting her eyes.

"Were you blind because you don't want to punish him? Skraw doesn't mind helping me. Go get him," Elder Woman said to Whit. "Now!" she said when he hesitated.

He quickly went out. Jay waited awkwardly nearby. His feet shuffled a few times as if he wanted to go with his brother.

Elder Woman stared at Leaf in a way that only increased his dread about what was coming. Whit soon returned with Skraw. Leaf's eyes went to the large stick the boy held. He tried not to show his fear, but Elder Woman had seen the look he'd given the stick.

Under her heavy brows, the large hooded eyes became frighteningly pleased. "Harrumph. You will be beaten every time you attempt to leave us until you stop trying." She motioned at Skraw, and he moved forward.

Blows began raining onto Leaf's shoulders and head, but they weren't so hard as they'd been the first time. The boy was at least using some restraint. Leaf gritted his teeth, determined to endure the beating in silence. Elder Woman suddenly raised a hand. "No more!"

Skraw hesitated then threw down the stick, his frustration apparent at being stopped so quickly.

"No more." She mumbled as if talking to herself. "Or he won't be of any use." She waved the two brothers over. "Take off all the ropes," she said in her usual strident voice.

Stunned by her sudden change of heart, Leaf waited quietly as they unwound the coils. He didn't want to say or do anything that would give her an excuse to retie him. Only after he was completely free did she leave, her two sons and grandson following. He'd tried so hard to get the ropes off, and they'd suddenly done it for him. The brothers were sliding the boulder back in place, but maybe Leaf could somehow move it once they were gone.

First, though, he had to limber up. His arms and legs still felt deadened, although he'd been able to at least use his legs when they took him outside. While breathing loudly, he waved his arms and stomped his feet even though it hurt to do so. He stopped and gulped in as large a breath as he could manage so that the extra air in his body would help mute the pain. With cheeks puffed out, he held his breath, but strangely, Leaf still heard heavy breathing.

He whirled around, the air exploding out of him. Someone else was in the chamber. He saw a pile of furs in the corner that hadn't been there when they'd taken him outside. The breathing seemed to be coming from a rounded mound under them.

Ignoring the pain in his legs, he rushed over and snatched off the top covering. He backed away as a woman, making a small sound, sat up quickly. She was a young Longhead woman, completely nude, her light-colored skin glowing in the firelight. Leaf's mouth fell open as she scooted sideways until she was crouched against the wall, her arms folded protectively across her chest.

Leaf looked at her closely and realized that the greenish-brown eyes staring back at him were vaguely familiar. The girl was one of the Longhead children who had been part of the group when he and Raven had lived with Elder Woman's band. She would not have been much older than a toddler then. He stepped toward her, intending to throw the fur over her nakedness. A sudden cramp in one of his legs made him stumble, and the skin landed in front of her instead. He dropped heavily onto it and began massaging his calf through his leggings. She watched him with wide eyes, her shoulders rising and falling with each breath.

"Don't be frightened." He looked at her out of the corner of his eye. "You were one of the children. Which one are you?"

She turned her head away slightly but kept her eyes on him. "I am Coo."

He nodded, motioning at himself and at her. "Do you remember me, Coo? I used to play with you."

"Yes." The recollection seemed to reassure her. Her body relaxed, and she unfolded her arms.

Leaf didn't know where to rest his eyes. He tried to keep

them on her face, but they insisted on going down to her abundant breasts. "You are all grown up now," he said awkwardly. A memory came to Leaf, one of himself as a captive boy lying pillowed against the chest of an older Longhead woman. He felt queasy. "Why are you in here, Coo?" His voice was cold. "In this room, alone with me. From what I've seen, there are many rooms, enough for you to stay somewhere else. Elder Woman can find you another place."

"She wanted me to come in here."

"Did she give you a reason?"

Her eyes didn't waver. "She wants you to mate with me."

Her revelation wasn't unduly surprising. He couldn't think of any other reason for a young nubile girl to be deliberately left naked with a man who wasn't her father.

"Why does Elder Woman want us to mate?"

Without speaking, she signaled that she didn't know, a quick movement of hands and shoulders.

Sourness rose in his throat, and Leaf wiped the back of his hand against his mouth. If the old Longhead woman thought she would control him that way, she was mistaken. Elder Woman was wrong if she thought he would forget Raven so quickly. The happiness he'd found with her couldn't be repeated. Since the day he'd first seen Raven, he hadn't desired any other woman. On occasion, various ones in the band had let Leaf know they would be willing to slip away with him, if only for a short while. He'd never even been tempted. And he'd never considered taking a second woman to his hearth through ceremony like many tribesmen did. Leaf was more like the Longheads that way. They seldom took a second mate under any circumstances.

Raven, forever alert, always noticed when another woman gave Leaf too much attention, and she would tease him about it in that probing way she had. When Leaf told her that he only needed one mate the way the eagles seemed to, she'd called him something different. Nothing inflamed him more than to hear her whisper "my eagle man" in his ear while they were mating. He would lift himself momentarily from her embrace, and she would lovingly whisper the words again while he watched her lips.

Coo was sitting with downcast eyes.

"You don't have to be afraid," he told her. "I'll leave you alone."

Her eyes darted up in alarm. "I am not afraid. Although I have never mated, I do not fear it." Her fingers fidgeted among the furs, belying her words. "The People don't feel fear. Not like your tribesmen."

Leif snorted. "So those are the stories now told at your hearths." Coo had a thin line of reddish hair that led down her belly, the same color as the fly-away fluff on her head. Such a strange color for hair. He forced his eyes to look at her face again. "Your grandmother will have to find someone else."

"She will be angry. She will slap me many times."

"That has nothing to do with me." He shrugged the Longhead way, indicating his distance from Coo's problem. "Just tell her that we did mate."

Coo breathed out with that loud sighing sound the Longheads always made when exasperated. "She said that you are cowardly, as all of Them are."

Leaf shrugged again. "What she says doesn't matter." But then curiosity got the best of him. "Did Elder Woman say how I was cowardly?"

"She told me that you were afraid to close in on an animal whenever you hunted. Perhaps you are a coward in other ways also."

"I've always provided. You were too young to remember how I helped feed the People when the starving time came upon them." Leaf was tired of the way they'd always tried to make him feel inadequate. First, the group that captured him as a boy had made him ashamed of his more lightly built body, then Elder Woman's band later had decided that he lacked enough courage to be a good hunter. He shook a finger at her. "You could have died then if I hadn't helped. Tell Elder Woman that the next time she tells you her lies." He waved a hand at the walls. "How long have the People lived in these chambers?"

Her fingers fluttered like fast-moving waves. "Many turns of the seasons."

"Without ever living elsewhere?"

"No, we always stay here," she said sullenly.

He looked at her sharply. It was unheard-of for a band to stay in one place for so long. The resources within an area would eventually become depleted. Perhaps that didn't happen if a group was so small that its tracks were light upon the land. "How many of you are here?"

A tight little frown on her face let him know that he'd touched a sensitive area.

"Very few, I have a feeling. Perhaps if I'd never left the People, more of you would have survived."

Coo gave him a petulant look. But then her expression suddenly changed, her features convulsing into a tortured grimace. The Longhead women, as well as the men, rarely displayed any strong emotions. But Leaf had learned the hard way that they were like erupting volcanoes when they did. He wasn't caught entirely off guard when Coo lunged forward without warning, knocking him over and landing on top of him. She began hitting him in the chest and head.

He struggled to push her off, but he was fighting a lioness. He'd forgotten how strong the women were. Leaf wasn't a child, though, like he'd been when they'd handled him roughly whenever he rebelled. With her clutching at him, Leaf rolled both of them over so she was underneath. He struggled to restrain her arms, but she managed to swing up a fist, catching him in an eye.

Leaf cried out, and all the anger he'd felt after finally escaping them as a boy returned. He raised his fist to retaliate. But then he remembered Coo as a toddler, the ribs showing on her broad but starving little Longhead chest. Not even a hint of her future lushness had shown during those days. While he hesitated, she grasped his arm with both hands. A mindless frenzy of tangled limbs ensued. She scratched and bit at him while he tried to subdue her.

He could not have said afterward exactly what had happened. His loincloth had somehow come off as they fought, and he was suddenly mating her like a frustrated stallion, clutching her body roughly from behind even though her ferocity had given way as quickly as it had begun. His thoughts had completely ceased.

The next thing he knew, they were both lying on their backs on the cold stone floor, gasping and panting for breath. The pain from his bruises that had gone away during their tussling returned. He ached all over. When the boulder grated across the entry, he groaned and sat up, still dazed from what had occurred.

Elder Woman came in with Jay. The other man averted his eyes, and Leaf once more had the strange impulse to cover Coo with one of the furs. At least Jay was only her uncle. Leaf could hear Whit, Coo's father, somewhere in the corridor, talking to someone. Elder Woman had at least displayed some sense by not bringing him in to see that his daughter had been taken without first undergoing a proper ceremony. Elder Woman looked down at them. She clapped her hands, signaling that she was pleased. A sound of disgust escaped Leaf. Her attention focused on him.

She stopped clapping. "I didn't mean that you were to blind him."

Leaf's hand went to his swollen eye for a moment as the old woman's words sank in. He crossed his arms, that simple action reminding him that the ropes were still off. "You told her to attack me?"

Elder Woman didn't bother denying it. "Get up, Coo, and leave us. Cover yourself before you go out."

Leaf pointed at Coo. "Why did you want me to mate her?" he asked, although he thought he knew the reason. And indeed, Elder Woman gave him a hard look as if the answer should be obvious.

"Harrumph. I want more grandchildren. If Chukar and Raven could make a child, then you should be able to do so with Coo."

He didn't think she was taunting him with Wren's origins. Longheads didn't waste much time needling others. They learned early on that disrespect could get them killed. But she'd obviously instructed Coo in what to say and do in order to goad Leaf enough so that he would forget himself.

Somehow, Elder Woman had understood that their low opinion of Leaf's hunting style had always dismayed him. She knew he didn't want to be called a coward. Her manipulation of him was an unexpected deviousness that forced Leaf to realize that even after living with them on two different occasions, he still didn't understand Longheads as completely as he'd thought he did.

Elder Woman looked again at her granddaughter. "I told you to get up, girl."

Coo rose so slowly that Leaf thought she might be in shock. Jay, having given up his attempt to distance himself from the situation, was looking at her with open dismay. After collecting a large fur from the cave floor, Coo turned toward the opening.

Leaf sucked in a sharp breath when he saw the backs of her upper thighs. While hunting, he'd always felt excitement when his spear hit its mark and the blood started flowing. That bright color meant a kill was probable. A bleeding animal proved he had the skills to provide for his family. He was a man to be reckoned with.

But the blood smearing Coo's legs made Leaf feel something entirely different. Eyes down, Coo wrapped herself in the fur and went out. Shame bored into Leaf so strongly that his voice came out little more than a hoarse whisper. "So, what are you going to do?" he asked Elder Woman. "Keep me here, making babies with her until I die?"

"No," she croaked in a maddeningly calm voice. "I will be satisfied with just one if it's born alive. I have no desire for your death. You can leave then if you survive being tied that long."

She'd never liked him—nor Raven, for that matter—so he wasn't sure Elder Woman had meant it when she said she didn't wish him dead. Hot anger seared him. At the moment, he wished her dead. He wished all Longheads were dead, wherever they stayed. And the last thing he wanted was for Coo to bear his child. Looking down, Leaf saw the girl's blood on his body and leggings.

He grabbed his loincloth and pushed himself up to put it back on, looping the ends once more over his mid-string. After yanking the tunic down over the loincloth, he turned back to Elder Woman. "You're an old hyena fighting to keep your kind from emptying off the land the same way those miserable creatures seem to be vanishing. Maybe every last one of you, the People along with the hyenas, should go…"

His fury faded as he realized that by his words, he was also wishing Wren gone. And maybe he'd been a little too insulting. More than likely, Skraw was in the corridor, just waiting for Elder Woman to lose her temper with him again. But instead of becoming angry, she simply looked perplexed.

# CHAPTER 7

*Elder Woman*

E LDER WOMAN WAS TAKEN ABACK. She didn't know what Leaf meant by calling her a hyena. No one had ever said that she was an animal of any sort, much less a hyena. Before she decided how best to respond, he rudely interrupted her thoughts.

"I need to clean myself." Jay had been about to wind one of the ropes around Leaf's upper body. Ignoring him, Leaf moved closer to Elder Woman. "In the stream. Tie as many ropes around my neck as you want, but let them take me down there."

Elder Woman sniffed the air. He did smell, but so did they all much of the time, especially during the colder moons. The audacity of the man to demand such special treatment. But perhaps bathing would make him more amenable. "Very well, but not in the stream. Jay and Whit will bring you water in the morning."

"If that's the best you can do. And I don't want Coo. I already have a mate, so don't send her to me. Your tricks won't work next time."

"Harrumph! It may take more than one mating for her to become with child. You'll stay at this cave until she does. Don't you want your freedom?"

"What if she never becomes pregnant?"

"I think she will. After all, Chukar and Raven made Wren." Elder Woman gave Jay a pointed look. He went forward with the ropes, but before he could start, Leaf's hands and arms were moving in agitated speech.

"That happened before Raven began living with me. I only desire her. I don't desire Coo. I won't mate her again."

Elder Woman spoke with a confidence she didn't feel. "We will see about that." He was just as she remembered him, a very stubborn man, but his response made her realize something interesting. Leaf didn't like for her to bring up Wren's origins.

Perhaps she annoyed him, but he also made her uncomfortable. They had to bind him again before he decided to run out of the room. She went to the opening. "Whit, Skraw," she called. Elder Woman hoped the pair was still around a curve down the corridor.

Whit's voice boomed toward her. "We're here."

"Hurry down and help Jay."

She hadn't wanted Whit to see his daughter with Leaf, so she'd insisted that the two wait at a distance so that Coo could leave in the opposite direction to go to her room. Like a good son, Whit had obeyed without asking why she was taking Jay along but not him and Skraw. He would find out what happened soon enough from Jay, then Elder Woman would have the task of explaining what she was trying to accomplish. When Whit and Skraw slipped past her into the chamber, she walked out, knowing that Leaf would be safely secured once more.

As Elder Woman meandered through the tunnels, she was finally able to think about what Leaf had said earlier about hyenas. Leaf used the correct word and his hand-talk had indicated the animal, his cupped palm moving down in a rounded slant the way a hyena's back sloped toward the tail. She hadn't been mistaken.

Torchlight grew her shadow long as she strolled along with bowed head, her thoughts running deep. A hyena was a hyena, and a person was a person. They weren't at all alike. Leaf's face when he'd said her people were like them had shown as much disgust as if he'd taken a bite of hyena meat and found it lacking. That made no sense. Although hyena wasn't something they normally hunted, their fresh meat tasted good enough, especially if there was little else to set one's teeth into.

She made a frustrated growl of a sound at her inability to divine his meaning. What he said, however, about the scarcity of hyenas was true. A long while had passed since she'd seen one. And that was good. The People had always killed the beasts whenever they had the chance. The presence of hyenas near a camp frightened away the tastier animals. She also had a memory, one that occasionally surfaced as a bad dream, of a hyena running with its head and tail held high, a screaming infant in its jaws. The band had given chase, throwing rocks at the beast, but the baby boy had gone quiet before the hyena dropped him. Everyone saw then that his throat had been crushed. She didn't know why so few hyenas remained, but they wouldn't be missed.

What he meant finally came to her. He was saying that her people were disappearing just like the hyenas. Perhaps Leaf's kind were killing the People or driving them from good hunting lands the same way the People chased away hyenas with rocks or killed them if the chance arose.

It had always been said that Them were trouble and should be avoided wherever possible. That was why she'd been against Leaf and Raven living with the band during that winter. She'd thought it odd at the time that her sons had demanded the pair be allowed to stay. "They will help us hunt and forage," they'd all insisted. Even Elder Man had said those same words, so she'd relented.

Leaf and Raven did help provide food, but that wasn't the real reason her sons and Elder Man had interceded. Elder Woman found out much later that Leaf had told them Raven was bearing Chukar's child. Chukar hadn't denied Leaf's claim, thereby creating an obligation. The men had agreed to keep the peace by keeping their mouths closed. They were afraid constant fighting would break out between the women and Raven once everyone knew. It was an insult that Raven was pregnant by Chukar when Chirrup was not. Although she'd been angry at them all for not telling her beforehand, Elder Woman soon stopped wishing Raven was gone. The woman had her grandchild, and there was a special place in the hearts of the People for their young ones.

Elder Woman reluctantly accompanied Finch, Chirrup, and Coo when they went out foraging that afternoon. By the time the sun rose high in the sky, her aches and pains usually became less. But on that particular day, her hips still hurt long after midday. When more children were born and grew large enough to help, Elder Woman could stay at the cave and do chores beside the warm fire.

Happily, food was still easily found close by. If they had to go long distances, Elder Woman wasn't sure she would be able to keep up on the return trip. Bags filled with roots, berries, and the occasional rabbit they came across were becoming increasingly heavy.

A more numerous band consisting of several families would have already been forced to move on. Elder Woman had never lived for long in a large group, but there were occasions during her childhood when other bands joined hers. Those melded bands had traveled during the summers into the mammoth lands. After the hunting was over and before the land froze completely, the bands parted company, each group going their own way to seek milder weather. She found it unbelievable that all those people she'd known had completely vanished, but they had. And for some reason, no young ones had taken their place in the world.

The women soon found a patch of blooming dandelions and started ferreting out the roots with their fingers and digging sticks, collecting the plants whole. Elder Woman heard a crunching sound and saw that Coo was eating a flowering stalk. When the girl saw her grandmother eyeing her, she quickly swallowed. They weren't to eat while collecting food, so they could go back quicker. At times, they did eat while gathering, but they'd come out later than usual.

Elder Woman became aware that wherever she foraged, Chirrup remained close by her side. Her daughter had something to say that she didn't want Coo and Finch to hear. Elder Woman began easing away from the other two women so that they could talk. When out of habit the others followed, Elder Woman pointed to a white oak tree down near the riverbank. "Finch, you and Coo should keep pulling dandelions. Chirrup and I will search for mushrooms under that oak tree."

When they reached the large oak, edible mushrooms were actually growing between massive roots that snaked down the bank. Elder Woman sat on one of the roots, motioning for Chirrup to sit across from her on another one.

"Why have you become my shadow today, daughter?" She began pinching caps off the nearest mushrooms.

"I understand why you took Wren. She is your granddaughter."

Elder Woman stopped plucking the mushroom caps. She didn't care for the way Chirrup was emphasizing her speech with brusque finger movements. She waited before chiding Chirrup to hear what else she had to say.

"I know you are worried that if Leaf returns to Them, he will bring men back to find Wren. But we all have good memories of Leaf. He was never selfish during the winter that Wren was born. He and Raven shared their food until it was gone. It pains this daughter of yours and your sons to see him suffering. He doesn't want to be here."

That her sons felt the same way as Chirrup could prove to be a problem. Elder Woman held her temper over the hint of rebellion. "Leaf wanted to live with us that winter. I practically had to chase him and Raven off when spring came."

"That was different. Leaf chose to stay with us then—and he was with Raven. They've probably had many children throughout the turns of the seasons. He and Raven may have let Wren come stay with you if you'd asked them."

Elder Woman's back stiffened. All those angry-sounding words coming from her normally docile daughter were highly unusual. "If he returns without Wren, Raven will make him come back here for her. That woman will not be generous with Wren even if she has as many children as there are fingers on her hands." She stared stonily up into the branches full of leaves and acorns while she mulled over how much she should tell Chirrup.

Elder Woman's daughter and sons had always been respectful, and they were, she knew, even a little afraid of her. She'd always succeeded in tamping down their little mutinies—if she didn't include Chukar's waywardness. He, however, had become of little importance. But if she lost Chirrup's goodwill, then Whit and Jay could possibly defect. Then Elder Woman's plans would come to nothing.

Of all her children, Chirrup could always be depended upon to restore order whenever quarrels broke out. Her cheerful voice was as soothing as the sound of the river presently bubbling below them. Elder Woman would explain what she was doing and hope that was enough. Even if Elder Woman forbade the men and Coo to let Chirrup know what was going on, she would find out anyway once the girl became pregnant.

She looked at Chirrup steadily. "I have other reasons for keeping Leaf."

Chirrup's head tilted to one side, her face full of uneasy curiosity.

"I want him to give me a grandchild—with Coo—if he will stop resisting the idea."

Chirrup's eyes went wide.

Elder Woman's voice and hand movements became slow and deliberate so that Chirrup could think carefully about what she was saying. "We have become too few. Maybe Jay and Finch will have another child, but that won't be enough. Hopefully, Wren will accept Skraw as her mate and have many children, but I also wanted a mate for Coo, a man who is not of our family so that the baby will have a better chance of staying alive long enough to be birthed. I will give Leaf his freedom once she has a child. Then the People will leave these harsh plains and go back to the mountain valley we came from."

"If I were bearing children, perhaps you would not be doing these strange unheard-of things," Chirrup said, struggling to keep her voice down.

"That is what I am trying to tell you." Elder Woman's hands wrung out meaning as she spoke. "All those miscarriages you had with your brother. Babies die when close kin mate. We need someone for Coo who is not an uncle or close cousin. Leaf is all I could think of. Don't worry. I'll send him back to Raven someday."

Chirrup didn't reply right away. Her eyes stared emptily into the distance. Then she took a quick breath. "I think I can help you. Leaf and I were friends. Let me be the one to explain what you have told me. He needs to understand before you put him and Coo together."

A pause ensued. Several wrens landed in the oak tree over them. When the birds noticed Chirrup and Elder Woman, they began scolding the women.

"She's already been with Leaf."

Chirrup gave Elder Woman a startled look before turning and glancing up the bank to where Coo was working. Her face shone when she faced Elder Woman again. "I wonder if she's with child."

"Maybe, but until we're certain, I'll put the two together as often as I can."

"I still want to talk with him."

When Elder Woman nodded her permission, Chirrup brightened the day with a big smile. She began picking mushrooms with an enthusiasm Elder Woman hadn't noticed earlier.

Relief washed over Elder Woman. Chirrup wasn't any longer a worry now that she thought there might soon be a baby in the band. She'd badly wanted a child with Chukar, and Elder Woman remembered how much her daughter had enjoyed helping mother Wren—as had they all. She moved away from Chirrup, slowly working over to where mushrooms were the thickest. She spotted wort farther down the riverbank. Though not nearly as effective for pain as the poplar bark in her lost medicine pouch, the plant would still help. She sent Chirrup down to pick some.

They soon started back after gathering only a small amount of food and medicinal herbs. The milder summer weather was too warm to keep plant foods fresh for long. No one enjoyed eating shriveled greens and roots, especially since meat was everyone's preferred food anyway. And she'd soon have her hands full with all the medicinal plants she'd picked on other days. They were dry enough to crush into powders.

The serenity that had settled over Elder Woman after confiding in Chirrup lasted only until the women reached the cave. They'd no sooner entered the mouth than she heard a shriek. Dropping her bags, she quickly limped through the front chamber, and without stopping for a torch, she went into the corridor from where the sound had come. As she moved deeper inside, groping the walls as she went, thumping sounds reached her. The noise was coming from the room where Wren was being kept. It was too dark. As soon as Wren could be trusted enough for her room to stay open, Elder Woman would tell Jay to keep more torches burning in the passage.

When almost to the boulder blocking Wren's chamber, she collided with someone. Her granddaughter was attempting an escape! She grasped at Wren's clothes, trying to stop her. If the girl got outside, and they couldn't find her right away, she would perish on the steppes. Elder Woman fought to keep a grip on the wriggling body. Her fingers dug through thick hair all the way to the scalp, and she yanked downward, forcing the girl to sit.

"Let go of me, Grandmother!"

At first, she thought that Wren had somehow learned the People's language overnight, but the deep voice wasn't that of her granddaughter. Elder Woman realized that the tightly held hair belonged to her grandson. "Skraw, what are you doing here?"

"I just want to see her again. You keep her closed in. Why can't she come out?"

"Harrumph. I'll let go of your hair," Elder Woman said. "But do not get up." Elder Woman was about to yell for Chirrup to bring light when she and Finch came into view, bearing torches. Elder Woman checked the large rock blocking Wren's room. It had been moved aside, leaving a small opening. "Why didn't you ask me to come with you instead of frightening her? Wait here. I'll go in first."

Firelight from within outlined the crack between boulder

and wall. Elder Woman had barely squeezed through it when something hard pelted her. She raised her arms in front of her face, protecting her eyes as Wren bent for more rocks. "Stop it, girl!"

Wren straightened with her fists full. When she saw Elder Woman, she hesitated.

"Drop them right now." Her hand movements showed Wren that she should let go of the stones. Seeing the defiance blazing in her eyes, Elder Woman thought that Wren might not comply, but then she opened her hands, and the rock weapons tumbled onto the gritty floor. Wren moved back, pressing herself against the wall.

"Chirrup, you and Finch come in here," Elder Woman yelled over her shoulder. "Bring Skraw in with you."

Chirrup came in first, nodding and smiling. Wren's face actually relaxed a little, such was the effect that Chirrup's presence had on others. The girl's expression changed quickly when Skraw squeezed through. Her fingers twitched on her tunic as if she wished she still had the rocks. Finch entered afterward, standing to one side.

Elder Woman waved her hand to get Wren's attention. "Skraw," she said, pointing at her grandson. Then she said Wren's name while pointing at her.

The two young ones stared awkwardly at each other. The burning bear fat that coated the twine-wrapped ends of the torches sizzled in the silence. Elder Woman would have liked to tell Wren that Skraw was the grandchild of her body just as Wren was, but of course, she wouldn't understand.

Elder Woman looked at their wary faces. With Raven as the girl's mother, surely the two weren't so closely related as to keep their children from thriving. The boy's features were much larger than Wren's abnormally small ones. His eyes were a lighter brown, and his hair and skin were paler. Wren was a good bit taller than he was. The pair didn't look very much alike, so perhaps they were different enough in spite of being kindred.

Without Leaf to interpret, there wasn't any use staying longer. Her sons were away hunting, and until they were around to help control Leaf, she would have to do without his help. The women might not be able to stop him if he tried to escape. Elder Woman took a closer look at Wren. She thought about telling Chirrup to cut off the girl's ridiculously long hair, but she had a feeling that would destroy any friendliness Wren presently felt toward Chirrup. The hair could wait. Elder Woman motioned that they should leave.

Elder Woman held the torches while Finch and Chirrup helped Skraw slowly wrestle the heavy rock back in place. She wondered how he'd managed to move it enough to force his way in. A strong suspicion crossed her mind. Perhaps his reason for going into Wren's room was quite different than what he'd said. All creatures sought a mate once they were old enough, and the need ran rampant through their blood until they managed to find one. Elder Woman had seen animals push themselves to exhaustion, even fighting to the death, for the chance to rut.

As soon as the rock was in place, she handed one of the torches to Finch and whirled on Skraw, slapping him across the face with her palm. "Impatient youngster! You'll wait until after the ceremony. Do you understand?"

Chirrup and Finch's startled faces turned toward her, then the two women wisely walked away so as to not witness his humiliation.

Skraw responded with anger, his eyes flaring at her, but then he caught himself and lowered his head, showing shame instead. "I understand, Grandmother." He left, stumbling away through a different dark corridor than the one the women had taken.

"Everyone else has gone," she called out loudly. "And now I'm leaving." Elder Woman waited a moment longer then shuffled down the passage that led to the main hearth.

She told herself to be patient. The girl would want company sooner or later. Elder Woman didn't know what would happen if Wren refused Skraw after the rites were performed. The boy would be hard to restrain. *He* certainly wouldn't be patient.

She strongly preferred that her granddaughter not be treated roughly, but at some point, Elder Woman had to step back. Otherwise, there would be no babies. Elder Woman gave a long sigh. She'd never felt so alone. Elder Man had died too soon, leaving her by herself with the difficult task of maintaining peace while assuring that everyone still did what was best for the group's survival.

*\*\*\**

Before many more days had passed, Elder Woman gave up working skins with her jaws and teeth. The pain was continuous and had become too great. She decided that she'd use bone tools for the task instead—she'd make lissoirs. They'd eaten red deer the night before when the men returned from hunting near a distant lake surrounded by forest. Red deer ribs were a good size for making lissoirs, neither too large nor too small.

First, she cleaned one of the ribs at the stream. Then after drying and polishing it with smooth bits of stone, she went in search for a skin to try out the newly made tool. She remembered how Leaf had always made beautifully finished leather using red deer ribs to deftly rub and work the skins. If he wasn't always trying to escape, they could bring him to the hearth fire some nights so that he could help.

Unprocessed skins were kept in one of the many smaller chambers. Upon entering the room, she stumbled and almost fell. Thinking that someone had carelessly dropped a skin in the wrong place, she lowered the torch. Instead, she saw her medicine pouch. Several packets had fallen out.

The bag had been lost for at least half a moon. Perhaps she'd left it there, but that didn't explain why she hadn't noticed it before. The others also worked skins, and they hadn't found it, either. She noticed, while putting the packets back inside, that some were missing. That bag was forbidden to anyone but herself. No one besides Elder Woman could touch it or dispense medicines from it. She realized at once who the culprit must be. He was the only one capable of breaking such a taboo.

Holding her medicine bag tightly to her chest with one hand, the torch in the other, she hurried to the main hearth. Finch and Jay were about to leave the cave.

"Stop," she yelled, hurrying up to them. "Have you seen Chukar?"

Jay hesitated, looking at the bag, then pointed toward the cave mouth. Elder Woman threw down the torch, pushed past him, and went outside. She immediately spotted her errant son sitting next to one of the large spear-like boulders that dotted the landscape. He appeared to be lining his moccasins with grass. The rocks skittering beneath her feet, she almost tumbled down the slope in her desperation to reach him before he disappeared. Chukar heard her noisy descent. He quickly stuck the moccasins on his feet and stood.

She slid to a stop in front of him but managed to keep her balance. "You should have asked me for medicine if you were ill."

Saying nothing, he only watched her.

"You should not have taken the whole bag." It crossed Elder Woman's mind that he might not have wanted the herbs for himself. "Who were the people that needed treating?"

He looked away from her to the ground.

Elder Woman took a closer look at him. Since he'd been living alone, Chukar was always unkempt, his furs torn, his face smudged, and his body dirty. Because he was by himself, he had to work all day, every day, making tools, gathering food and firewood, trapping, and hunting without much time to tend his personal needs. But on that day, his furs were mended, and his face was clean, his hair shining and free of nits. Chukar also had a self-satisfied air about him that made her think that he'd somehow found a woman. *But how can that be?*

A dreadful thought poked her. Raven, that wandering Them woman, must have come searching for her daughter and Leaf, and she'd somehow crossed paths with Chukar. Elder Woman narrowed her eyes. By the looks of him, Raven had recovered if she'd been ill. "Harrumph. You're staying with her, aren't you? Raven."

His eyes met hers and held.

"It must be Raven." She started to warn him not to bring her around, but then she had a thought. If Leaf knew Raven was with Chukar, he might be less inclined to resist Coo. "Bring Raven here if she is sick. She will get well faster." Elder Woman heard the goodwill in her voice, even if her motives for wanting Raven at the cave had nothing to do with helping the woman.

He looked at her as if she were jabbering nonsense.

Elder Woman tried to think of what to say that would convince him she was being sincere. "Raven helped feed our bellies when she stayed with us. I will do the same for her while she recovers," she said, feeling almost benevolent.

"We are not hungry." He began striding past her.

Crickets whirred in the grass as she watched him slowly

disappear into the horizon. Even if she hadn't persuaded him, it didn't matter. Raven might have forsaken Leaf, but sooner or later, she would insist upon seeing Wren. One didn't forget one's children so easily. He would bring Raven along with him before long. It would be interesting to see what happened when they came. After a lifetime of understanding that jealousy should be avoided, Elder Woman was forced to think differently about that destructive emotion. Jealousy made a good weapon.

Elder Woman climbed back to the cave. Huffing from exertion, she followed the passage that led to where Leaf was being held. She stopped in front of the boulder. Even if her sons had been with her to remove the stone, she wouldn't have gone inside. Although it was irrational, Elder Woman could envision Leaf leaping on her in spite of his bonds. What she was about to say was going to infuriate him.

"I'll bring Coo in again before long," she yelled so that he'd hear every word.

"I told you that I already have a mate," he yelled back. "You have a bad memory, old woman."

"You're wrong. I have a very good memory. This old woman remembers a baby's birth. Chukar wanted Raven, and Raven wanted Chukar. That is how Wren came about. And when you and Raven lived with us, he still wanted her and she him. That was why you asked for the joining ceremony. We made a good ceremony for you and Raven, but in spite of our efforts, they still wanted each other."

A long pause. "They were never together again."

His calm reply disappointed her, but she pressed on. "How can you be sure? None of *us* are."

"I am sure."

Elder Woman decided not to reveal any more at that moment. Her verbal spears had jabbed him well enough, and when Chukar brought Raven to the cave, Leaf would remember his conversation with Elder Woman. He'd not be so calm then.

# CHAPTER 8

*Raven*

DURING THE DAYS FOLLOWING CHUKAR'S seductive cleansing, Raven tried not to think about the future. For a while, she was successful. Chukar's ever-attentive presence helped mute her worries; he rarely left her side. But she couldn't loll on furs forever in front of a fire because hearth flames had to be fed with something—as did her body.

Soon, Chukar would be forced to hunt, or they would go hungry. That unpleasant thought loomed in her mind when one morning, she awoke before he did and refreshed the fire with a few pieces left from what had once been a large stack of aurochs' dung. After the patties were ablaze, the grass seeds in them popping, Raven slipped back under the furs. She turned on her side and began lightly tracing one of his collarbones; it was amazingly long. He stirred but stayed asleep while her fingers followed its length across his broad shoulder. Perhaps if he'd opened his eyes then, the memories submerged in the deep lake of her mind wouldn't have started rising to the surface. At least not for a while.

She suddenly saw in her mind's eye Wren and Leaf as they'd looked one particular day in the recent past when they'd brought her that rarest of foods, the sweet honey that Wren had found and Leaf had helped gather. How eagerly they'd anticipated her delighted response with small, almost-silly grins on their faces. The memory provoked a painful longing to see them. Raven felt her wrist, searching for the narrow woven bracelet made from her hair mixed with Leaf's. The small plaited circle was gone, probably lost during the flood. She'd only just noticed its absence; the loss made tears come to her eyes.

Raven eased over to the far side of the pallet. She would soon be completely well, then she would demand once more that Chukar take her to Wren and Leaf. But what then? Leaf was no fool. He would take one look at her and Chukar together and know what had passed, and she had no idea how Wren would react when her mother arrived with a Longhead man. That Chukar was her father was probably no longer a secret. Raven assumed that Elder Woman had somehow let Wren know that she was her grandmother.

Raven pressed a thumb over the gap between her top teeth. Perhaps telling Leaf a partial truth would suffice for his forgiveness. She could say that she'd done what she had to in order to survive long enough to find him and Wren.

Chukar sighed in his sleep. Raven bit down on the thumb pressing against her teeth. She couldn't just go out by herself to look for Wren and Leaf. If she showed up without Chukar, Elder Woman would take her prisoner. If she arrived as Chukar's woman, that was a different matter. She knew enough about Longhead families to know how seriously both men and women took that bond. They would not be so quick to part her from him, and Elder Woman would be thwarted—for a time anyway. Regardless of what Leaf and Wren might think, it was best that she arrived at Elder Woman's lair by Chukar's side.

He let out a gentle snore. She glanced over her shoulder at him. How shamelessly she was willing to use him, but if he refused to help her, would she be able to just walk away? At the thought, a keen sense of loss came over Raven. She groaned and flopped over on her back. Other than his help, she wasn't sure what she actually wanted from this man—besides satisfying her lust for him. She moaned softly.

His eyes flew open at the sound. He looked at her, brows squeezing together in a frown. "Do you hurt?"

"No," Raven said, although her thoughts were indeed paining her. She reached out and caressed his puckered forehead until his face relaxed. He took her wrist, pressing her fingers against his face, then pulled her under him, entering her in one smooth movement. Responding with a kind of desperation, she grasped him tightly, holding him deep inside.

Afterward, he remained lying on her like an enormous heavy cover, their bodies still joined. With a shock, Raven realized that she wasn't any longer protected from pregnancy by nursing Windy. That was one of the things she'd been hiding from herself about what was happening. Although drowsy again, Raven fought not to sleep. She might dream about raven hatchlings like she had the day Wren was conceived.

She enjoyed the way he always stayed with her afterward, covering her, closing out the world around them. But Raven had learned a lot about the way the body worked. She suspected that his amorous lingering might be the Earth Mother's way of keeping her still so that his seed could more easily take hold within her womb. But even though she wasn't nursing Windy, Raven's illness had suppressed her moon blood. So, with relief, she doubted that she could become pregnant.

Because Raven hadn't returned, her sister-in-law would have had to forcibly wean Windy. Sky had been left with a lingering insecurity when Raven put him aside to become pregnant. Sadness welled within her as she thought with regret about her deserted children. Chukar's weight stopped being pleasurable; his desires and needs along with Raven's own conflicting ones were pulling her in too many directions.

Later, as they broke morning fast, she tentatively broached again the subject of them leaving to find the Longhead band.

"When will we go find Wren?" she asked.

"You need more strength before traveling" was all he said.

The paucity of his verbal interaction didn't surprise her. The Longheads had all too often seemed uncomfortable with her and Leaf's desire to chat with them, signaling their displeasure not with words but with a quick, cold look. If a conversation went on for too long, they sometimes abruptly walked away, reacting as if their ears were under assault. Chirrup, Elder Woman's daughter, was the only one of them who ever conversed for any reasonable length.

It wasn't that Chukar couldn't talk more, but he seemed to feel that a few quick hand movements or a glance was often enough. The only topic he didn't mind hearing her discuss regularly was Wren. At those times, she had his complete attention. Raven told him how strong and brave his daughter was, relating stories of her more audacious exploits.

"She's a lot like her father," Raven often said.

He always responded with one of his noncommittal huffs, but she could tell the compliment pleased him.

Raven suspected his present silence partly had to do with his desire to postpone the inevitable trip they must take, because he replied at length to her next question. Although she'd never seen Longheads eat human flesh, Raven knew that Leaf had witnessed the practice during his childhood captivity. She found the idea abhorrent. Raven didn't believe that any amount of starvation could weaken her aversion, but she was morbidly curious as to why they didn't find eating their family and friends repulsive. She decided that day to satisfy her curiosity.

"I hope the coming winter won't be overly hard and long," she began.

"Ot," he said.

She interpreted his response as meaning he hoped not. Raven thought for a heartbeat about how she might turn the conversation in the direction she wanted. There didn't seem to be any subtle way. Clearing her throat, she charged ahead. "Winter is a time of starvation—for people as well as animals. When you were very hungry, did you ever eat the flesh of others in the band who had died?"

Chukar's head lifted in surprise at her question. "Yes."

A small noise of disgust slipped from her.

His eyebrows rose. "You never have?"

"No, I've never seen anyone in my tribe do that."

He frowned for a moment; she could almost see his mind working. "That does not mean it has never been done by your people. Perhaps it just doesn't happen as often." His shoulders twitched dismissively. "Your people are not as large, and they eat less. I don't understand why it makes you unhappy. Many animals eat their own kind if they are hungry enough—for a reason. Some need to stay alive in order to birth young ones."

His answer made perfect sense. She hadn't thought about it in that way. Sending a silent prayer to the Earth Mother, Raven hoped she never experienced hunger that severe.

Because they'd talked about death and hunger, Chukar must have thought Raven was complaining about their low food supplies. He arose from their meal and dutifully prepared to go out hunting that morning. The day was warm, and insects lifted off the steppes below in thick swarms, their humming and buzzing easily heard from the cave mouth.

After she smeared red ochre on his face and arms to provide a barrier against biting flies and mosquitos, Raven watched him walk with his familiar rolling gait away down the slope.

When almost at the bottom of the incline, he looked back to see if she was watching him. She raised a hand, her heart beating with quick, painful thumps. That awkward affection she felt for someone not of her own kind was an unfathomable mystery.

She turned abruptly and went inside the cave. The one thing Raven knew with certainty was that she couldn't remain with him forever. Her life was with the tribes. Every time she'd thought about Chukar after his assumed death, grief had draped her with a heavy sorrow that wasn't easily cast aside. She was afraid that when she left him to return to the Wind band, she would experience a different type of pain, a discontentment that would rake her at times, from knowing that he was alive, but that she could never see him again. Eventually, if she lived long enough, she would begin to wonder if he was already dead.

Crystalized drippings on the cave wall behind the hearth glistened wetly in the firelight. While observing them, Raven became pleasantly lost in a daydream. She imagined living with both Leaf and Chukar, the three of them dwelling together in harmony. But when she went so far as to see herself returning to the Wind camp with both men at her side, her reverie quickly faded. She made a derisive sound. What an uproar that would cause. Fin and the others would never let Chukar stay. He would be cast out on the steppes—if they didn't decide to kill him first. When she took Leaf into consideration, Raven chastised herself even more for imagining such nonsense. He would never share her with anyone, much less Chukar.

No wonder others thought her odd at times; her thoughts were often out of the ordinary, and people picked up on that. She looked away from the shining wall, her eyes darting restlessly around the chamber. Her glance fell upon Chukar's rent leggings draped on a nearby stone. Mending them suddenly became all-important. Sewing straight, strong stitches required concentration. If forced to stick with what was directly in front of her, she might stop thinking such strange thoughts.

By her request, Chukar had trapped birds a while back so that she could make bone needles. Heat weakened the bones, so the birds had been defleshed without cooking them first. After several leg bones were clean enough, Raven had split them into slivers and drilled a hole in the end of each one with a splinter of stone. She threaded one of the needles she'd made with sinew and took the leggings with her outside, where she sat a short distance from the cave mouth. The light was better there for mending, and a warm summer breeze gently caressed her face and hair while she sewed.

A herd of great-antler deer came into view after she'd been outside for a while. They were heading for the pool by the spring, grazing small plants as they went. Raven tutted, shaking her head. If only Chukar hadn't already left. He'd gone hunting farther abroad that day when he hadn't needed to.

Because Chukar hunted alone, he often set up ambushes or relied on pit traps to make a kill. So that she wouldn't accidentally fall in while gathering kindling, he'd warned her about a trap he'd dug not too far from the cave. Raven wondered if he'd gone first to that trap. If so, he may have glimpsed the deer on their way to the water and would soon return.

How she wished that a male was in the herd. They were a breathtaking sight with their huge slabs of antlers branching at the ends. But then a stag did trot up, being chased by yet another one. The first arrival bellowed and stopped to face his challenger. Both males lowered their heads and began maneuvering around each other while turning their antlers from side to side in a formidable display. The muscles in their legs bulged to maintain balance because of the heavy loads on their brows.

Their fighting dance was slow compared to other smaller kinds of deer.

Without warning, they moved forward, the sound of their heads ramming together a loud clatter. It struck Raven that their antlers were shaped like enormous hands with broad palms and wickedly curved fingers tipped by sharp fingernails. She didn't know how their heads bore the weight. The big but hornless females all stopped eating the low-growing foliage to watch as the males pushed back and forth, neither achieving an immediate advantage.

A movement to one side caught her attention. A large red fox was sitting not far away. It was also watching the deer, but at Raven's glance, the animal swiveled its head to look at her. The green eyes had a wistful, almost thoughtful appearance instead of the usual slyness. The fox abruptly broke eye contact, its gaze going over her head to the sky. Its expression changed to one of wide-eyed alarm, and it leapt up and fled. The fox's behavior mystified her. As far as she knew, hawks and eagles never risked attacking an animal that size. Raven looked skyward to see what had frightened it.

The moon always waited until night to cast down showers of firestones, so Raven was startled when she saw a bright flash slanting across the sky toward the earth. The great-antler stags still fought below, but Raven ignored them. She jumped onto her feet, her eyes following the light's path. The firestone streaking across the day sky was so large and bright that Raven decided it must have been cast by the sun instead of the moon. It grew as it traveled, developing a round head of fire followed by a long tail—a fiery creature that heated her upturned face. Her clothes suddenly felt too warm, and Raven felt a flicker of fear as it became obvious that the Earth Mother was in peril. She was under attack from the sun.

Loud thunder belched from above, and a flash split the sky,

accompanied by an even louder boom that shook the earth. A sound of falling rocks came from within the cave. Raven remained where she was, frozen in place. Then the world went completely quiet, but the eerie stillness was soon filled with a roaring sound. She glanced at the deer just as a powerful wind hit them with so much force that they fell onto the ground. Before she could move, an overpowering gust knocked Raven off her feet, and her fingers clutched the earth to keep from tumbling away. Plant debris and small stones pelted her as she fought to stay in place.

The wind quickly died. When after a short while, nothing more happened, Raven shakily pushed herself up. All the deer had fled except for the stags that were still on the ground. They squirmed in the grass, fighting to stand, but the curving prongs of their antler tips had become entangled so that their heads were held tightly together. Raven tore her eyes away from the strange sight and anxiously looked in the direction Chukar had gone, hoping that the sun creature had spared him. The plains were completely silent. The droning masses of insects had gone, all of them blown away.

She ran to the cave entry. Dust billowed outward from a pile of fallen stones on one side of the main chamber. The opening to their sleeping chamber was on the opposite end. Raven started in, but fearing the ceiling might fall once more, she fled back outside. She again searched the plains for Chukar, desperate to see his bulky form coming toward her. He was nowhere in sight. Her face stung. Running her fingers over her skin, Raven realized she had several small cuts.

The stags snorted below. Even though their antlers were still entangled, they'd managed to get onto their feet. One of them pushed forward, and when the other retaliated, they resumed their slow shuffling dance.

The weather had been bright and clear that day but not

anymore. Although the sky was still cloudless, the day had darkened abnormally. Raven shaded her eyes and looked upward. A heavy haze covered the morning sun; only a dim brownish light lit the world. The Earth Mother had retaliated against her brother, the sun, by blocking him with dust. Raven shuddered. All living things needed both earth and sun to survive. The two shouldn't weaken each other by quarreling.

Nervous about what else might happen, Raven looked into the distance. At last, she spotted Chukar. He was returning from a different direction, running quickly over the plains. To reach the cave, he would have to cross the gully. She shivered, hoping it was still dry and not flooded by a river dislodged from its usual route by the explosion. But shortly after disappearing into the depths, he climbed over the edge. Upon standing, he looked in her direction. Raven gave a little wave and pointed toward the stags up the slope from him. He reflexively crouched so they wouldn't spot him, not immediately realizing that the only thing they could see was each other.

As he slipped toward the animals, Chukar straightened suddenly at noticing how their heads were stuck together. They'd finally given up fighting and were trying to separate their antlers. He dropped the bag from his back to the ground and rushed forward. Coming from behind the closest deer, he rammed his spear into the front lower chest of the one opposite, the spear's point searching for the buck's heart.

With a sharp bellow, the deer's legs collapsed beneath it. Chukar lurched backward, pulling the spear free. He jammed the point in again. A loud cracking noise sounded, and the other deer staggered away, a huge antler tumbling onto the ground. It turned and ran, head held high, the remaining antler resembling a small tree sprouting from its skull.

Raven and Chukar looked at each other over the short distance. Chukar's chest heaved from the exertion. His expression was full of triumphant ferocity. She'd never been with him on a hunt or seen him kill an animal before that day, and she thought that he seemed part wolf. He reinforced the notion by throwing back his head and howling. Listening to the timbre of the wail, Raven realized that it was his howl instead of a wolf's that she'd heard while lying almost dead in the cave. Chukar cut the cry short but remained with his head tilted, staring at the sky. Raven followed his gaze but saw only dirty air. He must be remembering what had happened earlier.

Chukar started up the slope, and warmth pulsed through her. Instead of butchering the animal right away, he wanted to know how she'd fared during the strange event. Upon reaching her, he looked Raven up and down as if reassuring himself that she was fine. She stepped forward and wrapped her arms around his large chest. He immediately hugged her back. Raven had never seen a Longhead man and woman hugging. In spite of her concern over what had happened that day, his response thrilled her. When several drops of blood splattered her arm, she broke their embrace. A cut over an eye was leaking blood.

She tapped the skin over one of her eyebrows. "You have a wound."

"Rocks blew into my face when I fell on the ground." He reached up and touched the cut, his fingers coming away red.

"The wind also knocked me down." She turned toward the cave. "And a small part of the cave collapsed. But I think it's fine to go inside. I'll go for water."

He grasped her arm before she took more than a few steps.

Raven looked over her shoulder at him. "I have to go inside to get water for your cut."

The medicine bag had disappeared several days before, so she didn't have anything more than water with which to treat the small wound. Raven hadn't asked where he'd taken the pouch. She planned to make her own bag as soon as possible.

Chukar went in with her. The dust had already settled. He looked up at the section that had fallen.

"I don't think the ceiling will fall anymore," she said to reassure him. The celestial infighting seemed to have ended.

Chukar nodded his agreement, and she dampened a scrap of leather at the hearth. He sat down in the mouth so she could see better while tending his face. As Raven quickly cleaned the cut, she saw how well his large brow ridges protected his eyes. The steady trickle of blood had simply run across the top of his brows rather than blinding him.

"What happened in the sky?" he asked abruptly.

Clearly, he was as unsettled as she was, but Raven almost smiled. He wanted her to talk. "A firestone exploded like an overheated hearthstone," she told him. At his quizzical look, she continued. "You've seen falling firestones at night when they streak through the sky. This large one fell during the day."

"It was as bright as the sun."

She nodded. "I think that flaming firestone *was* a part of the sun." She wanted to tell him how worried she was that the sun had attacked the Earth Mother, but the Longheads didn't know about the Earth Mother. The few times she and Leaf had tried to talk to them about the spirit, they'd reacted with doubtful faces and shifting feet, as if the two of them were telling lies.

The day was still young, and they worked frantically, processing as much meat as possible before predators were drawn to the kill. Chukar brought heavy loads to the cave for Raven to slice and air-dry. She soon ran out of room to hang strips on the few drying racks they'd been using for any meat they didn't immediately cook. Chukar went to the spring and cut down saplings growing around the pool. They used them to make poles for more racks, stripping off the bark and branches with small hand axes.

By late afternoon, a few vultures circled overhead in the murky sky, and ravens began arriving. Although no land predators had yet come along, Chukar gave up salvaging any more of the deer. At Raven's request, he sliced off a piece of the hide that she could use to make a bag for medicines. Afterward, he helped cut thin strips for the racks. Twilight came earlier than usual, accompanied by a dusty sunset that covered the entire landscape with a muted red glow.

Chukar collected firewood for cooking and to keep any curious animal that came to feed below from climbing toward the cave. In spite of her exhaustion, Raven looked forward to the feast they would have, and she planned a little surprise. She thought Chukar would enjoy having his hunting prowess recognized—as did all men everywhere.

The spear had damaged the heart, but the organ was still edible. She cooked it before anything else. While serving him slices, she improvised a song about how he'd killed the deer with a single blow. She hadn't been singing long when Chukar raised a hand to stop her.

He smiled, but his hand speech was hesitant, hinting at embarrassment. "They could not run away."

Raven gave a little shrug. "But still." She thought that most men would have been too rattled by the firestorm to have killed the animal so cleanly. It had always seemed to Raven that Chukar, and the Longheads in general, accepted and adapted to life's events quicker than did her own tribesmen, who discussed to death whatever had happened in an effort to feel in control.

After they'd eaten their fill of the meat, Chukar went to the cave mouth, where Raven joined him. He nodded at the dark forms slinking around the deer carcass. "Cave lions."

She glanced down the incline then looked up, distracted by the sky. It was still aglow, although sunset had long passed. The exploding firestone had obviously affected a very large area. Raven thought anxiously of Sky and Windy. They had to be far enough away to not have been injured by the explosion. After all, the flash in the sky had not occurred in that direction. They'd probably escaped harm, but what about Leaf and Wren? She knew the location of the Wind band; she didn't know exactly where Leaf and Wren were.

Loud snarling drifted up to where they stood. Trying to impart her urgency, Raven shook Chukar's arm to take his attention away from the lions. "Sunset is past, but look at the sky. That light is left over from the burning firestone. The glow spreads far and wide, so the wind knocked down people everywhere. Other caves may have collapsed. Doesn't your family stay in a cave?"

He nodded, his response somewhat reluctant.

"I want to know if Wren is safe."

Letting out a sigh, he looked at her, and his hands began moving. "We will go there. But if my mother tries to capture you the same way she did our daughter, I will not let her." His eyes were tinged red from the glowering sky. "I will stop her."

She didn't know for sure, but Chukar seemed to be saying he would kill Elder Woman if things went the wrong way. "I don't think it will come to that."

Raven tried not to show elation that he was at last taking her to Wren and Leaf. She glanced at his grim face. What would he do if she somehow freed Wren and Leaf then left with them for the Wind tribe? Raven swallowed, remembering what Leaf had once said about the Longheads. "The important thing for the Longheads is keeping the peace," he'd told her. "They are slow to anger, but once they're upset about something..."

# CHAPTER 9

*Leaf*

THE MORNING BEGAN LIKE ALL the others. The two brothers undid Leaf's arms and gave him a small meal of meat and roots left over from the band's breaking of night-fast. They occasionally gave him berries sweetened with honey, but that day, there were none. As usual, they untied his legs and put on a leash. Jay tied the loose end of the leash around his own middle, perversely reminding Leaf of the way a birth cord attached an infant to its mother. After he relieved himself, Leaf was led back to his chamber and retied. And as she did almost every morning while Jay and Whit were working on the ropes, Elder Woman came by to make sure his bindings were secure. The two men went out into the corridor to wait on her after they finished.

He eyed her while she walked around him, scrutinizing the ropes for frayed areas and tugging at them to make sure they weren't loose. More than a handful of days had passed since the incident with Coo, but Leaf still had his guard up. The two women wouldn't surprise him again. Upon reentering the chamber after his short outings, he always checked the furs in the corner for suspicious bulges.

Elder Woman circled one last time while he tried to ignore her. She stopped, finally satisfied. "Harrumph. Coo says you hurt her. She's afraid of you."

Leaf let out an incredulous sound. "I'm the hurt one. Look at my eye. It's still painful from how hard she hit me."

"I explained to the girl that she bled only because it was her first time."

Realizing that Elder Woman wasn't referring to their brawling but to the actual coupling afterward, unwanted regret invaded his thoughts. He had indeed been overly rough with Coo. A small shuffling sound came from the corridor. Leaf realized that the young woman stood outside the opening.

"Coo thinks you are made differently than the men of the People." Again, Elder Woman's meaning wasn't readily apparent, but the hand gesture at the level of her crotch was sufficient clarification.

He spoke loud enough for Coo to hear, although what she thought didn't matter. "That's ridiculous. There is no difference." He gave a small snort. "Who's being cowardly now?" He immediately regretted his taunting. If Coo felt reluctant about cooperating because she believed joining with him was painful, then he shouldn't disabuse her of the notion.

Elder Woman raised her voice. "You heard his words, granddaughter? Stop your foolishness and come on in here."

Leaf had to somehow get over to them that he would not provide a repeat. He refused to demean himself again. "No," Leaf shouted. "I won't mate her. Stay out there, Coo."

Elder Woman waited expectantly, watching the opening. Leaf wondered if the girl's father and uncle would drag her in or if Whit was finally displaying some spine about Elder Woman's treatment of his daughter. The old matriarch's wide mouth turned down over her receding chin. She called out once more, "Girl, you know what I'll do if you don't obey."

Her head bowed, the young woman quickly shuffled inside. The ridiculousness of the situation suddenly struck Leaf. He began laughing, a raw, contemptuous mirth. Coo's head jerked up. Her look was part hurt and part defiance. Leaf went quiet. She thought he was laughing at her. But what if she did? If she thought him callous, that was to his advantage. He began laughing again, but his heart wasn't in it, and he stopped almost at once.

Leaf expected Elder Woman to call for the brothers to untie him, but she began walking away, waggling a finger his direction. "It is partly my fault that your first meeting went badly. A couple should keep company before the ceremony and the mating that begins afterward. You cannot be trusted to behave properly during a ceremony, so we will not have one. But I will leave Coo here so that the two of you will become used to one other."

"Isn't it a little late for that?"

Elder Woman hobbled through the gap in the wall, leaving Leaf waiting in vain for a reply.

Leaf and Coo stood without speaking. She looked down at the cave floor, while he observed her unhappy face. Now that the pressure was gone, he felt sorry for the young woman. None of it had been her idea.

"I apologize if I was rough and you were hurt," he said.

She rewarded his apology with a furtive glance. Straining against the ropes, Leaf squatted carefully so as to not topple over, then he flopped down to sit on the floor. He nodded toward the corner. "You could rest there on the furs if you wish."

Coo hesitated then went and sat, her smoky hearth-fire smell wafting into his face as she passed by. Once settled, she threw another glance his way. "I'm sorry about your eye."

A long silence ensued. Leaf noticed that the chamber had been left open. Perhaps that had been one of the girl's conditions for coming inside. That tantalizing hole in the wall didn't provide an opportunity for Leaf to escape, though. Not fettered so completely as he was. And although he couldn't hear anyone, Leaf suspected the men were still guarding the corridor.

Leaf ran his gaze over her, noting once more the large greenish-brown eyes and short reddish-brown hair, remembering how she'd looked as a small girl. As he'd already observed, her body had morphed into something very different since he and Raven had parted ways with the group. She looked to be almost fully grown. Other than the wolf boy, Coo was the only child he'd seen from those earlier times. Maybe there weren't any others. She fidgeted under his scrutiny, her brow tightening. Leaf knew he was being rude. Wide-eyed staring was usually reserved for selecting a herd animal to take down during a hunt.

"Coo, what happened to the others in your band?"

Sadness crossed her features, and her hands made the plaintive gestures of loss. "Soon after we came here, they sickened and died."

"I'm sorry. Was it because of hunger?"

"No, fever took them." She glanced his way. "We were in a hungry time though, so everyone was weak."

"Were the dead ones eaten?"

After another quick sad look, she nodded, affirming Leaf's assumption about how bad things were at the time. The girl had been faced with eating her kinsmen, perhaps even her own mother. Coo stiffened, her back straightening, emotions playing over her face. She looked out across the room with unfocused eyes.

"With the flesh of our people, we will survive," she intoned. Those ceremonial words, uttered before making a meal of the departed ones, were entirely familiar. Leaf had heard them several times during his childhood captivity. Although he'd been held by a different Longhead band then, the chant was exactly the same.

His voice joined hers. "They become part of us until our own deaths."

Leaf had never told Raven how he'd participated in those feasts. His cravings during the starving times were overpowering, and Leaf had devoured whatever scraps they'd given him. As he remembered the revulsion he'd felt afterward, several tremors went through his body.

To Leaf's bewilderment, the chamber walls trembled in response, and he heard a loud clap of thunder, the sound clear even underground. An even louder boom followed. Pebbles rained from the ceiling, and dust filled the air. With a cry, Coo leapt up and ran from the chamber. Leaf struggled onto his feet and hopped after her. His fear of being buried alive made him clumsier than usual. He fell but managed to rise. When Leaf reached the corridor, he collided with Coo, who had come back. He almost fell again, but she steadied him. Bending down, she scrabbled at the ropes around his legs, yanking at the knots.

And then Chirrup was kneeling beside Coo, helping to untie him. As soon as the ropes were off his legs, the three of them ran for the cave mouth. Conveniently, there were torches stuck in wall niches throughout the passage, probably put there at Coo's request so she could easily leave Leaf's chamber whenever she wanted to. But without his arms to help maintain balance, Leaf stumbled so often that he soon lost sight of the two women. When he was finally outside, they were already with the rest of the band at a distance from the cave.

With relief, he saw Wren standing beside Chirrup. They were both staring up at him, and he knew that Chirrup had told Wren how she and Coo had undone his legs so he could come out.

Dust that smelled like ashes filled the air. Leaf looked in

amazement at the leaves and uprooted bushes thickly covering the ground. A great wind had blown over the area.

Everyone's eyes were on the sky, their heads tilted back. They were speaking excitedly of an explosion, hands moving rapidly, their fingers imitating how a large fiery stone had exploded as it flew overhead. Leaf looked up. The sky glowed weakly as though day were ending, and the landscape around them became tinged with a muddy clay color.

Something untoward was going on. Leaf once more found himself wishing that Raven was there. She'd help him make sense of it all. His next thoughts were for the Wind camp. He wondered if the band had been in the path of the heavy winds. Everyone was still living in summer tents, so at least they wouldn't have been harmed by a cave-in. The tents may have blown down, though. He hoped Sky and Windy hadn't been too frightened when their home collapsed. A deep frustration at his powerlessness to see about them focused him once more on the group below.

They were distracted, everyone's attention still on the sky. That was his chance. He could slip away and hide until he somehow rid his arms of the ropes. Wren's rescue would come later when he had more help. But Leaf hesitated. The dim blood-colored sun troubled him. Standing apart from the others, the world seemed a dangerous and lonely place.

Drawn to them in spite of himself, Leaf approached the group, treading carefully through the debris so he wouldn't trip. His next escape attempt would have to wait until he was certain another firestone wouldn't explode out of the sky right away. Anyone caught out in the open could be hurt by that kind of blast. From what he'd heard them say, the stone in the sky had been huge.

Leaf needed to find out if anyone had actually been out of the cave during the explosion. He walked over to Whit. Every bit of skin that hadn't been covered by clothing—his forearms, lower legs, and face, had small bleeding cuts. He'd obviously been outside and survived.

"Did you see what happened?" Leaf asked him.

"A thundering firestone flew through the air like it had been thrown. It split the sky, letting loose a great wind. Then it blew apart and fell to the earth."

"Is that how you got your cuts—from flying pieces of firestone?"

"No, the wind knocked me down, and I was hit by pebbles blowing along the ground." Whit rubbed at his face, smearing the blood. "No one has seen this happen before." The large man looked at Leaf as if he could perhaps provide an explanation.

Leaf shook his head. "The elders never told stories about thundering firestones. Firestones are quiet and aren't usually seen during the day. I've never seen one explode." His gaze went once more to the sky. The disk of the sun had darkened even more. "The explosion sure made a lot of dust. I hope the sun won't go out like a smothered flame."

Whit gave him an uneasy look.

Everyone had begun moving around the clearing, uncertain if it was safe to return inside the cave. Since he'd arrived, Leaf hadn't seen them all in one place. Their numbers had dropped precipitously from when he'd last seen them. Whit and Jay remained of the men, and of the women, only Finch, Chirrup, and Elder Woman seemed to have survived. Coo and Skraw were the remaining children.

The faces of the other children who hadn't lived flickered through his mind. He felt a twinge of sorrow, but his sentimentality faded just as quickly as it had come when Elder Woman walked toward him. He already knew what she would say.

"Take him back inside," she ordered Whit. "The cave held strong. Whatever happened has passed."

Whit started over but stopped when Leaf backed away a few steps.

"No." Leaf couldn't stand being stuck in that badger den of a room again. "I have to find out if my family and tribesmen were hurt. I want to leave."

"They are several days' walk from here. Thunder can't reach that far."

He sucked in an exasperated breath. The ashy dust hit the back of his throat, leaving a bitter taste. Her single-mindedness was daunting. She hadn't been frightened by what had happened. He felt that even if all the spirits of earth and sky threatened her, Elder Woman still wouldn't be deterred from her plans for him. "You don't know that the wind didn't go that far. I want to leave now. I'll return once I see that they're fine."

"You expect me to believe you? Haven't I lived long enough to know when a man is lying?"

"I wouldn't desert Wren."

"Tie him." She eyed Whit, waiting for him to comply with her command.

Leaf's throat tightened with rage at having missed his opportunity. He'd made a mistake by not slipping away when they were distracted by the sky. After the strange happenings, he'd momentarily become childlike, seeking reassurance. And besides Wren, the Longheads were the only ones there, so he'd gone down the slope. But at that moment, Leaf loathed them. He despised how their large bodies constantly overwhelmed him with their bear-like strength. He hated Elder Woman with her impossible demands and how Coo stirred his pity as well as his lust. They should have all died from the fever that had decimated them.

Leaf lunged away. He'd only covered a short distance when someone pushed him hard between the shoulders. He stumbled on the debris and slammed onto the ground, the air knocked out of his lungs. Several hard kicks dug into his ribs. He heard Wren scream, but when he rolled over and saw Skraw over him, Chirrup was the one pulling at the boy's arms to keep him from hitting Leaf.

"Enough," she yelled at her nephew. "He's down."

The sound of a slap cut through the air, followed by Elder Woman's voice. "If you'd taken him inside when I told you to, then he wouldn't have attempted to escape again."

Whit's face, one cheek reddened, loomed overhead. Even as he struggled to breathe, Leaf felt amazement at how the big man, the largest of Elder Woman's sons, accepted his mother's dominance without protest. Whit yanked Leaf to his feet. Leaf strained to pull away, and Jay came to his brother's aid, grasping Leaf's shoulder.

Elder Woman pointed a finger at Chirrup. "And you, daughter, leave the commanding to me."

Chirrup bowed her head submissively. Leaf tried to catch her eye to let her know he was grateful that she'd stopped Skraw, but when Elder Woman turned her back on Chirrup as further reprimand, she trotted up the slope toward the cave.

To his surprise, he found her waiting inside the chamber when they got there. Chirrup spoke softly to her brothers while they wound the ropes around Leaf's legs, telling them she wished to talk with him alone for a short while.

"What if she comes in while you're here? You'll get me slapped again," Whit told her.

"It doesn't hurt that much. And if it makes you feel better, you can slap me afterward. Close the chamber and wait close by. I won't be long."

Although still seething, Leaf was wryly amused. He'd observed the Longhead pecking order many times. They often behaved as though they were steppe-hens. If Elder Woman chastised one of her sons, then he in turn would be rude to his mate, and she might end up slapping a child over some minor matter. Eventually, the ill will ran its course, and peace returned.

Whit's face showed his reluctance, but he nodded his assent, then he and Jay went out. Grunting as they pushed, the two men slid the stone over the closure.

Leaf struggled to let go of his anger, smiling wanly at the short, compact woman. "Thank you for stopping Skraw before he broke my ribs." He inclined his head toward the corner. "Those furs are comfortable for sitting," he said by way of inviting her to stay.

"Only if you join me." She sat down, her face full of pity as she watched him struggle to lower himself without falling.

Leaf remembered how she was always easy to be around, never neglecting to speak pleasantly, whereas the others had often ignored him and Raven. "I appreciate you helping Coo untie my legs." He cleared his throat. "I can't help but notice how small the band has become. Coo told me about the illness that struck the band." Despite his earlier wish that they would all die, he managed to sound concerned. "The illness seemed to be especially bad for children."

Chirrup gave him a sad look. "The children are very much missed. Regrettably, no more have been born."

He looked at her sharply; she sounded a bit like her mother. A fresh spate of anger threatened to destroy his resolve to treat her like an old friend. He doubted, though, that Chirrup had helped with Elder Woman's plans. She was just voicing distress about her young tribesmen's deaths. He'd almost relaxed when she fueled his distrust once more.

"It shocked me when my mother admitted what she was

doing with you and Coo. It's understandable that you're upset by what she's demanding before she'll allow you to leave." She looked him in the face. "But, Leaf, would it really be so bad to get Coo with child? To give a woman her own baby is a great kindness."

He couldn't keep suspicion out of his voice. "Did Elder Woman put you up to this?"

Chirrup's head shook vehemently. "No. I came here because I wanted to."

Leaf looked at her sidelong, not sure if he should believe her.

She fidgeted then opened her palms in appeal. "I told my mother that what she'd done was wrong. She shouldn't have stolen you from your people. But, Leaf, now that you are here, perhaps you will find it in yourself to help us."

"No. Elder Woman doesn't deserve my help, and none of you seem to understand how I feel about Raven. She's the air I breathe, my sun, and my moon. Without her, I'm an empty tortoise shell." By the look on her face, Leaf knew she didn't grasp his meaning. He remembered Elder Woman's confusion at being called a hyena. After thinking a heartbeat, Leaf came up with how to explain.

But then he hesitated. If Leaf understood Longhead women at all, the things he was going to tell her would pain her. He cleared his throat several times. "Remember when Chukar ignored you because he wanted to be with Raven? And how he tried to catch her alone by sneaking away from a hunt, forcing the band to shun him? You still wanted to be *his* mate even though his attention had wandered elsewhere. You only desired him. That's how I feel about Raven. I only want her."

Chirrup didn't seem overly upset. She calmly smoothed fine grit from her tunic as she considered his words. "I think

I understand," she said, dusting her hands. "I just didn't grasp what you meant about the tortoise shell."

"I know," he said with gentle sarcasm. "The People don't grow shells."

"I never blamed Raven. Chukar was the one behaving badly." She sat quietly, lost momentarily in thought before speaking again. "Now, because there are so few of us, everything has changed. Everyone is behaving incorrectly. The old ways seem to be gone. I've heard of stealing women from other bands but never a man. Yet, here you are." She pulled at the wisps of hair around her face. "But I do not think Raven would be upset if you gave Coo a child before leaving us. She was always kind. My mother says it's too difficult for close kinsmen to have children together, and I believe that to be true. Raven would understand that we have too few men here to make children."

Chirrup was right about Raven. Always generous, she enjoyed nothing better than helping others whether it was a chance to rid them of their ailments or to feed them when hungry. If he told Raven, upon returning, that he'd made Coo pregnant so that he could have his life with her back, she would be happy not only for his sake but for Coo's besides. He wasn't ready to yield, however. Even though intrigued by Chirrup's practical view of things, Leaf found her reasoning flawed.

If he gave in, not only would Elder Woman get away with what she'd done, but she would still have Wren. And that was wrong.

Chirrup began talking again. She spoke with an oddly weakened voice, her limp hands barely moving along with her words. "I wish to speak more with you about Coo. As we all have, she has seen all manner of animals mating on the steppes. And she may have thought that what passed under her parents' furs was similar to lions mating. Her mother and father fought often, you know—both day and night."

His embarrassment almost matched hers. "I didn't want to hurt her. I'm sorry she was made afraid. But when—"

Chirrup's raised palm stopped him. "It's only that the girl doesn't yet understand that there is nothing to fear from mating a man in whom kindness is mixed with desire."

Leaf looked at her with awe. He believed her to be extremely wise. "I'm sorry that you and Chukar didn't have children before he died."

Her eyes widened. "But he didn't die. He is still alive."

Leaf's mouth dropped. He hadn't just imagined that Chukar came into the chamber while he was barely conscious. A spike of delight went through him that the other man had survived his wound. In spite of their rivalry over Raven, he'd admired Chukar's steadfastness when it came to other matters and had found it difficult to dislike him. "But where is he? I didn't see him with the rest of you earlier."

"He doesn't stay here. He only comes for short visits. Chukar is just another brother now since he's no longer my mate."

"I'm glad he didn't die."

"If only my mother felt that way." Chirrup arose from the furs. "I'll leave before she comes. She's allowing me to see you, but she might change her mind."

"What of Wren?" Leaf quickly asked. "I saw you standing beside her outside, but are you allowed near her very often?"

"I see her every day. I'm teaching her the language of the People. Wren can make many words now and even uses her hands properly when she speaks." Chirrup moved toward the opening. "She's slowly becoming more content."

After giving Leaf a farewell smile, Chirrup called out to Whit and Jay. The boulder slid open a crack so she could squeeze through, then it moved back in place. Leaf heard her talking as they walked away. He listened for her lilting voice until he could hear it no more.

Chirrup needn't have left so quickly to avoid Elder Woman. She never came by that day nor the next one. Her absence baffled Leaf. Perhaps she'd decided that Whit and Jay could be trusted to keep him from escaping, but that didn't explain why she'd given up trying to push Coo on him. Maybe the exploding firestone had rattled her after all so that she'd forgotten about her desire for another grandchild.

It wasn't until three days later that Elder Woman finally returned. Whit and Jay had only moments before redone the ropes after his morning outing. She seemed agitated and even more impatient than usual.

"Quickly," she told them, "undo his legs and take him outside."

The two men looked at her hesitantly. They'd just brought him in.

"Do I have to untie him myself?" she asked.

Whit and Jay bent down and started undoing the ropes once more.

Elder Woman didn't seem menacing, only hurried, so Leaf didn't worry that she planned to harm him in some way. He was curious to find out what she wanted from him once they were out of the cave. The sun had remained darkened. The nights had also become colder since the firestone fell. Perhaps she wanted his opinion of how the dim sun and colder air were related. She hadn't yet discussed with him the celestial event, but Leaf had come up with several bothersome beliefs about what would happen.

If the sun didn't become brighter right away, summer would be over shortly. Plants would die, and the snows would begin earlier than usual. Leaf had to make Elder Woman understand that he must leave soon if autumn had already begun. It was too dangerous to wait until the earth was completely frozen.

As they rushed him through the corridor, he looked forward to being in the open air again. When they'd gone out earlier, the day had been windy. Even though the dusty air irritated his throat, he'd taken in large breaths, enjoying the scents of dried rosemary and thyme that came from nearby bushes.

Wren was sitting at the main hearth with Chirrup when the brothers hustled him through the chamber. He was glad Elder Woman didn't keep the girl imprisoned for the whole day. Wren didn't get up or smile when she saw him. After a quick stare, she turned her head. Hurt sliced through Leaf; Wren was still angry that she'd been deceived for so long. He would demand to talk with her again.

The old woman raised her hand as soon as they were outside, halting their haste. He waited for her to explain, but it was the brothers' huffed exclamations that let Leaf know someone was approaching the cave. He turned his head, and his breath became trapped in his throat. Raven was walking toward them, only a short distance away. Even in the dim light from the hazed sun, there was no mistaking that sweet face surrounded by a river of long dark braids. He gasped, his heart almost surging out of his chest. It was a moment before Leaf realized that the man beside her was Chukar, but that didn't mean anything to him at first. He was completely focused on *her*.

Leaf saw the exact moment when Raven spotted him. She raised her hand in a wave and began running, but then Chukar loudly called her name. She stopped and turned back. Their rapidly moving hands told Leaf they were talking, although they were still too far away for him to make out what was being said. Then Chukar took one of her hands in his, and they started forward once more.

Leaf felt as though he'd been gored by a large wooly rhinoceros. In the Longhead's world, a man taking a woman's hand signaled to everyone that the two were a pair and no one should interfere. His gut was clenching so strongly, Leaf thought he would vomit. After everything he'd done to keep her bound to him—going through the Longhead mating ceremony, loving her desperately, giving her strong children, accepting Wren as his own—this was the way things had turned out.

He didn't know how Raven had come to be with Chukar, but he had no doubts about what went on between them nightly and probably daily too. Leaf had always been her eagle man, but Raven was not, it seemed, his eagle woman. She never had been. The woman had proved to be as cunningly deceptive as the bird she was named for.

The brothers gave Leaf long curious looks, watching for his reaction. Humiliation filled him. He stiffened his spine and stared back at them. "Take me inside."

For once, Elder Woman didn't protest that her initiative was being usurped. Leaf took a quick look at the wrinkled face before they went through the cave mouth, and the satisfaction he saw there caused his stomach to spasm anew. He looked forward to the day when he would not have to see her again, but as soon as he was in his chamber, he started yelling for Elder Woman at the top of his lungs.

Whit and Jay stared at him warily without making any move to retie his legs. When he heard feet shuffling in the passageway, Leaf stopped his raucous calling and went over to them. "You may as well start untying my arms."

Elder Woman hobbled briskly through the opening.

"Bring me Coo," he told her. "I need to work on making that girl pregnant right away. When the skies are falling, a man's life could be shortened."

# CHAPTER 10

*Raven*

W HEN CHUKAR FINALLY TOOK RAVEN with him across the steppes, they walked until sundown before stopping to make camp under a rocky overhang he'd used in the past. Unusually frigid weather for late summer was settling over the plains. The night became quite cold, but with a blaze going and bundled together under quilted fox skins, they remained warm. Chukar awoke a little before dawn to rebuild the fire. When he slipped back under the skins, he pressed against Raven, gently at first, then insistently.

Banishing all sleep, the unrestrained desire he so easily sparked in her set Raven alight before the kindling began burning well. The fire was putting forth little heat as yet when she momentarily stepped out of the overhang to pull off her tunic and loincloth. All the heat trapped under the coverings escaped onto the plains. Shivering, she slid under him, welcoming his warm body.

The glimpse she'd caught of the land while stripping lingered in her mind, however, and muted her desire by dredging up the past. The last man she'd slept with on the steppes had been Leaf, during their long search for the Wind tribe. At that time, she'd thought Chukar dead. Raven tried to still her mind, but along with Chukar's body, memories of those days pressed heavily upon her. The same lack of concentration had happened several times when she coupled with Leaf. Thoughts and memories of Chukar unexpectedly interrupted her pleasure.

She recalled the wayward delight she'd felt so long ago at seeing the two men together during the winter of her pregnancy with Wren, enjoying each other's company while they made tools and helped each other with various tasks. Raven had recognized during that time that she had strong feelings for both men. And that seemed not only greedy but also perverse. She didn't understand how she'd become a woman for whom one man wasn't enough.

Sensing that she no longer responded, Chukar stopped and slid off to the side. He propped on an elbow, gazing down at her in the early light weakened by the dusty air. With the fingers of his free hand, he began tracing her mouth, nose, eyes, and all the features of her face, over and over. His hand seemed to talk to her, reminding her of their connection.

*This is what you did to my face the day we made Wren.* That day by the pool, she'd explored his differences with her fingers, his heavy brow ridges, big nose, and large jaw that sloped back. By the time she'd stopped, her fear of him was gone.

Raven realized as he caressed her that Chukar wasn't in any way lacking when it came to communication. It was only a matter of opening her mind to find meaning elsewhere besides in his words. The revelation caused her skin to tingle all over, and she marveled that he'd carried and cherished his memories of her during all the turns of the seasons that had passed.

His fingers didn't stop with Raven's face as hers had with his so long ago. They moved on, exploring even more intimately than they did whenever he cleansed her with the scraper. Her every thought was soon obliterated, and she clasped at the thick hair on his chest until he covered her once more. With eyes closed and gasping down the dusty but familiar smells of the steppes, she moved with him in ancient rhythm.

***

Later that morning, the pair trudged on beneath a pale sky, both coughing occasionally because of the grit in the air. When Raven spat out phlegm, it was streaked with gray. The landscape they were presently moving through had fewer trees than the area surrounding the cave they'd left, but wind damage was still noticeable. As far as she could see, the ground had a cluttered appearance. Bushes were uprooted, and the blast had scoured the earth, chewing up much of the low-lying vegetation.

Minced, rotting plants and grass soaked by morning dew and smelling like a stagnant pond soon coated Raven's and Chukar's leggings. The extent of the attack upon the Earth Mother alarmed Raven. Even the birds had been affected. Their early-morning calls seemed fewer, and the feathers on some of them were sparse, as if they'd been partially plucked. There was no way of knowing what had sparked the sun's temper tantrum. Because Raven was a camp healer, if she were in a Fire Cloud or Wind camp, she would join the elders in an attempt to soothe the earth and sky spirits with a ceremony.

Although Raven woke refreshed, she found herself tiring by midafternoon. The exertions of the journey were challenging her fragile recovery, and her pack seemed too heavy. She tapped Chukar on an arm and stopped walking. He paused, breaking his stride.

"I'm sorry. I need to rest," she said.

Chukar dropped his spear and looked into the distance as he loosened his backpack. "We are close." He pointed out over the steppes. "It will only be a short walk once we start out again."

If she strained, Raven could make out huge stone outcroppings mottled with gray and white that poked up out of the plains. An edgy excitement flew through her. "I didn't know we were so close. I can make it that far."

He hesitated with lowered head, taking in the way her feet shifted impatiently. With a sniff of resignation, he retightened his pack ropes and picked up the spear.

After they'd walked a short distance more, tall pointed stones shaped like enormous fat knives came into sight, dotted around the landscape near the outcroppings. Raven looked at them in amazement. Someone would have to be as big as a mammoth to use those as a tool. A little farther along, and Raven picked out a large cave mouth centered in the middle of the outcroppings. Smaller openings dotted the cliff farther down.

When they were almost there, Raven saw a figure coming down the slope in front of the cave. Noting the low, broad shape, Raven determined that the person was a Longhead woman. By the way she slogged along, the woman was old. She had to be Elder Woman.

Raven glanced at Chukar and knew that her guess was correct. His mouth was twisted as if he were holding back a snarl. Even though Elder Woman was his mother, Chukar obviously hated her. They had come to Elder Woman's den only because Raven had left him with no other choice. Hoping that Chukar wouldn't desert her and bolt away over the plains, she looked again at the approaching figure.

Elder Woman suddenly turned around and hobbled quickly back up the slope and inside the cave. Chukar started walking so slowly that Raven thought he might stop. She matched his snail-like pace.

"She's gone for the others," he eventually muttered when they were closer. "I will not let them take you."

Although he seemed to be talking more to himself than to Raven, she was about to reply when Leaf came out of the cave. He was followed by Elder Woman and two burly forms she recognized as Chukar's brothers. She realized that Leaf had seen her, and her mouth went dry. She waved her hand and attempted to call to him, but only a croak came out of her throat.

Leaf didn't wave back. Raven cringed inside, thinking that he wasn't reacting because she was with Chukar. Then she saw the ropes. He couldn't respond even if he wanted to. Of course, they would have Leaf tied to keep him from escaping. That, after all he'd done for Elder Woman's band. *How dare they treat him that way!*

Outraged, Raven found her tongue, letting loose an oath. Forgetting all caution, she started running. Leaf was a legendary hunter and tracker. To truly exist as the man that he was, he must be free; she would strip off those ropes.

"Raven," Chukar called out.

The panicked urgency of his voice stopped Raven in her tracks. She looked back, but he was already beside her.

"Raven, hold my hand, and do not leave my side. They will understand then that I will fight them."

"Surely, they wouldn't take me prisoner," Raven cried. But she didn't pull away when he tightly grasped her hand in his. If taken captive, she would not be able to help Leaf and Wren, and she would never forgive herself if Chukar killed someone or if he were killed while trying to free her. They resumed walking. Raven hoped that their intertwined fingers sent enough of a signal to deter any aggression, but she knew with faltering heart that the sight of them holding hands would disturb Leaf.

His voice blew toward them on the wind, so Raven heard Leaf perfectly when he yelled for the brothers to take him back inside. She wasn't close enough to make out his expression, but she saw his jaw lift in defiance. It was a gesture she'd seen him make many times when angered by some perceived injustice. But in the past, his indignation had always been directed at someone other than Raven.

Leaf and the Longhead brothers disappeared inside the cave. He wasn't even going to give her a chance to explain. A painful surge of despair made her realize how tired and weak she was. Raven forced herself to rally as they approached the old woman who was once more in front of the mouth's gaping maw, her gray hair whipping in the wind.

They were partway up the slope when Elder Woman's head inclined toward the opening as if she were listening to something within the cave. She turned and went inside.

Chukar's eyes met Raven's, his forehead wrinkling. They moved slowly onto the ledge, stopping short of entering. All the smells of a lived-in cave floated out to greet them: smoke, cooking odors, pungent animal skins undergoing softening, and the muskiness of the people living there. Chukar let go of her hand and motioned that she should wait. He cautiously peered around the edge of the mouth. Satisfied that no one waited in ambush, he reached again for Raven's hand and pulled her through. She immediately let her heavy pack flop onto the floor and turned to look at the main hearth.

Two women and an almost-grown boy were sitting beside the dim fire. The older of the two women grunted in surprise. Raven recognized her as a woman named Finch. The young man glaring at her from across the fire was unfamiliar, but he was probably one of the children she'd known. She turned her attention to the young woman sitting beside Finch. Her gaze met a wide-eyed stare, and swirling confusion filled Raven's mind. She decided later that it was the fly-away, shorn hair that prevented her from immediately recognizing her own daughter.

"Mother," Wren screamed. She leapt from the hearth and raced toward the cave mouth, her feet scattering firewood as she went.

Raven's hand slipped from Chukar's grasp, and she rushed forward. Wren tripped over a piece of firewood just as she reached her mother. Raven caught her in an embrace. A snorted hoot came from the Longhead boy.

Tears flooded Raven's eyes as she hugged the frantically sobbing girl. "It's all right. I've found you now." Wren seemed healthy, but she wanted to see if her daughter's skin had cut places like those on her own face and arms. Raven leaned back, trying to get a better look, but Wren held on with all her strength.

"Take me with you. I want to go back to our tent. Please don't leave me with these strange people." Wren was shaking as if racked by chills.

She kissed Wren's cheek and forehead to calm her. "We'll leave as soon as we can." Exhaustion threatened to overwhelm Raven. "Come sit by the fire," she said. With Wren still hanging on tightly, Raven struggled over to the hearth.

Juices from a spitted boar haunch sizzled onto the coals, creating a wonderful aroma. The Longhead boy started at seeing a strange woman sit down beside him. He jumped up and left. Wren buried her head in her mother's lap and continued weeping.

Her clinging despondency worried Raven. Wren had been a spirited, independent child, even as a toddler. She'd always chafed against her mother's desire to protect her. The winter after Wren had passed six summers, several of her playmates had run into the lodge where the Wind band was living during the hungry moons. Their feet prattled excitedly on the stone-paved entryway, snow falling off their leather boots. "Wren is fighting with a wolverine. She says she's going to cook it for us so we won't be hungry." Their words froze Raven with fear. Although ordinarily just scavengers, wolverines occasionally preyed on animals as large as elk.

Several men had remained at the lodge that day to knap flint. Grabbing their spears, they, along with Raven and the other women, hurriedly followed the girls to a wooded area. A few of the children had wisely climbed trees, but the others were standing nervously at a distance, turned sideways in preparation to dash for the lodge if the wolverine should come their way. Only one child was helping Wren against the wolverine, an older boy of eight summers named Ash.

The wolverine wasn't yet fully grown, probably only birthed the spring before. The animal's immaturity was what saved Wren and Ash from its powerful jaws and claws. That and Wren's spear. Wren hadn't been content with the small slingshots, bolas, and throwing sticks that girls were traditionally given to play with when they tired of their stick dolls. She'd demanded that Leaf make her a spear.

The wolverine faced Ash and Wren. From the blood on its chest, Raven realized they'd already wounded the animal with their spears, making it potentially more dangerous. Before the men could reach the children, it lunged. Wren jabbed her spear, finding an eye. As the creature writhed on the ground, the men rushed over to finish it.

Raven reached Wren just as she was recovering her balance after the men had shoved her aside. The girl was eyeing them hostilely, irritated that they'd interfered.

"You know better than to go near a wolverine," Raven told her. "Even the hunters leave them alone."

Wren gave her a hurt look. "I thought you'd be happy we had something to eat."

She'd fixed her daughter with a gaze of utmost seriousness.

"And what if that creature had jumped upon you and torn out your tongue? You would never have tasted it."

Conformity was the way of the tribes. Raven knew that many in the band disapproved of her daughter's headstrong ways and thought her spoiled. But even while chiding Wren, she'd been secretly proud of her daughter's hunting prowess. The spear—and the hunting—set her apart from the other girls, just as Raven's healing skills had always made her different from other women. The pity of it, though, was that Wren could very well be treated with the same aloofness Raven had known throughout her life.

Elder Woman entered the chamber from a side corridor. Raven snapped out of her reverie. A young woman trailed behind Elder Woman as they passed quickly through, her eyes kept on her feet. Raven wondered who she was, doubting that the young woman had even noticed someone different was at the hearth.

A fresh round of jagged sobs brought her attention back to Wren. Raven held her closely, whispering into the disorderly nest of hair. "Be calm, my heart, my firstborn child."

Wren stiffened then pulled away. She stood up and looked down at Raven with accusatory eyes. "Besides being yours, whose child am I? Everyone here says that Leaf isn't my father. He says that he's not my father." For the first time, Wren noticed Chukar standing nearby. She went quiet as she stared at him.

Raven chastised herself for not having decided how to go about explaining Chukar. She'd been so concerned with finding Wren that she hadn't given much thought about what would come afterward. The storminess rearranging her features—the tightly pursed lips and lowered brows—reminded Raven of Chukar when he was irritated. However, Wren always expressed her displeasure, whereas Chukar rarely did.

Chukar suddenly closed the space between himself and Raven. Wren gave a little hop sideways as he grasped Raven's hand and pulled her up. He linked his fingers with hers so tightly she thought he would crush her bones. A gasp of pain escaped her, then she realized that Elder Woman was standing right behind them.

Wren backed away as she looked at Chukar's fingers intertwined with her mother's. She made a strangled sound. "So, it is true." She ran sobbing from the room.

Raven found it impossible to pull her hand away from Chukar's grasp. "Let go," she hissed, and he immediately spread open his fingers.

She darted in the direction Wren had gone, trying to keep her in sight as they ran through a warren of passageways lit by smoldering torches. When Wren slipped inside an opening, Raven followed. Upon entering, she found Wren facedown upon a sleeping pallet, bawling into the fur coverings as though her heart would break.

Raven fought the irritation that Wren's emotional displays often stirred. True enough, her daughter had been through a bad time. But still. Before Raven decided whether she should comfort Wren or scold her, Chukar came in, carrying Raven's pack. After placing it on the cave floor, he walked over to the pallet and stood quietly, looking down at his weeping daughter.

Out of the corner of her eye, Raven saw Elder Woman walk through the opening. Again, weariness pulled at her, caused not only by the trip but by the stress of being once again with so many other people and all their wants, needs, and demands. If only the old woman would leave them alone for a while, Raven could go lie down beside Wren and tell her about Chukar.

After glancing at Wren and Raven, Elder Woman's eyes fell

on the bulging pack that Chukar carried on his back. "I see that you've had good hunting—if there's food in that bag."

Chukar whirled around at hearing her voice.

Elder Woman held out a hand, crooking her fingers, beckoning for the bag. "Give it to me."

Wren stopped crying, making Elder Woman's next words seem louder than they actually were. "Harrumph! Maybe it's better after all that you didn't remain dead."

Raven could have imagined it, but she thought a flicker of hurt crossed Chukar's face.

"I will share, but this bag remains with me," he said.

"Then you will have to leave for all the good you are." She jabbed a claw-like finger at Raven and Wren. "The woman and your daughter will stay."

Raven was taken aback by the strength of their animosity. She spoke loudly to draw their attention. "Whether Wren and I stay is for me to decide."

Neither one looked at her. They were giving off so much heated ill will as they faced each other that Raven became afraid of what might happen. To try to break the tension, she spoke up again. "And you should both go elsewhere now so I can be alone with my daughter for a while."

She recognized the danger. This was more than just a spat between mother and son. They were glaring slit-eyed into each other's faces like lions about to fight. Chukar's hand was slowly moving toward the knife he wore at his hip, and she knew what he would do to win the battle. The world froze as probable futures quickly unraveled in Raven's mind.

If Chukar killed his mother, the band would be forced to drive him from the cave. But that wasn't the worst that could happen. Doing in one's own mother was very much against the natural order of things. The Earth spirits would turn against Chukar, and he, in turn, would perish, perhaps by being caught in a rockslide or taken by a predator. But even if he did survive whatever the spirits threw his way, his mind would be affected by what he'd done.

The small chamber jolted back into focus, and Raven rushed between mother and son. She faced Chukar, forcing him to look her in the eye. Although she and Chukar didn't always agree, Raven had come to believe that she'd long ago become his sole desire. She poured all her feelings for him into a warm gaze, the words clinging to her breath as she softly whispered her warning: "If you do this, then we will no longer be together."

# CHAPTER 11

*Elder Woman*

WHEN RAVEN DARTED IN FRONT of Chukar, sharp relief momentarily blunted Elder Woman's contempt for the other woman. But surely that whelp of her loins had only been bluffing. He wouldn't have harmed her—not with Wren there. No girl would ever have anything to do with a father who was capable of cutting her grandmother. Raven had overreacted, Elder Woman told herself, but her rapidly beating heart indicated that she had her doubts.

Wren's snuffling had once more turned into crying, so Elder Woman couldn't make out Raven's lowered voice as she talked to Chukar. Raven's hand movements showed that she was pleading with him. Perhaps she was telling him he should hand over their bag of food. At the thought of Raven taking her side over Chukar, Elder Woman's brows lifted. The woman's life had been completely disrupted when Wren and Leaf were stolen away. Instead of helping Elder Woman, she should want her punished.

Irritated by how Raven had always confused her, she reacted without thinking. "Then keep your food for now. We will discuss the matter later." She was immediately disgusted that she'd given in before finding out if Raven had indeed convinced Chukar to turn over the bag. Her voice was gruff.

"You'll have your pick of a place to stay. The cave is full of large and small chambers."

After giving Chukar a lingering look, Raven went over to comfort her daughter. Elder Woman didn't hold it against her that she hadn't responded to the generous offer of shelter. Wren's blubbering made it difficult to think, much less hear. The girl had been calmer once Elder Woman got over to her that Raven would soon arrive. She'd begun accepting Chirrup's company more often and had recently started tolerating the others. And there'd been no more hissing whenever Skraw was around, so her present behavior greatly disappointed Elder Woman. She should be happy now that Raven was at the cave.

One of Wren's hands slipped from beneath her cape to dash away the tears. She said something in her own language, and Raven replied, shaking her head. Elder Woman guessed she'd told her daughter that they weren't leaving anytime soon and that they would have to stay at the cave.

Wren lifted her chin. Her eyes met Elder Woman's. "Ot."

Elder Woman flexed her fingers. She saw a slender willow branch among the firewood. That girl deserved more than a slapping; she needed a good switching. A child's discipline was usually reserved for the parents, but Elder Woman's patience had been worn down. She picked up the thin branch and turned toward Wren. Chukar was watching Elder Woman with hooded eyes. She hesitated. He and Raven might react badly upon seeing her hit their daughter. Elder Woman threw the switch on the coals. Sparks streamed upward as the crackling fire consumed it.

How Elder Woman hated that she would constantly have to worry about how they might respond to her actions. Even though she'd said so, Elder Woman didn't really want Chukar to leave; she'd only been trying to make him give her his food pouch. In order for Leaf to remain focused on Coo, both

Chukar and Raven must remain at the cave—as a constant reminder of Raven's disloyalty. If necessary, she would instruct Jay and Whit to once more barricade Wren in her room. Her mother would never leave without her, and Chukar wouldn't leave without Raven. Elder Woman lifted her voice. "Harrumph! I suppose the two of you will pick out a chamber."

Raven heard that time. She glanced around the room. "There's no need to look for another one. We'll move in here with Wren."

Elder Woman shook her head. She would not allow it. Wren had to be kept somewhat isolated from her mother so that the girl would continue interacting with everyone else. "Ot. Pick out your own chamber. They are plentiful. This is the only passageway well-lit with torches. You'll find more torches at the main hearth to help your search." She edged toward the opening, careful not to turn her back to Chukar. "Enough talk. I have work to do. I don't want to find you staying in here when I return."

"What harm would it be for us to sleep with our daughter?" Raven asked. "She's never been alone that way. Please reconsider."

"Ot," Wren said from the corner. "I want to be by myself."

Elder Woman understood every word. Chirrup had been successful in teaching the girl how to speak at least a few words.

Wren crossed her arms and hunched her shoulders, unaware that her stance and lowered brows made her somewhat resemble her father. Staring at Chukar, she spoke once more. "Ot."

A frown flitted over his face, and Elder Woman almost felt sorry for him. The father faced the same rejection the girl had shown her grandmother.

Raven kept her gaze on her daughter. "Well, then. I suppose we'll go now and search for a room."

Wren's response was to turn her face toward the wall. Raven squeezed her eyes closed for a moment then abruptly stood and strode out. After giving Wren a final glance, Chukar followed.

Elder Woman went to the opening. "I am also leaving, granddaughter. If you tire of being alone, come sit with Chirrup at the hearth." She wasn't expecting a reply, and she didn't get one.

As she hobbled slowly along, Elder Woman rubbed her chin with glee. She had everyone exactly where she wanted them. How fortunate that she'd been in front of the cave just as Chukar and Raven arrived. Her vision was still sharp enough that even with the sun darkened, their approach caught her eye. Elder Woman had immediately brought Leaf outside, and his response at seeing the pair together had been everything she'd hoped for. He hadn't just agreed to be with Coo again; he'd demanded that she come.

She thought about the potential number of babies that might be birthed before long if everything went well: one from Coo and Leaf—and once she put them together—one from Skraw and Wren. Perhaps even Finch would get pregnant again. And she was sure that Chukar was doing his best with Raven whether she wanted another baby with him or not.

Elder Woman scratched at her neck. Even though everything was going her way, she was still nagged by uneasy thoughts. Babies had never been planned in such a deliberate manner. They always just happened, a joyful outcome of the ritual ceremonies that sanctioned the natural urges. She remembered how Chukar had so blatantly held Raven's hand when they arrived, making a claim to that which wasn't his.

Leaf had reminded Elder Woman about his rights regarding Raven, and what he'd said was true. Elder Woman herself had guided him and Raven through the ceremonial rituals that bound them for life. With her own lips, Elder Woman had played the flute for the proper chants, and with her own hands, she'd served them a generous cut of elk. Elder Woman herself had fully recognized them as a bonded pair within the band. Then there was Leaf and Coo. Elder Woman was directly responsible for their unnatural coupling.

The firestorm and heavy winds had been unusual, but they hadn't frightened Elder Woman much at the time. They came, then they went. But her present thoughts pushed a cold shiver down her spine, and she wondered if the band's broken customs and the unusual event were somehow connected. Chukar had defied the sacred ways when he fathered a child with a Them woman. Perhaps combining the two different types of peoples was against the order of things, and the spirits were angry. Elder Woman's plan for Coo to have Leaf's child might have provoked them even further.

A light sweat broke out under her clothing. But any wrong-doings by a small insignificant band like hers couldn't have brought forth such a huge response. After all, they'd survived. The cave hadn't collapsed and killed anyone. The incident had happened because of some other unknown reason. She hoped she was right, or more chaos would follow.

When she entered the hearth chamber, Whit, Jay, Finch, and Chirrup were talking with their heads cocked together, their hands chopping the air, no doubt discussing Raven's arrival with Chukar. Upon seeing her, everyone stilled then separated.

"Did Chukar and Raven come get torches?" Elder Woman asked.

"I gave them several," Jay replied.

Finch and Chirrup resumed picking pine nuts out of a pile of cones, and the two men returned to whittling small sticks into various types of useful tools. Elder Woman sat down between her sons. The sounds of their knives scraping against wood filled the silence. She planned to wait a while before sending them to release Coo from Leaf's room.

Skraw sat near the cave mouth, apart from the others, using the better light to shave the end of a pole into a point. Elder Woman was glad that he was making something with his hands. She occasionally berated his uncles and aunts for not taking enough time with him so the boy could improve his toolmaking. They'd done so for only a short while after his parents died. The result of their neglect was that his wooden and bone tools were barely adequate, and his stone ones, particularly the spear points, were unusable more often than not. Elder Woman had to admit that their reluctance was partly Skraw's fault. He became frustrated easily, sometimes throwing his ruined work at whoever was working with him.

Elder Woman munched on a few pine nuts while she waited. One of them became lodged in a rotted tooth. She helped herself to one of the pointed toothpicks Jay had made and started probing. The gum around the tooth throbbed painfully until she finally pried out the nut.

After enough time had gone by, Elder Woman tapped a finger first on Jay's arm, then on Whit's, and pointed toward the corridor where Leaf's room was located. They jumped up and went out.

A short while later, Coo walked in. To avoid staring, Chirrup and Finch only glanced her way. Skraw didn't have it in him to be so subtle. He put aside the pole he was working on and openly looked Coo up and down. Elder Woman disliked the curious, lustful expression on his face.

Skraw's room was all too near Coo's. Elder Woman didn't put it past him to try pestering her some night. But Coo wasn't for him. Their kinship was too close. Elder Woman's mood soured. The boy was one more thing to worry about, but she

couldn't really blame him. He wanted his own mate. Elder
Woman might have to set up the ceremony soon, even if Wren
hadn't started her moon blood—yet another taboo that would
be broken.

At least Coo wasn't upset the way she'd been after her first
time with Leaf. Her face had a soft, relaxed quality, and her
cheeks were as pink as meadow flowers in spring. Coo hadn't
been outside the cave to see Leaf's reaction when he saw Chukar grab Raven's hand. It was possible that Coo might not
even remember Raven. The girl didn't yet understand what was
behind Leaf's sudden interest in her. Seeing that she was the
center of their attention, Coo's face colored even more. She
crossed the chamber, heading for the cave mouth.

Elder Woman quickly grabbed two of the empty baskets
that had held the pinecones and pushed herself up. "Coo,
come with me. I found a small blueberry bush hiding in a
crevice. We need to pick them while they are still good."

The girl dutifully joined her, taking one of the baskets.
As they passed Skraw, he made a rude sniffing sound. Elder
Woman decided that she would ignore him just that once.
They went outside and followed a path that went around the
cave complex wall to where the blueberry bush was. Soon, they
were picking. Even before Elder Woman could ask, Coo spoke
up.

"We didn't fight at all."

"Harrumph. I am glad there wasn't any need for that."
Elder Woman shivered in the wind. The weather was too cool
for late summer. "You were in there a good long while." When
Coo didn't respond to her gentle prying, Elder Woman eyed
her with an unrelenting gaze, insisting on a response.

Coo's gaze slid shyly away from hers. "We mated several
times. I hope that pleases you."

Elder Woman nodded encouragingly, glad that the girl was

confiding in her. "You were always a good child. And perhaps someday soon, you'll have one just like yourself."

Coo dipped her head, a smile playing around her lips. As she moved around the bush, plucking off berries, she began humming.

Elder Woman threw a bemused look Coo's way. The girl behaved as though it were the morning after her joining ceremony. Leaf didn't strike her as someone who knew how to please a woman, but then she didn't really know that much about Them. She remembered that his shaft had looked normal enough when the band had bathed in a river long ago one warm spring day.

Forgetting themselves, everybody had gawked at Leaf and Raven when they'd stripped before entering the water. The differences were readily apparent: their bodies weren't as muscular, their skins were darker, and the hips and rib cages overly narrow. They appeared almost gangly because of their longer arms and legs.

But Raven had birthed Wren by then, so Elder Woman knew with certainty that apart from appearances, they were enough like the People for the two groups to mate. That was something Coo seemed to have happily discovered, but the girl's hums might become squawks once she realized that Leaf's interest in her was because of jealousy, not because he couldn't wait to lie with her again.

"Should I pick all these dried ones, Grandmother?"

Elder Woman looked closely at the bush. Almost half the berries had withered since she'd discovered them only a few days before. "The ones like pebbles are no good. Just pick those that still have a little plumpness. We'll mix them with dried meat and fat."

She glanced at the darkened sky. The heavy clouds weren't the entire reason for the gloom. Even without clouds, the day would still be dim. Every day had been like that lately. Blueberries needed full sun to thrive. She looked at the surrounding foliage tossing in the wind. Many of the leaves were already changing color. The world was slipping out of summer into late autumn, skipping early autumn altogether. A strong gust went through the blueberry bush, and several yellow and red leaves twirled away.

Her granddaughter interrupted her thoughts, speaking loudly over the wind. "I wonder if he could be untied for more of the day."

*My goodness, but she is proving to be a lusty girl.* "Being with him wasn't so bad then, eh?" Elder Woman said. "The first time I brought up the idea, you reacted as if I was demanding that you mate a boar."

Coo flushed. "I didn't ask so that he could be with me more often." She twiddled her fingers among the leaves. "He could help the men hunt."

"He told you to ask me, didn't he?" Elder Woman eyed her sternly.

Coo didn't lie about it. She lowered her eyes and nodded. Elder Woman pursed her lips thoughtfully. It *was* a shame to have a hunter going to waste, but if Leaf was freed, he would run away immediately. Then he would bring back his tribesmen and demand Elder Woman give over Wren and Raven. Her people were too few to defend themselves against an attack. "I think we'll wait until you birth a little one," she said to mollify her. "Then we'll see."

Her granddaughter's request worried Elder Woman more than she let on. Surely Coo wasn't so naive that she thought he would remain with the band just because of her. Elder Woman wouldn't dampen the girl's happiness yet, but sometime soon, she needed to explain that if Coo became so bold as to untie him, the band would be forced to flee across the steppes.

While they finished picking the blueberries, Elder Woman again mulled over her willingness to break sacred customs and bonds. The spirits could punish an old woman who continued down such a path. She pushed the thought aside. If Elder Woman didn't fight for her people's survival, no one would, and their numbers would continue dwindling.

But Elder Woman worried that at some point, they might all fall upon each other in murderous rages brought about by the changes. Bringing Leaf and Wren to live with the band had stirred discontentment. It was Chukar and Raven, though, that she was most uneasy about at. Her control of them wasn't tight enough. As soon as she and Coo returned to the cave, Elder Woman took up a torch to search them out.

She should have been more specific about where they could stay. They weren't in any of the rooms closest to Wren as expected, but she had to admit that none of those were adequate, as they were very small. After going down several corridors without finding the pair, Elder Woman saw torchlight coming toward her. She slipped into a wall niche that partially hid her, and soon, Skraw walked into sight. He paused when he got close enough to notice her light, but realizing she'd already seen him, he continued toward her.

"Harrumph. Always snooping around."

He gave her a wary look before lowering his eyes.

"Well, where are they?"

He pointed back the way he'd come then started edging past her.

"Did you talk to them?"

He shook his head and eased away.

If only her other grandson hadn't died, Skraw wouldn't be so aimless. The two boys had been inseparable, wrestling, playing with toy axes and other tools their fathers made for them. But that boy had died even before Skraw's father.

After a short distance more, Elder Woman saw a glow. She went inside the room from which it came and breathed in the smoky smell of dried meat. Several long slices were heating on a stone near the fire. She'd been right about the contents of Chukar's bag.

Raven's back was turned, her fur-draped form bending over a small rock-lined hearth as she minded the fire. Chukar was enlarging a hole in the far wall that they could store things in. His stone ax ground heavily into the sandstone so that a pile of grit was gathering at his feet. He stopped working when Elder Woman entered. The room went quiet, and Raven glanced over her shoulder. She straightened upon seeing their visitor.

They would not take her seriously if she danced around what was on her mind, so Elder Woman was blunt. "Leaf is my prisoner. And a prisoner he must remain—for the band's safety. Once he escapes or is freed by someone here, he will bring men back with him from his tribe." She nodded at Chukar. "The last time a group of Them showed up, you were stabbed in the chest—a death wound."

It hadn't been her intention, but he gave her an angry look as if she'd again insinuated that he wasn't alive.

She ignored him. "If Leaf does somehow leave, I'll lead my people to a place where we can't be easily followed." She looked pointedly at Raven. "And your daughter will come with us."

Raven's baleful glare was similar to the dark gaze Wren had given Elder Woman earlier. She'd never thought mother and daughter closely resembled one another, but she saw it then. Just like the daughter, Raven needed a good whipping. *One of these days, when Chukar isn't around...* "You look well enough. I am glad my medicines were a help."

Raven started and glanced away, a flush creeping across her cheeks.

Elder Woman took a closer look at Raven's face; small scabs

similar to Whit's marred her skin. "How did you get all those scratches?"

"We were outside when the firestone exploded. Chukar has cuts also."

"So, you were staying close by to us then?"

"No. We walked a day and a half to get here." Raven's expression became concerned. "Was anyone in the band hurt?"

"Only a few scratches like yours." That Chukar and Raven had witnessed the firestone blowing up at such a distance was surprising. Elder Woman hadn't realized that the effects of the explosion were so widespread.

Raven faced Elder Woman, giving her a little bow. "If you will permit me, I'd like to speak with you about that day."

Her politely worded request and bow soothed Elder Woman a bit. And in spite of herself, she was curious as to what the other woman thought about the event. Raven appeared to be thinking deeply about what she would say, her head lowered, so Elder Woman patiently waited.

Chukar was watching Raven, his expression full of something that resembled contentment. Although his attraction for that strange woman had always repulsed Elder Woman, she had to admit that Raven was able to subdue her unruly son, whereas she never could.

Taking a deep breath, Raven looked up. She spoke using forceful hand movements. "The Earth Mother was attacked by her brother sun, using his firestone weapons. We, the peoples of the earth, are her most-favored children, and so it is our duty to support her with ceremony. But we must appease brother sun and the other spirits as well, using ceremony."

The things she spoke of weren't entirely unknown. The People occasionally performed ceremonies honoring the spirits or to ask for their help, but Elder Woman had never heard of a ceremony to appease them. The spirits did what they wanted, and there wasn't anything to be done about it. And the Earth Mother she talked about—Elder Woman knew nothing about the spirit.

The Them woman had gone on about that Earth Mother the last time she'd lived with the People. Everyone had just ignored her, understanding that her beliefs weren't theirs. But Elder Woman did agree with Raven that the exploding firestone had something to do with angry spirits. And it was as though the sun had attacked the earth.

Raven continued, her face animated. "During the rites, I'll plead with the sun spirit to never attack his sister again. And I'll ask the Earth Mother to disperse the fog of dirt she's thrown across her brother's face. I will beg her to understand that by shunning him, she also punishes her children—they must stop their quarrelling."

Elder Woman gaped at her. Raven's fervent intensity was unsettling, and she had a lot of audacity to suggest that she should lead any rites whatsoever. Elder Woman closed her mouth. Never would she allow it. Never. So small a band could have only one leader.

"Oh," Raven said. "I almost forgot to say that the spirits will be more inclined to listen if everyone attends the ceremony and adds their prayers to mine."

Glancing at the bags sitting against a wall, Elder Woman wondered how much of her precious medicines Raven had stuffed in them. A vein pulsed on the side of her head at the thought of the woman rummaging through the packets of herbs in Elder Woman's wolverine pouch. Raven sighed, impatient for a reply, but she wasn't ready to speak yet.

Elder Woman wished she could just close Raven up in one of the rooms, but that would mean imprisoning Chukar too. Whit and Jay already weren't hunting as much as they should because guarding Leaf and Wren took up much of their day.

Besides, she'd begun doubting their loyalty. They might refuse to restrain their brother. She must try to keep the peace. Perhaps it wouldn't be so bad if Raven participated in a ceremony that Elder Woman headed. A traditional ceremony was easy enough for Elder Woman to do, and her people would be soothed by the familiarity.

But what if a traditional ceremony wasn't enough? A twinge of guilt went through Elder Woman as she once again admitted to herself that she might be partly to blame for the spirits' wrath. She really had no idea how one would go about pacifying all those spirits. Just trying to grasp the concept made her head hurt. Elder Woman had the disturbing thought that Raven possibly understood the land and sky spirits better than she did—especially the all-important sun.

She thought about the sun, how it heated the world, and with a flash of insight, she knew exactly what must be done. The People were in possession of a type of useful rock that, when scraped into a powder and mixed with wood shavings, helped fires start quickly. The stones were called rock tinder. They were thought to fall out of the sky at night.

She cleared her throat, at last ready to speak. "I don't know anything about that Earth Mother, but if it was an attack from the sun, then we need to appease the sun with an offering of heat and fire. I'll do a ceremony with scraped rock powder— the kind that burns." Elder Woman had never done such a ceremony, but she could come up with one. She waved her arms emphatically. "We have rock tinder stored in one of the caverns."

She had to smother a smile at seeing Raven, for once, at a loss for words. The woman obviously knew nothing about how to make fire with rock tinder, just as Elder Woman knew nothing about the Earth Mother. "I will show you our rock tinder," she said, motioning that Raven should follow her.

Chukar took up a torch and made to go with them.

"I'll be fine," Raven told him, slipping the torch out of his hand.

He gave his mother a meaningful look but returned to making the shelf.

Once in the storage cavern, Elder Woman held her torch high. She pointed to the small irregular blocks of stacked stone. Here was something one could actually see, not like that vague Earth Mother. "You grind the rocks into powder and sprinkle it over wood shavings. You'll have a good fire much quicker than without it."

"Why was none of this at the cave where you used to live? I never saw you make fire that way."

To hear Raven's voice become sharp and dry like a scolding sparrow pleased Elder Woman immensely. Her knowledge surpassed Raven's when it came to the important task of making fire. She gave a smug smile. "Rock tinder stones weren't as easy to find there because of the forests. Here, they are scattered all across the plains." She waited, hoping to see another display of envy.

But the other woman only politely cleared her throat, indicating she was about to ask a favor. "Perhaps you'd take me with you when you gather more? I would like to learn how to spot them." Then she gave a small bow from the waist, admitting her inferiority in the matter.

Her response was so appropriate that Elder Woman couldn't help but nod, granting her request. Raven cleared her throat once more. Although irritated that Raven wished another favor so soon, Elder Woman waited to hear what else she wanted.

Raven raised her head to meet Elder Woman's eyes. "The large exploding stone in the sky was a warning message to the Earth Mother from the sun, one whose meaning we don't understand. The Earth Mother's response, I think, was clearer. It's a message also but one that is better understood."

On Raven went, talking about that Earth Mother once more. Unable to hide her derision, Elder Woman reflexively spit phlegm onto the cave floor. The gesture didn't seem to upset Raven. She kept talking, and Elder Woman was forced to listen.

"By throwing up a dirty haze to cover her brother, the Earth Mother has let him know that she will fight back. Your offerings of fire and heat during a ceremony will work to calm the sun spirit. But the Earth Mother has to be dealt with. If the air doesn't clear, the coming winter will be overly long."

Elder Woman hadn't considered the possibility of a winter harsher than usual. It was true that the sun's light and heat had become weaker as if late autumn had already arrived. Every living thing would perish off the land if winter's biting cold began early and continued for too long. Coo and the other women would starve without ever having their babies. *That must not happen.*

What if Raven was right, and other rituals were necessary to keep the spirits from wreaking havoc? As much as Elder Woman disliked the idea of giving Raven a large part in a ceremony, she couldn't risk ignoring the woman. And although Elder Woman had said she would perform rituals for the sun, she had no idea what to do about that vindictive Earth Mother.

Raven's words went again through Elder Woman's mind. She'd said the explosion was a message. The word *message* echoed around inside Elder Woman's head, and she realized that the event did indeed have a meaning. An overwhelming elation filled her. Raven might not grasp the significance, but Elder Woman did—because the message had been about the People.

Elder Woman would participate in a joint ceremony, but

the rites she intended to perform would have nothing to do with calming the sun. The sun spirit had sent a sign to Elder Woman that included a warning to the Earth Mother and those who followed her. The violent hatching of fire from stone was to tell them all that the People would not perish from the earth. They would soon be reborn.

# CHAPTER 12

*Raven*

RAVEN'S EYEBROWS DREW TOGETHER IN alarm. Elder Woman had completely stopped listening and was staring wide-eyed into the flames of Raven's torch with a strange expression on her face. She wondered if the older woman was taking something for her aches and pains and had perhaps overdone it. Whether treating oneself or others, a healer had to be careful. Herbs that were helpful in small amounts were harmful if a person ingested more than necessary. They could also cause hallucinations.

But she mustn't rush to conclusions. Hallucinations didn't come about solely because of medicines. A man brought to Raven by his worried granddaughter had claimed he often saw things that weren't there, including his dead mate. As far as the granddaughter knew, he hadn't eaten or drank anything to provoke such a reaction. A very old man, he'd lost count of the summers he'd lived. Raven decided that his visions were because of his vast age. He'd outlived all of his children and most of his grandchildren.

The torch crackled and sputtered, almost dying before catching again. The older woman's skin appeared mottled in the flickering light. Raven looked into her unseeing eyes. They were a dull brown and lightly tinged with green, very unlike Chukar's bright orbs that sparkled like dew-covered grass. Elder Woman didn't seem quite as old as the man who'd outlived his children, but Raven wasn't sure how quickly Longheads aged.

After waiting uneasily a few more moments, Raven spoke softly. "Thank you for showing me your stored rock tinder. I look forward to seeing how it works." The older healer finally focused on her; she'd only been lost in a daydream. "We should have the ceremony before too long," Raven said. "Hopefully, the haziness in the air will then fade away."

Elder Woman frowned. "We will do the ceremony, but the wood shavings and rock tinder must be prepared first. So don't be impatient. A goodly quantity is needed. Readying everything will be mostly up to the women. The men aren't hunting enough as it is, and now they tell me that the bison are leaving because they don't want to eat grass covered with dust. Harrumph. The women must hunt too, or we'll go hungry."

The longer they put off the ceremony, the more dust would fall, and the more animals would leave. Raven didn't dare voice her opinion, though. She was once more adapting to the Longhead world; they were similar in many ways to the people she'd lived with most of her life but quite different in others. From experience, she knew to tread carefully.

"I'll gladly help hunt," she said.

The older woman gave her a sidelong look, and Raven knew she was thinking again about the bag of dried meat they'd brought with them. Certainly, they would share as Chukar had told her, but they would not just hand over their stores. That food gave them a better footing within the band. And if Elder Woman decided to cast them out, they would at least have sustenance.

There was one aspect of their living arrangements that needed clarifying. Elder Woman hadn't banned Raven from being around Wren, but Leaf might be another matter. "I wish to see Leaf," she said. "I want to talk to him."

"Didn't I already forbid you from doing so? And don't think you can just walk up to him. He's being held in a closed room for most of the day."

"You said I shouldn't help him escape. Nothing was said about me not talking to him." She held out her hand that didn't hold the torch, opening it in a plea. "Hear me. Leaf is still my mate through ceremony, even if he's presently your prisoner."

An unsure look crossed Elder Woman's face. "I will think about your request." The uncertainty quickly passed, replaced by a sneer. "He may not want to see you. After all, you forgot about him when Chukar crossed your path."

Caught off guard by the sharp words, Raven winced, ducking her head slightly. Catching herself, she straightened to her full height. "I was almost dead when Chukar found me. Besides, he and I also have a bond—your granddaughter."

Elder Woman's free hand made one large gesture. "Enough of your chatter. I know you will have to make several trips for firewood. After that is done, I do not want to see you anywhere near us for the rest of the day. Nor do I wish to see that shadow who was once my son."

Raven walked away, leaving Elder Woman standing beside the rocks that she'd so delighted in showing off.

Upon entering the small well-formed cavern they'd chosen, she saw Chukar had almost completed the shelf. Relief crossed his face at seeing her. He put aside the tools, yawned, and stretched, his bulging chest threatening the seams of his tunic. Elder Woman was wrong about her son; he wasn't a shadow. Chukar had proved to be overwhelmingly substantial in a variety of ways, and Raven didn't understand why his own mother was aggrieved that he'd lived.

Even though she was exhausted, sleep didn't come easily that night. A cricket in the firewood kept chirring noisily in the darkness. The insect would die inside the cave, away from the sun. The cricket's plight made her think of Leaf. He was surely suffering. Somehow, Elder Woman had to be persuaded that he should be outside for more of each day. After listening to the cricket for a while longer, she finally fell into a restless sleep.

*** 

When Raven and Chukar ventured from their room the next morning, the sound of grinding reached their ears long before they reached the main cavern. Upon entering, Raven saw the band's women and Wren scraping rock tinder stones with pieces of flint. She was pleased that Elder Woman had taken seriously the idea of having a ceremony sooner rather than later. Powdered rock formed small peaks on the leather scraps they were using to collect the grains.

The Longhead women paused scraping for a moment, their heads nodding a greeting, and Raven was heartened to see Wren's face light up at catching sight of her. That eager look turned sullen, though, when Chukar came up beside Raven. Wren huddled back over her work, grinding the stone with quick jerks of her hand.

It shocked Raven to see how few women remained in the band—if indeed all of the band's women had been gathered for the task. Besides Elder Woman, she recognized Finch and Chirrup, the latter smiling and nodding several times more in greeting. The same young woman Raven had seen going through the hearth chamber the day before was also there. Raven quickly recalled the names of the children she'd known in the past. How their faces changed when they became older, the features becoming larger and heavier.

"Is that Robin I see?" she asked.

Raven frowned when the girl didn't look up. Either she wasn't Robin, or she was ignoring the question.

"That is Coo," Chirrup said finally.

The girl fidgeted and glanced up. Her eyes met Raven's for a fleeting heartbeat.

"Ah yes, now I recognize her. It's just that the child I remember is almost grown."

Snorting, Elder Woman slowly pushed herself up. "She has been a woman for two full turns of the seasons." Her eyes barely flickered Chukar's way as she jerked her head toward the cave mouth. "The men are shaving wood in front of the cave."

When Chukar didn't make a move to leave, Raven gave him a quick glance. He went outside.

When he'd gone, Elder Woman cleared her throat, making sure she had everyone's attention. "The sun had long risen before the pair of you left your sleeping pallet this morning," she said, her eyes running down to Raven's belly. "But that's how babies are made—lingering with a man under covers. Have you missed your moon blood since taking up with him?"

Raven's jaw dropped at the rudeness. The woman must have been spying on them to know how long they'd slept.

Elder Woman stood with her fists on her hips, elbows wide, seemingly pleased by the unease her bluntness caused. "Your mouth is open big enough for a bat to fly into," she said. "Don't behave like a shy girl. We are all women here—no need to guard what we say."

Raven pressed her lips together and looked over at Wren. Her daughter's eyes stayed on the rock she was scraping, but her face reflected Raven's discomfort. *Does Elder Woman think Wren a woman as well?* Even if she was taller than everyone around the hearth, she was still a child. Raven glanced at Coo and the other two women. They were pretending that nothing had happened out of the ordinary, even though Elder Woman's earthy comments and prying question were shockingly unusual for a Longhead woman. Not to answer Elder Woman would show disrespect in front of the others.

"No," Raven said hesitantly. "No, I haven't missed my moon blood."

Elder Woman's attention, however, had already turned elsewhere. She nodded at Coo. "Your impatience is obvious, girl. Go tell your father and uncle to move the boulder for you."

The center of Coo's cheeks flamed red as if stung. Averting her eyes, she put down the stone she was working on. Raven watched the young woman go outside, curious about the task she was being sent to do. After a few moments, Coo returned with the two men, and the three of them quickly disappeared down a corridor. Raven gazed around at the various openings that branched from the room. The cave resembled nothing more than a rabbit warren. One could easily become lost if not careful.

Elder Woman sat down and began working again. Relieved at being spared any more pointed questions, Raven took a rock from the stack and went to sit beside Chirrup.

She turned the rock in her hand, looking it over carefully. Then she held it to her nose. It smelled a bit like charcoal. Perhaps these smaller stones fell from the sky all the time. They either didn't catch fire before dropping to the ground, or the air extinguished the flames before they burned up completely, like a breeze blowing out a burning twig. The firestone that had caused such calamity had been a much larger rock. Raven shivered. The sun's power to cast down something so big was frightening. Elder Woman had shown wisdom by agreeing to a ceremony of appeasement for the sun. If only she were astute about other matters.

Raven had only ground a small pile of dark grains when Whit and Jay came back from the same side passage they'd gone down with Coo. Raven didn't stop working, but her body tensed. Jay was carrying several empty bowls. She didn't think that he, Whit, or Coo had been eating from them. He put the bowls down before going outside with Whit. Her breath caught in excitement as she glanced at the opening they'd come from. Somewhere along that dusty corridor, she would find Leaf—if she could slip away unnoticed.

Opportunity arose sooner than expected when Elder Woman suddenly halted their work. "Enough for today. The men will leave shortly to go hunt. We women will hunt also—but closer by. I have decided that the meat of any animals the men bring back should be dried and stored for winter. We women must find smaller game, so that everyone can eat tonight and tomorrow. We'll leave when the sun is directly overhead and won't return until dusk. Everyone should bring their slingshots and throwing sticks."

Raven wished they could have worked longer on the rocks, but she found Elder Woman's reasoning about the utilization of their kills flawless, although surprising. Leaf had tried with little success in the past to persuade the Longhead band to put aside more food for winter. Maybe Elder Woman had decided after living through so many starving times that he'd been right. With colder weather coming, food must be gathered—and a lot of it. Raven could only hope that the Wind band had come to the same conclusion.

A small sigh escaped her. Upon setting out to find Leaf and Wren, Raven hadn't known she would end up stuck in a place from which she couldn't extract herself. The present situation was like a pile of ropes all knotted together with Raven, Wren, Leaf, Chukar, and the other Longheads making up the separate cords. Somehow, the knots had to be undone so that Raven could be with her youngest children again.

The work had blackened their hands. A small pit in the floor near the hearth contained semi-liquid fat used for tasks such as cleaning, rubbing tubers before cooking, and fueling stone oil lamps. While the other woman cleaned their hands with the fat, Raven tarried, slowly emptying her ground tinder into the bag set aside for safekeeping the loose grains. She was hoping that Wren might also linger, but after wiping the fat off her fingers with a leather cloth, the girl left without even glancing over.

Raven wasn't about to let Wren ignore her so easily. She put down the bag and hurried to the fat pit, planning to follow her daughter as soon as her hands were clean. When she was finished, though, Raven realized she was completely alone and changed her mind about following Wren. She took up a torch and slipped down the corridor Whit and Jay had come from earlier.

The dark passage, lit only by a few widely spaced torches, wound first one way then another. Raven was fascinated by the cave complex. She'd never seen anything like it. Tunneling corridors ran through it like large, dry wormholes. The ceilings were low in some places, but in other areas, they soared high overhead. Occasional gaps opened in the walls that led into fully formed chambers. Large boulders dotted the corridors everywhere. Perhaps a river had run amok underground, creating the wormholes and carrying along the boulders until they dropped. To help keep herself oriented, she trailed a hand along one side of the wall.

At some point, she began hearing a faint sound drifting through the passage, a low bleating like that of a baby snow sheep. But the farther she went, the noise sounded more like moaning. Alarmed that someone was ill and needed help,

Raven walked faster until she came to a large boulder that covered a gap in the wall. The moans seemed to be seeping from around the stone. Raven knew at once that she'd found Leaf, but the fear that he was injured or sick diminished her excitement. She almost called out his name but stopped when it struck her that the sounds were more those of pleasure than pain.

Leaf's voice suddenly broke out over the moaning sound, a thickened murmur of encouragement in the Longhead tongue. Raven froze, her eyes widening. He was with a woman.

Because of Chukar, Raven knew she had no right to be upset, but she couldn't control the thumping in her chest and the sudden lack of breath as a sharp sense of betrayal pierced her. *But who is with him?*

Elder Woman had sent Coo away from the hearth. The girl had been ordered to find her uncle and father to help move a boulder. Raven's eyes focused on the massive stone in front of her.

Surely Leaf wasn't with Coo. Even if she'd become a "woman" as Elder Woman had said, the girl couldn't have passed more than twelve summers. It was hard to imagine Whit delivering up his young daughter that way. And what was wrong with Elder Woman that she might do such a thing to her granddaughter? If Coo was indeed with Leaf, the old bully had a lot of nerve sending her to him with Raven sitting there. She gnawed her lip, her thoughts going in every direction at once.

Perhaps Elder Woman had stopped their work suddenly because she'd observed her eyeing the empty bowls. She knew that Raven would search for Leaf and find him with Coo. The thought chilled her. If that was so, then Elder Woman was in control of everything and everyone at the cave complex.

Determined to know the truth, she went a short way down to where she'd glimpsed what appeared to be yet another chamber. The entry to the room was so small that she had to crawl inside. She put the torch behind a pile of rocks so that the light wouldn't be visible from the corridor, then she knelt to wait in front of the opening. From living in crowded lodges and caves, Raven had learned to ignore the noises made by others while they mated. But that day, she couldn't stop listening even though every throaty moan and grunt tormented her.

She was to the point of covering her ears when the sounds stopped, giving way to muted conversation. Soon, the quiet voices were interrupted by the noise of stone forced over stone. Peeking from her hiding place, Raven saw Whit and Jay moving the boulder. They went inside. Coo immediately stepped into the corridor and began walking slowly toward where Raven was hiding. Raven moved back so she wouldn't be seen. When she thought Coo had gone by, she looked out again.

Whit and Jay remained inside for a while longer then fought the large stone back in place before leaving in the opposite direction. Again, Raven wondered how Whit felt about the situation. Perhaps he didn't have a say about the matter.

After retrieving the torch, Raven crawled out and returned to the closed room. She hesitantly placed her free hand on the boulder, unsure about what to do. In finding Leaf, she'd discovered he was lost to her. Raven pressed her palm and fingers against the stone until pain from the ridges traveled down her arm and made her breathe in sharply.

"Who's there?" Leaf called from within.

She fled without answering. The central hearth was still empty when she rushed through. Once inside her and Chukar's chamber, Raven searched for a throwing stick and slingshot. She looked forward to the outing that afternoon. Hunting was an all-consuming activity that required a person's complete attention and left little room to think about anything else.

***

Raven and the other women waited while Elder Woman scanned the surrounding landscape from the hilltop where she'd led the group. The older woman began giving them directions while slowly turning in a circle. "We will hunt in pairs but still be within calling distance of each other." She pointed into the distance. "Coo and Finch, go follow the riverbank to where the brush is thick. Try to surprise some ducks."

Despite her earlier intention to focus only on hunting, Raven's eyes raked Coo from head to toe as the girl and Finch obediently trekked down the hill. Unbidden images of her lying naked in Leaf's arms came to mind. She turned to look at Elder Woman, forcing herself to listen.

The older woman jabbed her finger in another direction. "Chirrup and Raven will search that cluster of boulders. I saw ground squirrels there not long ago. Good place for rabbits too." Then her finger swiveled over to Wren. "You will come with me to the trees where we gather firewood." She looked directly at Raven. "Any food caught will be shared with everyone. Is that understood? No hiding rabbits away in your own supplies."

Raven nodded, trying not to frown. The woman wouldn't give up until she and Chukar had turned over every shred of their dried meat. She was disappointed by not being paired with Wren. Much better, though, to be with Chirrup than Elder Woman. Chukar didn't want Raven anywhere near his mother and had asked that she not accompany her. Raven told him that she had to go or risk seeming lazy. Raven glanced at Wren. Her face showed dismay at the prospect of being alone with Elder Woman.

A look passed between mother and daughter. Raven pursed her lips as she began down the hill. She gave a little shrug, her eyes rolling, mimicking the way Wren often reacted at being told what to do. Wren frowned, but before she turned away, her cheeks dimpled, and the corners of her mouth quirked up. Hope stirred within Raven that the warmth of their past relationship might soon be revived.

How good it felt to be active again after her illness. The only thing marring the day was the bad air. She doubted if even rain, whenever it finally came, could clean the dirty sky. The inside of Raven's nose felt raw, and like the others, she occasionally had sneezing fits. She hoped a bout wouldn't come on and scare away prey. Raven followed Chirrup's stocky form with quiet footsteps as they approached the group of boulders Elder Woman had indicated earlier. She kept her slingshot at the ready, having already slipped a rock into the weapon's small leather pocket.

When they reached the maze of stone, Raven heard sharp chattering close by. She and Chirrup crouched behind some rocks. Below them, several squirrels were in a bowl-shaped grassy depression, quarreling over seed-filled grass stalks. Raven lightly touched Chirrup's arm then signaled the word for net, her brows raised in question. Chirrup nodded and quietly reached into her bag.

Raven remained at the ready with her slingshot in case either of the squirrels escaped when Chirrup threw the net, but she didn't get a chance to try her luck. Both animals became entangled when they attempted to bolt from the hollow. The two women rushed down and put an end to their struggles.

Afterward, Raven intoned a quick thanks to the Earth Mother over the animals. Chirrup watched her whisper the words and make the ritual hand movements. Because she seemed intrigued by the prayer, Raven repeated the chant in the Longhead tongue, using the same gestures. Chirrup rewarded her with a smile of amazement. Raven had tried in the past to teach her about the Earth Mother, but the other woman hadn't been interested then. That was long before the firestone fell. Perhaps the event had made them all more receptive to learning about the spirit. Raven fervently hoped so, or else the ceremony she and Elder Woman were planning would have little success.

Pleased with how quickly they'd acquired game, she passed Chirrup a squirrel for safekeeping and slipped the other one into her own pouch. The grass stalks the squirrels had fought over were still lying in the hollow. Raven picked up some of them. They were withered and yellow, the seeds small and immature.

She looked around her at the browned landscape. The day was abnormally quiet. No birds sang in the foliage, and the swarms of humming insects were missing. Although glad about the lack of insects, Raven once more felt a nagging discomfort at the way the blast had affected the earth.

Raven dropped the stalks and picked up her pouch. Once it was secured on her back, she turned to Chirrup, signaling that she wished to talk. Because of the noise they'd made while catching the squirrels, they weren't likely to see any more, so she might as well take the opportunity to find out whatever she could about Leaf. Chirrup nodded her agreement and waited, her head tilted respectfully toward Raven.

"Do you know if Leaf is healthy and well?"

"He is not happy being a prisoner, but he is well."

"I wish Elder Woman would release him, but I doubt that will happen. She told me she's afraid that he'll bring Them back to the cave." Raven felt strange referring to her own tribesmen as if they were some menacing group that was best avoided.

Even by Longhead standards, Chirrup waited a long time before responding. She stared down at her moccasins while she thought. One foot began nudging small rocks into the hollow where the squirrels had been. Raven looked up from watching the cascading pebbles when Chirrup cleared her throat. "Elder Woman has another reason for keeping him captive that she hasn't told you. You will eventually find out, so I will tell you now—even though it is difficult for me to do so."

After that morning, Raven believed she knew part of what Chirrup wanted to tell her. To put the other woman at ease, she spoke calmly while her hands moved slowly and evenly. "It's all right. You can tell me anything."

"My mother wants the band to grow larger. The People seem to have disappeared from the Great High Plains, and she despairs because there are so few of us. Her greatest wish is to have more grandchildren—like Wren. So, with that hope in mind, she sends Coo to mate with Leaf."

What Chirrup told Raven was disturbing and a little embarrassing, as matters related to mating often were, particularly when one's family was involved. But the angst she had carried inside since hearing Leaf and Coo together actually abated a little. What Elder Woman had done to Raven's family was deplorable, but Chirrup had explained the old healer's behavior in such a simple, succinct way that her actions had become somewhat understandable even though they remained despicable.

The intensity with which Chirrup scrutinized her made the back of Raven's neck prickle. It was as if their safety or lives depended upon how she responded to what she'd heard. She didn't know what Chirrup hoped for. The best she could do was to be honest. "I don't like what your mother did, but I understand her desperation. I'll admit that I'm saddened that so few of you remain."

Something like relief crossed Chirrup's features. "You are not angry that another woman is in your place?"

"It causes me grief, but who am I to feel put upon?" Raven's face grew hot. Not from ire but because of her discomfort. "I became injured while searching for Leaf and Wren. Chukar stumbled upon me. He saved my life and then… well. I am now with Chukar, who once was *your* mate." She searched the other woman's face for animosity but saw none. "I'll ask you the same question. Are you angry? I hope that you are not."

"No, not anymore. I was angry at Chukar when I first found out about Wren. But that all happened long ago. Now he is only another brother."

Raven knew that she would never be able to completely forgive Elder Woman, but she found Chirrup's ability to put aside hard feelings enviable. She would follow her example and try not to think badly of Coo. "If it takes a baby for Leaf to win his freedom, I hope that Coo will have one soon."

Chirrup twiddled her fingers nervously before using them to speak, spreading them away from her stomach. "I—I wish my belly would grow as well," she stuttered. "I want my own baby."

Raven drew her breath in sharply. Had Elder Woman also sent Chirrup to Leaf? Or perhaps Chirrup was trying to say that she wanted to be with him the same way Coo had. Indignation caused Raven's back to stiffen. These Longhead women were treating Leaf as though he were a stallion in a herd of mares. Even so, the abject wistfulness on Chirrup's face moved Raven, and she swallowed her anger.

Before she could think of what to say, caws filled the quiet air, sounding almost like crows, though not quite. Both women looked in the direction the caws were coming from. Those cries of warning were the signal used by the Longheads to let anyone within hearing distance know that help was needed in warding off predators. Several more caws came, and Raven's heart sank as she realized they were coming from the small cluster of woods where Wren had gone with Elder Woman. Her first impulse was to race there at once, but she held herself

back. Matters wouldn't be helped if she ran straight into whatever animal menaced them. She and Chirrup began moving
cautiously toward the trees.

Upon entering the woods, Raven glimpsed a large black
bear through the brush. The two women approached as closely
as possible without being spotted by the animal. The bear was
standing on its hind legs, head swaying and jaws snapping
as it faced Wren and Elder Woman. Raven's throat caught at
seeing her daughter in such danger. The animal only seemed
curious, but of all the Earth Mother's creatures, bears were
the most volatile. Elder Woman talked soothingly as she and
Wren slowly started edging sideways, telling the bear that they
were leaving. Out of the corner of her eye, Raven saw Coo and
Finch ease behind a large bush.

If the bear stayed in place and allowed Elder Woman and
Wren to leave, then it was best that none of them interfere.
Raven thought about what might happen, though, if the
bear charged. Being slower, Elder Woman would probably be
caught, giving Wren a chance to get away. Raven realized right
then that even if Elder Woman's death gave Wren a chance to
escape, she didn't relish knowing that the elderly healer might
come to a violent and painful end. Bears didn't always kill their
prey before feeding. They would all risk injury if they tried to
drive it away from her once Elder Woman was on the ground.

Because she knew the bear hadn't been finding enough food
since the firestone fell and was probably hungry, Raven decided
that she must distract the beast to provide Elder Woman and
Wren a chance to escape. She reached inside her bag for the
squirrel, intending to throw it at the bear. She quickly changed
her mind and stuffed it back inside. The small animal wasn't
heavy enough to go that far. Instead, Raven scooped up a rock
and tied one of her leather rags around it.

She'd no sooner secured the rock than the bear huffed

once, popped its jaws, and started dropping to all fours. Before its front feet hit the ground, Raven had thrown the rag-tied rock so that it plopped down a short distance in front of the animal. The bear loped forward and nosed the covered stone. Wren grasped the opportunity and bounded into the trees. Elder Woman followed closely. Raven and the other women also fled.

Everyone except Elder Woman was soon gathered back at the cave. They stood in front of the mouth, trying to decide if they should search for her, but then she limped into view.

"That bear was only bluffing a charge," she said when she got closer. "There wasn't any need for you to give up your catch. What was it—a squirrel?"

Raven shook her head. "It was a rock covered with leather." Perplexed by Elder Woman's mistake, she opened her bag and pulled the squirrel out by its tail. "Here's one of the squirrels we caught. Chirrup has the other one." The older woman's sight was failing her—not a good trait for the leader of a band to have.

"Harrumph." Elder Woman stopped in front of the squirrel Raven was holding out to her. "Not worth sharing. You keep it. I had hoped to catch enough game to make a meal for everybody, but with that bear around, we can't hunt anymore."

Raven put the squirrel back in her bag, almost amused by the rejection. She doubted that the others would refuse to eat some, even if only a small portion.

"We found several geese nests under some dead rushes, Grandmother," Coo said. "They'd been abandoned, but I think the eggs are still good." She carefully placed her bag on the ground and pulled out several large eggs. "Finch has three more."

Finch took out her eggs, placing them beside the others on top of Coo's bag. She rubbed their smooth surfaces as she spoke. "These eggs scrambled with cooked squirrel meat will help fill our stomachs." Finch gave a small appreciative nod in Raven and Chirrup's direction.

Raven nodded in return.

Finch continued. "If the men bring back game, we can have some of that besides." She looked timidly at Elder Woman as if afraid of being reprimanded for voicing her thoughts.

"I suppose so," Elder Woman groused. She looked up from the eggs. "Well, we're not cooking until later. If there's something you need to take care of, go do it now."

Raven knew better than to remind them that they'd planned to dry and store all game brought back by the men. She had a feeling they would say that their larger bodies required more food than her smaller one just as Chukar had explained it to her not long ago.

When Wren went inside, Raven quickly followed, almost stepping on a skin mounded high with wood shavings that the men had left just inside the mouth. As she trailed after Wren across the room and down the turns and twists of the corridor, Raven heard Elder Woman's loud complaints that the pile wasn't nearly big enough.

Just as she entered Wren's room, her foot hit a small stone that went skittering across the hard-packed soil. Wren whirled around at the sound. The panicked look in her eyes took Raven by surprise. The kidnapping had traumatized her, as it would have anyone. But by now, her fear of Elder Woman and the other Longheads should have abated somewhat. It must have become obvious that they wouldn't hurt her.

"It's just me, sweet one," Raven said.

Wren visibly relaxed.

"How did it go hunting with Elder Woman?" she asked, trying to find out if there was something she should know.

Wren shrugged. "She's grouchy, hardly ever nice."

"But the other women are kindly, are they not? Finch, Chirrup, and—that young one, Coo." She wondered if Wren knew what was going on between Coo and Leaf. "She's only a few summers older than you are."

"I hate them," Wren snapped. She paused a heartbeat. "Except for Chirrup. She's not so bad." Her hands kneaded the front of her tunic. "They stole me. Why do you want me to like them?"

"I know what happened was bad, very bad, but—"

"And why are you with that Longhead man?"

Raven winced. "I haven't forgotten your stepfather, if that's what you believe. But life isn't always simple. Chukar saved me. I was almost dead when he found me. I'm with you today only because he took care of me when I couldn't help myself."

Wren's eyes went wide as what Raven said sank in. Her daughter's reaction was gratifying. Wren still loved her. "Long and Short were helping me search, and Short did die. He drowned in a flooded ravine. Long may have died too, although I didn't find his body."

Wren's face suddenly crumpled. For once, she cried almost soundlessly, her mouth partially open as though she were silently screaming.

Raven pulled Wren in close, her hands rubbing and patting Wren's back. She was still only a child; perhaps Raven shouldn't have been so abrupt.

"Somehow, things will get better. Don't cry. You'll make yourself ill."

Wren hiccupped several times. "Elder Woman wants me to be with that awful boy."

Raven had to think a moment to work out whom she meant. "Do you mean Skraw?"

"He sneaked up on me one day, and I threw rocks at him. Now he leaves me alone."

"What? Does Elder Woman know about that?"

"She told him to go away, but then later that day, I heard her say something about a ceremony soon with Skraw. She thought I couldn't understand her. But I did. I've learned a lot of their words from Chirrup. I don't want him. He's ugly and mean."

*A joining ceremony?* Raven stepped back from her. "Elder Woman can't do that. Only women have ceremonies. Until your moon blood flows, you're still a girl." She looked carefully at Wren's guarded face. Perhaps her daughter was leading up to telling her that she'd become a woman already. "That hasn't begun yet, has it?"

Wren vehemently shook her head. "Not yet—no." She opened her mouth as if she'd say more but then closed it. Her feet shuffled on the floor.

"What is it, my heart?"

"When the moon blood does happen, I already know who I—I want for my mate."

"And who is that?"

"I want Ash." Her jaw lifted defiantly. "Not that disgusting boy who lives here."

The son of a couple who'd supported the group's move inland, Ash had always been close friends with Wren. Raven remembered again how he'd valiantly helped Wren kill the wolverine so the band would have something to eat. She nodded. "He's a nice boy. Do you think Ash knows that you, uh, wish to have the ceremony with him someday?"

Wren nodded with an enthusiastic bounce. "He knows. We played the ceremony game many times."

Raven tapped several fingers against her cheek. She wondered how far the games had gone. Occasionally, children were found pretending to mate and have babies, playing at fulfilling the duties sanctioned by the rites.

Wren rubbed her eyes then gave a big smile. "I can't wait to see him again and tell him about all this." She waved her arms at the walls as she spun around.

Her mood had changed while thinking about the boy, a bit of boisterousness returning. Raven decided that she wouldn't risk destroying the girl's good humor with embarrassing questions about their games. Ash had matured more slowly than Wren; it was unlikely he'd accomplished anything more with her than hugs and kisses.

"No one will force you to have a ceremony against your will," she told Wren. "Not while I'm here."

Wren's face showed uncertainty as if she knew that her mother's sway at the cave was somewhat limited.

Raven decided it best to change the conversation. "Your hair is so short and unkept. I like your braids better."

"They wear their hair this way. Why shouldn't I? You had to go and have a baby with a Longhead."

Raven didn't care for her provocative tone. She started to retort that without Chukar, Wren would have never been born. Instead, she changed direction once more. "Come with me to work more on the rock tinder. Do you understand why we want to use it during a ceremony?"

"Yes, I heard Elder Woman, and then Chirrup told me. We want the Earth Mother to stop fighting with the sun."

"Then you understand that the sooner we have the ceremony, the better. I don't like how quickly winter is falling upon us. We must put forth our pleas immediately." An expression crossed Wren's features. It was one that Raven hadn't seen for many seasons.

She'd realized when Wren was little more than a toddler that her daughter was enthralled by her mother's influence within the band. She watched every move whenever Raven chanted an invocation along with the elders, ochre streaming from their hands into the wind. That childish fascination had blunted over the turns of the seasons, but Raven had just glimpsed a bit of it.

***

While Raven and Wren sat at the main hearth, scraping stone into powder, Whit, Jay, and Skraw returned.

Elder Woman came in just as they arrived. She shook her head in disgust when she saw they hadn't brought back game. "You'll just have to go again tomorrow."

A flash of anger crossed Whit's face, and he flexed his huge body as he spoke. "Two men and a boy can't always accomplish much."

"And Chukar?" Elder Woman asked.

Whit shrugged. "He went to set some traps."

"Chukar needs to hunt with you if he wants to live here."

Raven wondered why Chukar hadn't gone with his brothers. He could have set the traps later. All the men should be concentrating on large game so the group would have enough meat to put up for winter. Whit's frustration infected her, and she forgot her earlier decision to bide her time before confronting Elder Woman about Leaf's confinement. "You left a good hunter behind, rotting in a hole in the wall." She looked at Whit as she spoke, then Jay.

When they ignored her, Raven knew she should back off. But her lack of sleep because of the cricket the night before had caught up with her, stoking her irritation with them all. She turned abruptly to face Elder Woman. "He'll sicken and die staying in the gloom every day. He needs the sun's touch on his face, dim though it has become." She bowed her head slightly as she spoke, her hands held out in supplication, attempting to put forward the words as a plea instead of a criticism, but Elder Woman blew up anyway.

Frenzied, she waved her arms over her head. "Hold your tongue! We won't accept you telling us what to do." She lowered her hands, eyes boring into Raven. Her fingers curved stiffly like spider legs as she talked. "What do you care about what happens to Leaf? You should be in there with him, but you stay with another man."

Raven wished that Chukar was by her side. He hadn't realized that everyone would return so quickly. She lowered her eyes submissively, but Elder Woman continued her tirade.

"Since you disagree with how we do things, then you should leave us." Out of the corner of her eye, Raven saw her point at the cave mouth. "Go back out on the steppes."

Her breathing became panicked. She'd been through so much to find Leaf and Wren, but because of her lack of patience, she was about to be right back where she'd started.

"I told you to leave. Either you go now, or we will throw you out."

Her eyes met Wren's distraught ones, and she knew what she must do. Raven threw herself on the floor at Elder Woman's feet. She turned her head to the side and pulled away the braids covering her neck.

Raven had only once before seen someone plead in such a manner, using the extreme gesture of exposing the throat to indicate submission. A young child who was denied food to punish his bad behavior had fallen down screaming in front of his mother, pulling his parka away from his neck. Of course, the woman hadn't harmed the boy. She'd snatched him up and slapped him. Afterward, he'd been allowed to eat. Raven wasn't sure if the present situation would resolve with as good an outcome, although Leaf had told her he'd never in his time with the Longheads seen anyone's throat cut after exposing themselves that way.

Complete silence filled the cave, then Wren began crying.

She had no idea what her mother was doing. Sweat popped out all over Raven's body. Elder Woman was taking her time ending the situation. Finally, rough fingers grasped her arm and pulled. Before Raven fully stood, the slap came. She went down again in a heap. The blow hadn't hurt that much; Bear, her dead sister's mate, had once hit her much harder. Raven closed her eyes and lay still, shutting them all out.

"Go to your chambers. We are finished here until later, when Chirrup and Finch cook," Elder Woman said.

Quick footsteps pattered toward Raven.

"Go to your room, girl," Elder Woman bellowed.

Wren's footsteps hesitated, then Raven lost track of them in the noise made by the men leaving.

While Raven waited with her lids tightly clenched, she thought of Windy and Sky and how much she missed them. She hoped they wouldn't forget her, but she didn't want them to miss her too much. Perhaps she was deceiving herself as to her importance in their lives. From time to time, orphaned children were absorbed into the band, and they thrived. But Windy and Sky weren't orphans. Both parents were alive, and it was time their mother spoke with their father. She wouldn't hesitate to speak with him like she had earlier.

The chamber had gone so quiet that the wind could be heard whistling across the cave's mouth. Raven opened her eyes. She was by herself once more.

Rubbing her stinging cheek, she hurried down the corridor with a torch. When she arrived at Leaf's room, Raven found that luck was with her. Whoever had last moved the boulder hadn't pushed it over far enough, leaving a gap near the bottom. Excited that she would actually be able to see him while they talked, Raven went down on her stomach and began wriggling through.

# CHAPTER 13

## *Leaf*

LEAF ALWAYS KNEW WHAT ANIMALS were moving toward him in the forest even before spotting them. Out on the steppes, sight was all-important for a successful hunt, but in a wooded area or other close spaces, smell and hearing were just as important. By using the same skilled awareness that he'd honed since childhood, Leaf knew that Raven had come to the boulder earlier. He'd sensed her effortlessly, and the small familiar sounds she made while breathing and moving about confirmed her presence.

So when a shuffling sound started near the bottom corner of the boulder, Leaf was already aware that Raven was again in the corridor. He watched as she struggled to crawl through a gap that Whit and Jay had unwittingly left on one side of the opening.

When the familiar face came into view, one cheek reddened from scraping against the stone, the anger that he'd felt since seeing her with Chukar evaporated a bit. He didn't know how it had come to be that she was with his old rival who'd also been his friend. Perhaps fate had forced the two together. Leaf understood she may not have had a choice, but even so, bitterness gnawed at him whenever he remembered how the Longhead man had clasped her hand, marking her as his.

Coo was the only reason that his jealousy wasn't all-consuming. Even though the reprieve was short, he'd found that he could forget Raven for a time while he taught the young Longhead woman the various intimacies of mating. Leaf dared to hope that Raven could give him an explanation about her behavior that he could accept.

Leaf watched in agony as first shoulders then hips slowed her progress. He struggled reflexively against the ropes, desperate to help her through. Finally, with a final writhing twist, she slid inside, sprawling on the stone floor in front of him.

"Now I know how a baby feels while being birthed." Raven stood, swiping the dust off her clothing. Her attempt at levity died when she took a good look at him, her smile replaced by dismay that she didn't bother to hide.

He was sitting as he did for much of every day, his back against the wall, his arms clamped against his sides by the ropes, his tied legs thrust out in front of him. Lately, no one had brought him any extra water for cleaning, so he smelled bad again. Her distress was satisfying, but Leaf knew he resembled nothing more than a filthy boar piglet kept trussed until it could be slaughtered. Before he overcame his mortification enough to greet her, she spoke.

"Are you injured or ill?"

Always the healer—just like her to think about his health over anything else. He shook his head, one of the few movements he could easily make. "I was beaten, but those bruises are gone. As far as being ill, I'm sick of being inside this cave." He hated seeing the pity in her eyes. The only way that would change was for him to be free. "Untie me."

He expected her to immediately rush over and tear off the ropes, but she didn't. Her response was to raise her hand, palm out in the Longhead way, to indicate she had more to say. "Were you harmed by the exploding firestone?"

Leaf cocked his head. He'd made it clear enough that he

wasn't injured. "No, I was inside, bound like I am now, when the thing exploded." The way she stood there without making a move to help him hurt Leaf deep inside. His breath came in shallow sniffs, the smell of soot from the stone ceiling above him filling his nostrils. He tilted his head back and stared for a moment at the layered blackness left over from the fires of previous occupants. Feeling only slightly calmer, he met her eyes again. "Maybe together we can move the boulder enough for me to squeeze out. Untie me, Raven."

"The air is so dirty now. Every living thing will suffer if that doesn't change soon. The band is preparing a ceremony to bring about peace between the Earth Mother and the sun so that the air will clear and the earth will heal. I'll demand that Elder Woman allow you to attend."

Stunned by how she was ignoring his pleas, Leaf barely heard her until his surging anger forced him to focus once more on her chattering.

"Not only is the sun colder, it's become smaller now that autumn—"

"I know about all that," he yelled at her. "I see the sun every morning and evening when they take me out to piss. Why won't you untie me?"

Her glibness disappeared at last. She gave him a long look. "I can't. If I help you escape, I'll never see Wren again."

"Have you even asked Elder Woman to free me?"

"Yes, and for my trouble, she told me to leave. I can't cross the woman right now, or she'll force me out of the cave. Please be patient."

"Patient! Don't you care anything about my misery?" His voice dripped with contempt. "Are you sure that losing Wren is what's stopping you from helping me—or is it her father that keeps you from your duty by me?"

"If you think that I'm not angry about you being a prisoner, then you're wrong." She gave him a reproachful look. "It's awful how they have you bound, but the way forward isn't clear. The situation we're in is as full of twists and turns as this cave is."

Unsatisfied, he eyed her disdainfully. "Well, something has become very clear to me. It's obvious that for you, one man's stoking is as good as another's. First it was Bear, then Chukar, Bear again, then me, and now Chukar once more. Those are the ones I know about."

Her face became ashen. "Chukar saved my life. Long and Short weren't so lucky. They were helping me search for you and Wren when we were surprised in a canyon by a flood. I found Short's body. Long probably died too. I survived by climbing a tree, but a branch cut my leg."

Sadness at hearing about the two brothers silenced him a moment, but he wasn't ready to give up his anger. "Cut your leg? What does that have to do with Chukar?"

She yanked her tunic and loincloth up and turned a leg slightly outward. "I was unconscious from wound fever when he came across me."

He sucked in his breath at seeing the long pink scar in the firelight. She could have died, and he would have never known what had happened to her. His gaze wandered a short way higher. He'd always cherished the shapely way her upper thighs curved into her groin. The knowledge that a man other than himself was regularly lying between them was more than he could bear.

"And so out of gratitude, you became his woman? Is that it? Or did you decide that a big man like him is better than the puny men of your own kind?"

She jerked her clothing back down. "Let's not fight, Leaf." She pressed her palms together as if praying. "I just need to sort out what is best for everyone, especially Wren. Elder

Woman can't be reasoned with. I don't know what she'd do to me if Chukar weren't around."

"Forget Elder Woman. Forget Chukar and forget Wren. He foisted that girl on you. You were afraid to fight him off that day by the pool, and that's the truth behind her birth." He nodded toward the boulder. "Together, we can move that stone enough for me to get out. I can outrun them, and you always ran like the wind." Leaf realized at once from her scowl that he shouldn't have asked her to desert Wren, but that wasn't what she chided him about.

"I *was* afraid of Chukar at first, but how did you know we were beside a pool?" Her eyes went wide in exaggerated surprise. "Don't tell me that you were somewhere nearby. You were, weren't you? You always did follow me around, stalking me as if I were a doe. Well, since you were watching, you must have seen that I soon lost my fear of him."

Her words landed on a sore place. He remembered all too well how her rapturous cry rent the air when for the second time the Longhead covered her body. They'd never before talked about what had happened to her on that particular day. Hearing her speak so frankly about it left him speechless.

Raven eyed him. "What about you? I heard you rutting with Coo the first time I risked my freedom trying to see you. And I don't remember hearing that you wanted those women in your past to leave you alone, either."

He refused to feel guilty about Coo, and she had some gall to bring up those Longhead women without mates who'd taken him into their pallets on cold nights during his earlier captivity. She didn't really have an argument; that had happened long before he'd met her. Leaf had been a boy at their mercy. Resistance had been out of the question.

He'd never told her about several women in the Fire Cloud band who'd found a way for them to be alone. Those casual encounters had ended the moment Leaf had first seen Raven. From then on, he was a one-woman man. She, however, had never entirely committed herself. After promising to join with Leaf in ceremony, she'd forgotten him for Bear. He'd eventually overlooked that betrayal because he wanted her so badly. Leaf shook his head sadly. In spite of everything, he still wanted to be with her. If she fled the cave with him, then he would easily forget his rancor. They could return to their children and take up their old lives. She would be forgiven.

"Leaf, Leaf! We need to stop hurting each other. It *is* terrible how you're being treated. I will do my best to get you freed, but you may be better off satisfying Elder Woman's whims, waiting her out."

Leaf wished he could hold his hands over his ears. He lay down and rolled over several times, slowly angling his feet in the direction of the wall. His sneezes from the disturbed dust drowned out her voice but for only a moment.

"I know that Elder Woman has promised to let you go if Coo becomes pregnant. Chirrup told me so, and I've had to accept it. And I'm telling you now that just because I'm with Chukar doesn't mean that I don't—"

"Go away, Raven. Leave me." Leaf twisted himself up once more and sat with his back facing her, his legs stretched out, toes touching the stone wall.

She breathed in loudly, a wavering sound that caught in her throat, then he heard her struggling to crawl back out of the room. His heart felt as cracked as the stone wall in front of him. Raven was going, and he didn't know when he would see her again.

After a short silence, her voice came from the corridor. "Chirrup says that she'll come soon. I hope you'll be kind to her."

He heard a few footsteps, then complete quietness surrounded him once more. He frowned as he thought about her parting words. As far as Leaf knew, he'd never offended Chirrup in any way. She'd visited him once, and he looked forward to seeing her again.

***

The days went by slowly. At times, Leaf craved the companionship of someone other than Coo. Someone a bit more mature. Not that he wasn't grateful for her company. Besides keeping his mind off his disappointment in Raven, Leaf's enjoyment of her was as much about relieving his solitude as his lust. He prolonged his intimacies with Coo for as long as physically possible, because he soon discovered that Jay and Whit would leave her with him, the boulder remaining firmly in place, until all sounds of their mating ceased.

He hated to see her go because when he was alone, his thoughts often spiraled into deep holes, where everything bad that had ever happened to him came to mind. Leaf hoped that Chirrup would visit again soon. He desperately needed her easy cheerfulness to help lift him from those dark places. When almost half a moon went by without her coming, he wondered if she'd misled Raven.

Then one morning, Chirrup was at the main hearth by herself when Whit and Jay led Leaf through. She called out a morning greeting as they entered, and he spotted her squatting by the fire, pulling several grouse from a spit. Leaf smiled and responded, as did Jay and Whit. Returning his smile, she stood and watched them take Leaf outside. When he was brought back in, she was still there, and they swapped smiles once more. To his delight, she appeared at his chamber opening just as Jay and Whit were finishing with the ropes. In her hands, she carried a drawstring bag.

"Close the entry," she told her brothers, fingers clutching

the small pouch tightly. "I wish to talk with him at length. You can go away for a while."

Both Jay and Whit gave her odd looks, noting the bag in her hands, but they went out without comment and slid the stone back in place as she'd asked.

Chirrup didn't speak again until their footsteps had faded away. Then she opened the bag. "It has been a while since you've been able to get clean."

He watched her pull out a water bladder, a soft length of finely worked leather, a bone scraper, and a small bowl. The fragrant smell told him the bowl contained a cleaning unguent.

Her thoughtfulness warmed him, but he wondered how she thought he could possibly clean himself while tied as he was.

As if she knew what he was thinking, she nodded. "I wish to undo the ropes. But first, you must give me your promise that you won't try to move the boulder."

"I suppose you'd do something to stop me if I did."

Her smile went away. "I wouldn't have any choice."

"Don't worry," he said. "I know how your mother would react, and I won't do that to you. I give you my word." He realized that he meant what he'd said.

She was taking a chance. If he escaped, Elder Woman's wrath would be limitless. His eyes watered from the gratitude he felt. Chirrup was offering to take off the ropes when not even Raven had done so.

Chirrup's short stature and arms kept her from easily reaching the ropes going around his upper chest, so he sat down while she unwound them. After those were removed, he stood so she could undo the knots on the lower ropes. He looked over her bent body at the enormous boulder that he'd promised to leave alone. His eyes wandered to the bottom, where it met the cave floor, leaving no gap at the side like when Raven had come in. Chirrup was overestimating his strength. He would never be able to budge it by himself, not even a little.

Chirrup walked around him, unwinding the ropes from his thighs. "I have something good to tell you. It's not something a woman should discuss with a man, but I want you to know that Coo didn't have her moon blood when she should have." Chirrup straightened to look at him for a moment, then she knelt to undo the knot that bound his calves. "Everyone is delighted that the band may soon have at least one child." Her voice was wistful. "To see and hold a little one again after so long..."

He wondered why Coo hadn't told him. "Then do you know if Elder Woman will release me soon?"

Chirrup's hands paused on the ropes. He regretted how harshly he'd put the question. Leaf couldn't see her expression, but he didn't think she was pleased. No doubt she'd told him about Coo because she thought that bit of information would make him less inclined to make a break for it.

"I do not know," she replied, undoing his ankles.

Once the ropes were off, he stretched to loosen his muscles and get the blood flowing. When he saw Chirrup wet the piece of softened leather, he pulled off his filthy tunic then reached out to take the cloth.

But she didn't give it to him. Her hands kneaded the material. "If you'll sit down, I will clean your back."

He was mildly surprised. Offers of cleansing were usually only made by a friend of the same sex or family members such as one's mother or mate. His rankness must be quite noticeable if she was willing to help clean him. Leaf gave her a wry smile and nodded at his pallet in the corner. "I'll pull a fur over near the fire for us to sit on so that we'll be more comfortable."

While she warmed the waxy substance, he thought about

Coo being pregnant. A few drops of happiness trickled into his heart. He was fathering a third child. Leaf didn't know why that should please him. If all went well, he wouldn't be around long enough to see it. Perhaps that was why Coo hadn't told him. She knew he would ask to leave right away. He breathed in deeply. The dried flowers in the unguent had dampened the room's soot odor.

Chirrup sat behind him to wipe down his back with the cloth, then her hands were on his skin, massaging in the warm wax. An intense pleasure flowed through his body, and he closed his eyes. To his dismay, she stopped after only a short while. He looked back at her.

"I can't do this," she said. "I have not been truthful with you. Raven once told me how your tribe's people enjoy being clean whenever possible, just as we do, especially before—" She swallowed loudly behind him. "Before—so I thought that I could somehow..."

His suspicions about her willingness to clean him pushed away the contentment Leaf was feeling. He recalled Raven once telling him that Chirrup's childlessness made her distraught. Only a few days before, she'd told him to be kind to Chirrup. What she'd meant by "kind" was becoming clearer. Raven had seemed jealous about Coo, but she and Chirrup had obviously planned his cleansing.

They had a lot of nerve to manipulate him so crudely. And what if Elder Woman was in on their plan? That meant that Raven got along better with the old woman than she'd let on.

"Does your mother know about this?" He twisted his upper body so he could see Chirrup's face.

Her eyes were serene, although she was flushing. "No, she does not know," Chirrup said, standing up. "I'm sorry. I should not have thought to do this." She walked around him and over to the boulder. "Whit," she called. "Jay, are you out there?"

Leaf thought that she'd told him the truth. "Wait." He stood up. It had occurred to him how he could use the situation to his benefit. Whit and Jay were fond of their sister. They would go along with Chirrup's plan to get pregnant. And on the days he was helping her achieve that desire, Leaf would be untied for more stretches of time.

He went over and gently took her arm. "Why don't you finish cleaning me while I become used to thinking of you as someone other than a friend." Actually, she seemed more like a sister, and feeling that way, Leaf wasn't sure he would be able to help her. Unlike the Longhead acceptance of sibling pairings, mating with one's sister was a taboo of the highest order within the Wind tribe. Leaf sensed her hesitation. "It's fine. I want to." He was being sincere. *Why shouldn't she have her own baby?*

As she worked on his chest and abdomen, Leaf kept reminding himself to relax. The earlier pleasure her hands had given him didn't return, and he felt almost certain that he would end up failing her. The irony of it crossed his mind. Here he was, being pressured into impregnating other women, yet he wasn't allowed to lie with Raven, the only female with whom he truly wanted more children. It dawned on Leaf then how he might be able to fulfill Chirrup's hopes. He would imagine that she was Raven, although that might not be easy, considering the physical differences between the two women.

After Chirrup scraped the unguent off his upper body, he removed his leggings and stood. She knelt and began cleaning his legs. When her timid hands tugged at his loincloth, he helped remove it, realizing suddenly that he wasn't going to encounter any problem whatsoever. He wouldn't have to pretend he was with Raven. If only he could forget her entirely.

***

Elder Woman found out in less than a day. Jay and Whit's astounded faces had signaled their disapproval when they retied him after letting their sister out of the room. The Longheads gossiped far less than the Wind and Fire Cloud peoples, but perhaps the shock of seeing Leaf completely free of the ropes and without his clothes on had loosened the brothers' tongues. Leaf couldn't help being amused when Elder Woman complained to him that she'd been the last to know. He wondered who exactly had told her.

"Chirrup didn't have to come begging you. She only had to say she wanted to be treated the same as Coo," Elder Woman said. "I should have thought of it. Several babies birthed close together are better than one. If a mother dies or doesn't have milk, then the other one can suckle both. But I'm getting ahead of myself. I don't know if she can get with child." Turning her head, Elder Woman spat on the floor to show her uncertainty about Chirrup's fertility.

Leaf twitched within the ropes at her lack of thoughtfulness. He would have to avoid sitting in that spot for a while—that was not so easily done in such a small space. And he didn't like the way the conversation was going. "Our agreement had nothing to do with Chirrup. She told me that Coo is probably pregnant. If that's true, then I'd like for you to set me free, as you promised."

Although she was in good spirits, her typical annoyance with him quickly resurfaced. "Chirrup shouldn't have said anything," she snapped. "We won't know with any certainty until Coo's belly grows. Don't be in such a hurry. With how quickly winter is coming on, you may have to stay until spring. You can have Chirrup's company until then whenever my daughter wishes to see you."

Leaf's heart sank. The bodies of the Longhead women were naturally rounded. When he'd lived with them as a boy, they'd often had a baby before he'd even known they were pregnant. A long while could pass before Coo's pregnancy became noticeable. The idea of living all winter tied up in the chamber infuriated him. "How do you think I can keep living this way? I see less sunlight than a hibernating bear."

She lowered her brows. "You speak many of our words but are often difficult to understand. Raven told me that you'll sicken and die out of the sun. Is that what you're saying?" She looked at him suspiciously. "For all I know, she's been here, and the two of you made that up to fool me."

"I haven't seen her," he lied. "Although I would like to. But yes. I will eventually weaken. I won't be able to walk far—or be a bull elk for your women." He waited for her derisive reply about the comparison.

She stared at him, frowning. But then she grinned and even chuckled. "There you go, saying that people and animals are the same. You told me before that the People are hyenas. Now you call yourself an elk, even though you could never be one. The beasts are strong, not like Them at all. Being so tall and thin, you have to bend over when walking into the wind—or else be blown onto the ground." Shaking her head, she chuckled once more.

He wanted to tell her that even if his tribe didn't have bodies quite as muscular as those of the People, at least his kind were able to easily see over the tall grasses of the plains. He held his tongue, though. She was less likely to be harmful when in a good humor. Without waiting to see if he would answer her jabs, she called for Jay. He came in from the corridor.

"Did I hear earlier that you and Whit will be making birch bark glue today?"

Jay nodded. "Whit's outside, digging a pit for it."

"Listen carefully then," she said loudly, as if her son were hard of hearing. "Untie Leaf's legs and take him outside. Then bind his legs again and undo his arms and hands. Put him to work helping make the glue. Make sure you do not leave him completely untied or alone at any time."

***

The air was still so murky that anyone who stayed out in it for long started coughing. Even so, Leaf whistled happily under his breath as he sat weaving a small screen of green willow wood that would be used in making the glue. Not only was he outside for longer than he'd been in almost two moons, but he would have the opportunity to once more see how the tarry substance was made. Nothing did a better job of binding a spear point to a shaft. The Wind tribe people hadn't any knowledge of the tar. None of the tribes did. Leaf had tried several times unsuccessfully to reproduce the process after becoming reunited with the Wind band. He would have a chance that day to find out where he'd gone wrong.

Being alongside the Longhead men reminded him of all the times in the past when he'd worked or hunted in their quiet company. The difference was that instead of being a companion like in those days, he was their captive. Then there was the matter of Coo. Even though his taking her without ceremony hadn't been Leaf's idea, the three brothers as her kinsmen ordinarily would be obliged to punish him for breaking with custom. No one had shown him any ill will, but Leaf was still uncomfortable around them.

The wolf boy hadn't come outside, and that was just as well. Leaf could not care less if he ever saw the boy again. He took a long sideways look at Chukar, who was breaking sticks of firewood into smaller pieces, and Leaf's joy at being outside dwindled a little. Not that Chukar had displayed any belligerence at having to be around Leaf. Chukar was ignoring him, but Leaf couldn't help despising the man.

Leaf had been magnanimous enough to put aside his jealousy during the winter he and Raven had lived with the Longheads. Chukar had seemed to think that Raven should be his because she'd borne his child. Neither Chukar's family nor Leaf had gone along with the idea. Leaf had befriended the Longhead because that was the best way to keep the peace until he and Raven left the following spring. Chukar had died right before they'd parted ways with the Longhead band. But then he'd somehow managed to return from the dead so that he could finally be with Raven.

The thought of the pair together caused hot sparks to flash behind Leaf's eyes. A sharp-edged stone lay on the ground near his feet, but it wasn't large enough to do much damage even if Chukar had been within arm's reach. It was a good thing that, after Elder Woman's admonitions, Jay had bound Leaf's calves a bit tighter than usual. Even though the stone was inadequate, he might have tried something that he'd regret.

He gave up being discreet and openly stared, willing the brawny green-eyed man to look his way, and Chukar, under the intensity of Leaf's gaze, finally did glance over. Their eyes held for only a heartbeat. Chukar's unchanging expression disappointed Leaf. Although Chukar had acknowledged the accusatory stare, he'd shown no discomfort whatsoever. Leaf focused once more on the intricate latticework under his fingers, forgetting for a while his antagonism as he hurried to complete the screen.

Whit had been busy making a small tightly woven bowl out of birch bark, which he placed inside a small pit in the

ground. He took Leaf's finished screen and placed it across the
top of the pit. After several flattened rolls of birch bark strips
were layered over the screen to Whit's satisfaction, he trickled
small pebbles over and around them, as well as over the rest of
the screen. He then sealed the whole thing with a thin layer of
earth, creating a mound.

Chukar placed part of the kindling onto the dirt mound
and lit it using pieces of hot charcoal from inside the cave.
Leaf understood then that during his tar-making attempts, he
hadn't used pebbles to keep dirt from sifting into the birch-
bark bowl that was underneath to collect the pitch from the
cooked bark rolls. Such a simple thing. The tar was overly goo-
ey because of all the dirt in it and hadn't set up correctly. Much
to his shame, Leaf had given up before solving the problem.

The fire had no sooner started than Raven and Chirrup
came out of the cave, bearing several meat-filled skewers. All
three brothers looked at the women then over at Leaf. Jay's and
Whit's glances were curious, but Chukar's face had an oddly
sharp expression. That was how Leaf knew for sure that Chukar had found out what had passed between him and Chirrup.

As he took his share of the food, Leaf fidgeted under the
men's gazes. He thought that it wasn't so much the mating of
their sister that titillated them as it was the fact that something
had happened in the cave without Elder Woman's permission.
Leaf realized then that if he got Chirrup pregnant, he would
have achieved what Chukar never could. He swallowed a bite
of meat and looked directly into the other man's face, struggling not to smile. Leaf had a chance to best him in a very
important way.

Leaf also felt Raven's eyes on him. He stared into the fire
burning over the mounded dirt, refusing to acknowledge her
presence. She asked Whit what they were doing. During the
short time Whit was telling her about the glue, Leaf forced

himself not to look at her. Just as the women were returning to the cave, Leaf had a coughing spell. Out of the corner of his eye, he saw Raven pause and look back before going inside.

Leaf glanced at the dust-blurred sun. Raven had mentioned some sort of ceremony she was planning that had to do with the Earth Mother and cleaning the air. Leaf had been so consumed with his own unhappiness, he hadn't paid much attention to what she was saying. Even though he was angry at her, he hoped her ceremony would be successful.

After a time, most of the old coals were raked from the mound, and more wood was added. The men worked on spear points while waiting for the heat to transform the sap into glue. When the fire had burned down for the third time, Chukar brought over the spear shafts. The pit was then opened. Once the glue in the basket had cooled a little, it lost some of its stickiness. The brothers then worked bits of it into small malleable balls.

Leaf watched Jay notch the end of a shaft and then put a spearhead on using the pitch. "Could I do one?" he asked.

Jay nodded good-naturedly and passed over a sturdy pole, along with a ball of pitch. Leaf fit the point he'd completed as he normally would then pressed the still-warm ball of pitch around where the stone and shaft connected. When it was finished, he reluctantly gave the spear to Jay. He knew better than to ask if he could keep it.

The spears were quickly finished, eight of them in all. Whit stayed outside to keep an eye on Leaf while Chukar and Jay began carrying the spears inside the cave a few at a time, holding them separated from each other so the ends wouldn't stick together. They wouldn't be ready for use until the pitch hardened and the shaft tops were wound with gut string. Misery settled over Leaf as the last ones were carried in. He dreaded returning to his dank small chamber even though the air was slightly better inside.

Dark dreams had begun interrupting his sleep. They happened even when he was napping. In those nightmarish episodes, his legs and arms became withered. Leaf couldn't run or toss a spear. He could barely walk. During his conversation with Elder Woman several days back, he'd told her that he would eventually grow weak because he was so rarely in the sun. In his dreams, however, a raven had told him that the cause of his weakness was a lack of movement.

He twisted his upper body from side to side and flapped his arms.

Whit watched for a moment, his eyes filling with pity. "We have hides that need to be worked," he said. "I could bring some out here for you, along with antler bone."

Leaf didn't respond right away. In his mind's eye, he saw himself as a boy, working day after day over hides for his Longhead captors, scraping them and polishing them with red-deer rib-bones. His right arm was still larger than his left one from overuse during those moons. He'd once sworn he would never again be a slave for the Longheads. That oath mattered little now when he was pining to stay outside longer. He nodded his reply.

# CHAPTER 14

*Raven*

THE CEREMONY WAS TO BE on the morrow during late afternoon. Everything necessary for the rituals had been readied for some while, but it had taken the sky's sudden release of large wet snowflakes for Elder Woman to feel any urgency. The flurries lasted only a short while, but none of them had ever before seen snow during summer—not even Elder Woman. She couldn't justify delaying longer.

Raven was relieved to finally be moving forward with their plans. If the explosion had happened during winter, then prompt attention to the matter wouldn't have been as crucial. It had happened, however, during late summer when hunting should have been at its best. Many of the grazing animals had already left the area because the layers of dust and ash had deprived them of sustenance just when they needed to fatten.

Chukar wasn't sleeping yet if his restless tossing was any indication. They'd argued earlier when he'd voiced his opinion to her and his brothers that the group should follow the herds. Raven had mixed feelings about leaving. She certainly didn't want to starve, but the farther out on the Great High Plains they went, the larger the distance between herself and her two children. Even if she couldn't go to them, she found solace in knowing they were only several days' journey away. Elder

Woman, of course, would have the final say as to whether they left or not.

Raven needed sleep so that she would be alert during the ceremony, but she had to do something first—just as soon as Chukar slept. Finally, his breathing became slow and even, his large chest rising and falling. She carefully turned over to lie on her back. Raven wished for dreams, but she also wanted some control over any that came during the night. Lucid dreams that revealed probable futures were her desire.

Knowing what might come to pass would help guide her when she asked the Earth Mother to put aside all animosity toward the sun spirit. The asparagus root tea she'd drunk earlier was good for prompting someone to dream with vivid awareness, but a chant for the dream spirit was also in order. She squeezed her lids together and kept her voice little more than a whisper so as to not awaken Chukar.

"Sweet sleep, swoop me up on wings of night. Keep me dreaming till comes the light. Take the webs from my eyes. Let me see where the future lies." Raven chanted the simple phrases over and over, infusing her mind with them.

A sudden gust of wind swept her prone body. Raven opened her eyes and sat up. She found herself perched upon a small stone platform that crested a windy mountaintop. A man was climbing one side of the broad, conical incline. She awaited his approach, shivering slightly, the strong breeze lifting the braids off her neck. He was still at a distance, slowly winding upward, minding his step, carefully avoiding what appeared to be small leather-wrapped bundles covering the slopes.

High-pitched mewling noises drifted over the wind, the sound arising from every direction at once. Raven jumped down from the platform. She sniffed the air; a familiar odor floated on the breeze. When she recognized the scent, Raven's breath caught in her throat. The bundles lying everywhere below were babies, infants swaddled in skins. The distinct intoxicating aroma was that of a newborn child, the smell strengthened because there were so many.

Scarcely believing her eyes, she looked from the babies to the man climbing through them. The clothing he wore was most unusual. He had on a parka made of leather, although she'd never seen one made that way. The front wasn't held together with ties but was somehow tightly closed from chin to below his stomach without any gaps whatsoever. His bluish-colored leggings were made of a material other than animal skin. Raven remembered seeing that same type of leggings worn by a man in another dream she'd had in the past.

She tried to catch a glimpse of his features to see if she recognized him, but the parka hood hung over his face as he kept his gaze down to avoid stepping on the newborn babies. When at last the man stood before her, he pulled the hood back from his short black hair.

Raven saw the same fine features and fair skin that she'd so admired during that long-ago dream. His serious brown eyes considered her for a moment, then he showed her what was in one of his hands. She recognized the red quartz blade lying across his palm, the glowing stone throbbing like a beating heart. The knife had been her father's once. She'd left it in a cave by the sea.

Raven realized she was dreaming about some future time after the man had discovered the knife. She imagined that he often cleaned game with the blade's sharp edges. Raven hoped that it also helped keep him safe. At the thought, she began trembling, and her eyes rolled back in her head. A violent scene of chaos filled her mind. Men fought while explosions like bursting firestones rent the air. She forced her eyes to focus, and the noise faded away.

The man was still there. "Keep the knife," she told him in

the Fire Cloud language, hoping he would understand. "You will have the greater need of it."

When he dipped his head in a quick nod, she knew that he'd grasped her meaning. He slipped the knife into the side of his parka so that its red glow suddenly vanished.

The babies had quietened, but their wails began once more. Raven looked again at his face. She made a sweeping motion with her hand to indicate the numerous infants. "Are any of these the children of your body?"

"A few," he replied. "But all of them are of yours."

Astounded, she stared at him, openmouthed. No woman was capable of bearing that many children. The man's face suddenly began changing. His forehead grew rounder and his nose smaller. He'd been taller than Raven, but for a heartbeat, they were exactly the same height. She looked directly into his eyes, then she had to lower her head as he shrank slowly downward. The fine tunic and leggings became too large; they swallowed him whole as he collapsed onto the ground. To keep him from smothering, Raven quickly bent and pulled back the hood that had flopped over his face.

The baby had the beautiful, warm brown eyes of the man he'd been. He moved his arms and began fretting, his cries joining the others. In the distance, lightning flashed. A storm was brewing. Raven looked about her, hoping to find shelter—an overhang or a cave into which she could put the babies—but the mountaintop was only bare earth and rocks. A feeling of horror settled over her as she understood that the infants were meant to die. They'd been deliberately exposed, but for what reason, she didn't know.

Occasionally, a newborn was left upon the steppes if its parents considered the child too burdensome because it had been born during a famine. And a baby was usually abandoned if considered defective. The exposed children soon died from thirst or the weather—if predators didn't find them right away. She'd always despised the tribal practice of leaving babies to such a cruel fate.

Raven ran frantically from one side to the other, trying to come up with a way to save them. Her frustrated cries for help were lost among the wails around her. She was only one woman, and they were too many. Her eyes lit upon the baby who had been the man from the future. His light-skinned face was red, his eyes squeezed shut as he screamed. At least Raven could take this one with her while she looked for a safer place. She bent to pick him up.

Someone was shaking Raven's shoulder. Her lids flew open. Chukar's face loomed over hers. "You were moving about." In the dim glow from the dying fire, his eyes under the heavy brows appeared hollow.

"I had a dream. A bad one."

He lay back down, pulling her close. "Sometimes the hunt goes badly in my dreams too."

How odd that he assumed she'd been dreaming about hunting. Raven wondered if that was all Longhead men dreamed about. Surely not. The dream had been one of the strangest she'd ever remembered after waking. It left her uneasy, and she meant to ferret out its meaning before going back to sleep, but the warmth of Chukar's body soon lulled her into a dreamless slumber.

Raven felt a moment of panic when her eyes next opened. Because they slept deep within the cave, she never knew upon awakening exactly how long the sun had been up. She threw off the covers and arose to rebuild the small hearth fire. There was much to do before the afternoon ceremony. Her stirring about awakened Chukar. He soon left for the main chamber, seeking hot food with which to break night-fast. While she dressed, Raven practiced the chants she would use later, chang-

ing the familiar words she'd learned as a girl into Longhead
ones.

She planned to teach the women a dance that morning
to accompany the chants during the ceremony, a dance she'd
participated in during Fire Cloud gatherings. The songs usually emphasized safety, fertility, and abundance of food—all
the things necessary for a contented life. Because the overall
purpose of the ceremony was to bring about peace between
the sun and earth, Raven was reworking the phrases so that the
chants would ask only for safety and food abundance, the two
things most affected by the quarrelling spirits. She figured that
if those important needs were fulfilled, then fertility would follow. She wanted to downplay the significance of the sexuality
that helped prop up the male-female bond. Her pairing with
Chukar was contentious, and the way Leaf had ended up trying to impregnate both Chirrup and Coo was highly unusual.
The less emphasis on discord within the group, the better. The
ceremony should invoke harmony not only between the spirits
but also among themselves.

Upon remembering the dream, Raven realized it wasn't
going to be of any help during the ceremony. Its meaning remained as obscure as it had been the night before. Since there
was no use dwelling on it, she hurried to the main hearth.

Wren and the women were the only ones sitting by the
fire, eating dried meat that had been warmed. Chirrup passed
several strips to Raven when she sat down.

"Where are the men?" Raven asked.

"They've gone hunting," Elder Woman said.

Although annoyed at them for leaving on such an important day, Raven wasn't surprised. Everyone who'd been at the
cave the day before had rushed to the mouth and peered up at
the ominous flakes coming down. Whit had gone outside and
shaken his fist at the sky. Raven had shuddered inside, hoping

that the spirits of snow and ice weren't taking offense. While the women soon returned to the fire, the men had remained just inside the cave mouth. They'd stood with their broad shoulders hunched forward, staring up at the flakes and muttering as their hands moved in subdued worry.

"But will the men return in time for the ceremony?"

"Of course. Harrumph. They promised me to be back before midafternoon," Elder Woman said.

"What if they don't find game so quickly?"

Elder Woman bristled. "I told you they will be here."

Raven lowered her head meekly. The woman became riled so easily. Getting through the ceremony without a major blow-up would be more difficult than navigating a canoe down a river full of boulders.

No one had even considered taking Leaf along hunting. Raven would insist, though, that he be allowed to participate in the ceremony. Even if they didn't completely untie him, he must join the group. Raven had made a small drum that she wanted him to beat while the women danced. She hoped he would agree to help her by playing it.

\*\*\*

The men returned during the afternoon as Elder Woman had promised. Raven shared the other women's disappointment at seeing their empty hands, but on that day, it was just as well. The lack of game only proved how crucial it was to do the ceremony right away. Besides, the whole thing would have been put off if the men had brought back a large animal. Once the cooking and feasting were over, no one would want to do anything else.

Later that afternoon, everyone helped Raven and Elder Woman carry the objects needed for the rituals to the clearing in front of the cave. After a bonfire was set, Raven asked Jay to fetch Leaf, explaining that once outside, Leaf's legs should be retied and his arms and hands unbound. Jay hesitated a moment, glancing over his shoulder at Elder Woman, but then he left, an eager spring in his steps. It said something to Raven that he was willing to do her bidding without first checking with his mother.

Raven didn't approach Leaf right away after he entered the clearing. She waited until the ropes were changed from upper body to lower before bringing over the small drum. Jay had helped Leaf sit upon an upended log and was pushing a large flat-faced stone behind his back for him to lean against. Raven smiled at the short muscular man, touched by his thoughtfulness. She noticed that he'd also made sure Leaf wasn't sitting anywhere near Chukar. Jay acknowledged her smile with a quick nod before walking away.

She knelt beside Leaf. He looked at the drum in her hands. "I imagine that Coo has told you about the ceremony."

He nodded curtly.

"I'll be leading a dance while shaking a gourd. All you need to do is beat a rhythm like you used to in the past when you helped with ceremonies."

Again came the emotionless nod.

"I am grateful for your help." Chilled by his silence, Raven stood and walked away. She didn't really blame him, but he was treating her with the same wariness one would show a stranger.

While Elder Woman was busy organizing the rock tinder, Raven began painting the other women's foreheads and cheeks. Then Chirrup painted Raven's face. When that was finished, Raven looked around for Elder Woman. The matriarch was standing a short distance away, watchful and aloof.

Raven went over to her. "I'll mark you if you'll come with me. Then we'll begin."

After a pause, Elder Woman followed Raven to where the

paint was, her expression suspicious. She pointed at Raven's face. "What do those marks mean?"

"The red dots across the forehead are for the band's children—that they grow strong under our care. The yellow circles on the cheeks are for prosperous hearths. The two lines under the circles are because women both hunt and gather to feed the band. The ochre dot between my eyes and on my chin mark me as a healer. You will have those and a circle painted around your chin besides, because you're a healer and an elder. You'll feel the shapes go on as I make them."

Elder Woman looked one last time at the other women's faces before turning to Raven. "Go ahead then, so we can start the ceremony." She stood stiffly, staring into the distance. Her closeness made Raven's fingers tremble as she dabbed on the paint.

They'd agreed earlier that all rituals for the sun spirit would be left to Elder Woman. Her rites were first. As soon as Raven finished painting her face, Elder Woman went to the fire. Jay handed her a large gourd full of wood shavings and ground rock tinder, which she emptied over the flames. The fire flared higher with a bright-red color, sending sparks floating into the dusk.

Elder Woman put down the gourd and raised her hands toward the sinking sun. "Oh, powerful spirit, hear these words…"

As she continued, Elder Woman occasionally nodded at Jay, who, whenever she looked his way, threw more of the flammable mixture onto the fire. Astounded by what Elder Woman was saying, Raven barely noticed the bright displays.

Instead of asking that the sun spirit temper its violence, Elder Woman praised the entity several times for its cruel and destructive strength. Then her rant took a more ominous turn. "Harm not the People with those large firestones that drive the beasts from the land!" she yelled as fiery tendrils reached for the sky. "Destroy our enemies instead. Drop your firestones where *other* tribes live." The word *other* echoed along the length of the cliff walls.

Raven was aghast. She didn't like to think so, but Elder Woman seemed to be asking the sun's help in destroying any tribes who weren't Longheads. Clearly, the elderly healer wasn't fit to lead the blended band that Raven had begun envisioning for the group. The focus should have been on healing rifts between the spirits. Not upon death and destruction. Even though the old healer was shamelessly using Raven and Leaf to grow her band, she wanted their tribesmen to perish. Surely, she understood that any children produced by their intermingling would be like Wren, combining aspects from both groups. For the first time, Raven feared for Leaf's life. The woman's heart carried too much animosity to let him return to the Wind tribe.

When Elder Woman began leading a chant, Raven had difficulty joining in. After the older woman threw a frown her way, Raven reluctantly started repeating the praises to the sun. At some unknown signal, Jay, Whit, and Skraw picked up the large skin holding the remaining wood shavings and ground rock. They carried the load to the fire and threw it all in, including the heavy skin. The flames began sputtering, smothered under the weight. Raven held her breath. Even though she thought Elder Woman's ceremony terribly flawed, the fire dying would be a bad omen. But the mixture caught again, throwing up an enormous flare that sent the men scattering back.

As the blaze lowered, Raven realized that Elder Woman was finished. The multicolored sparks gusting across the almost-dark sky had been so captivating that she hadn't noticed when the other woman sat down. Raven jumped up self-consciously and hurried over to where two drinking bladders had been left earlier. She'd decided to serve water mixed with fermented honey to the group before beginning her part. The drink had a relaxing effect and would make everybody more receptive to the ideas behind the rites.

She carried one of the bulging waterskins over to where the women were sitting. Raven gulped a swallow then began singing a low droning song, thanking the Earth Mother for the gift of honey provided by her hard-working bees. She gave the waterskin to Elder Woman, indicating with her hands that she should drink before passing the water on.

Each Longhead woman carefully smelled the mouth of the bladder before taking her turn. They'd obviously never tasted honey water before that day. Wren looked up in confusion when she was given the waterskin. Usually, only grown-ups drank the special drink. Raven nodded at her to go ahead. After taking a tentative sip, she drank deeply.

The men showed less trepidation when Raven brought them the honey water. They smacked their lips in appreciation of the sweet taste. Chukar's eyes were full of warmth as he took an enormous swallow, his enthusiasm supporting her. Because she could feel Leaf's eyes watching them, Raven refrained from giving him a smile.

After Jay drank, he gave the waterskin to Raven. Leaf was the only man left. She was about to go over to him but realized that the waterskin was empty. She hurriedly retrieved the other one. Still singing, she offered it to Leaf. He ignored her, looking everywhere but at the bladder her hands held out. Raven's singing took on a frantic quality. His rudeness threatened to spoil her part of the ceremony even though she'd barely started. He suddenly relented and grabbed it from her, tossing back a gulp that was as large as the one Chukar had taken.

Raven tied off the top as she ended the song then placed

the waterskin on the ground. She moved to the fire and reached into the bag crossing her chest. The handful of ochre only caused a small flare when she tossed it in, a timid display when compared to the powdered rock and wood mixture, but a heavy earthy odor immediately filled the air. Raven turned to face the group. She saw with gladness that their curious attention was all hers, even if the ochre offering hadn't been as impressive.

She opened her arms wide, tilted her head back, and spoke in her birth tongue at the top of her lungs. "Oh, Great Earth Mother, hear our plea!" The words bounced off the outcrop above where the caves were located. The returning sound was louder and clearer than Elder Woman's echoes had been. She resisted the impulse to give the elderly healer a self-satisfied glance. Once the echoes faded, Raven began speaking in the Longhead tongue.

The Longhead people were often unfathomable. Although their way of living was similar to that of the Fire Cloud and Wind tribes, their views regarding the spirit world weren't clear to Raven. They may never have thought about some of the things they would hear that evening.

Her arms and hands moved fluidly, and she cobbled her speech together with careful slowness so that they had time to reflect upon the ideas behind her words. "Honored spirit, we revere the four-legged beasts that walk the earth. We revere, as well, the creatures that fly through the air and the ones that swim the waters. And we respect their sacrifice so necessary to feed your ever-hungry children. With gratitude, we take your gifts of flesh and hides, and in doing so release their spirits to you once more. We give back what will always be yours."

Her speech flowed like a singing river. "We beg that you cease fighting with your brother, sun, so that the dance of life and death may once more result in renewal. The animals starve on this ash-covered land. They will die without birthing new ones to receive the dead ones' spirits. Without animals, the people will also die. The earth will turn into a wasteland of wandering spirits."

She threw another handful of ochre into the fire. With the pungent smell in her nostrils, she continued. "Forgive your brother, sun, just as we, the peoples of the earth, try to forgive those who offend us. Seek an understanding with him so that the both of you may dwell in peace."

Most of the faces in front of her reflected thoughtfulness mixed with mild confusion. The exceptions were Elder Woman and Leaf, who were glaring at Raven. They obviously didn't want to put aside their grudges and live in peace. She despaired of swaying them, and the enormousness of what she was attempting to bring about between the two peoples seemed overwhelming.

Raven's eyes flickered over the group. Wren was watching her mother with bright, alert eyes from under her well-formed brow that was so similar to the foreheads of the other women. Raven's gaze settled next on Coo, sitting with her hands folded over her stomach that had grown larger.

At that moment, the ceremony ceased being a plea to the Earth Mother and became a direct appeal to those sitting before her. She must find a way to make them understand. Remembering the strong Longhead affinity for birds, she continued. "All the peoples of the earth are the children of the earth. Sometimes they fight the way eagle chicks do when one strives to push a sibling out of the nest to die. That is natural for the eagle, but it's not the only way of surviving. The hatchlings of most birds live and grow peacefully in the nest."

As if supporting her message, a thrush began its nightly song. Raven grasped the moment. She began singing, blending her song with the bird's throaty trills. In the beginning, she groped for the exact words to put forth her vision for the band, but her voice soon gathered strength. Raven sang about Coo's baby who would soon be born and how the band must keep the child safe and well-fed just as the birds did their offspring. "Our hatchling," she called the future baby, hoping the Longheads would make the connection.

Raven glanced at Leaf and Elder Woman. They were no longer radiating ill will but were watching her with mouths partly open. The powerful combination of her voice with the thrush's singing was ensnaring hearts, and ideally minds as well. She owed the Earth Mother a prayer of thanks for sending the bird.

She ended the song. The time had come to dance, an activity she'd always enjoyed. The words tripped joyously from her. "Revered Earth Mother, we ask you to protect all mothers and their children, those born and those yet to be born. We, the women of this *tribe*—" Raven paused, letting the word *tribe* hang in the evening air. "We offer you a dance of life honoring Earth's creatures."

She motioned for the women to join her. While waiting for them to form a line, the meaning of the previous night's dream became partially clear—it had to do with the tribe Raven envisioned and that tribe's descendants who would be born for more turns of the seasons than anyone could imagine. The babies were threatened with death, so the dream had been a forewarning that her hopes of forming a new tribe could also die.

Raven pushed aside her worries. The night was young, and she had more to offer. Readying herself to lead the dance they'd practiced that morning, she nodded at Leaf, holding his eyes with an intense gaze. He must help her. She began shaking the rattle to pace their steps and had the satisfaction of hearing his drumbeat quickly follow.

Following Raven, they danced in single file around the fire as they chanted. Happily, Elder Woman allowed Raven to guide their steps without interfering. The dance was sedate, unhurried enough to make sure that one foot was in contact with the earth at all times. Before taking a small step forward, each foot gently tapped the ground twice to the drumbeat.

Raven glanced behind her at the line of women. Elder Woman was doing amazingly well. Because the dance was slow, she didn't hobble, and from all appearances she was enjoying herself. A small grin on her face, she bobbed up and down along with the drumbeat as she tapped each foot, the fringe on her tunic swaying.

When the time came, the women formed a large circle, spacing themselves wide apart from one another. Raven had been the first one to dance alone in the center during practice, so Chirrup gave her a surprised look when told to go inside the circle. She hesitated only a moment before briskly walking into the middle.

After Chirrup had danced a while, Raven motioned for Coo to take her place. She then sent out Finch, Wren, and Elder Woman, in that order. During her turn, the older woman danced with a serious face, concentrating on the rhythm. When Raven signaled for her to leave with a final flourish of the rattle, Elder Woman threw over a dour look as if Raven had deliberately shortened her dance time. Following Raven's lead, Leaf stopped pounding the drumskin, and Elder Woman joined the other women.

Raven went to the center of the circle. The air was still, the night steeping in silence. The world seemed to hold its breath. After a few moments, she began rattling a fast rhythm, and Leaf's pounding joined in once more. Departing from the sedate shuffling and dipping of the earlier dance, Raven trotted around the circle's outer edge, staying in step with the beat.

Suddenly, she was a deer, bounding around the enclosure of women, her feet loosening the dust. Then during a leap, she became a raven. She flapped up into the night sky and looked down. Her human self was still below, swirling and swaying. The women were clapping their hands, matching the cadence of drum and rattle. The Longhead men also began clapping. They arose and joined the circle.

Although she knew how few they were, seeing the small group from on high pained her once more. Only two handfuls of people watched the dancing figure. For a new tribe to be born, their numbers had to increase dramatically. After a while longer, she swooped down to merge her raven self with the dancing woman. Then everything was quiet again, except for her own panting. Dizziness blurred her sight, but the unsteadiness passed quickly, and her breathing slowed.

"Everyone stay exactly where you are," Raven commanded. She felt the strength of her own power when everyone immediately froze in place. "The women will now honor the men for their hunting prowess," she said loudly enough for them all to hear. "With our painting of the symbols on their bodies, we will show our gratitude." She dropped the rattle and broke through the circle to retrieve the small bags of ochre mixed with fat.

Raven had earlier shown the women the symbols to be made and had also designated which man each woman was to paint. Wren wouldn't be helping because she was still a child. The men remained still as Raven passed out the bags to the women.

Coo and Chirrup went over to Leaf. Raven hadn't wanted to risk offending either woman by assigning one of them to paint Whit instead of Leaf. That left Finch with having to paint both Jay and her brother-in-law. Raven saw her motioning for the two men to join her. After a moment, Elder Woman turned to Skraw, who was already standing at her side. Raven walked over to Chukar and faced him.

She expected Chukar to be startled; Raven had been so intent on preparing the women, she'd forgotten to tell the men they would be included in the ceremony. But Chukar didn't seem at all bewildered. He reached for one of her braids, grasping it in an untypically playful gesture. A strong fermented odor wafted from him. He must have been drinking the left-over honey brew while the women were dancing.

"We praise your prowess in providing water creatures to slake our hunger," Raven chanted. She marked Chukar's fore-head with three wavering lines.

At her touch, his eyes narrowed. He let go of her hair and clasped her waist with both hands. Raven gently loosened his fingers from around her, the red color on her fingers smearing his skin.

He took his hands away, but as she sang out the chant for the animals of the air, they returned again to her waist. Raven glanced toward Leaf to see if he'd noticed Chukar holding her so intimately. Whit and Jay standing in front of Finch blocked her line of sight. If she couldn't see him, then fortunately he couldn't see her.

Raven continued marking Chukar, but while she painted clouds over his cheeks, he began gently touching her breasts through the tunic. Once more, she pulled away his fingers, but they immediately came back to wander high over her thighs. Raven wondered if any of the other women were experiencing the same problems. Her voice breaking from the desire hum-ming through her, Raven called out that the women should make lines representing the land animals. She rapidly dabbed paint under Chukar's mouth and over his jaw while his hands traveled wherever they wished.

The ceremony had taken an unexpected turn. Wry amusement tempered Raven's irritation. Her attempts to downplay the importance of fertility in favor of food and safety had been futile. She wasn't unhappy about her failure, however. In restoring what Raven had sought to ignore, the Earth Mother was signaling that the tribe's numbers would indeed grow.

# CHAPTER 15

*Elder Woman*

WITHOUT THE SOUND OF DRUM and rattle, the clearing seemed overly quiet. Raven's chanted directions for making the symbols had also stopped, but Elder Woman wasn't finished dabbing paint on Skraw's forehead, much less his cheeks and chin. An eagle owl on the hunt punctured the silence with a loud hoot as it flew overhead. Skraw tilted his head back to watch the large bird, his head lolling to one side.

Elder Woman lowered her hand. "Stop moving, boy." She stepped back to take a better look at him in the firelight.

He swayed on his legs.

"Are you ill? Why can't you hold yourself still?"

His unfocused eyes blinked several times. "It was that sweet water she gave us."

Elder Woman gave up on finishing the marks. "I drank the water, and I'm not about to fall down." She closed the drawstring bag of ochre and wiped her fingers on the moss she always carried inside her tunic.

He pointed to a collapsed bladder not far from their feet. "I had more than you did."

Elder Woman remembered then that there had been two waterskins, a small bladder they'd drunk dry before Leaf had taken his turn and a larger one that Raven had then brought him. After he'd finished drinking, she'd put it aside.

"You drank the whole bag by yourself?"

"No, we all did." He sat down heavily on the ground and put his hands over his face.

She nudged the empty waterskin with her foot. So, the males had been drinking the sweet fermented water while watching the women dance. Although Elder Woman hadn't cared for the flavor, they had obviously enjoyed their first taste and wanted more.

She looked over to see if anyone besides Skraw was behaving strangely. What Elder Woman saw startled her. Although Wren remained in the clearing, and Chirrup still stood beside Leaf along with Coo, the others were already leaving. Whit and Jay staggered along on either side of Finch, blatantly holding her hands as they moved toward the cave. Elder Woman already knew that both brothers were sleeping with her, but they'd always been discreet about it before that evening.

Elder Woman assumed at first that the men were leading Finch but changed her mind when she saw Jay tug his hand away from her grasp. He ran his fingers along Finch's neck. Giggling all the while, she grabbed his hand once more. Her feet dug into the slope as she pulled the two men along with her to the cave mouth.

Chukar and Raven were also holding hands on their way up the incline, but Raven didn't seem as eager to leave as Finch had been. She kept pulling back until he released her. Elder Woman couldn't hear, but if her hand speech was any indication, Raven was trying to reason with him. She gave up after noticing they were being observed from below and went along without further argument. The ceremony was over even if she hadn't intended for it to end so abruptly.

Because he'd been beating the drum and hadn't drank as much, Leaf didn't appear as affected by the honey water. He sat watching Chukar and Raven leave, his face set with bitterness.

Elder Woman saw Coo follow his gaze to the departing couple. The girl's mouth turned down when she understood the reason for his inattention. Leaf noticed her distress. He grasped her hand, and she turned toward him. He then reached for one of Chirrup's hands.

It was amazing that neither woman seemed jealous of the other. Elder Woman had witnessed fights when someone else tried to enter an established relationship; several had resulted in death. Only one of the fatal skirmishes had been between two women. The others were between rival men, which made Jay and Whit's harmonious sharing of Finch even more astounding.

The intimate pairing between the adults hadn't been lost on Wren. She gazed up the slope at her mother's vanishing form, her expression that of a lonely child. Elder Woman didn't feel the least bit of pity. It was Wren's fault if she felt deserted. Skraw yearned for her. If she could find it within herself to accept him, then she would have someone other than her mother to depend upon. She must indeed feel abandoned, because when Wren saw how Elder Woman watched her, she started walking over, uncharacteristically wanting her grandmother's company. Wren stopped in her tracks, though, her face wrinkling into an anxious frown, when she noticed Skraw sitting there.

Elder Woman ground her teeth even though doing so caused her jaw to ache more. The stubborn girl refused to give Skraw a chance, treating the boy as though he might bite her. Several moons had gone by since he'd frightened her. It was time she accepted that he was to be her mate. Elder Woman would plan a joining ceremony just as soon as the girl got her moon blood, if not before.

Her voice chilly, she asked, "May I help you with something, granddaughter?"

Wren's eyes darted nervously away from Skraw. "The honey

water made me thirsty. Do you have any fresh water? We used up every drop at the main hearth earlier, and my water bag is empty. It's too dark now to go to a spring, but I'll bring you more tomorrow."

Skraw lurched up off the ground and turned toward Wren. "I'll go with you to get water."

She started and moved back several steps.

Elder Woman yanked on his arm, pulling him back down. "You're not going anywhere. It's dark now, and anyway, I need your help with Leaf."

Skraw plopped back onto the ground.

She forced herself to smile at Wren, pointing to where the medicine bag lay beside a bush. "I have a bladder waterskin in my pouch. Go fetch the bag for me."

Elder Woman glanced at Skraw. The girl hadn't donned the parka again after taking it off before dancing. He was eyeing the way her tunic hugged her hips as she walked, his expression full of longing. Elder Woman couldn't help but notice the bulge in his groin that pressed against his clothing. She felt so very sorry for him. All the other men had someone for the evening. Naturally, he felt left out.

Elder Woman didn't have anyone, either. But at her age, she was beyond caring about all that. The memories remained, however. She and Eagle had been after each other constantly when they were young. Not content with just joining under their furs at night, they'd found places to meet during the day. Those couplings out on the plains behind boulders or in wooded groves had been highly satisfactory.

She snapped her fingers to get Skraw's attention. When he looked up, she motioned that he should cover himself. He eyed her sullenly, not comprehending until she pointed at his lap. Catching on then, he pulled his parka closed.

Elder Woman wondered how Wren would react if told she

had to stay the night with Skraw or else be beaten. The thought caused her shame. Even though she looked ripe, Wren wasn't yet a woman. Any attempt to force them together—either with or without a ceremony—would be a violation of custom. But nothing was normal lately. Elder Woman thought about how the rest of her family was carrying on that evening. Such deviancy would ordinarily have been punished. Instead, she was encouraging their aberrant behavior—or at least refraining from stopping them, as when she'd found out about Chirrup and Leaf. But then why should she stop them?

Hadn't the sun spirit recently ordained that Elder Woman grow her band into a tribe? She regretted that she hadn't insisted on blood offerings during the ceremony, a gift for the spirit to show Elder Woman's gratitude for the revelation she'd received. A small cut on each person's arm dripping a few moments into the fire would have made the rites even more powerful. But staunching the cuts would have delayed Raven's ceremony. Elder Woman was reluctant to admit it, but she'd been looking forward to dancing and had decided that any pain or messiness the cuts caused would have been too distracting.

Wren was crossing over with the bag, the firelight illuminating her. She stumbled over a stony patch of ground, making her chest bounce under her tunic. Skraw made a sound, part moan and part snort. The girl had breasts. How was it that the moon had been so negligent in starting her flow? At the thought, Elder Woman's eyes narrowed, and she became convinced that Wren *had* fully become a woman.

She was being deceived by both mother and daughter. How devious of them to deny her more grandchildren by not sharing such important information. With difficulty, she controlled her anger as Wren went out of her way to avoid Skraw, coming up on Elder Woman's side opposite from where he sat.

Elder Woman squatted on the ground and rummaged through the bag, searching for the waterskin. Her hand brushed across an herbal packet of valerian, used whenever she or anyone else had difficulty sleeping. An idea flashed into Elder Woman's mind. If Wren were in a deep sleep—a very deep sleep—then she wouldn't be in any condition to reject Skraw if he went into her chamber.

The recklessness of the idea made the side of her face twitch. But their lies hadn't left her with many options. They would learn to not be deceptive; the girl being mated without her mother's permission would be their punishment. An awful uproar would follow when Wren awoke the next morning and realized what had happened. Everyone would be angry with Skraw—and possibly with Elder Woman besides, if they thought the girl had deliberately been given too much valerian.

But Elder Woman believed there was a way around their anger. She thought about the odd lustiness of the men after the ceremony. The cause of their behavior could be directly attributed to Raven's honey water. Skraw's lack of restraint was Raven's fault, and Elder Woman would point that out. That honey water hadn't been necessary for the ceremony, unless Raven had deliberately been trying to inflame the men. Wren had asked her for water, so Elder Woman couldn't be accused of forcing anything on the child. She'd merely put in the same herbs she always used to help the others sleep. If Wren was too groggy to know exactly what was going on, then perhaps she was overly sensitive to those herbs. Elder Woman couldn't be blamed for that.

Elder Woman took out a stirring stick and bowl as well as the water and several packets. She began deftly pouring and mixing, making a special blend. After finishing, she raised the bowl up carefully so that Wren could take it from her. "I've mixed in a few pinches of herbs that will help you sleep well," Elder Woman said and pushed herself up.

The girl was indeed thirsty. Several large swallows went down before the bitter taste of valerian and yarrow made her pause. Elder Woman stifled a smirk at how Wren struggled not to make a face. Lifting the bowl once more, Wren took a tentative sip.

"Drink it up, girl. I don't wish to stand out here all night. Leading a ceremony is tiring. And don't you pour it on the ground."

Wren gave her a guilty look, as if that were exactly what she'd planned to do. Elder Woman flexed her hand, preparing to provide quick discipline if she wasted so much as a drop. But then Wren raised the bowl to her mouth. Elder Woman watched how her throat worked hard under the skin of her neck to swallow it all.

Taking the emptied bowl, Elder Woman spoke in a soft voice. "May your dreams be about family and the children you'll have someday."

Wren gave her an odd look and started toward the cave. "Thank you for the water, Grandmother," she said over her shoulder.

Elder Woman's heart gave a little jump. Wren had never called her Grandmother before. Sudden doubt assailed her, but she set her jaw against any weakness. She would not waver in saving the band. A hyena cackled out on the steppes. Her arms crossed reflexively over her chest at the sound. She and Leaf had been wrong about their disappearance. A few of them were still around.

"Get up, boy," Elder Woman said, looking down at Skraw. "Go bind Leaf's arms, so we can undo his legs and take him inside." She glanced over at Leaf and the two women. They were talking quietly, their heads close together in the shadows thrown by the dying fire. Once they had him back in his chamber, it would be up to her and Skraw to close off the room. Moving the boulder would be difficult, but the two of them could manage. She wanted to leave Leaf completely untied since Chirrup would be there.

She thought about making Coo go back to her room. As far as anyone knew, Chirrup wasn't yet with child, but Coo was already pregnant. Leaf's attentions would be wasted on her. Elder Woman had a feeling, though, that Chirrup would be upset if Coo were sent away to be by herself.

Skraw hadn't moved. He remained sitting on the ground with his eyes half closed. Elder Woman almost kicked him but then decided to use a different motivation to get him up. She knelt at his side.

"I've given Wren herbs that will make her sleep deeply," she told him in a low voice. "I know you want to be with her. Well, now you can. You can go into her room when she's asleep."

At first, Skraw didn't seem to understand, then the words sank into his honey-addled skull. His eyes glittered. "When she goes to sleep?"

"Yes, but first we have to take care of Leaf." She pushed up, her stiff back popping in protest.

Skraw stood up too. Although a little unbalanced on his feet, he walked steadily enough as they crossed over.

Coo and Chirrup stepped aside so they could work on Leaf's ropes. Although Skraw had recovered somewhat, Elder Woman supervised him closely. Never having helped his uncles, the boy didn't know the proper way to wind and tie the ropes. Leaf ignored them except for the occasional irritated glance at Skraw fumbling with the knots. His expression lightened, though, whenever he looked at the two women waiting patiently. Eventually, the ropes were done to Elder Woman's satisfaction. They put the leash on Leaf, and everyone went inside.

To Elder Woman's surprise, Chirrup stopped before the hearth. "No one has eaten tonight. I wonder if I should cook," she said. Her plaintive voice gave her away. She didn't actually want to cook. She was only taking into consideration Coo's claims on Leaf.

Elder Woman didn't break stride as she walked past her. "You'll come with us. That honey water took away everyone's appetite." She heard Chirrup's footsteps scrambling eagerly after them.

Elder Woman told the two women that they must not untie Leaf's arms until she and Skraw closed off the room. The boulder once more covered the gap after only a short struggle. Although not yet grown, the boy's strength was close to that of his uncles'. He seemed almost fully himself again as they walked together in the flickering torch light. Perhaps the others had been stingy with him and hadn't let him drink as much.

She stopped a short distance from Wren's room. "Wait here. I'll see if she's asleep."

At first, Elder Woman tried not to make any noise. Realizing that being quiet wasn't a good way to determine how deeply Wren slept, she cleared her throat as she sank heavily onto the pallet. The only response was a light snore. Elder Woman poked her torch into a wall niche and pulled back the furs. The girl was lying on her side, facing away from Elder Woman. Only her loincloth had been removed before she'd been overcome by the need to sleep. Her tunic was still on but was bunched up over her hips, leaving her plump buttocks exposed.

The complete vulnerability of her granddaughter's bare backside almost caused Elder Woman to snatch the covers over her again. She remembered how she'd cleaned her as a baby when her moss-lined breech clouts became fouled. Raven had kept the child close, but occasionally, Elder Woman had insisted on caring for her.

An impatient cough came from the corridor. Her brow tightened. If everything went right, the girl would be getting her own baby soon for Elder Woman to help keep clean. She tugged Wren over on her back. The girl's mouth fell open, and her eyelids fluttered several times, showing the whites, but she didn't awaken. Wren's slackened face was cause for concern. The drink had been made with a lot more valerian than normal. Elder Woman leaned over to listen to her breathing. She sounded fine.

Skraw's gasp let Elder Woman know he'd entered the room. She looked up. His eyes were fixated on the girl. Once more, Elder Woman had the impulse to yank the furs back over Wren's exposed body. She wished to hide from him that place where the hair was so freshly grown that it was still downy. But instead of covering her, Elder Woman struggled onto her feet. She would not stop him. Skraw mating Wren was part of her plan for the band's rejuvenation. Without looking back, she shuffled into the corridor.

***

Elder Woman lay sleepless in her furs, thinking about everything that had happened earlier. With pleasure, her mind returned to the dancing. All eyes had been on her when she'd moved into the circle of women. The unabashed awe on her children's and grandchildren's faces had spurred her on. Forgetting her aches and pains, Elder Woman had performed the steps with a surprising surety considering that her feet were often unsteady. Not that her own rites had been weak by any means, but she should have also put together a dance—one dedicated to the sun.

She admitted with reluctant respect that Raven's performance had been extraordinarily powerful. When Raven danced alone, Elder Woman thought at one point that she'd seen a large raven flying up from the fire toward the sky. The hair on the back of her neck had risen at the sight. No normal bird would come so close to a fire. She tried to remain focused on the raven, but its blackness had melded with the night. Elder Woman believed that what she'd seen was a spirit.

That a woman of Them could conjure the spirit of her namesake bird by ceremonial means was astounding. For the only time since she'd first seen Raven, Elder Woman felt a bit afraid of the other woman. It was amazing that Raven hadn't retaliated in some way the afternoon Elder Woman slapped her.

But as Elder Woman thought about Raven's rather benign chants, her discomfort waned somewhat, even though she wasn't entirely sure that she'd understood them all. The part about the baby birds being babies of a tribe was somewhat difficult to grasp.

Eventually, something close to understanding had taken hold—at least to Elder Woman's way of thinking. Raven had wisely sung the same chant over and over in the traditional manner so that everyone could think about the words. What she'd meant had become slowly clearer. Just as birds protected their hatchlings by laying their eggs in a nest, Raven had implied that the dwellings of the clan were like nests for their infants. If that was what Raven had meant, her ideas were similar to Elder Woman's when it came to taking care of babies.

She dared think that the mother might not be completely dismayed once she found out what had taken place with her daughter that night. If anything came of it, Raven would be a grandmother. Raven would cherish the child just as much as Elder Woman would. That comforting thought soothed her for only a heartbeat before reality returned. The next morning was going to be awful if Raven found Skraw in Wren's room.

Elder Woman sat up on her pallet. She had to get Skraw out of there. He'd seen enough animals and people mating during his lifetime to know how it was done. He must have finished already. If Wren hadn't woke up, and if Elder Woman made Skraw leave before he fell asleep, then perhaps no one would realize what had happened. Because it was her first time, Wren would bleed, but she might just think she was getting her moon blood. Elder Woman arose. She stuck a torch deep within the coals until the end of it caught fire.

Elder Woman found upon reaching the room that she had no desire to see her ravaged granddaughter. "Skraw, come out of there," Elder Woman called in a low voice from the corridor. She waited, but when he didn't respond, she had little choice but to go inside.

"Grandmother."

Elder Woman jumped at hearing his voice so close by.

"I wanted to make sure that it was just you." In the dim torchlight, his naked body was a shadow flattened against the wall beside her. At least he realized what he was doing should be kept hidden.

Elder Woman's eyes were drawn against her will to the pallet like a moth to flame. She saw with relief that Wren's body was covered. Only the top of her head was visible, a bit of tousled hair showing over the fur blanket.

Elder Woman's worries about the valerian returned—the mounded form was lying too still. She went and leaned over Wren, listening again for her breath. The sounds of air entering and leaving the girl's chest were normal. She straightened and whispered to Skraw, "Put your clothes on and go to your chamber."

"Can't I stay with her longer?" His hand went down self-consciously to cover his erect member.

Elder Woman averted her eyes, wondering how many times he'd already been at her. "No, then I'll have to come back again to make sure you don't fall asleep." Her voice was a menacing hiss. "Haven't you thought about what might happen if her mother finds you here? Or your uncle Chukar? You know, don't you, that he is her birth father?" She realized by his surprised look that he hadn't known. "Never mind. Put on your things and go."

To make certain that he did leave, Elder Woman stayed in the room while he dressed. He had a cocky air about him whenever he looked over at the pallet. She worried that he couldn't be trusted to keep his mouth shut around Jay and Whit now that he'd rutted like a man. "Don't tell your uncles about this," she told him. "And don't try to sneak back in here. I'll plan a joining ceremony for you and Wren. But if that doesn't come about right away, I'll give her sleeping herbs again for you."

He nodded as if he understood then went into the corridor without bothering to take a torch. Elder Woman followed, holding the light high until he disappeared around a curve. She hoped that he comprehended the seriousness of what they'd done.

***

The next morning, Elder Woman was the only one at the main hearth even though light entering through the cave mouth showed that the day was well underway. She envied how long and well the others slept. Elder Woman had awakened throughout the night because of her aching teeth, and every time she opened her eyes, worries over Wren kept sleep from easily returning. She looked around the empty chamber, eyes drooping with weariness, glad to be alone a bit longer.

A noise down the corridor made her start. She didn't know whom she was the most nervous about seeing, Wren or Raven. When no one came in, she decided the sound had been a falling rock.

To clear the fog from her head, Elder Woman wanted to make rosemary tea, but the stone water vat was still empty. She found that her waterskin was also empty. In her nervousness the night before, she hadn't closed it well after making Wren's drink, and the water had leaked out. She immediately left the cave to get more water.

Unless she was fooling herself, it seemed to her that the sun was a bit brighter than it had been the day before. Elder Woman stood still for a moment on the path, looking at the sky. Perhaps their rituals and incantations had helped. She continued on.

When Elder Woman returned, no one as yet had come in to search for food or warmth. She hung a cooking bag of water over the barely live coals. Only a few bones and patties of bison dung were stacked nearby. Elder Woman tossed them into the fire pit. Scowling, she looked around unsuccessfully for more fuel. Winter was almost upon them, and no one had thought about gathering enough branches, bones, and dung for when the blizzards came. That would be the afternoon's task for all of them, she decided, except for Leaf, of course. They could use one of the empty chambers for storing however much fuel they found.

Thinking about Leaf, she remembered that Coo and Chirrup were still with him and couldn't get out—unless the three of them had cooperated to move the boulder aside. She didn't think Chirrup would go along with that. Above everything, she wanted to become pregnant. The thought that Leaf could possibly persuade them to set him free was unsettling enough, however, for Elder Woman to make her way down to where Jay and Finch normally stayed. She'd assumed Whit was with them and wasn't surprised at seeing the three of them sleeping huddled together for warmth.

She shook Whit's shoulder until he awoke. "Take Jay and go open Leaf's chamber."

He grunted and sat up. She caught a glimpse of their nude bodies as she turned to leave. Perhaps between the two men, they would get Finch with child—if she wasn't too old. That happy possibility lifted Elder Woman's spirits until she reached her granddaughter's room. Although the prospect of seeing Wren filled her with dread, Elder Woman felt obliged to find out if the herbs had left any lingering side effects. Thinking Wren was probably still asleep, Elder Woman intended to just check on her then leave.

Wren's chamber, however, was empty. Elder Woman stood looking at the empty pallet, unsure what to do next. Wren may have gone directly to her mother upon awakening because she remembered parts of what had happened to her during the night. Elder Woman straightened her spine. If that were the case, she might as well go ahead and face their wrath. She couldn't avoid them all day; there was work to be done. When almost to the room where Raven stayed, Elder Woman heard Wren's voice.

Elder Woman stopped a short distance from the entrance, remaining unseen in the shadows. She saw Raven holding out a small pile of moss to her daughter, who seemed reluctant to take it. Although Elder Woman couldn't follow her gabble, Wren seemed to be asking questions. Raven began answering her, then Elder Woman heard language that she did understand, words that she'd once learned from Raven. She heard Raven say, "moon blood."

She understood at once that they hadn't been lying. Wren wasn't yet a woman. Elder Woman started backing away from the room as she absorbed that dismaying piece of information. Her foot slipped into a small hollow, and a cry erupted from her throat as the torch flew out of her hands. She fell hard onto her knees. Before she could rise, Raven was standing there, her unbraided black hair falling over her shoulders as she reached out a hand to Elder Woman.

"I can get up by myself," she said.

Raven stepped back, letting Elder Woman struggle to her feet.

"I just came to tell you and Chukar that we will be gathering kindling today to store for when the blizzards come." Her knees stung painfully, but she wasn't about to complain.

"I don't know where Chukar has gone, but I'll gladly help."

Elder Woman forewent her usual tirade about Chukar's constant elusiveness. Her mind was elsewhere. Perhaps it was better to pretend that she hadn't heard what they'd said. That way, she could find out if either of them would tell her about what they mistakenly thought was Wren's newly changed status to womanhood. "Will you find Wren and tell her to come with us? I haven't seen my granddaughter yet today," Elder Woman lied.

Raven's face gave nothing away as she stood blocking the room entry. "Yes, I'll fetch her after I braid my hair."

Elder Woman nodded. She picked up the almost-extinguished torch and limped back through the corridors, careful not to fall again. Although relieved that Wren hadn't suffered any harm from the sleep medicine, Elder Woman was overflowing with outrage that Raven hadn't immediately told her about Wren's blossoming. That must mean Raven didn't want her daughter to join with Skraw in ceremony.

*Well, I will see about that.* Wren couldn't remain a child

forever. Her true moon blood might start any day. They would change their minds if the girl became pregnant.

\*\*\*

That afternoon, while the band gathered limbs and whatever else they could find to burn, Elder Woman again noticed that the day was brighter than any since the explosion. She almost remarked upon it but decided to keep her thoughts to herself. Perhaps the cloudless sky was deceiving her old eyes, or the breathtaking cold had something to do with the better light. Elder Woman eased over to work near Wren for a while, eyeing her stealthily. As Wren broke off pieces of dead brush before throwing them onto a carrying skin, the girl seemed distracted, her normally smooth brow wrinkled as she worked erratically. The cracking, popping sounds from the dry branches often paused for long periods.

Elder Woman was about to chide her over how slowly she worked when Wren bent over and picked up the skin, bundling the brush into it. A quick flash of pain crossed her face as she straightened and swung the load over her back. Elder Woman stopped working to watch her walk toward the cave. The expression had been stronger than a mere wince. Although Wren had no recollection of Skraw's attentions from the night before, her body had a memory of its own.

What Elder Woman had done fully sank in as Wren disappeared inside, the truth of it colder and sharper than an icicle. She'd enabled one grandchild to take advantage of the other one, who, according to the norms of her people, was still a child. Elder Woman didn't know if she had the wherewithal to complete what she'd started. She mentally shook herself. *I must continue.*

Although she'd grown strong as she approached womanhood, Elder Woman had been puny and timid as a small child.

Her mother admitted that she'd almost exposed Elder Woman at birth. She would have done so but for the newborn's insatiable desire for the breast that convinced her the baby would thrive.

Elder Woman had remained alert her entire life, fighting any weakness that needed correcting, whether a failing of the body or mind. She'd become all too aware that old age was a fight she would ultimately lose. No matter animal or human, death was the penalty for being born. To give in without a battle, however, wasn't in her nature. Elder Woman refused to succumb until she'd accomplished the survival of her people. She would go out defiantly, leaving as many descendants as possible.

# CHAPTER 16

*Leaf*

A BITTER COLD CLUTCHED THE LAND in an unrelenting freeze that took hold much earlier than usual. Instead of late autumn, the weather had become more like deep winter. Or it would have been, except that it hadn't yet snowed much. For that, Leaf was grateful. Hauling firewood on his back with his arms bound was difficult enough without having to wade through snowdrifts.

He had only himself to blame for being out in the weather instead of inside the relatively warm cave. When he'd complained about the small amount of firewood Whit brought one morning, Whit told him they were traveling a lot farther from the cave to find fuel. Everything nearby had been used up. "I'd rather be hunting," Whit had muttered.

Fetching firewood was usually women's work, but Elder Woman always demanded that everyone do their part. Craving fresh air and wide spaces, Leaf volunteered to help. To his surprise, Elder Woman had consented. The band took him along that very afternoon. Even though his arms weren't untied to gather wood, they could use him to carry it.

After everyone gathered a load and an extra amount for Leaf, the whole group started back to the cave. Leaf was the last one in line, following the women as they walked through the dense wooded area that surrounded several springs. Elder

Woman hadn't come with them, so he wasn't being watched as carefully. He wondered how quickly Jay and Whit would catch on if he stood still and simply let the others walk away from him. Once they were out of sight in the trees, he could turn and run. The forest covered only a small area. Provided that the sticks poking out of the bundle on his back didn't sideswipe a tree and knock him down, he would soon reach the plains, where he could move faster.

His body tensed in anticipation of quietly stopping. Coo was ahead of him in line. She knew how badly he wanted his freedom; perhaps she wouldn't call out an alarm if she noticed when the sound of his footsteps behind her ceased.

Coo was a very affectionate young woman. He would miss her, and Leaf imagined her angst once he was gone. Chirrup might also be dismayed. She'd only told him that morning that she could be pregnant. She was holding off telling Elder Woman until completely sure. What would she think if he vanished without warning?

Irritation went through him at how his unwanted consideration of the two women weakened his resolve. But perhaps escape didn't make sense at the moment. The sun had already sunk low in the sky. He would have to somehow rid himself of the heavy firewood on his back and find a jagged edge of a boulder to cut the ropes around his arms. He might freeze to death if he didn't manage to start a fire before nightfall. Leaf eyed the lowering sun again then shook his head. Escape was not possible that day. At least that was what he told himself, hoping he wasn't just making excuses to not leave.

Why they'd put him last in line, Leaf didn't know. Apart from the fact that he could escape more easily, being hindmost would have made sense only if his arms weren't tied and he had a spear. His branches were longer than those the others were hauling, preventing him from easily twisting his torso. As it was, he couldn't watch his own back, much less protect the people in front.

He spoke out loudly in the Fire Cloud tongue, the words meant for Raven's ears. She was the first woman in line after the other men. "Perhaps you'd walk in the rear and scout for us, Raven." His breath created a cloud that blew over Coo's laden back. "My load is overly wide. I can't turn around if I hear something following us." Any of the others were just as capable of scouting behind, but he wanted to make her respond to him, to come closer.

She didn't answer.

He frowned as the silence dragged on, the tight icy muscles of his brow scrunching painfully.

"We're almost out of the woods," she finally called back. "Then we won't have to walk behind each other."

Several moons had passed since Raven snuck into his room. He was tired of being ignored. Even if she wouldn't leave with him, he needed her help in persuading Elder Woman that he should be freed before the heavy snows came. The old woman kept insisting that he wait until Coo's baby was born before he left. Raven may have forgotten their two younger children, but he had not. The passage of time had only made him more anxious to know if they and his sister's family had survived the explosion.

He didn't understand Raven's lack of concern. "Cold-hearted lion woman," he muttered under his breath. She'd taken another mate, leaving her cubs from her time with Leaf to fend for themselves. At least Windy and Sky weren't around for Chukar to kill off the same way a male lion would have eliminated the cubs fathered by another male.

Leaf knew in his heart that those thoughts were unfair and that Chukar would never do such a thing. But the comparison stoked his anger, keeping him focused on freedom. Coo, Chirrup, and their coming babies were distractions that he must fight. Leaf realized that if he left, he would never see the two women again, and on a certain level, the thought saddened him. Without them, he would have lost his mind. They'd been nothing but good to him—if he didn't take into consideration that neither had helped him escape.

He decided to try another tactic on Raven. "I thought a large amount of fuel had been stored for the winter. Not that I'm above hauling firewood, but I could help more if they'd let me hunt."

To his chagrin, Raven answered in the Longhead tongue so that their conversation was no longer personal. "We did have a goodly pile of wood and dung and bones besides, but we've already burned most of it." She paused. "Elder Woman didn't listen when I brought up that one of her best hunters was being wasted."

Leaf's disappointment diluted his gratitude that Raven had spoken to the old matriarch about the matter. She obviously hadn't tried hard enough. His voice was harsh and dry. "Then your plea wasn't any more effective than that Earth Mother ceremony. I remain tied and useless, and the sun still has enough dirt across its face to make the earth a cold—"

"The sky *is* somewhat clearer. Be patient. The spirits don't always respond quickly."

Chirrup cleared her throat loudly, interrupting their conversation. "Whit and Jay have talked about taking you hunting."

Leaf imagined that the two men's ears perked up at hearing her say what they might have discussed in secret. The trees were giving way to brush and dead grass. He trotted around the women and went up beside Whit, who was leading the group. Careful not to scrape him with the branches sticking out from his back, Leaf turned toward Whit slightly. "Did you ask Elder Woman if I could go with you?"

Giving Leaf a warning look, Whit quickened his stride. "We haven't mentioned it yet," he said over his shoulder. "We will do so soon." The rigid set of the man's broad back under his wolverine cape discouraged Leaf from pushing his cause. He stood aside.

"Father," Wren blurted in the Wind tribe tongue as she passed by him.

He thought she wished to ask him something, but then she frowned and turned her head away.

"My daughter," Leaf replied belatedly, but she didn't say what was on her mind. He dropped back in line behind Coo, trudging with the group back to the cave.

***

Some days later, Elder Woman came, accompanied by Whit and Jay. After pushing the boulder aside, all three entered. Leaf was alone at the time, both legs and arms tied. He hadn't seen Chirrup or Coo since the afternoon they'd all collected fuel. He hoped that Elder Woman hadn't forbidden them to visit anymore once Chirrup told her that she was pregnant.

Elder Woman pointed at the brothers. "They've asked that you join them in a hunt. They want you to spear an animal your way." She shrugged. "Harrumph. I don't see how the point is able to puncture the hide, but they say that you have killed animals from large distances by throwing your spear." With a flip of her hand, she let Whit know that he should talk.

Whit's fingers made the symbol for aurochs. "Aurochs are using a trail through the forest to reach a spring. The path is too narrow and full of tree roots to dig a pit trap. It is a very small herd, led by an old female. When we set an ambush and charged them, she heard us running through the dead leaves and bellowed a warning. The herd scattered back through the woods, running toward the steppes. We barely saw them before they were gone. They will stop using the trail if we keep trying and failing."

Leaf nodded. "I'll help, but your spears are too heavy for throwing. I'll have to make one first."

"We have the spear you carried."

At first, Leaf didn't know what spear Whit meant, then he realized they must have brought his with them the day he was captured. The two men had often made fun of Leaf's spears and the way he hunted, but now they wanted him to use his supposedly defective skills. "So, I'm no longer a coward because I throw my spear from a long distance?"

All three Longheads looked at him blankly. He realized they didn't grasp that he was being sarcastic.

"You are not a coward," Jay finally said.

"Ah, now that we understand each other, I'll help. But I also have a request." He looked up at Elder Woman. "Could we talk alone?"

She paused then indicated with a curt flick of her hand that Whit and Jay should go into the corridor. As soon as they'd gone out, she asked, "Well, what is it?"

"I will be happy to hunt those aurochs. But first, I want to be alone with Raven for a while."

Elder Woman watched him closely, her expression unsure.

"I am her mate, after all. We had your ceremony. You were there."

Her expression became sly as she grasped the reason behind his request. "And when Chukar finds out?" She tapped her head. "That one is unpredictable. I have little control over him. Whit and Jay are sharing Finch, but I don't think Chukar will want to share Raven. Men die fighting over women." Her bad teeth showing, Elder Woman flashed a smile as if his potential demise pleased her greatly. But then she shook her head. "You can't hunt if you're dead."

"But I won't hunt unless I see her. Chukar doesn't have to know," Leaf said hurriedly.

Her brow lowered menacingly as she contemplated him. The way Skraw's face had looked as he wielded a stick went through Leaf's mind.

He pressed on. "Raven won't tell Chukar. She doesn't want trouble, either."

Elder Woman grimaced. "You are a greedy man. I'd think that Coo and Chirrup would be enough." She turned toward the opening. "You can be with her *after* the hunt—once there's meat in the cave."

He watched her go. The coming hunt provided the chance Leaf had been waiting for. They would have to untie his legs as well as his arms and hands; no one could effectively throw a spear with his legs tied. He'd wanted another stab at persuading Raven to come with him. As it was, he would have to leave without seeing her again.

***

Leaf had shed both hand mitts and a large parka so that he could freely cast the spear, but his shivering threatened to spoil his aim. He gritted his teeth against the cold. Skraw's head came around at the small sound. The boy signed that he should be quieter. Leaf threw him a biting look, his frustration at a slow boil.

Not only had they left the boy guarding him, but Leaf still had ropes to contend with. Even though his arms and legs were free, several ropes tied around his waist kept him tethered to a tree. He would have to put down his weapon in order to untie them, leaving himself open to an immediate attack from Skraw. If Leaf defended himself against Skraw by using his spear, then Jay would hurry over. Then Leaf would be forced to kill or at least wound Jay, but Leaf didn't believe he could bring himself to harm the man.

Although his hoped-for escape was thwarted, Leaf admired their planning. They'd clearly anticipated that he might try to get away. The brothers had also set up a type of ambush they'd never used before. Hidden behind a leafy screen of branches, Leaf was to wait until the hindmost aurochs was going by on the path before throwing his spear through an opening in the foliage. As soon as the injured animal panicked, Jay was to rush forward and howl at the beasts, making them all surge forward. That would ideally prevent them from turning around and fleeing back to the steppes.

Chukar and Whit would then charge out of their hiding place. If Leaf's spear hadn't killed the aurochs outright, then they and Jay had the job of isolating and finishing off the animal. Skraw's only participation, other than being a guard, was to help frighten the aurochs by howling along with Jay. Leaf gave Skraw a quick look. If the boy resented having no part in the actual kill, he wasn't showing it.

A low grunting sound brought Leaf's full attention to the trail. The first aurochs, the wily old matriarch, was in sight. His stomach clenched. Everything—not only the fresh meat, but also his agreement with Elder Woman—depended upon his skill with the spear. She'd been adamant. Without a kill, he wouldn't see Raven. Leaf hoped that he could still throw accurately. Many moons had passed since he'd hunted.

But he needn't have worried. As soon as the hind aurochs was directly in front of him, his body knew exactly what to do. His arm drew smoothly back then snapped forward, his torso twisting slightly, his leg following through as he released the shaft. The spear flew across the opening and entered the beast exactly at the spot he'd aimed for, low under the right shoulder.

With a bellow, it leapt forward, mounting the aurochs in front, spear sticking out from its side. The entire herd surged forward. Skraw let loose a wolf howl; Jay's wail followed immediately. Leaf threw back his head and joined them. All the frustration of the previous moons poured from his throat. He became so lost within the mournful sound wracking him that he momentarily forgot his surroundings. He sensed rather than saw the boy's movement beside him as Skraw sprinted away down the path after Jay.

When Leaf realized he was alone, he stopped howling. That was his chance, but instead of immediately untying the rope around the tree, Leaf became frozen by indecision. If he ran, he would probably never again see Raven—the one person who'd made life worth living, until Sky and Windy had been born. Whoops of joy came from within the woods. The kill had been successful. If Leaf stayed and Elder Woman honored her promise, then he would be with Raven—but only for a short while. That was an unsatisfactory swap for freedom. Leaf groaned as he turned toward the tree. His children would have to be enough to keep him going.

The knots were cleverly made. Skraw returned while Leaf was fumbling with them. He snatched his hands away and stood still, hoping that the boy hadn't noticed what he was doing—but Skraw wasn't that dumb. He ran toward Leaf, holding his spear like a club.

Leaf dodged the blow, but his feet became tangled in the ropes, and he slipped. Upon landing on the ground, he flipped over onto his back. Skraw's features were contorted by bloodlust as he aimed the spear. Leaf sucked in a large breath. When Jay appeared beside the boy, Leaf nosily released the air.

Jay pushed Skraw's spear aside. He eyed Leaf, shaking his

large head, his lips pursed in irritation. "We'll put a load on his back," he said to Skraw. "But first, help me tie his arms." Jay reached a hand down to help him up.

Leaf grasped it, thankful that Jay wasn't overly upset. "The aurochs looked to have very little flesh on it," Leaf said, behaving as though he hadn't just tried to escape once more.

Jay played along. "Yes, but it's become harder to find any game at all. We will eat for a while now at least."

Skraw looked from his uncle to Leaf and back again, his confusion obvious. He shrugged then began helping Jay with the ropes.

As soon as the animal was butchered, Whit and Jay tied its legs onto Leaf's back. They weren't very heavy, the animal having been emaciated as they'd noted earlier. Whichever shoulder he looked over, Leaf could see two hooves sticking out past his body. Perhaps they would let him have one of the legs.

Regardless of the less-than-adequate kill, there would be feasting that night, but Leaf took little pleasure in anticipating the meal. His teeth ached from clamping them whenever he thought about how he'd become paralyzed once Skraw left. He'd wasted a good opportunity for freedom. All because of Raven. *Elder Woman better come through on her promise.*

Elder Woman had assumed he wished to assert his ceremony-sanctioned mating rights. And Leaf did want to do that, although if he had a choice, he would rather wait until Raven escaped with him. His breath quickened just at the thought of once more pressing into her familiar body. He enjoyed Coo and Chirrup, but they didn't stir the same level of desire that he'd always felt for Raven. Elder Woman was right. He was greedy—like those bull elks that rutted with many females. He hadn't been challenged by other males the way those animals continuously faced off against one another. But that might soon change.

He didn't desire to fight Chukar, so he hoped Raven would keep her mouth closed about whatever passed between them. But perhaps there wouldn't be any reason for her to lie about where she'd been. A bottomless misery opened when it crossed his mind that Raven might not want him that way anymore.

Surely, she would not deny him. They *had* been joined by ceremony. All peoples, including the Longheads, performed rituals that carried within their hearts promises of one kind or another. Without ceremony, they were like the beasts, thoughtlessly searching the land for food and shelter during all the turns of the seasons.

He shivered once again from the cold, wondering for the first time in his life how the animals managed to survive such frigid weather. At least the band had fire. As they trod along bent under their loads, he listened to the crunching sound made by the yellowed, frozen grasses under his feet.

***

Elder Woman brought Raven in during late afternoon, fulfilling her part of the bargain. After Whit and Jay opened his room, they began untying him as if nothing unusual were happening. Leaf didn't yet dare look at Raven. He wondered if Elder Woman had ordered the men not to tell Chukar that she was with him.

When Leaf was freed, Jay and Whit went into the Corridor, but Elder Woman didn't immediately follow them. "I told her about our promise," she said. "I brought you this." She dropped a bag beside him. "It's part of the liver." Astounded, he stared at the bag. She'd given him some of the choicest meat, for once showing a bit of gratitude.

After Elder Woman went out and the boulder was pushed back in place, Leaf allowed his eyes to finally meet Raven's. He thought she might be angry about the way he'd bargained for her as if she were a fine piece of flint, but her beaming face was full of kindly affection. The small gap between her top teeth was as enticing as ever. She'd looked at him in such a way the first time they'd kissed, and her gaze then had mended him and made him whole. *Oh no*, he thought, feeling something like panic. He must stay at least partly aloof.

Leaf rubbed his arms where the ropes had been. The numbness wasn't too bad. "Sit down," he said more brusquely than he'd intended. "I'll cook the liver. It's better cooked than raw."

She hesitated before sitting. "Wouldn't you like for me to do it?"

"No. I will." He wanted her to remember how he'd prepared food for her the day of their joining ceremony.

The liver was already cut into smaller pieces. They sat quietly as he made two skewers out of a couple of the thinner branches in his firewood. After filling each stick, he held them over the small hearth fire. The meat began steaming right away.

She watched him from the other side of the fire. "How did you persuade her to let you hunt?"

"I didn't have to. She came to me."

Silence filled the small room again, broken only by the sizzling drip of meat juices into the fire. Leaf tilted his head back, breathing in the rich aroma of liver. From under his lashes, he watched Raven swallow several times.

"The smell is making me dizzy with hunger," she said.

Bringing both skewers, he moved over beside her. "Then we shall eat," he told her solemnly. He took hold of a piece to slide it off but immediately snatched his hand away. In his eagerness, he'd burned himself. She laughed, and the sound was as pleasant as the burbling of a running brook. It had been too long since he'd heard her laugh.

"So impatient, but I know how you feel. I can barely wait."

Leaf gave her a sharp look. Perhaps he was mistaken, but

he didn't think she was talking only about the liver. She held his eyes; they were soft and knowing. His loins stirred, and he looked away to focus on the skewers, blowing on the meat to cool it. After a moment, he was able to slide off a small section. He moved it slowly toward her, and she opened her mouth. Her teeth grazed his fingers as he placed the piece on her tongue. She devoured it greedily while he watched.

Raven stopped chewing. "Aren't you going to eat?"

"I've lost my appetite at the moment—for food, that is." He stacked the skewers on a stone near the fire. "The meat will be warm enough later."

Without hesitation, she took off her cape, stood, and began pulling her tunic up and over her head. Leaf quickly took off his clothing. At least he wasn't worried about offending her with his smell. They'd brought him enough water to wash with the day before.

He'd never been one to rush his lovemaking, but now that he was finally with her, Leaf became frantic. He tried to take his time, to go slowly, to do all the things he knew that she enjoyed. But he quickly lost restraint, joining with her in a frenzy that ended all too quickly.

Leaf draped a fur over his shoulders against the cold and went to retrieve the skewers. "I was too fast," he said. Smiling wryly, he handed her one of the skewers and sat down. "You'd think I was an overly eager boy."

"I was no better. It's only because we've been kept from each other." She reached for her cape and, to his disappointment, also covered her nakedness.

He quirked an eyebrow. "Once we've eaten, and if they will leave us alone for a while longer…"

She was just before putting another piece in her mouth, but she paused first to give him one of her smiles, and it seemed so natural to be with her. But nothing was as it should be, he reminded himself. He was sure that never before had a man been stolen by a tribal matriarch to impregnate the women in her band.

"I don't know how much time Elder Woman will give us," he said, "but I do have something important to discuss with you."

"Then we'll have to take turns. I too have something that I want to talk about. You go first."

He took a quick breath. "The animals are scarce on the plains and in the forest. They've migrated elsewhere. The ones left are skittish and starved. As was the aurochs today." He waved a skewer in the air. "This liver and the marrow are the only fat to be had from that puny beast. We'll sicken without more fat. They'll ask me to hunt again. Jay and the other men need me—and my throwing arm." He gave her a sideways look. "I could have escaped today. After I hit the aurochs, they left me by myself."

"Why didn't you?"

"Because of you. Another chance will come, and when it does, I want you to come with me." He watched her closely. "Hide a cache of food and weapons somewhere in the direction of our old camp. Paint the Fire Cloud symbols you and I know so well on trees and rocks to show me the way to the cache. Then let me know when all is ready. The next time they take me hunting, go to the cache. I'll meet you there."

"And I'm to leave Wren behind?"

Leaf realized that he'd made the same mistake as the last time they'd talked by not including Wren. "Bring her if possible. If not, then we'll return for her in the spring."

She threw him a skeptical look.

"She's always been my daughter, Raven. I won't forget her." He began eating a small chunk of liver.

"Leaf, we don't even know if our children are still at the

same place." She cleared her throat. "We may have to search for them, and when we do, everybody here should come with us, Wren and the others."

His throat spasmed so that he choked on the liver. For a few heartbeats, the only sound in the room was his coughing. "What?" he sputtered, staring at her in disbelief.

"We'll all leave in the spring," she said. "By then, the babies will be born, or at least most of them. Finch won't have hers until early summer."

"Finch is pregnant, too?"

She nodded, an excited smile of joy lighting up her face. "Yes, the band will soon have three young ones. In order for mothers and babies to survive the winter, we must stay. We can't just sneak away."

"And Elder Woman will follow along, docile as a newborn mountain sheep when we leave. Have you been chewing morning glory seeds from your medicine bag?"

Raven's happy expression went away, replaced by a patient calmness that infuriated him. He'd seen that look on her face while she treated those who were bad-tempered during their illnesses.

"Elder Woman is in no condition to stop us," she said. "The pain in her mouth worsens daily. She says that she throws away the pain potions I give her, but she's lying. Elder Woman believes that Chukar's wound healed after I gave him pain medicine. She hopes the same will happen for her, but it won't. I've offered to pull her rotted teeth—she won't allow it. Elder Woman will either come with us or die alone in these caverns."

He couldn't believe that she was asking him to go along with such a scheme. "Even if Elder Woman died before we left, and the others agreed to follow us, I can't impose on the Wind band that way. And what about Chukar? Is he coming along? If so, then what just happened between us must not mean anything to you. Why is it that you won't leave him? I know that he saved you, but you don't belong to him. Cast him aside and be with me once more."

"I don't wish to cast anyone aside. Not him nor Elder Woman." She gulped, the strain of explaining beginning to show. "Leaf, listen to me. Elder Woman is desperate. They haven't come across another Longhead band for a long time. Although she's trying to save her band, what she's really fighting for is to keep her kind of people from vanishing completely." She raised her hands in a placatory gesture. "Not that I agree with how she's gone about it. But perhaps she couldn't think of a better way."

He banged a fist on the cave floor. "I can't believe you're taking her side. How can you ask me to forget the despicable way they stole me and Wren? Maybe they *should* vanish from the earth."

She made a small frustrated sound, and her eyes appeared watery all of a sudden. "I don't think Elder Woman will live much longer, but what about Coo, Chirrup, and their babies? They're your babies as well. Should they vanish also? I suppose you'll just say that babies die all the time, and there's nothing to be done about it."

Leaf squirmed as he struggled to harden himself against her tears. She couldn't be reasoned with. He looked away, focusing his gaze elsewhere, no longer wanting to spar.

But Raven hadn't given up trying to persuade him. She dashed away her tears and moved around in front of him, forcing him to look into her eyes. They were pools of sadness. "Aren't you concerned about the survival of your blood children—the children of your body?"

He sighed. "I don't wish them dead, Raven. But what you're planning just won't happen."

"And why not? We'll take anyone with us who wants to

come, and we'll go find Sky and Windy, and we'll ask your sister's family to join us in forming a new tribe. They weren't happy with Fin's leadership; many others besides them were also discontented."

Leaf's head was spinning from trying to put together everything she'd told him. He was unclear as to which man Raven would end up with in the new tribe she spoke of. She'd said something about not casting anyone aside. Surely she didn't believe he would share her. Leaf didn't want to think about her and Chukar mating, much less talk about it, but he had to know what she meant.

Finding the right words was difficult. Before he could ask his questions, the boulder scraped along the cave floor. Startled, they both turned toward the opening. Raven threw off her cape, grabbed her tunic, and pulled it over her head. Whit and Jay stopped short when they saw her dressing. They looked away while she struggled with her leggings.

"I'm almost ready," she told them. She thrust on her boots. "We'll talk again," she said to Leaf in the Fire Cloud tongue.

A keen resentment pricked him as he watched Raven stand and smooth down her tunic. Everything had been going so well until she told him her foolish ideas. They should have been lying together again instead of arguing. Picking up her cape, she starting turning away. Leaf held up a skewer. "You haven't finished your liver."

Anger rippled over her face at the derision in his voice. She snatched the stick from him. "I'll share it with the pregnant women. They need the fat," she said and strode out.

Jay and Whit picked up the ropes. They looked at him warily as if they thought he might bite them. Leaf was riled enough to put up a fight, but he knew better than to try them. He wouldn't accomplish anything other than a humiliating defeat.

She'd dressed so quickly, she hadn't put on her loincloth. Leaf wadded it up and threw it onto the fire. Smoke immediately began billowing into the room. Jay lifted out the strip of leather with a piece of firewood and tossed it aside.

# CHAPTER 17

*Raven*

RAVEN HAD FORGOTTEN TO TAKE along a torch when she left Leaf's room. Still grasping the stick that held the liver, she sat a short way down the corridor and cried. When Jay and Whit came out from retying Leaf, she stood to go with them. Forgetting themselves, they openly stared as she followed along. Raven was aware that the People considered unrestrained weeping an excessive display of emotion, but she couldn't staunch the tears. To not be offensive, she muted her sobs. They soon reached the passage that split off to her own chamber.

"Just give me one of the torches," she gasped. "I'll go on alone."

Whit passed his over, and she dipped her head, thanking him. She watched them leave, their bulky forms soon swallowed by the gloom. His expression had seemed to show concern. Raven wondered how the brothers would have responded if she'd explained her distress.

"I want us to become a new tribe," she said as if Jay and Whit were still there with her. "But Leaf won't even consider the idea. He's once more become the bruised bee he was when I first saw him." She waved the torch in the direction they'd gone. "One reason for his bad temper is that your people twice stole him from his family—when he was a child and now again." She sighed in frustration. Even if they did hear, nothing would change. They would keep following Elder Woman's orders, as always.

If he saw her, Chukar would wonder about her weepy-eyed discomposure. She hurried along the quiet tunnel, hoping to avoid him until she was calmer and had wiped her face with water. When Jay and Whit came earlier to take her to Elder Woman, he'd already left to go chop up large tree limbs he'd hauled to the cave the day before. She hesitated before the woven mat they'd recently hung over the opening to keep warmth from escaping. Not hearing anything within, she pushed the mat aside. He hadn't yet returned.

She'd almost finished cleaning her eyes and runny nose with a dampened chamois when he came in. As was his way, Chukar didn't say anything, just stood watching her. She finished with the rag and lowered her hands. His nostrils suddenly flared.

She thought he was smelling the liver that was on a stone near the fire, but after only giving it a quick glance, he walked over to her. He breathed in deeply, and Raven realized that she should have used the chamois on other more intimate body parts before her face. She'd often seen Longheads, men and women alike, sampling the air, their large noses up and twitching like wolves catching an interesting scent. His jaw tightened, his eyes narrowed, and she understood that he knew. Perhaps he'd even seen his two brothers, and though they hadn't told him where she'd been, he may have sensed something was amiss and had come to find her.

Many times during her life, she'd been faced with impossible choices. This was just such an occasion. But Raven refused to choose one man over the other. She only prayed that Leaf's bitterness would somehow fade and that he would eventually understand her better. She was capable of finding an equal place in the landscape of her heart for each man, just as she had for all three of her children. Leaf didn't yet realize that he could be happy following her vision.

At the moment, though, Chukar was the one Raven was faced with appeasing. She dropped the chamois onto the cave floor. "I will not leave you," she said. "I will live with you until one of us dies."

His chin lifted as he considered her words. For once, all of his emotions were there on his face, flitting across his features one at a time—hope, despair, then something darker.

Raven searched her mind for anything she could tell him that would help blunt what he saw as her betrayal. "Leaf and I were joined by ceremony. He's the father of my children. We—"

"Wren," Chukar said.

He didn't have to remind her of their unique tie. Their daughter was a gift from the Earth Mother, not only to them but also to the yet unborn peoples of the world. Her dream about the babies on the hillside had opened Raven's eyes to a startling possibility. Once Wren had children, and those children had their own children, and so on, then some blended part of Chukar and herself would live forever. Raven felt happy about all those special people who might come into existence because of what she and Chukar had done long ago beside the pool. A little smile sprang to her lips.

Her smile didn't placate him whatsoever. Perhaps he thought she made light of their bond. He grasped her arm in a painful grip as if she might flee him. Raven winced but stood her ground. He gave the tunic she wore a quick tug with his other hand, letting her know that he wanted her to remove it.

In spite of the chilliness, she began taking off everything, just as she had for Leaf. Raven realized after pulling the tunic over her head that she'd left her loincloth in Leaf's room. She glanced at Chukar, but he was busy shedding his own clothing and hadn't noticed it was missing.

When they were both unclothed, he looked down at her abdomen for a moment then placed his hand over the flatness between her pelvic bones. He raised his eyes to meet hers. With just the barest movement of her head, she let him know the answer to his unspoken question. As far as Raven knew, she wasn't with child. She hadn't been aware until then that Chukar had been hoping to impregnate her. As he pulled her down, guiding her onto her hands and knees, Raven understood that he was trying to reassert his claim. Chukar thought she would stay with him if she were pregnant with his child.

He began taking her roughly. Looking over her shoulder into his agitated face, she cried out in protest. He was more upset than she'd realized. His eyes focused on hers, and he pulled away. Raven lowered herself and turned so that she was lying on her back. Before he could think that she was rejecting him, she reached out her arms. He eased down, slowly pushing into her.

Although he was trying to control himself, Raven could sense the anger lying just beneath his skin. She hoped that Whit and Jay were at the main hearth and would stop Chukar later if he headed for Leaf's room. To her relief, he stayed with her for the rest of the day, only going out once to relieve his bladder in the distant chamber they sometimes used. Raven thought that he'd believed her when she said that she wouldn't leave him. She hoped to keep her promise.

*** 

Because of the freezing weather and limited kindling, Elder Woman told them one evening that the band would start sleeping together in small groups. Raven found it surprising that Elder Woman didn't demand that they all sleep in the same room. It said something about the tensions within the band that she'd deviated from the traditional way to keep warm during the coldest days of winter.

Finch, Whit, and Jay were already spending every night together. Chirrup and Coo happily agreed to stay with Leaf. They would go to his chamber during early evening and leave the following morning when Whit and Jay took him out for a short while. Skraw would move in with Elder Woman. Assignments were going smoothly until a heated disagreement arose over where Wren would sleep.

Chukar agreed with Raven that Wren should stay with them, but Elder Woman had other ideas. Her granddaughter should come be with her and Skraw.

Chukar responded immediately. "Ot!" His hand emphatically cut through the air.

Raven stole a quick look at Wren. She was ignoring the argument swirling around her, her attention on a digging stick she was sharpening, methodically slicing the end into a blunt point. Then Raven glanced over at Skraw. Elder Woman had obviously forgotten how he'd pestered Wren for a while after her arrival. When he saw Raven looking, the boy openly stared back, a smirk on his face. She frowned and turned to Elder Woman. Before she could open her mouth, Wren began shouting.

"I don't want to stay with anybody!" she yelled. "I'll cover up with more skins to keep warm."

Faced with Wren's vehement opposition, Elder Woman backed down. "Harrumph! Very well. But when we run out of kindling, you'll think differently."

Raven stared at the older woman in surprise. She'd given in so quickly.

Once alone with Wren, Raven begged her to change her mind. "Please stay with us. Then you won't have to worry about Skraw sneaking in on you." Raven remembered how he'd earlier gaped so smugly, as if he had a secret that she wasn't in on. "He hasn't tried that trick again, has he?"

"No. He knows I'd fight him off. Besides, he doesn't frighten me anymore," she said.

Raven doubted that was true, but she didn't insist again that Wren move in with her. Maybe if no one pushed her, she would decide to on her own.

Over the next few days, Raven gathered flat smooth stones for heating that everyone could put into their pallets at night, making sure that Wren had more of the small slabs than anyone else. To her amazement, the People had never heard of using heated rocks to keep warm. They took the stones from her, but she didn't think they would actually use them. It was such a simple thing, but it showed Raven how resistant they were to change. She worried that they might view her idea of forming a new tribe even more negatively than had Leaf.

As the days went by, Raven felt more and more like a fraud. Her efforts to bring back normalcy to the world hadn't achieved much, as Leaf had so cruelly pointed out. Although the sun did shine a bit brighter, the air remained clouded by debris. For all the good their ceremonies had done, she and Elder Woman would have been better off using their energy to store dried food and roots for the starving days of deepest winter. Fresh meat would become even rarer when the already-scarce game searched out hidden areas in which to shelter from the freezing winds.

Even though heavy snows always made life more difficult, Raven began thinking that snow was the answer to her hopes for a clear sky and possibly to shortening the winter. If the sun wasn't allowed to warm the ground, then spring might never return. The few flakes they'd received had freshened the air only a little. The world needed a snowfall so thick that even a hand held in front of one's face wasn't visible. A blizzard would surely scour the remaining dust from the sky.

Raven began chanting to the snow and ice spirits whenever she found herself alone, asking for the gift of heavy snowfall. She was far from sure her efforts would be successful. The powers of earth and air were capricious. That should have been obvious to everyone, including Leaf, but she decided it best not to ask the band to chant with her. Most of them were glad for the lack of snow that winter, and if it never happened, then Leaf couldn't point out how she'd failed again.

*** 

Another moon passed before snow finally did come. Blizzards formed, one after the other, trapping them in the cave. Wren's moon blood came upon her heavily during the cold, dark days. Her abdominal discomfort was even worse than when she'd first blossomed during the night of the ceremony. Raven recalled the strange symptoms Wren had shown then.

Her daughter had complained of experiencing bad dreams during the night after she'd awoken that morning lying on a blooded pallet, and she'd been lethargic for much of the day. Her arms and legs seemed to have lost some of their strength and were strangely floppy. All that was somewhat unusual, but Raven hadn't had much time to become alarmed, because Wren's bleeding stopped almost as soon as it started. She'd regained her arm and leg strength by afternoon. But after a handful of days, Wren had begun bleeding again for a short while. Then several moons went by before her present need for moss and thongs.

An uneasiness crept over Raven. They would soon be out of moss. She'd set aside a good bit for when icy weather kept her from finding more, but the supply was dwindling rapidly. Wren was also being abnormally silent about her suffering.

Perhaps she was simply becoming more mature, following the tribal way of enduring pain in silence. Raven decided to make a brew out of flax seeds to help lighten the flow. She'd started for her own room to locate the herb when Wren cried out, the sound a small shriek. Raven rushed back in and saw her writhing on the pallet while holding her abdomen.

Raven reached down and took her hand. "Squeeze my hand against the pain," she said. Never had she seen a woman react that way to what was a normal event every moon cycle.

Wren grasped her hand tightly, panting. After a short while, she started breathing levelly. "The pain is passing." She glanced at Raven hovering over her. "Don't look at me that way. I'm not dying. It was like a bad stomachache, but I'll need fresh moss." She used her mother's hand to pull herself up.

When Wren passed her the thong, Raven let out a strangled sound. The bloody mass nestled in the moss had the appearance of something more than moon blood.

"What is it?" Wren asked in alarm.

To hide her disquiet, Raven turned and emptied the used moss into an old ragged piece of leather. "You're fine," she lied. "But I'll make a brew for you that will help the cramping and slow down your flow." Raven rummaged in one of Wren's bags until she found more moss and a fresh thong. Struggling to remain calm, she handed both items to Wren. "Lie back down as soon as you put this on. I'll make the medicine and be right back." Taking the piece of leather containing the bloody moss with her, she rushed into the corridor.

In her practice of healing, Raven had seen enough failed pregnancies to believe that Wren was suffering a miscarriage. *How could that be?* But the most important question was—if she was right about the miscarriage—how did that come about? Although it was unlikely, Skraw came to mind immediately. Wren hated him—but Raven was positive none of the other men at the cave were responsible. The culprit had to be Skraw; he was the only one who made any sense.

Perhaps he'd raped her, and she hadn't told her mother out of shame. Raven discarded the thought at once. Wren, being Wren, would not have quietly put up with that kind of treatment. She'd said she wasn't afraid of him anymore. The boy had somehow gotten to her, persuaded her—but how?

Raven shook herself mentally, tamping down the anger that moved her like a whirlwind through the dusty corridor. If Skraw was mating her, then he would continue doing so. Raven intended to take care of Wren's immediate needs, then she would find out the truth. Whatever was going on must stop.

Chukar had gone when she slipped past the hanging mat. He was working skins with the other men in a room used solely for that purpose now that it was too cold to work outside. She wanted to be sure about Wren and what had happened before she told him.

Leaf, as Wren's stepfather, would also have to be told. He'd become part of the day-to-day life of the band. Once the blizzards started, they'd left him untied and his room open, unconcerned that he would leave. Only someone whose wits had flown would try to survive a journey in that kind of weather.

Since Leaf and Chukar were thrown together much of the time, Raven worried daily that one of them might eventually try to provoke the other. Wren's miscarriage wasn't going to help things. They might blame each other for failing to protect her. Raven put a stone cup near the fire and hurriedly searched through her packets of dried herbs, the anxiety caused by Leaf and Chukar overshadowed by her concern over Wren. Raven was going to press her daughter for the truth, and she hoped that her questions wouldn't damage their fragile rapport.

Before Raven returned to Wren with the brew, she folded the leather containing the used moss into a packet and bound it with twine. She'd hide the packet in a cold place until the ground was no longer frozen, then she would bury it. The bloody glob inside was possibly the unformed remnants of her first grandchild and as such should be treated with respect.

It turned out that Raven hardly had to pry at all. When Wren drank the crushed flax seeds steeped in warm water, she made a face. "Why do herbs taste so bad? This is worse than Elder Woman's tea."

Raven frowned. "She gives you tea? What sort of tea?"

"If you stayed longer every night, you'd know that she sometimes makes me a cup of chamomile tea for sleep before I leave the main hearth. She uses a different kind of chamomile than you do. More bitter."

"Elder Woman doesn't enjoy my company. That's why I leave early. Perhaps she mixes something with the chamomile. Stop drinking her tea until I find out what's in it. It could make you bleed more, and I think it's what makes you seem so tired some days."

"But what if she gives me a cup? If I tell her why I don't want the tea, she'll set up a ceremony with Skraw. She's always talking about him. It makes her mad if I don't listen. So I pretend to."

"Does she still constantly ask if you've had your first moon blood?"

Wren crinkled her forehead, thinking. "Not in a long while. I guess she finally gave up on that."

Raven wondered if Elder Woman's lack of interest meant something else. Perhaps she'd stopped asking because she believed her granddaughter had already become a woman. "Tell her that you can sleep well enough without the tea." Raven paused a heartbeat as an awful suspicion plopped unwanted into her mind. "No, don't do that," she said sharply.

Wren looked over, startled.

Raven wasn't about to share with her the unthinkable thoughts she was having. "You know how upset she gets if things don't go her way. You'll have to take the tea."

A plan was forming in Raven's mind. She concentrated on speaking calmly. "I'll sleep with you tonight, lest the bleeding gets worse."

Wren's expression became frightened.

"Not that I think it will," Raven added quickly. "I want you to do something for me. I'm curious about what she's putting in the tea. Ask her for a cup before leaving the front hearth this evening. But don't drink any of it. Tell her that you'll take it along to your room. I'll taste the tea when you bring it to find out what herbs she's using. If you have to, pretend to sip some."

"All right." Wren's face had brightened. She was enjoying the idea of them tricking Elder Woman. "But she always waits until I drink it then takes the cup."

Raven thought for a moment. "Do you drink it right in front of her, or do you sometimes move around the room?"

Wren shrugged. "I don't always stay right where she is."

"Good. I'll sit longer at the hearth tonight. After she makes the tea, I'll call you over for some reason or the other. My own cup will be on the floor beside me with nothing in it, and I want you to put the cup she gives you down beside it. She'll know if you return a cup that's not hers, so when she's not looking, I'll pour the tea into my cup, and you can pick up Elder Woman's empty one. After pretending to drink, give her back the cup and go to your room. I'll meet you there."

"Chukar's not going to stay with us, is he?"

"No, no. Just myself. I'll tell him you've been feeling ill lately." Raven gave her a chiding glance. "I wish you'd show him a little kindness. He was so proud to be your father when you were a baby. He still is."

Wren's gaze shifted to one side, but at least she didn't roll her eyes.

Raven left it at that. She needed Wren's complete cooperation to find out if her fears were actually well-founded.

That evening, after everyone ate a meager meal of dried meat, Raven sat in readiness. While waiting, she stitched a tunic she was making for Wren. Eventually, it became late enough for Wren to ask Elder Woman for the "special night-time tea."

The silence around the hearth wore at Raven as Elder Woman began preparing the tea. Subdued by the frigid weather, no one had felt like talking, and the usual night noises from outside were completely absent. Not even the wind could be heard through the plug of snow that covered the cave mouth. Elder Woman moving about was the only sound, except for the occasional popping of the fire.

When the cup was in Wren's hand, Raven called her over. "Put your drink down," she said. "I want to see if this tunic will be long enough. You've grown a lot lately."

As they'd planned, Wren put the tea near her mother's cup on the cave floor. Raven stood and held the partially finished tunic against Wren's body.

She saw the old matriarch's head turn their way, sunken eyes intently observing the fitting. Stymied by the attention from Elder Woman, Raven didn't know what to do. If she poured the tea into a different cup, it would surely be noticed. She pulled away the garment, folding it in half, and patted Wren on the shoulder. "Go let your grandmother see your tunic," she said.

That hadn't been part of the plan, but after giving her mother a quick look, Wren took it and dutifully meandered over.

Leaf was watching Raven with quick secretive glances, the

way he often did, but she didn't hesitate. As soon as Wren blocked Elder Woman's view, Raven bent and quickly poured the tea into her own cup.

After Elder Woman had looked over the tunic, Wren came back, handed it to her mother, and reached down to take the empty cup. Raven gathered up the tunic and other things along with the tea, readying to leave, her hands full. Luckily, she didn't need a torch to go down the corridor to Wren's room. It was usually well lit. She took a quick look at Leaf as she walked by him on the way out. He was staring at her curiously, very curiously indeed.

*** 

Later that evening, Raven lay beside Wren on a pallet near the far wall, waiting for her to fall asleep. Raven's body was rigid, her thoughts churning. Just as she'd thought, the tea had been full of various medicines, a strong brew crafted to make a person sleep heavily. When Raven took some into her mouth, the bitterness of valerian, yarrow, and ground antler skin had overwhelmed the chamomile. Other medicinal flavors as well, though not readily discernible, teased her tongue with mysterious pungency.

After a few moments, she'd vehemently spat it all out. "I don't know what all she put in it," she said to Wren. "But it's too strong."

Raven never gave yarrow to a woman who might be pregnant. It was dangerous for the sprouting bud that would grow into a baby. Surely, Raven's suspicions were wrong, and the tea was indeed only for sleep, but if Elder Woman's plot had been to impregnate Wren, then she'd doomed her own plan. Raven had always thought the other woman's healing skills were lacking—or it could be that she'd become forgetful about the dangers of certain herbs.

When Wren's breathing deepened, Raven quietly slipped out of the covers. She went and sat cross-legged within a large indentation in the cave wall near the corridor opening. The fire had burned down, but she wasn't overly cold. At her suggestion, they'd kept on their clothing to help keep warm.

Raven was dozing when a small noise alerted her. She lifted her head and saw that Skraw was in the room. The sight of him standing over her daughter shocked her completely awake. As she watched, he prodded Wren's side through the covers with a foot.

Rage seized her, and she had to refrain from rushing over and raking her fingernails across his face. Raven struggled for control. She must be absolutely sure before accusing the boy.

Wren didn't stir. If she felt his nudge, she mistakenly thought that her mother's arm or elbow had grazed her. Skraw pulled off his parka and tunic and let them drop, leaving him clothed only in his loincloth, leggings, and foot coverings. Raven hadn't truly realized how he'd grown until she saw his muscled torso in the glow of the hearth coals. A flicker of fear went down her spine. Everyone in the cave except for Elder Woman considered him strange and unreliable.

He reached down and pulled away the skins and furs. Raven jumped up, but the boy was so focused that he didn't hear or see her. Wren stirred, one hand groping for the missing coverings. Skraw took a small leap backward.

Her hand still searching for the covers, Wren realized that Raven was no longer beside her. "Mother?" she said and started sitting up.

"I'm right here."

Upon hearing Raven's voice, Skraw whirled around. The instant Wren saw him, she scrambled onto her feet. Pressing her back against the cave wall, she started screaming. Skraw let loose a loud hiss. He snatched up his clothing and fled into the corridor.

Raven rushed over to the pallet, alarmed that Wren's screams would awaken everyone. Now that her fears were confirmed, Raven needed to think about how best to approach the matter. She pulled Wren toward her. "Shh! He's gone. He won't dare come back."

Wren wrapped her arms around Raven so tightly she could barely breathe. "Thank the Earth Mother you were in here."

As her daughter babbled on in her ear about how awful Skraw was, Raven's heart became increasingly heavy. She was going to tell Wren the truth about what Skraw and Elder Woman had done even though the knowledge would fester like an open sore on Wren for many turns of the seasons. A punishing regret flooded every fiber of Raven's being. For so long, she'd given in to Wren's whims, allowing her to shamelessly manipulate those around her. She'd been a strong mother for Sky and Windy, but with Wren, her unusual and different child, she'd always been weak.

And Raven had to contend with her own ignorance. It wasn't common wisdom that a girl close to womanhood could become with child before having her first moon blood, but that was no excuse. What she'd originally mistaken for a natural occurrence had been something else entirely, and because of that error, her daughter had become pregnant right under her nose.

But Raven didn't believe she deserved all the blame. Wren should have been staying with her and Chukar all along. The girl had been born headstrong, and no amount of discipline could change that. It was time she learned, though, that ignoring her mother's guidance resulted in bad things happening.

Raven shushed her once more. "Be quiet—you don't truly understand what has happened to you." Wren leaned away to give her a wounded look. Something in Raven's face must have alerted her to the seriousness of what was about to be said, because she didn't say another word.

Wren listened in stunned silence. Even though the firelight was dim, Raven saw the color drain so quickly from the girl's face that she feared Wren might pass out. Then the crying began. Raven wondered if she'd been right to explain exactly what had taken place in the little room, not just once but, in all likelihood, many times.

Instead of the rage Raven had expected, Wren's sobs were full of hurt.

"My own grandmother did that to me," she burst out, and Raven realized that contrary to what Wren had always declared, she'd begun to feel some fondness for Elder Woman. The older woman's betrayal cut deeply.

Wren crawled under the covers, curling into herself. Raven knew there was nothing she could say to console Wren, so she rubbed her back until she stopped crying and fell asleep.

\*\*\*

When morning came, Raven sat bleary-eyed before the fire, an arm around Wren's shoulder, holding her devastated daughter closely. Having wept away her sorrow over Elder Woman's treachery before she slept, Wren had awakened full of dry-eyed bitterness. Raven knew her well. It was only a matter of time before she sought revenge. She might even demand that Skraw and her grandmother be put to death. And that was a normal enough reaction.

Within the Fire Cloud and Wind tribes, death for the pair of them would have been the likely penalty for their evildoings. At the least, they would have been whipped and banished. Elder Woman's status as a healer wouldn't have saved her. But they weren't living among the tribes, so Raven had to be cautious.

Nothing would please her more that morning than seeing Elder Woman's body lying frozen out on the plains, but that couldn't be Raven's decision alone. And she would not allow Wren to endanger herself by rashly taking matters into her own hands. She was a big girl, but Skraw was much stronger.

"I want you to come with me," Raven said. "I'm going to tell Chukar about this, and I don't want to leave you alone."

Wren's head snapped around. She gave her mother a ferocious frown. "No, I don't want anybody to know. Besides, you told me I need to lie still, so stay here with me a while longer."

"You can walk that far. Your bleeding has almost stopped, and you aren't having any pain. We have to tell the others. How else will Skraw and Elder Woman be punished?"

A shrewd expression played over her face. "You can make poisons. It will be our secret."

Never would it have occurred to Raven that Wren might ask her to kill the pair. "No. As much as I despise them, I'll not be the cause of their deaths. We'll seek justice through the tribe. Now get up."

"This is no tribe—"

Raven's voice rose. "I'm not killing them, and neither are you. But something must be done. I can protect you only so much, and what if something happens to me? If we don't involve Chukar, then you may find yourself one day bound to that boy. As soon as the blizzards stop long enough, the men will go hunting. This needs to be taken care of now." The strength of Raven's anger surprised her. The way Wren had dismissed her idea that the group should be considered a tribe had only added to her annoyance.

Reluctantly, Wren stood. Raven wasn't sure which part of her tirade had persuaded the girl. Perhaps Wren realized that under certain circumstances, she could very well end up mated to a man who had wronged her immensely.

Chukar was still asleep, but he awoke and sat up when they came in. Wren knelt on her heels, stonily watching the fire as Raven started telling him what had passed. His face darkened when she explained how she'd become suspicious of Elder Woman's teas and what they were being used for. When she told Chukar about catching Skraw uncovering his daughter, a word Raven hadn't heard before exploded out of him. Wren looked over, her sullen indifference vanishing.

Chukar threw off the skins and furs. He arose and started quickly dressing, his breathing taking on a noisy furiousness.

"All I ask is that you not hurt Skraw enough to kill him. Everyone should have a say in what needs to be done." Raven wasn't sure that he was listening. "We must *all* decide."

Without responding, he finished pulling on his clothes then strode over and snatched aside the mat covering the opening. It came loose from the stony projections holding it and fell behind him onto the cave floor as he went out. Raven hadn't asked him not to harm Elder Woman. She was suddenly very frightened. The band could break apart that very day, shattering into pieces like a poorly made stone tool.

Chukar had taken the torch that she'd brought with her. Raven hurriedly searched the area until she spotted the rope-wrapped tip of another one. She snatched it up and stuck it in the fire. As soon as the tip was lit, she grabbed Wren's hand and set out.

They hurried to the room where Elder Woman and Skraw were staying. That it was empty didn't surprise Raven. By then, Skraw would have told his grandmother about the night before. Until Elder Woman knew whether or not Raven had caught on to her involvement, she wouldn't want to be alone around Chukar. Once back in the corridor, Raven saw Chukar's torchlight farther down. To catch him, she almost began running but remembered that Wren shouldn't exert herself.

They were still a good distance away when he entered the main chamber. Within moments, loud shouting erupted from the room.

By the time they went in, Chukar was astride Skraw on the floor, hitting him in the face. Every blow sounded like meat being pounded before it was cooked. Elder woman was yelling for Chukar to stop beating him at once.

Wren moved closer until she stood near them. She watched as Chukar hit Skraw, her pitiless eyes wide with her loathing for the boy.

Elder Woman began whacking Chukar on the back with her hands. "Stop it!" she screamed over and over.

If Skraw had tried to defend himself before Wren and Raven arrived, he'd quickly given up. He didn't even attempt to escape when Chukar turned from him and violently shoved Elder Woman away. The old healer stumbled sideways and almost bumped into Wren, who scurried away just as she fell.

Finch, the only other person at the hearth, was watching in horror.

"Go fetch the others," Raven yelled, holding out the torch to her.

Finch took it and ran from the room. Chukar resumed hitting Skraw. The boy's nose and mouth were bleeding; his eyes were already swollen shut.

"That's enough," Raven shouted, but Chukar kept beating him. Raven ran to the cave mouth and scooped out snow, mounding it into a large ball. She rushed back and threw the snowball over Chukar's head.

He looked up, white powder sifting down his hair and face. She shook her head, her eyes pleading. Chukar held Raven's gaze for a long moment, as if listening to her thoughts. Then he dusted the snow off his hair and rose from straddling Skraw.

Grasping the boy's legs, Chukar began dragging him toward the cave mouth. By then, Elder Woman had managed to get onto her feet. Screeching at the top of her lungs, she limped after them. When Chukar was at the opening, he pulled Skraw upright and turned him so that he faced the cave mouth blocked with snow and ice. The boy stood unsteadily. Chukar backed up a little then pushed him forward with a hard shove. Skraw went flying into the whiteness, his body becoming suspended there like a fly stuck in milky sap.

When Elder Woman reached Chukar, she kicked and punched at him. For a heartbeat, Raven thought he might throw her in the snow also, but he warded off her blows until she stopped. Leaning into the frigid wall that surrounded Skraw, Elder Woman struggled to free her grandson.

Transfixed by the strange sight, Raven turned her head only when Jay, Leaf, and Whit sprinted into the room. Finch and the other women ran in behind them. They were all breathing hard as they looked from the cave mouth to Chukar and back again, trying to work out how Skraw had ended up stuck in the snow.

Raven straightened her shoulders, stoking up the courage to charge ahead with what had to be done. "You are all wondering why Chukar has thrown Skraw out of the cave." She pointed a finger at Elder Woman and spoke carefully as though each word had a bitter taste. "The fault lies with that woman."

Elder Woman stopped tugging at Skraw and turned to face her accuser. "How is it a fault that I want more grandchildren?"

A great sadness came over Raven that the old matriarch would try to insist her behavior had been harmless and benevolent. "I'm going to tell the band exactly what you did. Let them decide whether you've behaved correctly."

Bristling, Elder Woman crossed her arms and hunched her shoulders up high. "Everything I've done was for the good of this band."

Chukar took a step toward her. "Silence," he said. "Or you will join Skraw."

Elder Woman flinched. She gave him an evil look and moved a short distance away.

Raven held up a hand to stay him. "Being thrown into the icy snow might be the death of her. Elder Woman will be quiet. She knows that everyone must be told."

Fury reddened Elder Woman's face. She opened her mouth, but after glancing at Chukar, she closed it.

Raven turned to Chukar. "Please pull Skraw out for Elder Woman." He scowled but did as she asked, reaching over and pulling hard on an arm.

Skraw fell backward onto the cave floor. Elder Woman knelt and started frantically knocking snow from his body.

Wren was quietly slipping across the chamber. She didn't want to hear again the sad story of her violation, but Raven couldn't let her leave. "Stay in our midst, Wren," Raven ordered. "You must help decide what will be done."

Wren stopped and slowly turned around. She lowered her eyes to the stone floor when she saw all of them looking at her. Raven cleared her throat and began.

The telling wasn't yet finished when Chirrup turned her back. Raven's heart fell, but then she realized that rather than rejecting what was being said, Chirrup had begun a shunning. As Raven continued talking, Jay and Whit followed their sister's lead by turning around.

Raven could not help but be disappointed; shunning was a relatively mild punishment. But then shunning was probably the only penalty they could agree upon that wouldn't tear the band apart. Chirrup would never go along with her mother being killed, and if Elder Woman was banished—well, that was a slower death. If any of them did propose death, bitter contention would break out. Once Coo and Finch turned around, only Chukar, Wren, and Leaf remained. Their lack of response worried Raven.

She finished the tale of betrayal by telling them she believed Elder Woman's tea had caused Wren to lose the baby foisted on her by the depraved pair. All Elder Woman's schemes for Wren had come to that—a dead grandchild. Raven took a last look at the old healer's shocked face before turning her back to join the shunning. From that moment on, the woman and her grandson no longer existed. They were dead to her unless the group eventually reversed the shunning.

Chukar let out an aggrieved sound upon seeing Raven face away from Elder Woman and Skraw, but then he turned his back.

Leaf was staring at her, his face incredulous. "What? Is that all? A shunning?" He started toward Raven.

A rumble came from Chukar's throat, and with a quick look his way, Leaf paused beside the fire.

"It's what the group wants," Raven said.

"Considering what happened, it's a weak justice. Maybe I'm just a prisoner here and don't have any say, but I won't go along with it." He snatched up a torch from the hearth.

Wren was watching Leaf leave the chamber, tears streaming down her cheeks. Raven made herself stay still. Whether or not Wren left with him had to be her own decision. Ever so slowly, without looking at Raven, Wren turned her back.

# CHAPTER 18

*Elder Woman*

E LDER WOMAN LIMPED TOWARD THE main hearth, her torch bobbing with each agitated step, her shadow dancing madly along the walls. Upon awakening that morning, she'd noticed immediately that Skraw hadn't returned to the chamber to sleep. His bedding remained untouched, and she'd gone the whole night without realizing he wasn't there.

Several days before, she'd sent him out to spy. He'd told her when he came back that everyone had begun sleeping together in a distant chamber. So when she saw his empty pallet with the furs still pulled over it, Elder Woman thought for a fleeting moment that he'd been allowed to stay overnight with the others. But that kind of wishful thinking was foolish. None of them would ever go along with him sleeping in the same room as Wren.

Skraw often explored the cave complex alone. She didn't believe he'd become lost. The boy knew his way around too well. He'd told her about finding other openings that led outside so he wouldn't have to go anywhere near Chukar.

Dawn barely lit the cave mouth when she walked into the front chamber. Even so, Chirrup and Coo were already sitting at the hearth. From their tired eyes, Elder Woman knew they hadn't slept well. Something had changed during the night.

Perhaps Chukar had finally decided to kill Skraw. Panic

seized her at the thought. If anything happened to her grandson, she would be completely by herself.

Chirrup and Coo turned sideways in irritation that Elder Woman was imposing her company upon them. The constant vigilance necessary to maintain a shunning required energy they didn't seem to have that morning.

"I don't know where Skraw is," Elder Woman muttered as if talking to herself. Neither woman responded. "Harrumph. He didn't come to our room last night," she said a little more loudly.

Finally, Chirrup took pity on her. She sighed and looked at Coo. "Hopefully, Jay and Whit will be well soon. Then Leaf and Chukar won't have to rely on Skraw to help them hunt. If we weren't so famished, they wouldn't have broken off his shunning that way," she said.

Coo nodded. "I hope they will bring food back soon."

Elder Woman's spirits soared. *The group has stopped shunning Skraw!*

Maybe they would soon stop shunning Elder Woman. But then she thought about what Chirrup had said and the way she'd said it. Elder Woman's two oldest sons were ill and couldn't hunt. Once they were well, the band would go back to treating Skraw in the same scathing manner. Chirrup had put a lot of emphasis on the word "famished," her hand signaling distress by snatching the air in front of her mouth. Elder Woman took a quick look at the two women. Their bellies were large with late pregnancy. Not a good time to be starving.

Although the band always ignored Elder Woman's presence, they'd never failed to feed her, which was unusual for a shunning. Wooden bowls with food and water appeared every morning and disappeared once emptied, usually by afternoon. Part of the food always arrived chewed so that she could swallow it easily. The unchewed part Elder Woman gave to Skraw.

She suspected Raven had ordered her food softened. Perhaps she'd even done it herself.

Occasionally, Elder Woman struggled down to the main hearth, returning the empty bowls, but no one ever acknowledged her attempts to lessen their burden. Elder Woman remembered then that there hadn't been any bowls outside her chamber that morning. She'd been so upset about Skraw having gone missing that she'd barely noticed their absence. The band's food stores must be completely exhausted.

Chirrup and Coo left the room without glancing her way. Her unease over Skraw had helped her ignore the pain in her teeth, but the aching returned full force. She held her jaw, and all at once, it became clear to Elder Woman what had to be done.

She ran a trembling finger across one eyebrow. There was no putting it off. It was time. She'd been deluding herself by thinking that things would eventually return to the way they were before. Elder Woman well understood what she must do. *It is your duty*, she told herself.

Walking out into the snow was a time-honored way for an old one such as Elder Woman to shed a life that had become useless. A voluntary merging with the earth was the best way to cease being a burden upon the younger band members, to stop taking food from their mouths and fuel from their hearths— sustenance the old one no longer had enough strength to help replace. Tranquility settled upon her, and Elder Woman shambled over to look outside. A frigid hush rested over the pure-white landscape. She set out, feeling at peace once again with herself and, most importantly, with the band.

The snow was hip deep in places. After going a short distance, Elder Woman's legs began shaking with weakness, but she forced herself on. The waste must stop so the pregnant mothers would have more to eat. Elder Woman regretted that she would not be around to at least see the babies. Delivering them was out of the question. Raven would never trust Elder Woman near the mothers for fear she might give them the wrong herbs if they needed medicine. A small keening sound slipped from within her as she remembered how she'd unintentionally killed Wren's barely conceived infant.

Elder Woman couldn't blame her granddaughter for the hate the young woman didn't try to hide. She would have liked to beg Wren's forgiveness if she could have caught her alone. But no matter how quickly Elder Woman moved her shuffling feet, Wren always slipped away before she was close. The only part of her Elder Woman ever got a good look at was Wren's retreating back held rigid with rage.

The day that Raven told the band what Elder Woman had done, she'd called the medicine prepared for Wren "a poisonous tea made solely to force a girl who was barely a woman." Elder Woman hadn't thought what she was doing was so despicable until she'd heard those words. She realized then how she'd turned into something rotten. She'd been so blinded by her craven desire for Skraw and Wren to produce a grandchild that she'd forgotten how harmful the herbs would be once Wren became pregnant.

Elder Woman took a look behind. She hadn't come very far. The cave complex was still in sight, but it was time to hurry the process along. The strenuous walk through the snow had kept her warm—too warm. Before continuing on, she stripped off her parka, letting it drop onto the ground.

She hoped that Jay and Whit wouldn't die from whatever illness had sickened them. That would leave Chukar her only living son. Now that she was putting her life behind her, Elder Woman finally admitted to herself that she'd treated Chukar badly when he returned from the dead. Although he hadn't exactly been shunned, she'd encouraged the others to ignore him in an attempt to shoo him back among the spirits. Before he'd found Raven, Chukar must have felt the same loneliness that attacked Elder Woman daily, in spite of having Skraw's company.

Even though her children and grandchildren often remained at the main hearth when she entered to return the food bowls, their turned backs always greeted her. She'd been the center of their world for so long, then suddenly, she wasn't. For the first time in her life, Elder Woman knew the feeling of becoming no one. She'd shunned people herself, never realizing what they suffered. Without acknowledgment from others, a person became like wisps of smoke.

When she looked again over her shoulder, the cave was finally out of sight. No one could see her now; it would be a while before they realized she was gone. Elder Woman struggled out of her tunic and threw it aside. She sat down on a felled tree sticking out of the snow. Letting out a groan, she untied her shoes from her leggings and took them off her feet. Her eyes watered as she grunted and pulled at her leggings unsuccessfully. They should also be discarded, but the effort was simply too great. Giving up in exhaustion, she tumbled over into the soft powder.

Her death was all she had left to help the band survive. And so there she was, lying on the frozen ground, shivering from the cold while waiting for the moment when her thoughts would stop. Her body was quickly losing feeling. Elder Woman welcomed the creeping numbness because it took away the awful, freezing pain—and her teeth had finally stopped hurting.

In spite of her lessened bodily sensations, Elder Woman's mind was still somewhat alert. An increasing drowsiness reminded her, though, that she was rapidly approaching the final, endless sleep. Closing her eyes, she turned her mind to the past, bringing up pleasant memories of her youth so that her last thoughts might be good ones.

Elder Woman fell into a dreamlike state, but the faint crunching sound of a person's feet approaching through the snow snatched her back into the present. She felt a pressure on her neck as if someone's hand pressed her skin there. When Elder Woman tried to open her eyes, she found they were frozen shut, and when a voice called her name, her mouth wouldn't open to reply. The person began talking, but the sound echoed hollowly through her mind, distorted almost beyond recognition. She struggled to understand.

The unknown person told a story about how, as a girl, she'd rescued a healthy newborn boy who had been cast out onto the steppes by his mother to die. Even though the baby had been forcibly taken when the girl returned to her family, she'd discovered after many turns of the seasons that the boy still lived. The people of another band had accepted him to dwell among them. The woman's voice spoke of the happiness she'd felt upon seeing the child alive and well.

A spark of understanding thawed her sluggish thoughts a bit. The person speaking was most certainly Raven. The story was the healer's way of telling Elder Woman that she would dedicate herself to preserving any children born to the band. Elder Woman wished that she could still speak. She would have liked to thank Raven for giving her that peace of mind. Although Elder Woman's limbs were without feeling, she thought that Raven had taken one of her hands and placed it on her belly.

"Yet another baby will arrive during summer."

*So, Raven is pregnant.* Elder Woman wondered groggily who the father was then decided it wasn't important. All that mattered was that the band would be one person stronger.

Unease tugged at Elder Woman, then her thoughts lit up

one last time. There was something important she must tell Raven. She'd never told any of her children what her name had been before she became Elder Woman. It should be mentioned during her death ceremony. Her mother had given her a special bird's name because of the sing-song melodious cries she emitted whenever she wanted the breast. Elder Woman had always felt a bit happier whenever she heard that bird sing its beautiful song. Her last thought was that she wanted very much to tell Raven that her real name was Nightingale.

# CHAPTER 19

## *Leaf*

L EAF, CHUKAR, AND SKRAW WERE walking single file,
taking turns breaking a trail so that none of them became
unduly exhausted. The top layer was powder, mounded over
denser snow underneath, some of the deepest Leaf had ever
walked through. At his suggestion, they were headed for the
wooded area surrounding the springs. He hoped they would
find game there.

To keep from being covered by blowing snow during blizzards, many animals left the flat featureless steppes for the
protection provided by the forest. Although the latest blizzard
had ended during the night, deer or even bison might linger in
the woods to eat tree bark or paw out moss from beneath the
drifts.

Leaf stomped down the loose fluffy snow with every step,
moving along at a steady pace. After a while, he motioned for
Skraw to take over. As the boy passed, Leaf took a look at his
face. The last of the yellow bruises from Chukar's beating were
almost gone. He wondered how Skraw felt about being allowed
to go on a hunt again.

Not that Leaf and Chukar had been given much of a choice
in the matter. With Whit and Jay ill, they needed his help to
carry back food through the snow if they were lucky enough
to take down an animal. Even so, Leaf thought that Chukar

might protest his nephew coming along, but he hadn't. Raven had probably persuaded him that it was best by pointing out that not even a scrap of dried meat remained in the cave.

When it was Chukar's turn to lead again, Leaf followed behind him as the other man struggled through waist-high drifts. All three men had rubbed hearth soot under their eyes, but to help prevent snow blindness, Leaf focused on Chukar's wide, fur-covered back. For the first time in a long while, he thought about Bear, remembering how he'd speared the other man in the back to save Chukar's life. How easy it would be at present to spear Chukar in the very same place that he'd speared Bear.

Before they'd fallen sick, Jay and Whit had asked Leaf to stay until summer was under way, whenever that might be, at least until the babies were born. Chukar had been there as well, although he didn't say anything.

"I want to see my sister's family and, above all, my two children," he'd told them. "Don't any of you understand that?"

Jay had stroked his beard as he thought. "You will have two children here soon," he finally said. "We could do a ceremony for you and the two women."

Leaf stomped a foot in agitation. "But what about my family from before? You want me to forget them?"

Jay snorted and looked down at the ground. "It is too much to think about. All I know is that I wish you would live with us."

"Raven sent you, didn't she?"

Their silence was his answer. Under his harsh stare, Jay and Whit slowly averted their eyes. Only Chukar's gaze remained steady.

Leaf wagged a forefinger at him. "I don't know why you're even part of this. I'd think that you'd want me to leave." Leaf smiled bitterly. "Well, you can keep that woman. I'm going as soon as it's warm enough." He'd walked away, his stride more cocksure than he felt.

Leaf took his eyes from Chukar's back and looked down at his own skin-clad feet slowly trudging through the snow, the fur lining bulging out around his calves. How awful to want to kill a man who'd once been his friend. But a lot had happened since those days. Perhaps if Chukar were dead, then Raven would flee the Longheads with Leaf to search for their children.

He realized the hopelessness of that desire. Even if she would go, it was too cold; they might die trying to travel such a long distance. Leaf almost bumped into Chukar, not noticing that he'd stopped. The man's chest was heaving, his breath labored.

"I suppose it's my turn again," Leaf said. Chukar didn't reply but only went to the back of their short line.

He hadn't gone far as the lead man when a cracking sound split the cold dry air. Before Leaf could react, the snow under his feet began to give way. He leapt to one side, his arms and legs flailing, to avoid falling into the fissure opening below him. But the ice kept collapsing. As he went down feetfirst, he glimpsed Skraw, who was also falling.

Like a drowning man, he fought mindlessly to find something, anything to grasp hold of. When his panicked mind cleared, he was hanging by his gloved hands to a frozen ledge, a pit yawning beneath him. Hearing a moan nearby, he turned his head and saw Skraw a short distance away, clutching the same ledge.

Chukar was nowhere to be seen. He'd either fallen without finding a handhold or remained above them. Leaf realized that they'd stumbled across a canyon made by the meandering stream that originated from the springs in the woods where they were going. Although narrow, the channel ran deep, as did all the ancient streams and rivers that cut through the Great High Plains.

He looked upward, searching for a way to pull himself out, but besides the ledge, there was only snow and ice. A scrunching sound came from above, then Chukar's head appeared, surrounded by his fur hood. He peered down at Leaf.

"Uncle?" Skraw said.

Chukar gave him a glance then looked again at Leaf. Their eyes met briefly before Chukar edged his head back. Leaf's heart sank. How ironic that he'd been thinking about the death of his rival such a short while ago, when all Chukar needed to do was walk away to be forever rid of Leaf's claims on Raven.

The sound of Chukar's feet stomping and kicking the snow away from the side of the pit was such a relief that Leaf almost lost control of his bladder. Snow sprinkled over his upturned face. He quickly bowed his head as a large clump fell and broke over him. His fingers clutching the side had become numb. Both arms were losing feeling as well, but Leaf still felt the bone-crunching strength of Chukar's grip when the other man leaned over and grasped one of his forearms.

Both his hands came off the shelf so that he momentarily dangled over the chasm. Grunting, Chukar slowly pulled him up and back. Leaf clawed at the flattened area at the top with his free hand, his fingernails tearing holes in the tips of his gloves. Finally, he was able to swing a leg and foot over the ledge. He lunged out of the pit. Chukar fell backward to the ground, letting go of Leaf's arm.

Both men sat panting, the snow a low wall around them. Leaf glanced at Chukar, his joy at having survived tinged with the shame of remembering his murderous thoughts before falling. He wasn't sure why Chukar had saved him, but he couldn't bring himself to ask the man about it. Maybe he just wanted Leaf around to help him hunt. A shudder went through his

body when he turned his head and saw how snowdrifts surrounded the break in the snow behind him. The gully's path
was hidden, impossible to see. Even a short journey like
the one they were undertaking was dangerous. The brothers
needn't worry about losing Leaf's help anytime soon, not until
a major thaw cleared the snow.

Groans rose from below. Leaf carefully leaned back and
looked down into the fissure. Skraw was attempting to pull
himself out, his arms bent at the elbows. Leaf quickly sat up
straight again and stole a look at Chukar. He knew how much
the man despised his nephew and wondered if he would save
him. Leaf also despised the boy not only because of what
he'd done to Wren, but also for the way he'd relished thrashing Leaf on various occasions. Even so, the tortured sounds
of his struggles disturbed Leaf. He reminded himself that he'd
wanted death for both Skraw and his grandmother after Raven
had exposed their depraved behavior.

At hearing a scrabbling sound, Leaf turned his head. Skraw
was trying to climb up the snow at the edge of the chasm, the
top of his reddish hair barely visible. Leaf stared pointedly at
Chukar, who looked away. He seemed to be leaving it up to
Leaf as to whether or not Skraw would be saved. Leaf doubted
that any help would be forthcoming from Chukar if he did
attempt a rescue. Before he could make up his mind, a large
chunk of icy snow gave way and crashed over Skraw's head.

He screamed as he went down, the sound muffled by more
snow falling, then there was complete silence across the frozen
whiteness covering the land.

Leaf's rescue took on even more significance, although he
still wasn't sure what Chukar saving him meant. Shuddering,
he turned away from the crevice. "We need to hunt while we
still have light."

The normal route to the forest didn't cross the channel at

all, but because most landmarks were buried under the snow, they must have veered in the wrong direction earlier. Leaf and Chukar worked out that they'd come across a meandering loop in the stream. If they went farther out to the side before heading toward the woods, they could avoid the hidden channel. Using their spears, they punched through the snow at every step, just to make sure.

Before long, they came across a deeply trodden path made by deer and other animals all going in the same direction. When Leaf found deer droppings so fresh the pellets weren't yet frozen, he knew the animals were only a short distance ahead. Hurrying along the well-packed trail, they encountered the small herd at the edge of the woods. The deer were kneeling, frantically using their faces and antlers to dig up the snow and find any dried foliage underneath.

To keep from being seen, Leaf and Chukar squatted momentarily within the icy walls of the path while they quietly took off their backpacks, readying themselves. The deer were so engrossed with their efforts that Leaf and Chukar were upon the animals before being noticed.

Leaf speared a stag at close quarters. The wound was fatal, evident from the way the animal collapsed kicking onto the ground. Leaf pulled his spear out just as a small hind floundered through the drifts ahead of him. He leapt after her using the trail she made. Another good throw, and she also went down. Looking back, he saw that Chukar had also felled two deer.

They couldn't possibly carry all the meat in one trip. Leaf proposed that they drag the deer to a rock outcrop near the woods. They could build a fire against the side of the outcrop and butcher the animals there. The flames and heat reflected from the sheer stone face would warm them and keep away curious animals while they worked. Once the meat was in more manageable pieces, they could bury a lot of it under snow and rocks for safekeeping until they returned.

Chukar stood still, hands on his hips, gazing toward the sun slung low in the sky. "We will have to stay the night."

Leaf glanced up and saw that it was so. There wasn't time to finish with everything and return to the cave complex before nightfall. The winter afternoons were short and ended abruptly. "Then we have to pile up a lot of kindling," he said. "But let's drag the deer over first."

Finding firewood wasn't a problem because the weight of ice and snow had broken off many dead branches. Once they had enough, the two men only needed to clear the snow from a small area before making fire. The outcrop was on a slight hill, so melt water caused by the fire would flow downward, away from their camp.

The two men worked quickly after they butchered the deer, managing to bury the meat in snow and to cover the cache with sticks and stones before sundown. They ran out of light before burying the intestines and other discarded body parts, which they tossed into the woods. Wolves soon came around.

Since the creatures had already discovered the butcher site, there was no reason to keep down odors. Leaf and Chukar took out some of the meat they'd packed to take back to the cave the next morning and cooked it on stones around the fire. For the first time in a long while, Leaf's hunger was completely sated.

Leaf took first watch that night. Chukar was lying stretched out between the fire and heated rock face. Leaf looked out into the darkness, where shadowy forms approached. The smells had attracted yet another pack, but they were too late to contend for the cast-off parts. The animals came close enough for Leaf to see their eyes gleaming in the firelight. They sat on their haunches a short distance away, peering at the camp.

When a few of them began howling, Chukar arose. He sat beside Leaf and listened for a moment, then he threw back his head and began wailing his own deep-throated song. Leaf began howling along with Chukar, the pair of them competing with the animals. He allowed himself to become lost in the hollow, doleful cries just as he had when he'd helped the band ambush the aurochs.

He breathed in sharply after finishing several howls. Chukar was quiet beside him, and the glowing eyes were gone. Snarling came from the woods as the most recent pack fought among themselves for the scraps of the previous pack's feast. Chukar went back to lie against the stone, leaving Leaf alone with his watch.

The wolves were nowhere to be seen the following morning, but first light brought ravens and crows. Leaf couldn't imagine the birds finding much of anything unless they were eating the bloodied snow. One raven landed directly in front of their campsite. It watched while Leaf and Chukar helped each other load the packs of meat onto their backs. Leaf thought of Raven and her affinity with her namesake bird. Her mother had named her aptly; she was as opportunistic as the birds were.

No more snow had come down during the night, so the trail they'd made the day before was easy to follow. When the path branched away, heading for the fissure, they stopped to rest, dropping their packs.

After a while, Leaf turned to face Chukar. "Even though it's out of the way to keep on yesterday's trail, we'll reach the cave sooner than if we make a new one."

Chukar rubbed a hand across his face, and Leaf knew he was reluctant to return where his nephew had fallen. But then he nodded. "We will stay on the old trail." He stood, rapidly put on his pack, and took the lead, trudging forward.

Leaf watched him walk away, then he grabbed his own

pack and followed. Jealousy darkened his thoughts for the first time since Chukar had rescued him. The Longhead man was practical, but he had a good reason for not wishing to delay. Raven would be at the cave, waiting for him.

When they reached the collapsed pit, Chukar skirted around it, breaking new snow for a short distance. Looking over to where the yawning hole was, Leaf began trembling, a barely perceptible shiver. He held his breath for a moment, and the shaking ceased as quickly as it had begun.

When they were only a short distance from the cave complex, Leaf stopped and stared out across the white expanse. A figure stood in the snow. Someone had come out on the steppes. Leaf wondered why the person had made a new trail upon leaving the cave instead of using the one the men had left the day before. Chukar suddenly veered off the path. Leaf caught up with him and waded through the snow at his side.

The figure ahead waved, and Leaf recognized Raven. After a moment, she leaned over, looking down at the snow. Someone was lying on the ground at her feet. His heart jumped into his throat. Although Wren hadn't said so to Leaf, Chirrup had recently told him that the girl was going around saying that she wished she were dead. He hunched over a bit, distributing the weight away from his shoulders, and began running.

# CHAPTER 20

*Raven*

"WE OUGHT TO LEAVE HER where she fell," Leaf said. "It was Elder Woman's choice to die out here in the snow."

"No." Raven's emphatic shake of her head loosened her parka hood so that it slipped back. "No, I don't want us to be stumbling upon her bones for several moons after the snow melts." Straightening the hood, she turned to Chukar.

As one of Elder Woman's sons, he should have a say. He stood looking down at his mother. She wondered what he was feeling behind that face as calm as a still lake.

"We'll take her body farther out on the steppes, then." Leaf stuck his spear into the snow so he could adjust the pack on his shoulders. "I admit that her bones would bother me. I certainly don't want to come across parts of the old wolf bitch moon after moon."

Those weren't quite the words of a person who planned to leave the area as soon as possible, but Raven wasn't going to point that out. She widened her eyes at him for saying such a thing in front of Chukar. Even though no love had been lost between mother and son, he should have thought before he spoke. Leaf gave Chukar a quick look of apology, but the other man showed no sign of having been perturbed.

Mollified by Leaf's contriteness, Raven looked again at the

frozen body. Elder Woman had caused a lot of misery, but Raven couldn't abide her being eaten by predators. "Please, let's not leave her to the beasts. She was the band's leader for many turns of the seasons as well as a healer. We should bury her inside." Raven's sentimentality was genuine, but she also wanted it well-defined in everyone's mind that change had taken place.

She belatedly noticed Skraw's absence. "Where's the boy?"

Leaf inclined his head toward Chukar. "You tell her."

"Skraw fell in a hole. He could not get out." Chukar slipped the straps off his shoulders and dropped his backpack onto the snow. "Don't try to carry that," he said to Raven. "I'll come back for it before animals find it." He leaned down and hoisted Elder Woman over a shoulder. "We'll bury her inside."

Perplexed by his failure to elaborate on what had happened to Skraw, Raven watched Chukar walk away, his gait steady in spite of the burden. Leaf cleared his throat, and she turned in his direction.

"I suppose we could bury her in one of the chambers," he said. "There's so much room inside those cliffs that three or four bands could live there without seeing much of each other." He began kicking snow over Chukar's pack, and Raven helped him.

When it was sufficiently covered to keep an animal from noticing it, they followed Chukar's tracks that overlaid the trail Raven had followed to find Elder Woman.

Raven had a lot on her mind that she wanted to discuss with Leaf, but with Elder Woman dead and the band weak with hunger, it would all have to wait. Instead, she asked him about the hunt. He told her how he and Chukar had found the small herd of deer then killed four of them and how the wolves came around during the night. He said not a word about Skraw.

No one was at the main hearth when they entered. Raven

went immediately to warm herself by the fire. Leaf took off his pack then joined her. Shortly afterward, Chukar came out of one of the corridors, followed by the rest of the band, including Whit and Jay. Although not completely well, they'd begun to move around some. Raven tensed up when Chukar's glance took in the way she and Leaf were standing close together.

"I've put Elder Woman in her room," he said matter-of-factly. He didn't stop by the fire before going out to retrieve his pack.

She could tell that the others hadn't fully recovered from seeing Chukar suddenly walk in with the newly dead Elder Woman slung over a shoulder. Even Wren's face showed her shock, though she'd said many times that she wished Elder Woman would die. Raven didn't know what Chukar had told them, but she quickly took control, just as she'd been doing since the shunning began.

She turned to face them. "When I saw Elder Woman's tracks leading out of the cave, I followed them. I found her in the snow right before Leaf and Chukar came along." Raven doubted that Chukar had told them about Skraw. She hesitated a long moment. "Skraw didn't return with Leaf and Chukar. He died while hunting."

Wren's expression of shocked astonishment changed to surprised relief. Before anyone thought to ask what exactly had happened to Skraw, Raven went on. Leaf was the only one present at the moment who could answer that question, but for some reason, he didn't want to. "We will bury Elder Woman in her room," she said, "unless any of you suggest a better place." When no one spoke, she continued. "But first, we, the living, must eat."

After satiating their immediate hunger with raw meat and with the understanding they would cook and eat more later, everyone gathered in Elder Woman's room. The men softened the hard-packed dirt by pouring water over the cave floor. The group waited a short while for the moisture to soak in, then Chirrup and Coo began digging first so that they wouldn't have to crawl in and out with their enlarged bellies when the hole became a pit. The two women sank their digging sticks into the ground, turning the soil before moving it to one side.

The group dug the hole quickly, everyone throwing the dirt and stones out at a frantic pace when their turn came. In spite of their lingering illness, Jay and Whit insisted on helping. Chukar returned before the task was complete. He finished the job, digging rapidly until the pit was deep enough.

To Raven, it seemed as though they were all rushing, herself included, to put the elderly healer into the ground and out of their lives. No one could be blamed for wanting her gone, but by the time the hole was finished, Raven had become ashamed of their haste. "I would like to put Elder Woman's spirit at ease by doing a short ceremony," she said.

No one protested. None of them wanted the dead woman's discontented spirit wandering the cave's corridors.

After Chukar placed Elder Woman on her side in the pit with her knees drawn up against her chest, Raven passed around a bag of crushed ochre. She discreetly skipped offering Leaf the bag. He would only refuse to take some, and his sharp tongue would ruin the tranquility of the moment.

As each person stepped forward with their bit of the red powder, Raven explained to the Earth Mother the relationship that person had to the dead woman. When Raven's turn came, she paused. "What was her name before she became Elder Woman?"

After a moment, Chirrup replied hesitantly, "We were either very small or not born yet when she became Elder Woman. I asked her once. She said that if the name became known, her leadership as Elder Woman would be weakened."

Raven nodded at Chirrup, her face serene. "It doesn't matter." Although using the birth name was important to help calm the spirit, she didn't want them to worry. Raven sprinkled ochre over Elder Woman's head, the red color brightening her matted gray hair. "This woman was the grandmother of my first child," she said, motioning for Wren to come forward so that the ceremony could be finished.

Wren glared at her mother, showing her displeasure at hearing herself so firmly linked to the woman she'd constantly said that she hated. Faced once again with Wren's bad humor, Raven almost lashed out at her. But she caught herself. After what Elder Woman had done, Wren, just like Leaf, shouldn't be forced to take part. But a kinsman, particularly a granddaughter, refusing to participate was just the kind of thing that would keep Elder Woman's spirit from resting in peace.

An uneasy quiet settled over the room. Finally, Wren stepped to the edge and tossed all her ochre in at once. "A granddaughter," was all Raven said as the powder wafted over the body. She expected that Wren would leave the chamber immediately, but she stayed to help fill the grave.

After the last clods and rocks were piled over the burial mound, everyone returned to the main hearth and began cooking and eating. At some point, they started sharing food, murmuring "aulehleh" as they tempted each other with freshly cooked morsels. Chirrup and Coo were the first ones to lie down, curling up beside each other a short distance from the fire. Raven remembered all the times in the past she'd seen the Longhead band sleep together beside the cooking hearth after a large meal.

Leaf stopped eating next. He gave Raven a quick look before lying down and wrapping himself tightly around Coo. If Leaf was trying to make her jealous, then he'd failed. The only sentiment she felt was happiness that he'd returned safely from the hunt. He fell asleep at once, his light snore joining Coo's quiet breathing. If the kill was as large as he'd told Raven, then he needed to restore his strength by sleeping soundly. Unless Jay and Whit felt well enough to help, he and Chukar would make many trips to their cache.

Raven took Chukar's hand and led him over to where Leaf was lying against Coo. She felt his fingers tighten around hers when she was about to sit. They usually slept some distance away from wherever Leaf slept. Raven turned to face him. She waited patiently while he searched her face. When she felt his fingers loosen a little, Raven lowered herself, pulling him down with her.

Lying down, she turned on her side toward Chukar. After a moment, he stretched out beside her. When Whit, Jay, and Finch joined the group, the only one left sitting by the hearth was Wren. Raven raised a hand, motioning her over. Giving her mother a hard look, she went to lie down beside Chirrup.

At first, Raven couldn't relax. The strangeness of being so close to both men at the same time made her tense. Although she faced Chukar, Leaf had moved in his sleep so that she felt his side pressed against her back. Eventually, the satisfaction of having a full stomach, along with the warmth of the nearby bodies, loosened her tight muscles. A deep contentment swept over her, and she fell soundly asleep.

*** 

On a morning when it was her turn to bring in snow for melt-ing, Raven decided to check the stream to find out if she could break up the ice to melt. Just as it happened at every winter home base where Raven had ever lived, the snow close by the cave became unusable after the band started relieving them-selves there to avoid becoming lost during heavy snowfalls. Emboldened by hunger, wolves and other animals came around during the nights and dug their leavings out from under the snow. Those animals' tracks and scat were everywhere, dirtying the area further. Readily obtaining clean snow to make drinking water became harder.

Raven had already emptied the large woven basket filled with snow several times into the stone vat at the cave, but it still wasn't full enough. Besides drinking water, they also needed water for cooking and cleaning, and there just weren't enough people to do all the work. The frozen stream was closer than where she'd been collecting snow, so going there could possibly speed up the chore.

The day was bright and sunny as she walked along, balancing the empty basket on her head. Raven took a deep breath and found she didn't have to cough afterward. Her belief that the snow would eventually rid the air of dust had been correct. And perhaps she was imagining things, but the weather didn't seem quite as cold that morning. Raven looked carefully about her and spotted moisture dribbling down the side of a boulder where the sun hit it. Her spirits lifted. Even though the Earth Mother had relented, allowing the snow to cleanse the air, Raven still feared that spring would come later than usual. The harsh weather was certainly not going away overnight, but at least there were signs of the coming thaw.

All the Earth Mother's creatures had suffered cruelly, the hooved ones that depended upon foliage and grass most of all. The band scavenged the fallen animals whenever they found them, the frozen bodies augmenting their hunting. Raven hoped that enough grass-eaters were left to produce an adequate number of young ones; otherwise, hunting would be slack for some time.

As if her thoughts about hunting brought them, Chukar and Leaf walked by at a distance. From the determined way they strode along, she knew they felt lucky that day. The meat cached from the four deer they'd killed had lasted a good while, though not as long as Raven had expected. The dangerous hunts in the ice and snow were resumed even before half a moon passed. She reminded herself once more that the Longheads ate more food than what would be considered normal for her tribesmen because their bodies were larger.

After Jay and Whit recovered their strength, all the men hunted together again, but quite often, Chukar and Leaf went out by themselves. They were companions once more as they'd been in the past. Raven didn't know how that had come about, but she felt the reason was somehow related to Skraw's death.

When Raven pressed him to tell her more about how the boy died, Chukar told her that Skraw had fallen into a deep canyon covered over by snow. But his answer didn't explain the renewed friendship with Leaf. When she asked him about that specifically, he was slow to respond.

"I think Leaf wanted to kill me but changed his mind," he finally said. Alarmed to hear that, she tried to get him to elaborate, but he retreated into his usual silence.

The two men made a formidable pair, bringing back game more often than not. "Good hunting," Raven called out.

They each raised a hand in acknowledgement. Raven enjoyed seeing them together; she watched their progress a few more moments before continuing on to the stream.

Raven often caught Leaf watching her. She detected the same longing on his face that she'd noticed the first time they'd met. His eyes tore at her defenses, and her heart skipped a beat whenever her gaze met his. She knew that Chukar quite often noticed their intertwined glances. Having come to thoroughly know him, Raven was keenly aware of the sharp astuteness that lay behind his heavy, taciturn features. She did her best to hide her feelings, but she knew he wasn't fooled.

Although his desire was obvious, Leaf never attempted to

be alone with Raven. She had no idea how she should react if he did. Raven didn't want to be the cause of trouble between the two men now that they were friends once more, but she was well aware that the situation was vastly unfair to Leaf. She'd tied herself to Chukar when she promised not to leave him, and she didn't know yet how much slack was in those tethers.

Raven's namesake birds also enjoyed the sight of the pair leaving the cave carrying their spears. Whenever they hunted, a group of ravens accompanied them. Not long after the men passed, ravens flew overhead from their roosts on the cliffs, behaving for once as if they were a flock. She tilted back her head to watch them. Upon spotting Raven standing beside the stream, they vigorously flew around overhead, diving and swooping to show their happiness. A few of them even flew upside down for a while. Their raucous calls sounded playful, as if they were laughing.

They soon flew on, except for one extremely large raven, in all probability a male. He landed nearby, spreading his wings to keep from sinking into the top layer of snow, the feathers around his neck bristling. When Raven began breaking up the ice with a stick, he watched her intently.

Raven thought she recognized that particular bird. He was eyeing her in the same manner as the raven she'd seen the day Wren and Leaf were kidnapped. Her heart tightened with dread as she made eye contact, hoping his appearance wasn't an omen of more disruption to come. They stared at each other until Raven became impatient.

"I must work," she said. At hearing her voice, the raven beat the snow with its wings until it could lift up and fly away.

She began filling the basket with ice, her gloves slowly becoming wet. Before long, a big patch of the stream was free of ice. Surprised that it hadn't been frozen solid, Raven con-

templated the uncovered water, wishing she'd brought along a
waterskin to fill. Then something fell into the stream in front
of her with a small splash.

Raven glanced up and saw the large raven flying overhead.
She looked back down. A shiny pebble, different from the
other rocks, lay on the stream bed, the ripples above it radiating in all directions. She eyed it, amazed. The raven had gifted
her with the small rock by dropping it into the water.

She squatted to see the pebble better. The small oval stone
glittered with an unusual sheen, and a giddiness came over her
as she stared intently into the quivering liquid. Raven realized that she was slipping into a trance. At first, she fought
to remain lucid, but then it crossed her mind that instead of
the pebble, the real gift from the bird was a trance—sent by
the Earth Mother. She stopped fighting and let the trance take
over.

Raven heard two babies crying, one bawling huskily, the
other one letting out high shrill wails. She lifted her head from
staring at the pebble. The cries came from the basket beside
her. The woven container no longer held ice but was covered
over with soft furs. She was reminded of the dream about
the crying babies threatened by the storm. A glance skyward
showed only a few white clouds floating along. She decided
that the babies hidden in the basket were crying from hunger
instead of fear. At the thought, her breasts began leaking milk.
She pulled back the covers.

Although not newly born, they were still very young, only
several moons old. They were almost the same size, one a little
larger, and both wore identical tunics, but that was where the
likeness ended. The smaller child was dark skinned, and the
large lighter-skinned baby had a slightly longer head—the
same shape as Wren's when she was first born. Sensing her
presence, the babies opened their eyes at almost the same time.

The dark-skinned child had black-brown eyes; the large irises of the fairer infant were hazel colored.

Both babies had gone quiet at seeing her, but they began crying again, mouths opening wide as they screamed their displeasure that she hadn't picked them up to nurse. Raven took a quick breath when she looked at their mouths. The brown-eyed baby didn't yet have any teeth, but the one with hazel eyes already showed a few. The baby's two front teeth had a small gap between them.

Raven looked down at her abdomen. The small mound she'd developed over the past moons was missing. She groped her flat belly, then she understood the Earth Mother's message. Both babies were her children. She would deliver twins.

The trance broke without warning, and Raven found herself still staring at the pebble, her face so near the water that the tip of her nose was in danger of becoming wet. She straightened too quickly and flopped backward onto the snow, her arms spreading to lessen the impact.

Sparse white clouds floated above, the same clouds she'd seen in the trance. Raven slid a hand over her belly several times and was reassured that her pregnancy hadn't just disappeared. She became very still as she gazed into the sky.

Twins were rare enough, but for them to have different fathers, as the dream seemed to indicate, was something she may have seen only once. While living with the Fire Cloud tribe, she'd delivered twin boys so dissimilar that they didn't look related at all. One baby was born with exceptionally thick hair that had a white streak running through it above the forehead. A traveler had recently stayed with the band who'd also had a white forelock. During his stay, he'd told Raven that white streaks of hair were common in his tribe, no matter the person's age. The other twin didn't have the white streak, and as he grew, that boy came to strongly resemble the mother's Fire

Cloud mate. The child with the white forelock always had a different look about him.

Someone calling to Raven broke through her musings. She struggled out of the snow.

"Raven!" the person cried out again.

She recognized Chirrup's voice. "I'm down here."

"Come back to the cave," Chirrup called from somewhere up on the bank. "Coo is having her baby."

"I'm coming!" Raven yelled back. She dusted the snow off her clothing, picked up the ice-filled basket, and began climbing the bank, her heart beating wildly with excitement. If all went well, the band would soon have a new member.

After only a few steps, Raven remembered the pebble. She quickly went back down, remembering to take off her glove before thrusting her hand into the water.

# CHAPTER 21

*Leaf*

I T SEEMED TO LEAF THAT they were all happier and more alive after the babies were born. Even Wren had shaken off the gloom gnawing her for so long. Not only were the women entranced by the infants, but the men were too. Whenever the mothers brought their babies to the main hearth, chores went undone while the group gathered around. Smiles and exclamations met every hiccup and gurgle the little ones emitted.

Leaf was watching from the other side of the fire as Jay dandled Chirrup's and Coo's baby boys at the same time. When they began fretting, he gave them back to their mothers. Chirrup's face beamed as she soothed her child's cries. A pleasant surge of pride went through Leaf that he'd done his part in fulfilling her long-time desire.

Sitting apart from the others, he was assailed by a pang of loneliness. Before he knew it, Leaf was on his way over to be with them. When Finch saw him approaching, she struggled up, her baby pressed against her breast, so that he could sit next to Coo. Leaf felt bad that he'd dislodged her. She'd delivered her daughter only the day before.

He reached out his hands to Coo once settled. Giving him a delighted look, she passed her baby over. Leaf knew that his increasingly distant behavior disturbed her and Chirrup, but he must keep himself somewhat at arm's length from the situation. He hadn't been a prisoner for some time. Now that the snow and ice were melting, it wouldn't be too long before he left. The last thing Leaf wanted was to become attached to the babies; deserting the mothers was enough cause for the guilty feelings he was trying to ignore. Raven also remained a sore spot. His stomach clenched every time he thought about explaining to Windy and Sky that their mother hadn't returned with him.

When he'd told Raven about his intentions, she'd pointed out that a trip would be difficult until the earth dried out. She was right about that. Once all the snow from the extreme blizzards of winter began melting, land that had once been dry steppe became full of rivers, streams, and lakes that hadn't existed before. So he lingered, gazing out at the steppes from the cave mouth every morning to see if the waters had lessened enough during the night for him to leave. So far, they had not.

He looked at the infant nestled in the crook of his arm. The brown-black eyes with amber flecks twinkled back at him. Both Chirrup's and Coo's babies looked very similar. Their skin and eyes were almost as dark as Leaf's, but the downy red-brown hair was much lighter than his brown-black mane. He breathed deeply of the scent that was pure baby and gently smoothed back the infant's hair. The little one let out a noise that sounded like a giggle. Leaf couldn't help but grin.

The two boys weren't yet named. Nor was Finch's baby girl. Longhead mothers, it seemed, usually waited at least a moon before giving their children names to see if they lived. Finch had declared that she would forego the practice so that her baby could be named at the same time as the others. The naming ceremony was to be that very day, and for that reason, everyone was gathered at the hearth.

They were waiting for Raven, who was in her chamber, preparing a special water to bathe the babies with after the ceremony. She'd taken over many duties that Elder Woman had once done. How quickly they'd ceded those responsibilities to Raven, a woman not of their ilk. Then again, no one else in the band was stepping forward to fill the void. The men didn't seem interested enough in taking control to displace her. Chirrup was the only one Leaf could see taking Elder Woman's place, but other than counseling Raven at times, she seemed satisfied just being a mother.

Raven finally arrived along with Chukar. Her face lit up when she saw Leaf holding Coo's baby. Unchecked anger ran amok along the edges of his thoughts at seeing the indulgent smile she bestowed on them all. He brusquely handed the baby back to Coo; the sudden movement caused the child to let out a plaintive cry. Raven frowned slightly and looked away.

Leaf knew he was being churlish, but upon seeing Raven's smile, it had occurred to him that he was betraying Windy and Sky by interacting with the infant. He was giving affection that they should be receiving to the baby. Even if Raven no longer missed their children, he still did.

Once the group was standing in a circle around the hearth, Raven intoned a chant to the Earth Mother, giving thanks that they'd survived the winter. Leaf's gaze roamed over the group while everyone repeated the verses. He didn't know whether the Longheads were merely indulging her or if they'd come around to recognizing the Earth Mother as the powerful spirit she was. When Raven thanked the Earth Mother for the new babies, he looked over at Chirrup. The woman's usually calm face was fervent as she chanted along, her eyes ablaze. She seemed about to burst with feeling, and Leaf concluded that she, at least, believed.

After halting the chant, Raven asked the mothers if they had names for their babies. All three said that they had names.

Finch's girl was named Dove; Chirrup's son, Falcon; and Coo's, Osprey.

Leaf approved of their choices. They were good, strong names. Not like his. Although at that point in his life, he couldn't imagine being called anything else, he'd always wondered what his mother and father had been thinking to give him a name like Blowing Leaf. At least it had been shortened to just Leaf. He hadn't thought about his parents in some time and was busy recalling old memories while Raven spoke. Her words suddenly jolted him back into the present.

"We will form a new tribe," she was saying. "A tribe in which the People and any of Them who want to join us will live together peacefully and raise their children with one another's help. Our group here will be the first band in that tribe." She raised both hands toward the cave's ceiling then lowered them, her fingers moving as she spoke, each movement deliberate. "Oh powerful Earth Mother, please accept each person gathered here today as part of a new tribe formed in your honor— but only if that particular man or woman agrees to become a member of the tribe."

Leaf craned his head to look at the men. Shock and confusion had taken over their faces. And when Leaf looked over to where the women stood, Chirrup's smiling face was the exception. The others were just as shaken as the men by Raven's proposal. Their eyes were owl-like, wide and unblinking.

Chirrup stood. "I want to be in the new tribe you speak of."

Leaf hoped that Chirrup would be the only one amenable to Raven's strange proposal. He glanced at Chukar. The man's face was a thundercloud. Raven obviously hadn't told him about her plan. Leaf could barely hide his glee. Chukar and Raven might finally part ways. Since the day Chukar rescued him, Leaf had given up trying to persuade Raven to his side.

He'd finally understood why she'd remained with the man after he'd kept her from dying. But if the Longhead rejected her, all obligations were done with.

Raven was trying to maintain her composure, but Leaf knew her well. She could fool the others with that unnaturally serene face of hers, but he saw the worry in her eyes and the tenseness with which she held herself. The small quivering around the corners of her mouth meant that she felt humiliated by their lack of response. He almost felt sorry for her.

His sympathy vanished when Chukar stepped away from his brothers. "I wish to be part of the tribe."

Leaf had been outmaneuvered. Chukar knew that Leaf would have a hard time going along with Raven's ideas and would in all probability leave at once to go find his family. Leaf crossed his arms tightly over his chest to keep the scalding grief there from bursting out. He was about to lose her forever because he couldn't follow her down that new path she was determined to blaze.

Chukar stared over his shoulder at Whit and Jay as if challenging his brothers to join him. Leaf watched in disbelief as the two men and Finch came forward and stood beside Chukar, the three of them repeating the exact words he'd said.

Coo was the next one. She spoke quietly, so as not to awaken the baby sleeping in her arms. "I will be in the tribe." Coo then turned and looked directly at Leaf. She tilted the swaddled infant so that he could see Osprey's sweet sleeping face, her gesture impulsive but at the same time demanding. Leaf ignored her and glanced over at Wren.

His stepdaughter was gazing out at nothing, her brow twitching in thought. Surely, she would refuse Raven. He'd ask her to come with him. Together, they would cross the plains to find the people she knew best. But she quickly dashed his hopes.

"Why is everybody staring at me?" said Wren. "I'll be part of it."

Leaf made a disgusted sound. He suspected that she'd been persuaded ahead of time. The girl he knew wasn't so immediately agreeable. "Raven, you are really something," he said, speaking in the Fire Cloud tongue. He shook his head. "You've somehow convinced everybody here to forget their pasts. But I can't forget mine, and it hurts that you can so easily let go of yours. I won't join even though your new tribe seems to be the Earth Mother's will."

She replied using the Fire Cloud tongue. "I haven't forgotten anything—not our pasts and especially not our children. We'll find them and bring them into this group. I promise you. Please trust me, Leaf."

Tears glistened in her eyes, but he wouldn't let her manipulate him the way she had the others. "I'll leave tomorrow in the morning," he said. "Flooded plains or not."

Raven suddenly gasped. She pressed both hands over her stomach. He looked at her, alarmed. "Are you ill?"

She straightened. "I've never been better." She held out a hand. "Come, I want you to feel something."

Leaf hesitated, wondering what tricks she was up to. But curiosity got the best of him. He uncrossed his arms and went over.

She took his hand then reached out with her free one to Chukar. His face puzzled, the Longhead man walked over and stood on her other side. Raven took his hand as well and placed both men's hands upon her middle.

"I carry two babies," she said, switching to the Longhead tongue. She pressed Leaf's hand firmly over her tunic, and he felt her stomach move. "I think your baby is on this side."

Leaf's breath caught. The twitching under his fingers

caused a vibration that traveled up his arm and into his shoulders. As if from a distance, he heard her speak to Chukar.

"And yours is over here. They are both lively today."

Stunned, Leaf looked into her face. A shiver went through him so that he trembled, and hair everywhere began standing on end. She'd amazed him so often during the many turns of the seasons he'd known her, but until that day, he hadn't truly understood her nature. He thought that the Earth Mother had entered Raven a long while back, probably at birth, and she'd become a living, visible expression of the spirit. Leaf doubted that Raven even realized she was so much more than just another woman.

He didn't resist when she raised his hand off her stomach then Chukar's and placed them on opposite sides of her face. Gripping them firmly, she slid their palms rapidly away so that their two hands met in front of her with a clap. In her firm hold, his and Chukar's hands were pressed together as if praying.

"Earth Mother, make us as one," Raven cried. She became silent but kept their hands squeezed together.

Leaf knew then that she would live her life with whichever man did not pull away. Although she held them tightly for many heartbeats, Leaf didn't move, even though he believed that Chukar had no intentions of breaking her grasp. Their hands under hers remained palm to palm until she released them.

Exhausted by his emotions, Leaf felt as though he were only partly awake as he stumbled over to lean against the edge of the cave mouth. The land spreading away before him looked different, as it would during a dream, or perhaps he'd fallen into a trance the way Raven sometimes did. The plains still flowed with water in braided streams, but he saw them as somehow imbued with meaning that he alone was meant to understand.

His and Raven's lives, along with the Longheads' lives, were similar to the streams. They'd come across each other then separated and met up again several times over the moons, the Earth Mother braiding the two different peoples together— sometimes tightly and other times loosely—as they flowed toward a larger river.

# CHAPTER 22

*Raven*

THE DELIVERY OF RAVEN'S TWINS lasted almost a whole day but was less difficult overall than Wren's birth had been. Even so, she didn't have as easy a time of it compared to the three women who'd delivered before her, though their labors were hard enough. While helping Coo's child into the world, Raven had been unsettled when the baby failed to turn so that it faced downward like in all the other births Raven had assisted. But later when Chirrup's and Finch's babies were born in exactly the same manner, Raven realized that Coo's delivery hadn't been unusual. All three infants had squeezed directly out of their mothers, face up with their heads turned to the side. Raven concluded that the babies were born that way because of the way their mothers were shaped. The women's pelvises were wide enough so that a baby didn't have to turn during birth.

Raven understood then why Elder Woman had assumed she would die while having Wren. The old woman had run her rough hand across the relatively narrow span of Raven's pelvis. "Too narrow," she'd muttered, shaking her head.

Leaf's child was born first, her slick body tan like a fawn. Chukar's child followed soon, a boy whose eyes were hazel colored. Both fathers came in together to see the babies. She asked them to come up with names that would be formally given to each child during the naming ceremony. Chukar chose Owl for his son, and Leaf picked Willow for his daughter, naming her after Raven's long-deceased older sister.

The two men then left so Raven could rest. Chukar returned a short while later, bringing with him a bone from a raven. He'd cut notches into one of the sun-bleached sides. While she held it, he touched each notch, reciting a name as his fingers went down the bone's length. "Raven, Chukar, Leaf, Wren, Chirrup, Coo, Finch, Whit, Jay, Dove, Falcon, Osprey, Willow, Owl."

Raven smiled when she saw how he'd made smaller nicks for the babies, but those tiny lines left her apprehensive. The bone was a nice representation of their band, but it also pointed out that a good portion of the group were small defenseless infants.

But they were the founding band in a new tribe, regardless, as was shown so well by Chukar's raven bone. And as such, they should think of themselves as one. She took the bone out often, hoping that it would eventually inspire a tribal name for their unique group.

Raven guided the women in setting up a nursery inside one of the chambers. The mothers lived there with the five infants. Wren joined them from time to time. Raven found it difficult to watch her daughter whenever she held one of the babies. Wren's face was wistful, and the cooing sounds she made then were more like those of a mourning dove than a doting sister or aunt.

Because the mothers were all producing milk, they nursed one another's children and took turns caring for them. Two women minded the babies every day while the others concentrated on the unrelenting chores. Indeed, Raven had presented this unusual living plan as a way to increase the amount of time each woman could work without being distracted by the needs of a baby. Normally, women in a Fire Cloud or Wind band who didn't have small children would help their kinswomen or friends for several moons after a baby was born. Raven believed that Longhead women normally did something similar. But except for Wren, they each had newborns, so the workload of the mothers couldn't be lessened very much. The band had too few sets of hands to assure the group's survival.

Raven had another purpose for changing their living arrangements that revolved around other commitments and duties besides tending children. If a woman wished to pass time alone with the father of her baby during the evening, she did so but returned shortly afterward to sleep in the nursery. When Raven's body healed from childbirth, she went some nights to Leaf's room and other nights to Chukar's.

The changes overall weren't a perfect solution. Finding Chukar alone was never a problem, but to be with Leaf, Raven had to make sure that Coo and Chirrup weren't with him. Raven kept putting off discussing with the two women how they would share him. They might tell her that she should be content with one man. And she worried that Chukar resented sharing her with Leaf. Finally, Raven realized that he was tolerant enough to not be overly discontented. When no one complained after a while, she become more relaxed about the whole situation. That lasted until Leaf let her know that everything wasn't going quite as smoothly as she thought.

"They would never say it, but Coo and Chirrup are unhappy because I've been neglecting them," he said one night when Raven arrived at his room before either of the other two. "Sometimes when one of them comes by, I just talk to her for a while, then say that I'm tired and wish to sleep. I save myself for when I see you."

Raven feigned surprise. "But are you not the insatiable man who wanted to mate with me behind every boulder and bush during the time we fled from Bear?"

"Ah, but I was a boy then with not that many turns of the seasons behind me."

She smiled at him. "You're still a young man."

"Just not that young," he said and reached for her. "It's easier for a woman."

Raven knew he was thinking about her evenings with Chukar, but he hadn't sounded resentful. When he folded her into his arms and nuzzled her neck insistently, Raven wanted to stop worrying but couldn't. Even though Chirrup and Coo were mild mannered enough not to show jealousy, their discontent concerned her. "Let's try to keep them happy. On some of *my* visits, we can just talk."

He groaned. "I shouldn't have said anything."

"Only occasionally, Leaf. I suppose I am greedy, but I'd never consider giving you up entirely even if you'd go along with it. I realize, though, that things can't go on like this forever. Perhaps other men will join us when we find Windy and Sky—men without mates, that Chirrup and Coo might consider. I just hope that once the Wind tribe people see us living together peacefully, at least some of them will prove capable of putting aside any aversions they might have."

He pushed away slightly to look at her face. "And when will we search for them?"

She was grateful that he hadn't ridiculed her idea that some of the Wind tribe might agree to becoming part of the new band. "We'll go as soon as the twins have passed another half-moon. I give you my word."

"And if the camp has moved back to the coast?"

"Then we'll look for them there."

\*\*\*

True to her promise, Raven called a gathering in midsummer for the purpose of telling everyone that she and Leaf wanted to find their other two children and bring them back to the cave.

"But we shouldn't stay here for long upon our return," she said. "This is a place of bad memories. We were all happier at the river valley cave where we first lived together those many moons ago. That is where we should dwell."

She told them that anyone who wished to was welcome to come along when she and Leaf looked for the Wind tribe. The other option was to wait until they came back through again and join them for the journey to the other cave. Wren and Chukar promptly said they would go. Raven hadn't wanted to risk either of them feeling deserted by her when she left, so she'd explained her plans to the pair before the gathering. Neither one had needed much persuasion.

As it turned out, the whole group agreed to leave. No one wanted to be left behind, which was what Raven had secretly hoped for. Because everyone was coming, it was decided that they wouldn't return again to the cave complex. Packing went quickly as there was only so much they could carry on their backs. Some hides and furs went into the bags, but mostly, they took food—dried meat, berries, and roots.

Raven looked regretfully at the chipped-out stone vats and wooden bowls that took so long to make. She felt better about abandoning everything when she remembered that the dry cave where they would eventually go held the vats, tools, and bowls made in the past. Those items at least would be useable even if the old furs and hides were rotted or chewed through by animals and insects.

***

On the morning when the group arrived near to where the Wind tribe had lived, Leaf was suddenly by Raven's side.

"I see smoke ahead," he said quietly.

Raven peered into the distance. A faint gray haze spiraled upward on the horizon. "I see it," she said, awed yet again by his sharp eyesight.

Everyone was spread out in a single-file line, the men leading. No one other than Leaf had yet noticed the smoke. She looked around excitedly at the other women and was about to call out that their journey was almost over when Leaf stopped her.

"Wait," he said in a low voice. "Let's you and I go on alone. We should talk to whoever is at the camp before taking the whole group there. Remember all the bad things that were said about Longheads around those campfire gatherings? The people, especially Fin, might react poorly when they see our traveling companions. We'll come back later for them; they can stay here until we return."

Raven saw how he gnawed his lip while waiting for her reaction. He was right to be nervous about the two groups meeting for the first time.

"Why didn't we talk about this earlier?" she murmured more to herself than to him. She and Leaf had become so used to them that they'd forgotten how different the Longheads would seem to the Wind tribesmen.

Raven called a halt so she could explain to the group what had been decided. Wren raised a hand while Raven talked, impatiently waving her fingers. Raven gave her a chilly look. Wren lowered her hand but then began fidgeting so much that Owl, inside the sling across her chest, started crying.

Raven hurriedly finished what she was saying. "What is it, Wren?"

"I want to go with you."

Raven shook her head firmly. "You're needed here to take care of both babies while I'm gone." She started lifting the sling from around her neck that carried Willow. "I'm going to leave my pack here with you also."

A low frustrated sound came from Wren's throat as she took the baby, but she didn't try to argue.

"We won't be gone long," Raven told her.

The band settled down to rest as Raven and Leaf set out. None of them, except for Wren, had seemed upset that they were going on alone to the Wind camp. Raven knew that by leaving Wren and her babies with the group, everyone was reassured, especially Chukar, that she would return.

Raven glanced at Leaf after they'd gone a short distance. She knew that her own expression matched the nervous hopefulness playing over his face. For some time, they walked briskly toward the camp. When she smelled smoke, though, Raven stopped in her tracks. Leaf paused and looked back.

"If Fin is in camp," she said, "he'll insist that we go directly to his tent. I'd rather find Sky and Windy first before we become stuck explaining to Fin what happened to us and what that means now."

Leaf gazed down at his feet for a moment then looked at her. "Stay here while I go search for Shell's tent. I'll look for those strings of shells she hangs around the entry flap. Hopefully, that's where Sky and Windy will be. I'll come get you as soon as I find her tent."

Shell had always been fond of her namesake object, hanging strings of seashells everywhere that she'd brought with her from the coast. She also wore them as necklaces and bracelets.

Raven nodded. "I'll wait for you here."

Leaf set out immediately.

Raven nervously fiddled with her braids while he was

gone, but she didn't have to wait long. Leaf reappeared almost at once. He was smiling as she ran to meet him. "The Earth Mother sent me luck," he said. "Shell's tent is the closest one." The corners of his eyes crinkled. "I saw Windy and Sky playing outside with Shell's children."

Raven grasped Leaf's arm tightly, allowing what he'd told her to fully sink in. After being away from their children for so long, it seemed a wondrous thing that he'd actually seen Windy and Sky. "Thank the Earth Mother they are safe. You didn't speak to them?"

"I want us to be together when they see us."

Releasing him, she breathed out shakily. "Then let's go."

The children spotted Raven and Leaf as soon as they entered the clearing. All of them stood still, staring for a moment, before running to the tent.

"They think we're strangers," Leaf said.

Every child darted inside, except Sky. He held the tent flap open with a hand, watching as they drew nearer. Raven saw that her boy had become as slender as a sapling even though he'd grown taller.

When Sky recognized Leaf and Raven, his mouth dropped open. He let go of the flap and ran to them. Opening his arms wide, he attempted to hug both parents at the same time. They wrapped their arms around him.

"I told everybody that you weren't dead," Sky cried out in a choked voice.

Raven blinked back tears as the three of them huddled together. Sky was trembling, and she knew without looking that Leaf was also trembling.

"You were right. We are very much alive." She kissed Sky's cheek, the smell of his skin so familiar.

Leaf's voice wavered as he spoke. "I'm glad you didn't believe that, son. Is your aunt Shell safe and well?"

"She is—everyone at our tent is fine, but lots of people died."

"Oh my…" Raven saw Shell hurrying toward them, Shell's children and Windy trailing behind. They were all very thin. Windy had hardly grown at all during the seasons they were gone. Shell was trying to speak but was so overwrought by seeing Leaf and Raven that all she could do was gasp. Raven released Sky and went to her.

As she hugged the crying Shell, Raven looked over at Windy standing nearby. She realized at once that Windy didn't remember her or Leaf. Their girl was watching them suspiciously, no recognition whatsoever in those big beautiful eyes.

"Windy," Leaf said and turned toward her with his arms outstretched.

She ran away, stopping to look back at him only when she reached the tent again. Leaf slowly lowered his arms as Shell's children went over to join her. He exchanged glances with Raven then placed a hand on Shell's shoulder. "Let's go inside the tent," he said over his sister's muted sobbing. "There are some things we need to talk about now, before Raven and I see anyone else."

Shell took a couple of big breaths as she swiped away her tears. She turned to Sky. "Go tell your sister and cousins that they can play again."

While Sky ran to get them, Shell walked with Raven and Leaf toward the tent. The children soon slipped by with curious stares then hurried over to the make-believe camp they'd been playing in earlier.

"It's our mother and father," Raven heard Sky tell Windy as the grown-ups went inside.

So much needed saying that Leaf, Raven, and Shell were confusing each other, everybody trying to ask and answer questions at the same time. One thing Raven pulled out of her first frantic questions to Shell was that Long had returned to the band after being gone for a hand's worth of days.

"He'd been badly trampled by horses," Shell said before being distracted by answering something Leaf wanted to know.

"But is Long all right now?" Raven asked when she could jump again into the conversation.

Shell gave a quick sigh. "He only lived a day after he came back. Before dying, he told us that Longheads had captured Wren and Leaf." She raised a hand to her cheek, a pained expression crossing her face. "But where is Wren now? Is she…"

"Wren is fine." Raven was finding it hard to absorb the unwelcome news of Long's death. She'd hoped for so long that he'd survived.

"That's a relief. But then, where is she?"

Raven glanced at Leaf, who nodded for her to continue. "Wren is a short walk from here. We left her with Longheads who are friends."

Shell's face went blank as if she hadn't heard Raven clearly.

"We wanted to talk to you first before bringing her and the Longhead group to the camp." Raven took a deep breath before going on. "The Longhead who was behind stealing Wren and Leaf is dead. The others in her band never wanted the kidnapping."

Shell blinked several times. "But… but I still don't—aren't you afraid they'll hurt Wren?"

"I know what the Elders have always said about Longheads, but they are wrong." Raven needed to somehow ease Shell's confusion and misgivings. "The Longheads are people very similar to you and me," she said, repeating what she'd told Long and Short. "They feel joy and pain, suffering and sorrow, just as we do. Most of their band died from an illness not long ago. Very few are left. We couldn't just leave them to struggle and starve, so we brought them with us." Raven held up a hand, spreading wide her fingers. "And a hand's worth of babies are with the group, including my twins."

"Twins?" Shell exclaimed, grasping onto something she could easily understand. She smiled. "You've been blessed with twins?"

Raven nodded. "A girl and a boy." A chill went down her neck when Shell's smiling face suddenly crumpled.

"You say a lot of them died. Well, that's exactly what happened to us—right after that rock blew up in the sky."

"Did the explosion kill them?" Leaf asked.

"No, the explosion didn't harm anyone, but a fever sickness came along shortly afterward. It was thought that the blast may have released the illness," Shell said. "But I'm not sure I believe it, because our family didn't fall ill. I truly think that we survived because we were being shunned and weren't living in the winter lodges with those who were dying."

Leaf's head made a quick movement backward. "Shunned?"

Shell's expression turned hard. "When Fin refused to let anyone search for you and Raven, I cursed him." She shook her head while speaking, practically spitting out the words. "I threw curses at him every day, but it didn't change his mind. He ordered the band to shun me, and so our family left. We found a rock overhang at a good distance from camp, and we built our own lodge in it. I knew where you kept your food cache, so I took it with me." An anxious look crossed her face. "I hope you don't mind."

"Of course not," Leaf and Raven said at the same time.

"That extra food helped carry us through winter. We didn't know for a long while that most of the others had died. But when the fever took Fin and the weather warmed a bit, the remaining band members found us. We moved back to camp." Shell paused. "But tell me more about what happened to the both of you."

Raven knew that Leaf felt the same relief she did that they wouldn't have to try to persuade Fin that the Longheads should stay. "Why don't we gather together whoever is in camp today," Raven said. "And we'll tell everyone the story of our long disappearance."

***

Neither Windy nor Sky wanted to stay at the camp Raven and Leaf set up nearby with the Longheads. They, along with the rest of the Wind band children who'd survived the fever, were frightened of the different kind of people. And although it wasn't surprising, considering how young she was when Leaf and Raven vanished, Windy remained aloof whenever they tried to warm up to her. Raven and Leaf were disappointed that their children weren't living with them, but they allowed them to remain with their aunt, at least for the time being.

Although they weren't openly antagonistic, some of the adults were also wary of the Longheads. Others were fascinated by them and often visited with the Longheads in the neighboring camp. On the day when the men from both groups hunted together, Raven knew they'd reached a turning point. The time had come for her to implement the last part of her plan. Raven sought out her sister-in-law once more. Without Shell's family agreeing to come along when Leaf and Raven left with the Longheads, Windy and perhaps Sky wouldn't want to come.

She found Shell busy breaking up small limbs in front of her tent. After greeting her, Raven went right to the heart of the matter. "The Longheads will soon leave to return to a valley rich in game, fish, and plants," Raven told her. "It's the same place where Leaf and I once lived with their family. Leaf, Wren, and I will go with them. We want your family to come too. Not only because Windy and Sky are living with you and because it would be difficult to persuade them to leave but also because Leaf and I believe we won't ever see you again once we've gone."

Raven was almost holding her breath as she waited for her sister-in-law's response. Shell was still upset that Leaf and Raven had hidden their past association with the Longhead group from her for so long. Afraid of Shell's reaction, they hadn't told her yet that Wren wasn't Leaf's child.

Shell looked at Raven strangely for a long while. She bent over to crack off a piece of firewood. "Before you arrived, the band discussed returning to the coast. What stopped us from doing so was that we didn't know what we'd find there. We don't know if the people there are any better off than we are here or even if they survived the winter."

"I hope they did survive," Raven said. The woman Gale, whose headache Raven cured, had moved back there with her mate before the illness started.

Shell straightened and swiped back several braids that had fallen over her face. "It's completely unknown. Everyone here, though," she said to Raven, "can see that *your* band is thriving." Seeing Raven's startled look, Shell smiled and inclined her head toward the Longhead camp. "Yes, it's what we say when we talk about them: Raven's band."

Raven looked at her as the words sank in. *Raven's band.* That was what people were calling the recently arrived group. She felt weak-kneed just thinking about the responsibility.

Shell went on. "You might remember that our family had a falling-out with the group at the coast, so we're not so eager to go back."

Raven recalled that Shell's mate, Dune, had been set upon by several men and beaten almost to death. "So, you think that Dune will want to come with us?"

"He doesn't really have a choice if he wants to stay with me," Shell said.

Raven grinned at Shell's cheekiness, and her heart felt like it was bursting from joy. Shell had just made Raven's dream of forming a new band from the two peoples seem attainable. She grasped Shell's hands, whirling her around in circles until they were both dizzy. The two women laughed so hard that they soon ran out of breath and collapsed down among the firewood, still giggling like young girls.

\*\*\*

During the time they were putting aside food for the trip, three men decided they would come along when the mixed group left. The youngest was Ash, Wren's childhood playmate. Most of his kin had succumbed to the fever. The other two men lost their entire families, children as well as mates. Ash had grown into an able young man, and he and Wren soon renewed their friendship. Raven was happy for her daughter, although a little bemused. Wren had never been shy, but she was bashful around the boy. Raven strongly hoped that her daughter's bad experience with Skraw wouldn't somehow taint their future together.

The Wind people had already been told why Elder Woman had decided to capture Leaf. They knew that Leaf had fathered Chirrup's and Coo's children. Upon finding out, Shell had immediately befriended the two women. She even helped take care of her new niece and nephew.

But while telling the story of their unusual and hazardous adventures, Raven and Leaf had left out Raven's relationship with Chukar as well as Wren and Owl's true ancestry. At first, Raven decided to leave it that way. The truth would soon become obvious to any Wind people who joined the new band. If they were upset at first, then that would pass. But knowing how Shell disliked secrets, Raven decided to confide in her before the group began their travels. Leaf was at Raven's side when she told Shell.

Different emotions, including poorly hidden shock, came and went on Shell's face as she heard them out. Raven was afraid that her sister-in-law would desert them at once.

But when they were finished, she took Raven's hand. "If Leaf isn't upset, then why should I be? How unusual about the twins. Does Wren know you were going to tell me that Chukar is her father?"

A deep relief went through Raven. She hadn't lost her sister-in-law's support. "Wren doesn't know. I was afraid she wouldn't want you to find out. So, for now, I don't think I'll tell her. She hasn't yet realized this is something that can't be hidden forever."

Shell gave a little laugh. "I well understand. My niece could always throw an impressive tantrum. But Wren seems more subdued now. I don't think she'll be that angry when she finds out you've told me. All she can think about these days is Ash."

Raven nodded. "We'll do a joining ceremony for the pair when we reach the valley. You may be right that she won't care that you know."

***

They didn't tarry. The camp was a place of pestilence, and Raven pushed them to leave for fear that fever still lurked in the area. Leaf was all for beginning their journey right away so that they could reach their destination before summer's end. He'd well learned that the Great High Plains during winter were unpassable. Raven was disappointed that more of the Wind band wouldn't be joining them. The group had still grown considerably, though, with the three men who were coming, Shell's family of four, Windy, and Sky.

As they traveled, the band settled into new patterns.
Knowing that Leaf was the father of Coo's and Chirrup's babies, the two older men from the Wind band were hesitant for
a while about wooing the two women. Leaf quickly explained,
however, that he didn't mind. Coo's feelings were hurt at first
when he discouraged her from joining him at night. One of
the men was so persistent, however, that she soon yielded to
his attentions.

Chirrup remained close friends with Leaf, but she didn't
seem to mind staying with a different mate. She came to Raven
one evening, a twinkle in her eye as she spoke. "Coo wanted
me to tell you that she enjoys not having to share a man anymore."

When Raven heard that, she began planning joining ceremonies for Coo and Chirrup that would take place the same
time as Wren's ceremony. She would somehow blend the ceremonial practices of the two peoples.

Whenever they stopped their journey for the day, Raven
always set up her sleeping area apart from the others. If they
ended up in a cave, she took her babies to a far corner. When
they stayed in open-air camps, she set up a small tent. Windy
slowly began to interact more with her mother. She and Sky
occasionally even spent the night with Raven, although they
usually slept with their cousins because that was what they
were used to doing.

On some nights, Chukar stayed with Raven, and other
nights, Leaf was with her. She never asked how the two men
worked out who would come. During those times when the
group halted their travels to hunt or make tools, the three of
them were inseparable around the campfires. In the beginning, after realizing how close Raven was to both Leaf and
Chukar, the two older Wind men gave them perplexed glances
and muttered under their breaths. Leaf so obviously enjoyed

Chukar's company, though, that they soon stopped making anything of it.

Raven noticed one day that the spear points Leaf and Chukar were making looked different from the ones each man had made before. She asked Leaf about it that night when they were in her tent alone with the two babies.

"All our tools are different now. We took the best traits of his tools and mine and blended them," he said.

Raven thought about that for a moment, then she made a small sound.

"What is it?" he asked.

"I was only thinking." She pointed at herself then at him. "We—us and the Longheads—are becoming blended together the same way as the tools."

He gave her a slow look. "I had the same thought not long ago. We're becoming like a braided stream."

"Sweet Earth Mother," she exclaimed.

"You don't like the comparison?"

"No, no. It's wonderful. And I think you've just come up with a name for our fledgling tribe. We'll call ourselves the Braided Stream tribe."

"I guess it will do," Leaf said in a teasing voice. He was smiling, amused by her excitement, and she smiled back, happy the group had a name.

# ACKNOWLEDGEMENTS

I would like to thank all the people that helped directly or indirectly with the writing of The Braided Stream. Barb Schwalbert, I couldn't have done it without you. And, as always, a big thanks to my husband, Cleon for his constant support.

My appreciation goes once more to the talented editors and proofreaders at Red Adept Editing. Stefanie Spangler, line editor at the RAE, your eye for errors only improves with time.

I wish to express my gratitude, as well, to the members of the Prehistoric Writers and Readers Facebook site who continuously share their research and knowledge at that site.

Thanks again to family and friends for supporting my efforts. A special thanks from my heart goes to Valerie Greenman and Lena Smallwood. My early readers have been invaluable in giving suggestions for improvement.

I wish to give credit to John Hawks's blog for giving me the idea for the title. It was there that I first encountered the braided stream analogy to describe interactions between the various branches of early humanity.

Many thanks to Philip Newsom for allowing me to purchase and use his artwork of a Megaloceros herd for the cover. That beautiful but now extinct deer plays a major part during one of the book's scenes. When I saw Philip's painting, I knew that I had to have it for the cover.

Several books were helpful to the writing of The Replacement Chronicles because of the sheer amount of detailed information about Neanderthals they contained within their pages. Those works are The Neanderthal Legacy by Paul Mellars and Cafe Neanderthal by Beebe Bahrami.

# ABOUT THE AUTHOR

Harper Swan lives in Tallahassee, Florida with her husband and two sweet but very spoiled cats. Her interests include history from all eras, archaeology and genetics. She enjoys researching ancient history and reading about archaeological finds from Paleolithic sites. As well as writing stories with plots based in more recent times, Harper is also following a longtime dream of writing books that include the distant past, her inspiration drawn from Jean Auel. Harper is the author of The Replacement Chronicles, a four-part series.